The Tale of
Old Man Fischer

Russell

Russell

The Tale of
Old Man Fischer

Russell

Second Edition

Edited by

Kristen Grammar

DEDICATION

To Collin and Rowan,
Your endless thirst for understanding allows me to be
Continuously inspired by the endless mysteries of the world …
Love you both

Vickie —

Please enjoy a
piece of my madness

Read 2 Escape

Russell
'17

FOREWARD

When the pen hit the paper, I began the first few lines of *The Tale of Old Man Fischer*. As a result, several long years later, stealing moments here and there, I finished my freshman novel. As such, when I first published *Old Man Fischer*, I was a novice writer. Honestly, the First Edition was a raw piece as it were. Today, what you have in your hands, my dear reader, is a re-awakening. Honestly, I would never have thought that I would create a second edition of any work. Thus, given this opportunity, I would like to share insights behind this particular book.

Travelling to Central America, my interest focused on the splendid national preserves filled with lush rainforests and abundant wildlife. On one particular occasion, I took a tour of the rainforest in a motorized gondola ride over the rainforest that ran well over hundred feet above the forest floor. From the view, the abundance of indigenous plant life seemed to be untouched by man and sealed off from the rest of the world. As the tram rose above the canopy of the rainforest, the lush greenery, the movements of holler monkeys and flying colorful birds evoked me with awe and wonder as I took in the magnificent beauty. When I stared down into the depths of the forest, I was intrigued by the layers of shadows where the sunlight seemingly could not penetrate. Extraordinarily, the movement of life scurried, ran, slithered and flew amongst the limbs of trees, leaves and the ground. Perhaps, I began to feel like a new explorer, or even a research scientist.

While I continued my travels in Costa Rica, a trip to the Mount Arenal region made me appreciate Central American topography: The endless ridges and the deep gorges and coastline were created from a convergence of continental plates smashing into each other over millions and millions of years. While Central America, particularly Costa Rica, lays in center of an existing ring of fire, the local people today accept earthquakes, active volcanoes and the possibility of a dormant volcano to erupt. Being stated, I was fascinated about Mount Arenal's recent eruption. After being dormant for centuries, it erupted in 1968, which killed close to ninety people and buried three small towns in the surrounding area. I could only image the reaction of the people, regrowth of the life and reshaping of the area after a sudden natural disaster. Needless-to-say, Fischer's tale is roughly based on Arenal's eruption.

Thus, inspiration for this book stemmed from the sublime beauty and darkness of Central America. However, as the novel opens up, you will find Old Man Fischer in a depilated house in the Chicago area. Why transition from Central America to the Midwest United States? Simply put, I lived in the Windy City for almost twenty years. Even though I currently live in Up State New York, my thoughts return often on my pseudo hometown. In fact, Shane's neighborhood reflects a typical commuter town near Chicago.

For the duration of the novel, the characters will speak to you, my dear reader, in the first person. To me, it seemed the most natural way to describe the events. Also, it proved to be a daunting challenge in staying in each character. (On a side note, I actually wrote the Prologue last which is the reason why it is in the third person.) Thus, the story itself is told in two different perspectives.

The first perspective will be Shane. Writing Old Man Fischer, I was a new father. Shane's life reflected the early years raising my son in those formidable years before he entered middle school. The elementary grades are key stepping stones of progress as homework escalates, concepts of the world are discussed and actual friendships begin to rise. Adding another dimension to Shane's life, his parents both have full-time jobs in meaningful careers in the restaurant industry. Having been a chef for most of my life, the crazy and long hours took a toll on family life which led to a lot of compromise. You will see through Shane's eyes the reality of the food industry on a family.

The second perspective will be Dr. Hans Fischer. His perceptive was exciting and significant voice to add to the story. In my old restaurant life, I worked in many private clubs: One in particular consisted of a membership of older German men. On typical Men's nights, the men were robust and stoic and expressed their opinions about politics, sports, religion and young women. Usually they drank a plethora of manhattans, martinis and gimlets until close, wobbling haphazardly out of the door. How I imagined Dr. Fischer was the tone in which these men spoke: Long full described stories of yesteryear (which I believe is a lost art today). More so, their voices were guttural and robust and reflected the Old Country where the *s* sound was a *z*, *th* sound was just a blunt *t*, and so on. From that, Dr. Fischer's voice became an essential piece for the pages to come.

Couple of years ago publishing my freshman novel, I shocked many family members and close friends. Because I have a *full* life, they asked when I had time to write. Simply, I made time here and there. Yet without their endless support to this day, I would not be able to continue my adventure as a writer.

My dear reader, I offer to you a piece of my madness.

Please enjoy reading *The Tale of Old Man Fischer*.

Thank you,

Russell

Read to Escape!

July 2016

ACKNOWLEDGMENTS

I thank Kristen for her editing skills on this book. With her colorful insights, she helped to shape various moments within the story itself and allow Shane and Dr. Fischer become even more alive. Our collaborative effect brought the story and characters to a slightly different vision.

PREVIEW

Please Take a First Glimpse At

Russell's Exciting New Thriller

GAVIN

At the End of the Book.

"It comes like the thief in the glooming;
It comes, and none may foretell
The place of the coming –the glaring;
They live in a sleepless spell
That wizens, and withers, and whitens…"

--Herman Melville

PROLOGUE

Sitting in the darkened room, he heard the faint click of the large grandfather clock in the hallway as it echoed in the silent shadows just outside of his study. The desk lamp no longer worked, leaving only a lamp near the far window for any reading light.

No matter though. His thin hands carefully picked up the tattered magazine before him and opened to the exact dog eared page. Purposely ignoring his once youthful appearance, the memories of that expedition haunted the back of his mind. His eyes scanned the article briefly until he reached the right section.

He read the words out loud slowly and concisely, as if he were lecturing to a small group of students:

"Under the hot Central American rain forest canopies of the large indigenous plant life, I remained still and quiet although my body had been depleted by the day's humid conditions. I had waited for the prized species which has not yet been documented in this lifetime, in which this region has only been investigated the various subsets of creatures. My resilience for patience had mounted to this moment." After so many times, the memorization of the words had embedded within his tone. While his eyesight had been gradually worsened, the words were as fresh he had written the first time. "My resilience for patience had mounted to this moment."

In the periphery of his vision, he sensed some movement in the

1

corner of the cave-like, but nothing out of the ordinary.

The darkness of the night permeated what little light could be attained. Behind long-faded yellow curtains, The strong winds outside buffeted the windows. He had picked those curtains for her when they moved to this house. Yet in this light, just beyond his vision, he could see the quick silent movements of small shadows along the darkened floorboards

He looked away from the article, catching the faintness of dust and mildew in his nostrils. How long has it been since he had dusted in here? How long had it been since he dared to care for the house that he had long ago lavishly created for her? Then again, he now thought, how long had it been since he bathed, as he caught the faint scent of musk from his body as he shifted in the chair. He was getting away from the daily procedures of life.

The coolness of autumn had crept into the house, making the room feel cooler than it should be. With one hand, he drew his sweater closer to his body, trying to huddle his long, bulky frame closer to the desk. He dared not to turn the heat up sooner than necessary. The environment of the house would be off; he would lose valuable time. He made the sacrifice necessary to keep the temperature at a proper level. Sometimes, it had been necessary in his life to avoid the normal customs of everyday life in order to continue his research.

Seeing nothing in the darkness, he turned back to the article and continued from where he had left off.

"'On the edge of the decimated bark of a fern leaf, a colony of tribe *attini* used their sharp beaks to cut away the significantly large portions of vegetation for the hill. One-by-one these beautiful creatures encircled the plant, their large size of two-to--four centimeters in length, their translucent bodies were a dull auburn color perfectly exposed their thoraxes when viewed against the lush green backdrop. During the course of my research, I spent five hours a day for three weeks observing and cataloguing the species in its natural environ. As a result, I designed the path of *attini* on the forest floor that covered an impression fifteen hundred meter radius from the nest. I realized the nature of their aggressive behavior when an innocent *marcus felix* of an undiscovered species happened to be in their path. In an instant, the *attini* descended upon the offensive obstacle, using their beaks to snap and crack the creature's long body apart quickly. They stormed in unity, much like an army in battle challenging the foe. More so, the creatures marched instinctively past..."

A sudden loud bang shuddered from the back of the house.

He neither stirred nor was he shaken by this disturbance rapid fire loud thuds. Rising from the chair slowly, he placed the tattered bookmark at the crease of the magazine and closed it. He would leave it for another day, another time to *reread* his article on that moment in time. Back then, he had *her* in his life, where *she* helped him cope and see his vision clearly. Looking at the article, seeing the picture of that life, seeing himself and *her* beside him, it had all been meaningless after those days.

That was the past.

A thunderous crash sounded below his feet in the basement. A familiar sound.

Eerily the house was silent once again.

Soon the faint hum almost pulsated through the wood floor through his feet.

Outside, an energy of the wind whipped at his windows, banging heavily at the tired old panes, which hadn't been sealed for many years. Slowly, he ambled toward the kitchen, long drawn shadows pooling around his legs. The dark house was his domain, where he knew every inch as his tired eyes grew to adjust to the dim light. His footsteps were soft and quiet as he could hear slight scratching and rapid clicks on the floor boards. So faint, no one else could hear it; his trained ears were well-tuned to it.

Coming to the kitchen, in its disarray, he looked past the stacks of dishes and counters filled with papers and boxes. He opened the back door, the rush of cold air invading the warm house, and he shuddered slightly as he pulled his sweater closer to his thick chest. Hanging onto the railing in need of repair, he stepped down to the ground to see that the storm doors were wide open.

Looking beyond his immense fence, he could hear next door as a door slammed and then a female voice.

He stopped and craned his head towards the noise.

It was the young girl who lived with her parents next to him. Over the years he had watched from his window as she was brought home from the hospital for the first time as a newborn, to growing up with her brother, playing in the backyard on a tire swing, then putting on makeup on the front porch with her girlfriends, to dating a lot of boys who were questionable, and now she was a college student. Now he could smell her overuse of perfume and pictured her in her typical tight jeans and bright colored shirt, wearing an abundance of makeup. Her voice was loud; she must be on her phone. "Yeah, yeah. I'm leaving now. No. Not him. No. You talk to him. Shut the hell up—"

Then a car door slammed and no more noise.

The young girl had never been polite with him. As a child she had made sour faces, stuck her tongue out at him, and eventually she just looked nervous and afraid and didn't look at him at all as she hurried in and out of the house. It didn't matter.

Looking back at the open storm doors, he could see the very tip of his basement basking in a redden glow, like the back of a throat. In the silver white shine of moonlight, he glimpsed at the metal slide that replaced the cement stairs from long ago. Among the bits of mud and weeds, he could see the amber redness of blood, only a tiny smear, flowing along down into the shadows.

A grin crept to his face.

"So you had some dinner," he said aloud. He closed the doors quickly as the wind began to pick up, throwing more leaves down the gigantic chute. "Let's go see what you found."

Turning to go up the stairs, he muttered, "Well this will better a night then planned."

Closing the storm doors above him, the man walked into his warm house.

He made his way towards the open mouth of his basement which shown in that same brilliant scarlet light.

That same light had *first* embraced him thirty some years ago.

That same light that monopolized his whole life.

Part 1

The Dog Collar

"Dizzy in the head and I'm feeling blue
The things you've said, well, maybe they're true
I'm gettin' funny dreams again and again
I know what it means, but ..."

--The Who

Russell

ONE

"Honey, you have to wake up now. It's already ten to seven. We're going to be late," my mom said to me until I could not ignore her anymore. In my nice warm bed with the comforter up to my eyes, I had been trying to forget the fact that I had school today.

I rose out of bed looking at my dark blue walls, looking up at the sun that my mom had painted for me. It circled the ceiling, its rays stretched along the walls.

I walked along our narrow hallway towards the stairs. I had barely opened my eyes, my body just knew the way down to the kitchen where my mother would wait for me.

Mom had been dressed already as I turned the corner. I could smell her flowery perfume faintly over the burnt toast. My eyes opened slightly more even though the sunlight from the windows was making it impossible for me to see. Still, the lavender scent filled my nose, reminding me of days at Lynda's house when I was younger. Lynda was the first person who had taken care of me, while Mom and Dad went to work. I only remember the shape of her dark-paneled den. And Lynda's perfume. Mom stopped wearing perfume for a while because she was worried I would smell too much like her, not like a little boy.

With her back to me, she said, "Shane, your clothes are on the table. Can you brush your teeth real quick?" Then she slipped into the bathroom.

I turned at the sound of soft thuds to see Maggie running towards me, her long, blonde thin hair flapping behind her, her

7

favorite stuffed dinosaur clutched in one hand. Her little toddler body pushed me off-balance since I was still just trying to wake up.

"Morning, Maggie," I said softly and gave her a slight hug. She danced back to the television and sat down. I walked over to her, scooping up my clothes, then I plopped onto the couch near her. Her show was on. A bunch of little girls were dancing and singing to a friendly song. I was never thrilled with her shows, but it was soft enough to let me wake up slowly.

"Shane, are you hungry?" Mom called out from the bathroom. I knew that she was putting on her makeup, that was where she usually did that. Also, she was trying to escape from Maggie's grabby little hands.

"No," I replied. I just never ate right away in the morning. Besides, today was Tuesday. Usually Mrs. A made fresh muffins in the morning. I really liked the blueberry ones the best.

Maggie began tugging at my clothes next to me. She was already dressed in her play clothes. She would wake up early, always Mom's natural alarm clock. Well, that was what Mom called her.

"Stop, Maggie," I said, pulling my clothes back from her. She laughed and tried to pull harder, smiling.

"Stop it!"

"Shane, stop yelling at your sister!" Mom poked her head out of the bathroom. "Come on. You have exactly seven minutes."

"But Maggie is taking my clothes."

"How old are you?"

"Twelve."

"How old is your sister?" Mom was beginning to put some lipstick on.

"She's two and a half."

At that moment, Mom's cell phone rang, stopping her from saying anymore, but she still gave me a strong look. Mom reached over the kitchen counter to her purse.

Maggie stopped with me, and then ran to Mom, trying to grab the phone.

"Hey, hon. Yeah. Hmm." Mom always had a knack for doing multiple things at once. While she was finishing her make-up, she was entertaining Maggie with one of the other make-up brushes, then immediately went to straighten up the kitchen counter. Over the clanks of the dirty dishes being put into the dishwasher, she carried on this conversation on the phone.

I was shrugging off my pajamas, and slipped on my pants when Mom looked at me, and said, "Phone's for you."

"Who is it?" I was putting on my shirt.

"I'll give you three guesses," she smirked at me. Then she went about her business, Maggie following her every step.

I placed the phone to my ear.

"Hey, champ!" My dad's voice was always large and boomed like thunder in the phone. He still somehow felt that he needed to shout over the phone.

"Hey."

"Are you getting ready for school this morning?" In the background, I could hear the sounds of his work: the rolling carts, people yelling at each other, Spanish music playing far away. Dad's work was really active, to say the least, but hearing those sounds I could image my dad sitting in his office in the far corner of the kitchen near the back door with his door wide open.

"What's going on, Dad?"

"The usual: mixing cake batter, making cookies for a million people, blah, blah, blah. Ya know, doing baking things." He stopped at the sound of a loud crash of metal pans hitting the bakery's tile floor. I heard him put down the phone, and scream, "YOU BETTER PICK ALL THOSE GODDAMN BAGELS UP OFF THE FLOOR OR SO HELP ME, ANTONIO! NEXT TIME I'LL SEND YOUR ASS HOME!" It made the phone vibrate in my hand. Then I could hear a door slam and he got back on the phone, as he let out a heavy breath, and said "Make sure you listen to Mom."

Dad thought that I didn't move fast enough for Mom in the mornings.

"I always do."

"Alright, Mr. Man. Have a good day at school. Pick up you up after."

I was looking at Mom as she gestured for me to give the phone back to her.

"I gotta go, Dad. Here's Mom."

Before he could say anything, I handed the phone over to mom.

Mom and Dad continued their conversation briefly, then she hung up as she was putting Maggie's jacket on my wiggling sister when she said to me "Come on Shane, get moving and go brush your teeth."

A few short minutes later, I was outside with Maggie while I was forcing my feet into my new Nike shoes as Mom closed up the house. The bright sunlight didn't keep the unseasonably cool temperature from permeating the thin sleeves of my lightweight jacket. I could see my breath. I thought it was too early for the weather to change this suddenly. As I held Maggie's hand, I slung my heavy backpack over my shoulder. Within seconds, the click of the locks opened the car.

"Dad packed your lunch. He got you your favorite chicken nugget meal," Mom said rapidly as she went around the car to where Maggie was waiting to be put in her car seat.

"Yum," I replied as I slipped into my side, next to Maggie in the backseat.

"We are going to practice for your spelling test, right?" Mom said to me.

Above us the clear blue sky went on endlessly letting the sun shine brightly, showing off the beautiful colors of the tree leaves. A little wind picked up and some brown leaves blew into Mom's car.

"You know, I just cleaned out the car," she grabbed the leaves and threw them out of Maggie's door. To Maggie, she assured, "There you go sweet heart, locked and loaded."

I smiled at Mom. I like when she said boy things like that.

"What are you smiling about, mister?" she cooed. She closed the door, and got into the driver's seat, touching the button to close the garage door. She shifted her seat and started the car. I could feel cold air pump through the air vents. "Brrr. I have to start warming up the car earlier, don't I?"

I only nodded as I felt the car move us down the long driveway. Our house was an old farm house. Dad told me that this was one of the first houses ever built in the area, and one of the oldest in our town.

Our house was nestled between two other larger houses: It was the smallest on the block. While we lived just out of the city, our yard was small, but the city people would say that we had land. Its long thin windows, what Mom called shot gun windows, lined the thin wooden porch. Over the century, our house had some additions on it: the kitchen, the down stairs bathroom, the garage, and even the second story. The eaves on the peaks of the roof gave a glimpse how tiny the second story really was. As the car slid out of the long narrow driveway, I really liked the large tree in front yard where its branches drooped over our steep roof and seemed to touch the peaks. Somehow, the tree seemed to protect our house from everything.

As Mom and Dad said that we lived in a rather rich neighborhood, our house was much more inviting and less formal as the ones that hugged our very street.

"Momma, fast!" Maggie yelled from beside me.

"No, Momma can't go fast." Mom turned the car down our street, which was named Bend Road. Her eyes were on the road as her fingers fumbled around on the seat next to her.

There usually weren't too many people out at this time in the morning. There would be a rusty brown van throwing the papers on the lawns as we passed it. Inside, I saw a man smoking a thin cigarette. Just like me, he too was barely awake.

Our neighborhood had older houses all over and they all looked different. Some houses were large and majestic, with wrap-around porches. Some houses looked flatter and longer. Some houses were painted bright reds, yellows or purples; some houses were just plain white with black trim. The yards were in different shapes and forms, showing how much the people wanted to garden, long green lawns were beginning to be covered in leaves. The most I liked about our street were the large trees that hanged over the houses and street itself. In summer, their bright leaves shaded the street and helped cool me down. Because earlier this summer, I just got my new skateboard to keep up with Jack, my best friend, on his roller blades. In winter those trees usually were covered in thin ice and snow, sometimes long icicles hung from the low branches like dangerous glass spikes. Now, in the fall, the auburn colors blinked at me blocking the morning light, yet I could see more sky through the increasing number of pinholes in the canopy as more and more leaves fell to the ground.

I loved our neighborhood, and my friends' houses were scattered here and there, all within easy walking distance of each other. I had lived here all my life, and hoped that we would never leave this area.

"Shane, can you spell 'kindness'?" Mom leading her lesson from the front seat. She liked to quiz me on my weekly spelling words, but today I was not really in the mood. Honestly, I'd rather be on Minecraft but I forgot my iPhone on the kitchen counter.

Without much effort, I spelled out the word slowly.

Mom turned the car onto Ashland Road. This block had some smaller homes on it, but as we slowly crept forward, I knew whose house would be coming up. True, I enjoyed my neighborhood, but there was one house that would leave me temporarily dazed, as it often did when we drove down this street.

As I counted the houses, which were exactly seven, I spotted the gray roof of his house as we approached. I had no choice but to see the house every day because I sat on the right side of the car, I could avoid it by looking at Maggie, or looking straight ahead, or even looking at Mom while she drove especially through this part of the street. But this day was different for some reason: On this day, as we approached it, I found myself wanting to look at it, curious to study it and catch all its details.

"Good job. Now try, 'reassurance'," Mom's voice seemed to come to me from far away as I continued to stare out the window.

The gray two-story house that was unusually large in comparison to the other houses on the block drew nearer as we rolled down the street.

At 346 Ashland Road was Old Man Fischer's house. From here, as the sun was behind the house, the grayness of the wood siding seemed black causing the long shadow across its overgrown front yard to look even longer. There was an old tarnished iron fence in the front of the house while an usually high ten foot tattered wooden fence edged the sides of the house. Rumor had it that Fischer was known to like his privacy and space. It was closed that exposed a broken walkway leading to bulking porch. Along the upper floor, I could see broken pieces of wood dangle from the top. In the slight wind, I could see smoke slowly coming out much like a snake disappearing into the blue sky.

"Reassurance," I began, looking at the windows from the top to the bottom. That's when I noticed that someone was standing in the window to the right of the front door, just between the parted, dark grey curtains.

I had to stare hard as if my eyes refused to see him. But I did see him.

I was looking at Old Man Fischer.

12

I'd heard many stories on the playground about Old Man Fischer yelling at kids to shut up and get off his lawn, or off his fence or away from his hedges or out of his driveway. I heard stories of him standing out on his porch just staring at kids as they passed by his house. He liked to frighten the younger kids with a yell here and there. I never seen this ever happen, but there were enough stories to convince me they were true.

I tried to catch a glimpse of him each time we had passed his house. One time I saw a shadow of someone in the window. Another time, the door was closing and I only saw a figure hunched over a cane walking into the house.

But this day, I saw him. He was standing there, between the ripped curtains in a room just inside the dark wood front door. I could tell that he was leaning on something, and that his button-down shirt was striped and he wore a white t-shirt underneath that was poking out at his neck. His face said it all: the dark eyes laid deep in the round face covered in wrinkles and nasty brown spots; lips flattened tight and looking ready to pounce; a full nose cradled just above that fierce mouth. His eyes followed our car, and I knew he had seen me look at him, as his solid head on the unusually thin body slowly moved with us.

I felt a sudden pain in my left forearm, which made me turn towards Maggie. She was laughing as she hitting me hard with the shoe she had taken off.

"'Reassurance.' Are you listening to me?" Mom's voice was louder now.

As Mom stopped at the intersection at the end of the block, I turned back to see if he was there. Old Man Fischer had disappeared back behind the curtains. I felt that he was still there, just a couple of steps back, in the darkness still watching our car speed off the line.

I spelled the word absent-mindedly and looked straight ahead. I dared not to look back again.

I watched smoke rising from several of the large smoke stacks above the houses trying to block out the chilling image of hostile Old Man Fischer's face. School was only three blocks away. While we continue our journey thru the neighborhood toward the school I recited a couple more spelling words for Mom until she seemed satisfied that I was 'proficient' in this week's assigned vocabulary.

She pulled up to the north side of the school in an empty

parking lot that would be filled in an hour. Cold air assaulted me as I opened the car door and got out. As Mom unbuckled a very excited Maggie, I put on my back pack and hugged myself in my heavy coat.

"Me push, me push," Maggie yelled out as she ran towards the double doors to the school.

"Maggie, wait," Mom called after her.

"I'll get her," I said, catching up to her.

As Mom locked the car, I reached Maggie and let her press the button for the front office. Mrs. A was in charge of the Before and After School Care Program at school. Since Kindergarten, I had come here while Mom went to work at the hotel, and Dad at the bakery. Mrs. A and I really have a good friendship. She reminded me of a spare grandma.

Mom reached us just as the loud buzzer sounded and the door's electronic lock unlocked with a loud click. I pulled it open. Maggie charged between my body and the door and went inside.

Mom held the door open behind me and we walked down the stairs.

Down in Room 105, Mrs. A was busy getting trays of muffins ready for breakfast. Already her purse was on the desk and her coat was over her chair. I could smell the first batch already baking.

"Mmm, I smell muffins!" I said aloud.

Mrs. A turned towards us and said, "You are so on time, Shane. Hello, Mrs. O'Conner."

"Good Morning Mrs. Ackhart," Mom said, then to me, "Go put your stuff away and take Maggie along."

Maggie already had a head start down the hallway, and behind me I could hear Mrs. A asking how my mom was today, complimenting her dress, as well. Mom and she had brief chats in the morning because Mom had to get to work in hurry all the time. But Mrs. A always said my mom was "pleasant to talk to."

I caught up to Maggie who was trying to get a drink from a nearby fountain. I quickly took off my coat and threw my bag into a nearby locker, which were set aside for us kids who came early. The early mornings before school always seemed so empty because there was never much going on here, no noise. Then Maggie finished her drink and skipped towards me. I turned and followed after her back towards the Multipurpose Room.

"Come on Maggie, this way," I said. The sweet fruity smells of the fresh-baked muffins that wafted from the kitchen were making me hungry.

As I walked into the room, I overheard Mrs. A. ask Mom, "You heard about Mr. Whitley's prized German Sheppard?"

"No," Mom said, leaning against the counter, smiling at me.

I looked longingly at the piping hot muffins, catching an eyeful of my favorite blueberry ones.

"Well, it turned out that his dog went missing the night before. It's the strangest thing," Mrs. A said as she leaned on the counter, nearer to my mom. "He said that his dog wouldn't just run away. No, he took great care of his dog. Paid enough for it, if you know what I mean."

"That's too bad." Mom was looking at Maggie who was jumping on a chair near us. "Maggie, we have to go in one minute."

"Better yet," Mrs. A said in a softer voice, "I overheard from Mrs. Voilette say in the grocery store last night that his dog was actually stolen. Yeah, the leash was ripped right off the house. You can never know what people are like these days."

"You are correct about that," Mom replied, smiling and winked at me.

Mrs. A, who already was lost in her daily routine, turned towards the stacks of paper plates and napkins.

"Shane, you are going to have a good day at school, right?" Mom asked me as she gently touched my shoulder.

"Yes, Mom." I went to her for a quick hug.

"See you tonight." Her long arm wrapped around my shoulder briefly.

"Are you going to be late?"

"Not tonight, I think."

Maggie came towards me and hugged my legs. Then she zipped out of the room at top squealing toddler speed.

"Thank you Mrs. Ackhart," Mom said, then to me: "Be good to Dad."

I nodded.

I watched her go, then I went to the windowpane where I could see them a couple of seconds later going to the car. Maggie was hopping the last steps to the car then Mom lifted her up put her in her seat. I waved at them but I knew they didn't see me as Mom got the car started and went out of the lot.

Mrs. A said behind me, "Thank Goodness your Mom is like clockwork. Mrs. W. is running a wee behind this morning, and muffin mornings mean a little more work for me." She paused, "Can you help a little bit until Mrs. W comes? She'll be here very soon."

"Okay," I said.

I helped Mrs. A put out plates and napkins on the tables. She didn't talk much which was fine by me. I was still thinking about Old Man Fischer.

I could not get *his* dark eyes out of my thoughts.

TWO

Everyone around me was eyeing up the clock, watching the seconds tick closer to the final moment. Just minutes away, recess was the time for our minds to be free from the canned educational lessons being forced upon us. It didn't help that Mr. Fazio, my math teacher, decided to give us a pop-up math quiz and told us to be quiet during it. He himself went to his desk, which was neatly organized and sorted, and typed loudly at the computer the entire time. *Tap! Tap! Tap!* He was older, tall and thick through the middle with a huge bald spot that made his salt and pepper hair look like a crown. Probably, he was searching for a job like Mrs. Huessen, my fourth grade teacher, had been. There was no whispering permitted in our class, no signs of rustling papers and no signs of life from any of us. Moving only my eyes, I looked over to the others whose eyes darted back and forth to the clock.

With great relief, at ten thirty-five exactly, the bell sounded throughout the building. We all eagerly jumped up and made a run at the door.

"Everyone! You must complete your problems when you return from recess!" Mr. Fazio bellowed over the deafening clack of shifting chairs and joyful screams of the parolees.

I became a fish in the hallway, swimming upstream towards the open ocean against the current of other kids heading downstream on the older staircase towards the playground. Recess always meant that the hallway was instantly packed with friends seeking each other out and socializing. The girls usually greeted each other and immediately started talking in a series of high-pitched squeals and top-secret whispers and generally kept to themselves. As I made my way up the hallway I passed a group of younger boys I recognized as some first and second graders who were more into meeting a friend or two at the door. At the top of the stairs, as I passed through the door frame to the outside, some other, taller sixth-graders were booking down the stairs and knocked over some of the younger kids. I never understood why they felt the need to get out so quick. I knew when I got to middle school next year that you don't even get any recess.

That'll suck.

Finally, I was outside. I made it through all the pushing and shoving in the sardine can. I felt cool wind on my face and the bright sun beat down on me. The sun's rays reflected off the asphalt lot, leaving nowhere for shadows to escape in the far corners of the school grounds. I knew our outdoor recesses would be shorter soon. Once the weather turned cold and the first flakes of snow appeared, the principal would be the one to decide if we got to go out or not. I didn't like being in the dark, dank basement gym. It reeked like dirty shoes, body odor and leftover food.

"Hey Shane," a girl said to me as she passed me by to meet her friend on the edge of the blacktop.

"Hey Molly," I called after her.

Molly was a nice girl who sat next to me in my English class. We sometimes helped each other on reading assignments.

I just ran with the other kids, after saying quickly to Molly, "See you in Mrs. Hutchinson's class this afternoon."

She didn't reply but I did see her blond hair fall into the riptide current of girls running toward the jump ropes. I ran to the jungle gym in the far corner of the playground, where I already saw Jack waiting for me. I laughed as I watched a gust of wind whip his long dark hair into his face and fill his open jacket with air like a boat sail. He was my best friend, even if he did look ridiculous.

Other kids, mainly second and third graders, were already crawling all over the gym, swinging around, defying gravity, exhibiting their superhero-like strength and laughing and playing tag with each other. A couple of younger kids, first graders maybe, were pretending to be cops and robbers. For Jack and me, we liked to stand on the bridge and watch the playground.

"You're late, Mr. Shane," Jack stated, smiling. His eyes darted all over. I only wish I could look at everything that fast.

"How did you get here so quick?" I was breathing a little heavy after my quick run.

"I run like a zebra in Africa. That's what we were studying in our class just now. Did you know that zebras sprint quickly in the open African dessert? Did you know that zebras are not the only animals to have stripes? Did you also know that zebras are skilled climbers? Did you know that the same word is used in London for crosswalks?" Jack talked so fast . His long thin body hunched over the bars of the bridge between the two sets of the playground fixtures as he dangled his feet off the ground. His agile body twisted and turned rapidly like a wild monkey.

Far too soon, there were many whistle warnings sounding off around the playground. Near us, I saw Mrs. Wetzel, a larger older teacher, scolding at couple of third graders. These warnings usually were for climbing on the fences, or running too fast, or screaming, or anything else a kid shouldn't do. The school rules were always so rigid and detailed. Don't do this, don't do that. It's not like my teachers were my parents.

Jack continued to talk. "And then we were able to go online and do some research on Africa and some other animals in Africa. That was cool because you see the plains of the grasslands in Kenya. I would like to go to Africa one day. Wouldn't you like to go too? I just don't know what I'd go see first!" Jack was an easily excited person.

I just listened to him talk on and on about Africa. I didn't say a word; well I really didn't get a chance.

"Hey, Shane. What's up?" A familiar voice asked from behind me.

There was Lewis, a kid from my class. I met him in fourth grade. He was a good person to hang around as well.

"Hey, where were you the last couple of days?" I asked him.

Jack had stopped talking then to listen to us.

"Out sick. Got strep," Lewis croaked. He was quite the 'Word Economist', as my dad would say. Right, he did look rather paler than usual.

"You are always sick, Lewis," Jack said, with a somewhat dazed look.

"Jack," I said softly. Sometimes Jack would say out loud anything that entered his brain.

"It's true," Lewis shrugged as he leaned against the rail.

"Oh boy," Jack said, looking past me. He looked nervous.

"What?" I said as I turned around.

"Hey boys, can I crash your little party?" Mike announced himself, loudly. Great.

Mike was a sixth grader, second time around this year. He was tall and thin, and began to show his older side through the scruffy patches of fuzz on his upper lip and chin. To me it looked like a bad dark rash. He just stood there for a few moments, staring at me with his hands in the pockets of his football jersey stained with ketchup and mustard splotches. I didn't even want to know what the other stains were made of.

Lewis looked uneasy, then snuck off the playground the school entrance. Other younger kids also bolted toward the building.

I stood my ground. Jack slumped slightly, his code of best friend loyalty forcing him to stay by my side, he moved slightly closer to me, putting him in Mike's line of sight where I know he didn't want to be.

"Where there's Jack, there's a Shane?" Another familiar voice, somewhat squeaky from the Big Change. I looked over to the left side of the bridge. Larry, , stood smiling, or grimacing, with a show of delightful yellow-stained teeth.

"You two are like BFFs? Yeah? Like *fer sure?*" To the right, Tim, another of Mike's buddies mocked us from the other end of the bridge. He was leaning forward, twisting his body, looking around. The roll around his middle stuck slightly from the black t-shirt, which made "The Ramones", look like a big white tongue.

"What do you want?" I asked. I stood straighter.

"I need some money, Jack," Larry took a step forward.

"Don't have any," Jack said nervously.

"Knock it off, Lar," Mike said behind me.

Larry looked over at Mike, nodding then took a step back, grinning. He looked like a bag of bones dressed in a rocker shirt and loose dark cargo pants.

I could tell when Jack was becoming more nervous. He began to fidgeting, his hands fluttering as he touched every other fingertip to the other, quickly and randomly, over and over.

Mike and his little buddies always were on Jack for everything, and I tried to run interference for him as much as I could. At the end of last year, in one of the last weeks of school, Jack and I had been at recess. We had been doing our own thing, kicking a ball back and forth, not harming anyone as usual. Jack kicked the ball farther than I could catch and it passed me, and it ended up hitting Mike squarely in the back. Immediately, Mike had gotten angry and went after Jack on the playground. Of course I told a nearby teacher what had happened.

Mike was sent inside for fighting, his buddies following along behind him like always. As he was being ushered into the building with the help of some other teachers, he yelled back after Jack, "I will get you, you little punk!"

After school that day, I had walked with Jack down the hallway to the basement, to the After School program, where Mike, Larry and Tim were waiting in the staircase for us. There was a lot of shoving and I tried to get in between the bigger guys and Jack when a punch had been thrown. Before I knew, Jack had gone down the stairs and broke his wrist. Those guys just laughed at him. Because several teachers and the principal had seen what happened, Mike had been suspended for next three days. Larry and Tim got off somehow; I discovered later that their fathers were very influential people downtown.

When Mike returned from his suspension, he and two of his minions cornered us in the lunchroom. He went straight to Jack and pulled up on his shirt collar which made some other kids around us jump back. Mike growled at him, and said, "From now on, I am going to make you pay for what you did to me." He flung Jack back into his chair, as Jack grabbed his cast to his chest to protect his new cast. I thought I could see tears form in his eyes.

I knew then I had to protect my friend. No matter what the cost.

Since this year had started, Larry and Tim had been bothering about lunch money and some food. Other than that Mike had stayed away. Perhaps the humiliation of repeating sixth grade had gotten to him. Maybe for the second time, I wasn't sure.

As Mike approached us now, I could smell sweat and pee. "I want to talk to you," he looked at me, studying a nearby teacher who was busy talking to some younger students.

"What if I don't want to listen?" I replied defiantly. I looked the other way, to indicate my plan to ignore him.

"You will," he said so confidently.

"Why would I want to?" I felt a cool breeze cover my face, I trembled.

Tim looked at me and smiled, "Ah, he's shivering, Mike." He laughed deeply, or more fake than necessary.

I looked at Jack who was now nursing his wrist, imagining the pain he surely associated with the sight of these jerks. I just wanted to find a way to get out of this, but I couldn't come up with anything on the fly.

"A compromise," he offered.

"Didn't know you knew such a big word," I snarked.

Jack snickered.

Mike's smirk dropped from his face. He loomed closer to the bridge, where I looked directly down at him. He looked up towards the school building and scanned the area. An asteroid belt of red bumps marred his neck in a nasty pussy mountain range.

"Explain more," I felt my hands began to sweat. I looked over to a teacher with little kids around her, but she hadn't taken any notice of our little gathering here.

"You need to listen to somethin'," he said frankly.

"I don't think so," Jack whispered. He was nervous.

"Shut the hell up, geek boy," Mike looked at Jack with a look of disdain. Larry stifled a laugh.

Then Mike turned back to me, "What's it gonna be?"

I shrugged my shoulders, thinking that if I listened to what this idiot had to say then he would back off of us. "Tell me," I conceded with trepidation.

Jack looked at me with wide open eyes, no doubt surprised by my easy acceptance.

"Heard that Mr. Whitley's dog went missin' right?" He scratched at his neck, his dirty nails digging into his blemishes.

Gross. "Yeah, so."

"I don't think it is just a onetime thing." Mike's voice was different, less threatening as he slow meandered toward what I hoped was a point to this conversation that didn't involve bodily harm of Jack or myself. "My brother John told me somethin' last night that I can't get out of my head." His brother John was in high school, a sophomore on the football team. Big and strong, and actually smart too. I wondered what happened to Mike. This thoughtful, rational side of him couldn't last.

"Why tell us?" I asked.

"Shut up an' listen," he demanded. Larry and Tim stood

straighter, like soldiers would to protect the area. "John told me about our dog. Do I remember the dog? No. Only seen the photos. Mom was nutso about not havin' any living thing that needed taking care of in our house. Couldn't even get a damn goldfish. When John told me that we had dog once, and then I was like how come you had one, not me, you know?

"About seven years ago, he said it was like now, fall-like, cold, whatever. Mom, me and John were home that night. My dad was out-of-town that night on some sales thin' in St. Louis. John said Mom didn't really like being alone with us boys, so she made sure we had a large dog around. She loved that dog. Name was Ginger.

"One night when it was real windy, Mom put me to bed early. John had just gone to bed when he heard Ginger just barkin' crazy-like. He got up and looked out his window. He saw the back of the doghouse from his window but he couldn't see Ginger, but could tell she was at the end of her leash, tied to her house. She was barkin' louder and louder.

"John wanted to quiet her down, so he went downstairs. He met Mom in the kitchen.

"'What's Ginger barking about?' John asked Mom. She was dressed for bed. She didn't sleep good when Dad was gone. Still don't.

"'Don't know. Why don't you get back to bed?' She said quietly. 'I'll go see.'

"Then Ginger's yippin' went different. She was growlin' and yappin' low, like she was scared but she wanted to fight.

"That's when John just stayed in the kitchen. Mom grabbed the baseball bat from behind the door. She opened the door, and went outside. 'Stay inside, just in case Mike wakes up.' Then she closed the door.

"From the kitchen windows, he saw her walk around the house. He heard her call Ginger's name. Then he heard a loud noise, like wood bein' ripped up. He ran to Mom. She was screamin' real loud. He wasn't sure if the neighbors heard cause the wind was really strong. But when he saw Ginger runnin' down the side walk, her chain was still attached to part of the dog house. It wasn't slowin' her down, or nuthin'.

"'Get in the house!' Mom screamed at him and ran past John.

"He stood where he was and called after Ginger. Mom came

back out with the car keys and said, 'Get in the house. Stay here and watch Mike. I'll go look for Ginger.' Off she went, and John came inside. He didn't go back to sleep. He sat at the kitchen table For maybe an hour or so, until she came back. She was sad 'cause she loved that dog.

"'I couldn't find her,' she said.

"'What's wrong, Mom?' John asked.

"She said nothing right away, and then looked at him. 'I swear there was something Ginger was barking at.'

"'Another dog? A fox from the Forest Reserve?' John asked. He saw the weird look on her face.

"She shook her head, and said, 'It's nothing. Too much wind, things shifting all around.' She wiped away her tears and told John to go to bed. He turned to look at her, and she sat there, just looking out the window into the darkness of night.

"Mom an' John went from door to door lookin' for Ginger for couple of days. No luck. Mom was real upset, was promisin' never to take another animal, into our house. John said that whatever it was, it shook her up. Mom didn't sleep good for 'while, I guess.

"'About a month passed. John and his good bud, Charley, were walkin' to here, this goddamn stupid school. They happened to pass Old Man Fisher's house, when he looked down and saw Ginger's colla'. He stopped and picked it up." Mike's feet fiddled around in the mulch, and a look of seriousness washed over his pimply face.

"So did he talk to Old Man Fischer?" I asked.

Mike rolled his eyes and said, "It's John. Of course he did, you idiot. He got to the bottom step when the door opened, an' Old Man Fischer came out." Then, Mike leaned closer to me, his eyes wide with red lines dancing across them. "That crazy old man yelled at him, 'Get off my property!' John said he was waiving some long garden clippers over his head.

"'Do you know anything about this?' John asked an' showed our dog's colla'.

"'I swear I'll call the cops on you!' Old man Fischer yelled.

"'We've been missing our dog Ginger and I—'

"'I ain't no Lost and Found! Get off my property!' he yelled back.

"John just ran off. He knew Old Man Fischer has somethin' to do with all of this," Mike stated.

"With all what, Mike?" I asked impatiently. I already saw the first and second graders lining up to go back into the building.

"Do you know that not only Mr. Whitley's dog disappeared? On Green Tree Road, there went a cat missin'. There was another small dog on Sheridan Avenue that went missing too." Now Mike dug into his pocket. "You'll find out what I am sayin' ain't no lie."

"How would I know?" I looked down at him.

The first warning bell for recess rang and Jack, Larry and Tim took off with the other kids. From my view, it was like herds of wild buffalo being shepherded into the next pasture.

"This," Mike pulled out an old, tattered collar with Ginger on it and handed it to me.

I climbed down from the bridge and trotted toward the line of kids waiting to go inside. Mike kept a quiet pace alongside me. I finally asked, "So what do you want me to do about this?"

"Come on everybody! Hurry it up!" Mrs. Wetzel yelled out.

There were kids running past us, screaming and whirling around, with their jackets wide open and they looked like human kites against the wind.

"Find out if I'm right. 'Cause I know it's that old man," Mike said. At this close distance I caught a wiff of his stale body odor. *Hasn't this kid ever heard of soap?*

"Why me?"

"'Cause you can find things out." Mike began walking faster, so now I was scurrying to keep up. "Like last year," he said, answering my unspoken question.

I had discovered the hidden pool behind the After School room wall, which had just been a rumor from other kids. But there had been all this loud squeaking in the mornings after Mom dropped me off. Mrs. A claimed she didn't know what it was. Well, I had to find out where the squeaking was coming from. All I remember was that there were so many rats. But that's another story for another time.

Ahead of me, I had lost Jack in the crowd. I began to move my way through the crowd with Mike only a couple steps away from me.

"What's the compromise?" I asked as a girl looked at me funny, as if I was talking to her. I only smiled.

Behind me, he said, "You find out what happened ta my brother's dog, an' I will leave your little Jackie alone."

I stopped and he bumped into me. "You promise?"

Just then the second bell rang, louder than the first since we were so much closer to the building now, and the doors swung open, letting the kids inside.

"For you, only, yes," Mike agreed.

I turned to him, "How can I be sure you will keep your promise?"

He just smiled his yellow-toothed smile at me. Somehow, I knew I couldn't trust him, nor should I trust him, but I needed to try, to help my friend.

"Shane! Come on!" It was Jack yelling at me over the screams and chatter and blowing whistles.

I said nothing as I turned to go inside the school, when I heard Mike say behind me, "Find out if I'm wrong! And Jackie's off my radar!"

I didn't acknowledge his offer, just moved on to catch up to Jack who had anchored himself against the rail mid-way up the stairs.

"What was that about?" Jack said with a sour face, then added, "Creepazoid."

"Not sure," I lied. I had to lie. Swarms of kids were all around us and teachers were ushering us all inside. It was so loud and chaotic in the staircase filled with the echo of hurried footsteps excited voices, there was no way to fill Jack in on my exchange with Mike just then, and I couldn't tell him the whole story anyway. I wasn't quite sure what to make of it all myself just yet.

"Did you believe his story?" Jack asked as he turned to move up to the second floor where fourth grade classes were.

I slipped the remnants of the dog collar into my pocket, feeling the roughness against my leg through the thin fabric liner. I shrugged, then answered, "You know Mike."

"Yeah, he's a jerk," Jack said. Then like the a flip of the switch, he brightened and said with a grin, "Well, I will see you for lunch!"

"Okay," I said and smiled back at my friend.

I watched Jack merge into the stream of kids going up the stairs with an almost upbeat skip in his step. I noticed Mike, Larry and Tim slip in past me, without looking up. Instead they seemed to be going toward the inner halls of the school, toward their rooms.

"Young man, you better get to class," a teacher voice startled me from her station at the top of the stairs. Mrs. Gaines, I think, was a thin, older woman with long gray hair always tied in a bun.

I looked at her and smiled, but she looked at me shrewdly, as though I was up to something.

When I made it to class, the same math problems were still on the board for us to work on, but the kids were talking loudly and laughing, walking around to each other's desks, while Mr. Fazio tried to calm them down without much success.

I stared at the math problems, the same as I had before I left for recess. I still couldn't concentrate on them because my mind was back to Old Man Fischer. I could see him at the window. *Was he staring back at me? What about the missing animals?* I thought and thought, then looked up at the clock. It was going to be a long day. I could tell.

There was no way I could think about math today.

Russell

THREE

"Uh, huh. Steve add the flour slowly to the creamed butter and sugar mixture. Seriously, just follow the directions I gave. Yes, then add the chips and nuts. Yeah, then roll out two ounces, yeah, huh? Yeah. Yeah. Give me a call if you have trouble," my dad said into his phone.

Just as he was about to hang up his phone, he let out a huge sigh then continued his phone conversation. He was sitting opposite of me at the kitchen table.

Dad was always on his phone with the bakery, his work, which made homework time with him half the problem. Next to me was a bowl of cold macaroni and cheese. I wasn't hungry anymore. In front of me sat the math problems from earlier today.

Maggie was watching TV, as usual, already on the couch with her pajamas on and her herd of stuffed animals surrounding her. She usually went to bed around seven, and from the clock that was only an hour away.

"Dad," I said. I didn't like to interrupt him when he was on the phone.

"Steve, hold on one second," Dad sighed heavily. I could smell the subtle hint of cigarette smoke on him. He told me that he quit smoking a month ago. "Yeah bud?" He looked at me with tired, blood shot eyes. How could he stay awake for such a long time? I always about wondered that. Usually he woke up around two-thirty in morning, or so, to go into work. Maybe he took a nap in the afternoon when he got done at work around one.

"What does it mean by prime factorization?" I asked, and then looked down at my problem.

"Steve, I have to let you go," Dad said. He got up from the table to clean up the dirty dishes. "I thought it would make my life easier to hire a night supervisor for the store, but it's turning out to be a lot more work." He walked over to the counter and poured himself another cup of coffee.

"Dad, my question," I said louder.

He looked at me. "What does your book say?"

"I forgot it."

"Shane, what did I tell you about these things?" He came back to the table. My dad was a large, thick man with dark hair streaked with gray. He always wore his work clothes, which usually consisted of black-striped chef's pants and a white t-shirt that was always too tight on him. As he sat down next to me, I could smell the sweetness of bakery products: frostings, chocolate, sugar and baked cakes. The smell was no longer pleasing to me, and I wished that he would take a shower before I got home from school. But he always waited until Mom came home.

"'That I shouldn't leave my materials at school,' " I quoted him from a speech he had given me at the beginning of the year. I knew he was getting upset.

"That's correct," he said, looking at me. The glare of our chandelier gave him more wrinkles than he really had. "How can I help you with homework when you don't bring all your stuff home? Plus, you're at school all day. I'm sure that Mrs. A would allow you to go up and get anything you left behind."

"I know," I muttered as I stared at my problems. I just didn't want to do homework tonight.

I just didn't feel like it.

Maggie ran over to me and began pulling at my arm.

I looked at her. She was just giggling and rambling on, . "Look at show. Look at show." She wanted to me watch her show with her.

"No, honey," Dad said. "Shane has to do his homework first."

Maggie kept tugging at me. I pulled my arm back hard, which made her fall backward, landing hard on her butt on the floor and . she instantly started to cry.

Dad got up and checked her out. Dad knelt to Maggie's level as she bear hugged him, sobbing harder. His concern for Maggie took first priority at any given time, especially with her condition. Sometimes I wonder if he puts her on pedestal.

"There, there," he said to soothe her.

He glared at me, and yelled, "Shane, stop behaving that way."

"But I wasn't--"

"Enough!" His voice was rising.

"I said I didn't do anything!" I shouted back, then I pounded my fist on the table. I hated when Dad took her side.

That made Dad stand up and raised his voice, "I will have none of that. You get to your room now."

I got up and I felt my cheeks flush. "Sometimes I think you love her more than me!"

"Shane that is not true!"

Maggie released herself from Dad and began to say, "Sar-re." She wanted to come to me, but I wanted nothing more than to escape to my room in that moment.

"Leave me alone," I said and ran upstairs. Was I crying? I wasn't sure. But sometimes Dad and I just get into these things and he always takes Maggie's side. Maybe they would treat her different if she didn't have the on-going problems.

I didn't care about that. I ran to my room and sat on my bed. I didn't have a TV in my room; there was one in the guest room, Grandma's room. Dad would hear me if I turned that on.

So I sat.

Our family was different than most; both my mom and dad worked long hours at busy jobs. My dad owned the bakery, so he had to work all those crazy hours to make it successful. But lately, there seemed to be more stressful days in his life and he brought it home. He was often crabby towards me and never wanted to help me with homework. I could already hear him on his cell phone, it was ringing again and he was talking to one of his workers. He worked when he saw fit. I saw him mainly on Sundays because I would smell breakfast cooking, sometimes French Toast, sometimes blueberry or chocolate chip pancakes, sometimes corned beef hash. I loved Dad's breakfasts.

But when it came to school events, plays or open house, usually Mom made a point of attending these. I don't remember the last time Dad came to my school to meet with a teacher. I was sure that

Mom would tell Dad what was going on.

Dad was always working at the bakery.

When he bought the bakery five years ago, I remembered him saying, "Shane, having your own business is the American Dream. I am it. I promise that I will spend more time with you. This will be great." All I know is that he works now more than ever. If one of his staff calls off in middle of the night; he has to go in earlier. He's always such a tired person these days.

At least I had Mom to help with this though. Yes, unlike most of my friends, my mom did work. I always knew about going to someone's house and spending the day there. I always had very nice sitters, and I still remember them. Still, Mom helped me write them holiday cards this last Christmas. My mom enjoyed working, having the craziness of her job be part of her life. Once in a while, we would go to her hotel—that was a treat in itself. I would go with her to all the big dining rooms, check on the workers there, overlook the setup of the tables, and look at the fancy silverware and plates. The best part was when she and I would go back into the kitchen. It was huge with stainless all over the place, people running in and out, large pots and pans clattering everywhere, lots of fast talking between the chefs that I didn't understand but it sounded really cool. It was nothing like Dad's kitchen, where it was always quiet. I would go with her to talk to the Chef, who usually remembered me, and he would give me a small basket of French fries.

She made her job seem fun to me, where Dad seemed to make his job more difficult. Still, I knew they loved me. On weekends, we had always something to do, or someplace to go. My dad came from a large family, so we were always going over to my cousin's house. For the last few weeks though, we had stayed home, which was nice-doing nothing. I think that was the best part of the weekend.

I sat in my room for I don't know how long, lost in my wayward thoughts. Even though our house was older, below I could hear downstairs when Mom came home because there was a large squeal from Maggie. Mom and Dad were talking, and Dad's booming voice always carried. But I couldn't understand exactly what they were saying.

I heard someone, or something, slowly enter my room. It was our orange fluffy cat, who strolled in and looked up at me with his big dark sleep eyes as though he had just gotten up from an afternoon nap.

"Did you sleep okay, Billy Bob?" I asked, not really feeling angry anymore. I patted the bed to invite him up. "Come on, big boy."

He twisted his head to look down the hallway, and then licked his paw as if considering his options, then slowly walked over to me and jumped up. His fur was thick and soft as I slowly pet him, letting my fingers massage his neck. He instantly erupted into uncontrollable purrs.

That's when Mike's story floated back into my thoughts, as I stroked Billy Bob's fur as I began to think about the deal I was making to protect Jack, imagining how much I could count on this promise from Mike. But then I thought of the missing dogs and cats—people's pets—all the animals that had gone missing over the last couple of days. I knew that my family would be heartbroken without Billy Bob. I could remember picking him out at the shelter when I was four. He came to the front of the cage and purred when he saw me. I fell in love him at that moment. Perhaps that was why Mike's mom would not have another pet. These creatures were a part of our lives, a part of our families, and a part of our everything.

I pulled the dog collar from my pocket. Ginger's nametag was still on it. It was old, but looking at it, I noticed rips in it, as if it was torn off. Why was this at Old Man Fischer's house though? Was it just lying there? What had Mike's mother scared? What did happen that night?

"You look deep in thought," Mom said at the door.

I looked up at her, Billy Bob's purrs still going strong in the background, and I could feel their vibrations on the bed.

"I heard that you and Dad had a little blow up." She came over and sat on opposite of me. Billy Bob just looked up casually, content with being petted.

"Yeah," I said softly.

"Dad loves you," she said, running her thin fingers through my hair.

I looked at the collar in my hand.

"He only means well," she said softly. "He has been working a lot lately and that just makes him—"

"Crabby," I finished for her. I adjusted my glasses slightly on my nose.

Mom sighed. "Sometimes you two boys are so much alike that it's frightening."

"What do you mean by that?"

"Nothing. You'll understand one day." Then she saw what I was fumbling in my fingers. "Hey what's this?"

" A dog collar."

"I see it's a dog collar. Where did you get it?"

"From a boy at school. Mike."

"Isn't that the boy that gave your friend Jack a hard time last year?"

"Yeah."

Mom shifted slightly on the bed. "What are you doing with this then?"

I looked up at Mom. "If I tell you something, you have to promise that you won't say anything to anyone else. Promise?"

Her face was serious. Then she replied, "Promise."

I then told her Mike's story, about Ginger, about John at Old Man Fischer's house, leaving out the part about the deal with Mike not bullying Jack anymore.

At this point, Billy Bob must have grown tired of this spot, and leapt to the floor and slowly walked out of the room into the darkening hallway. Mom didn't say anything at first.

"What do you think?" I looked at her. I was anxious to know her response.

She took in a deep breath, and said softly, "Wait here. I will be back in a sec."

I did as she told me, listening as she walked down the stairs. Below me I heard muffled conversation with Dad, then I heard Mom tell Maggie to stay with Dad for "just a quick second." I listened to an airplane fly overhead, making a very faint screeching noise as it gained altitude and was finally above the cloudbank. The airport was only few miles from our house, which meant that we were sometimes in the flight path of planes as they took off and landed, when plane engines are always at their loudest. I didn't know any different.

Mom appeared a few minutes later with a glass of wine in one hand, and a glass of milk in the other. She handed the milk to me and took a sip of the wine before setting it on the nightstand next to my bed as she stepped over my of Lego structures and models. I felt slightly guilty for not picking those up from the weekend.

"Okay, Mom just needed that." She sat back down in the same spot next to me. I shifted over slightly, feeling the warmth of the cat's recently vacated spot.

"Well?" I prompted.

"Patience, young man," she said, smiling. "You need to learn some patience."

Outside, the wind kicked up a little and I heard the force of it press against my window. We both looked at the white blinds, hoping that another one of those gusts would not come again. Soon the pitter patter of rain droplets fell against the window, echoing a faint drum beat into my quiet room.

"Do you know why we bought this house, Shane?" Mom's voice seemed quiet.

I shrugged my shoulders.

"This may sound silly," she said, resting her hand on my knee. "It was the trees in our front yard."

I didn't know where she was going with this, so I said, "Mom, okay. What does this have to do with Mike's story?"

She ignored me. "The huge trees on the south side of our house, the maples and elms, being the avid gardener that I am. But anyway, they must have been planted them when this house was a farm in the eighteen hundreds. When I looked at them and saw how big they were, I fell in love with this house. They seemed to protect the house. The Realtor, her name is Barbara Freeman, showed me this house. She lives only one block over, and I see her occasionally at in the grocery stores from time to time. Her kids were your age when we moved here. Now they have moved onto college. Anyway, this house was stop number three. We pulled up in her car, on a rainy day in late summer, and the trees and the grasses were an unimaginably beautiful green. I saw the trees and I knew that this was the house I could spend the rest of my life in. Then, when I saw the porch, and how it made the house seem so quaint and welcoming, unlike any other house on the block, even before I set foot in the house, I knew this would be the house to raise our family in.

"I looked down the block after we toured the house. I saw the large trees hanging over the street. I could even see larger trees on other's land. It felt as if the trees were the watchers of our block. When Dad saw this house, he fell in love with the fireplace and the space in the kitchen, which we remodeled before you were born."

She stretched her legs slightly and took a sip of wine. Then she placed a thin warm hand on my leg, and continued without looking at me, but watching the rain outside.

"At the time when we bought this house, Dad and I were young. Hard to believe, right?" A small smile caressed her lips. "It's been fourteen years now, this month, to be exact. We were busy with our careers, almost too busy, I should really say, and did not have any clue about you and Maggie coming in our lives so soon. Dad worked out in the suburbs, I think in Schaumberg or Bollingbrook, I can't remember, in a large private club as a sous chef, working disgustingly long hours. I suppose he needed that job, and the countless, thankless ones after that too, in order to have the bakery today. A lot of the members from that club long ago are his clientele now. It always comes full circle.

"Me: I was on my way up the ladder too, earning my keep and learning the ropes in the business. I stayed in hotels, selling weekend business, booked thousands of weddings, funerals, bat mitzvahs, whatever it took. And in the nineties, there was a lot of that business too. I rarely had weekends off, much less a Friday off. I suppose your father and I were a perfect match for our jobs. When we bought this house, it was just the right time.

"Our little downtown here was not how you see it today. Oh no, it had two restaurants, a shoe shop, a hobby store, a candy store, a bar and the rail station going into Chicago. City Hall was in need of repair. Now, we see how much this town had grown, how busy it is, how many new restaurants there are, how many kids live here, how many new schools have opened. It is just amazing. But the trees, the trees were never torn down unless there was storm damage or disease. I think this was what made our town so nice over the years. I just couldn't imagine living in a new suburb without trees.

"Once we moved in here, we had just enough stuff from our downtown condo to get by, but our house felt rather empty and over time we managed to fill it up. We had enough belongings when we moved, especially for the kitchen. You can imagine that Dad was a little crazy, even then, about his kitchen gadgets," she smiled at me and then turned away, back toward the empty space. "And he still is today about that stuff, but don't say anything.

"Even with my long hours, I happened to have a Friday night

off. It was rare when that would happen, but none of my groups were booked on that day. It was a perfect day for me to get us sorted. Dad would not have a day off for a week or so. Our schedules always conflicted with each other, still does from time to time.

"That Friday night, it was cool outside, clear enough to see the stars above. That I do remember. I had just finished putting away all of the kitchen stuff, putting contact paper down on the shelves, scrubbing down the refrigerator, all those things that us crazy moms do. I was busy organizing, and cleaning, blah, blah, blah, I was just happy that it was done and I could do some other unpacking. So I decided to take a break.

"I went outside to our front porch. We only had couple of ugly yellow chairs that we got from your Grandmother. Once we got new furniture for out there, I was really happy to throw those out. There I sat with a glass of good cabernet, watching the neighborhood go by. It was quiet that night. I watched for some time as the houses slowly went to sleep. Soon the street got dark. For a couple of years, I would laugh about the houses going dark so early with my friends at work. Then you came along and I discovered quickly that lights do go out early when you have kids.

"That night, I sat enjoying the quietness of the street. Barely had I heard a car pass by. I'm still glad we picked Bend Street because Ashland has a lot more traffic noise, but our street still remains as quiet as it's always been.

"I looked out onto the moon-drenched street, in the darkness the shadows seemed almost to come to life. It was like when I lived in Michigan as a kid. At night, the shadows were always so big, and so dark. As a little girl, I looked out my window, and the single streetlight was never enough light. Here I loved the darkness of these shadows.

"There was something different that night in the darkness. I really couldn't put my finger on it. I thought because I had been inside most of the night, smelling the harsh cleaning chemicals that they had affected my eyesight. And honestly, I was just getting a little light headed, my dear. I thought it was just me, but there really wasn't that much sound in the neighborhood. I did not mind. You know how I like my quietness. This night was different though.

"It just seemed like there was no movement at all. There was no breeze. The trees were almost motionless. The leaves on the ground didn't move. I didn't hear a car going through our little downtown. How long this lasted I wasn't sure.

"I was about to get up and return to my unpacking project. when a dog's rapid barking caught me off-guard. I stayed still in my chair. I thought it sounded as though it was about five or six houses away. I did remember spotting a small Yorkshire terrier there the first week we lived here, but that small animal couldn't have made such a big fuss, unless it was in trouble.

"I sunk down in my chair, thinking about how I should blend into my own shadows of the house. The barking was so loud and continuous. I thought for sure that the neighbors would wake up from this, but nothing. No lights came on.

"Then, the barking just stopped. The silence returned. I stayed in my chair for a while longer, thinking that somebody may have noticed me. Then something happened that I can't really explain, except that across the street where the Dunn's' live, I saw in the shadows, something moved. Something alive. It was subtle, just a small movement, and I had to concentrate on the movement, to see what shape it was,. Like I said, I wasn't sure if the cleaning chemicals had gotten to me, or maybe it was the little bit of wine I'd had, but my eyes just couldn't make sense of the dark shape. It moved in a way that was unfamiliar to me. Whatever it was, it was something I had never seen before. Yet, there in the darkness, through the glare of moonlight, I would swear I saw something carrying off the body of a small dog. I still cannot say for sure." Mom stopped and took another, deeper sip from her glass.

The rain was a good noise now, feeling some comfort in its beat. I looked at my mother, as she stared off into space.

I finally spoke, "Did you ever tell Dad about this?"

Mom looked at me then. "No, I never have. I don't know why really. I just sort of put it out of my mind. But Mike's story just reminded me of that time."

"What about Old Man Fischer?" I asked. My voice was slightly anxious.

"Mr. Fischer," my mom corrected me. Then she said, "He is a nice old man."

"How do you know?" I asked.

"We used to talk to each other from time to time." Mom said as she sat up straighter. "We used to talk about gardening. When I walked past his house when you were little, I admired his gardens and he used to be fanatic about them. Remember him saying that he retired from the university and gardening had been his new passion. Now, well, now I think they were too much work for him and let them go."

"Do you still talk to him?"

She got a sad look on her face. "Well, no. Haven't for, gosh, I don't know how long."

I stood up, "Then how do you know that he doesn't have something to do with this?"

"Shane, that's a big accusation you're making. And, there's no proof." Mom stood up next to me and picked up her glass. She checked her reflection in the mirror above my dresser.

I held up the collar, jingling the tags. , "Isn't this proof enough?" I said bluntly.

"Anything could have left it there." She just looked at me. "Come on, young man. Don't you have some math problems to finish?" she asked as she left my room.

I followed behind her, not ready to give up our debate., "Mom, really, think about it. Why did Old Man Fischer want Mike's brother off his porch so bad?"

"Because he and his friend were causing trouble. I know Mike's brother, John. He was not as a nice kid as he'd have everyone believe." Mom put a hand on her hip, took another sip of wine, emptying her glass, then said: , "You have homework to do. No more stalling, mister."

I felt a flush of heat in my cheeks. I followed down the hallway, with Billy Bob close on my heels until he drifted off in the direction of Mom and Dad's room, disappearing into the dark shadows.

We were going down the stairs and Maggie came towards Mom excitedly. "I missed you too, Sugar Bear." Mom said instantly as Maggie hugged her leg.

I just wasn't ready to let this go. "Mom, there has to be something to this."

"To what?" Dad asked as he came from the kitchen drying his hands.

Mom gave me a stern look then smiled, "Shane's imagination." Then she said to me, as she pointed at my stagnant pile of homework, "Get to it." And that was the end of that discussion.

I obeyed, shoving the collar into my pocket. I started to do my homework, staring at the same problem as I had before.

I overheard Dad ask Mom, "What were you guys talking about?" As he followed her into the kitchen. I saw her grab her phone. She had her back to me. "And who are you calling?"

Mom said nothing, waiting for a response on the other end. Maggie was playing around her legs, giggling.

"Well, I'm going up to shower," Dad announced and headed up the stairs, shaking his head as he ascended to the next floor.

"Hello, Mr. Fischer?" Mom said into the phone.

I froze and felt the pit of my stomach fall into the chair. I was lost for words.

Mom talked joyfully, her voice like a fluttering butterfly. "It's me, Allison. Yes, Allison O'Conner. I know it's been a long time. Yes. Yes. Yes, they are, aren't they? I was wondering... No, no. You are too kind. Mr. Fischer, I was wondering if Shane and I could come by one day to visit?" Mom slowly turned toward me, biting on a nail. A clear sign that she too was nervous. "Tomorrow night? Are you sure that's okay? Then tomorrow night. Yes, I will bring home one of Donald's scrumptious pies. Lemon Meringue as you liked them? Yes. Good. Good. See you then."

She hung up her phone.

I could only stare at her in disbelief, unable to utter a word.

Mom finished her glass of wine and walked towards me.

"Shane, I do know Mike's mother. Emily is a good person, . I see her once in a while at the school, and once in a great while, I do get to spend some time talking with her over coffee. Emily is a good person. She's been through a lot, especially with the divorce and after, and now raising those two hellions on her own. She's hinted at that story once, the one about Ginger." I heard Dad come down the stairs then, and Mom said simply, "There, if you need the proof, we'll get it."

Mom was a very direct person, always getting to the bottom of things quickly. She did not have time to waste on foolishness. "Make sure you have your homework done at school tomorrow."

"But Mom," I protested.

"No buts, now," she replied and smiled. She kissed me on the head.

Soon Dad came in, fresh and clean, and Mom couldn't wait to tell him. , and followed him into the kitchen. Dad accused Mom of being nosy. She didn't really explain why we were going to Old Man Fischer's, but he decided he had heard enough.

I could barely get through my homework, thinking of the neighborhood in the darkness, covered in shadows.

And shapes I could, or could not, see.

Russell

FOUR

In class today, Mrs. Dolan, my social studies teacher, talked about the next assignment. We were to find a country of our choice, find some interesting facts, and then create a poster board of our findings. Finally, we were to discuss it in front of the class. That part was I too fond about because I didn't like speaking in front of the class. The buzz in the class between the other kids were talking about what country to choose. Mrs. Dolan gave us a jump start so she allowed us time to go the library.

On the way there, I scooted quickly ahead of the pack so I could get one of the four computers. Still tired from a lack of sleep last night, mom's story seeped into my dreams. making me wake up every so often. But I had to be awake. The trip to the library gave me a new mission.

Entering the school's library, it was a rectangular shape: On the left side, the bookshelves were arranged in order of reading levels; and, while the right side, the reference section held many magazines, encyclopedias and factual information. The center of the area consisted of several rows of small tables that six students could easily sit around. Because the library was in the heart of the three story school, no windows gave any hint of the outside. Above, the overhead lights shone brightly and chased any shadows out of the way.

Immediately, making a bee line to the right far corner, I wanted a computer. At home, mom and dad let me use the laptop whenever either one of them are not on it. They encouraged me to use as much as possible. If I did not know the answer to something, I googled it. Mom was proud how quickly I took to researching topics. Usually I would look for new video games, history stuff and a bunch of YouTube videos of stupid people doing stupid things.

Several of the kids went to the reference area and grabbed books. While couple other boys and girls went into the stacks of books. Behind me, I heard Natalie, Sam and Linda walking fast behind me as well, heading for the computers. Choosing the one that faced the wall, I sat down because it was a good location to see the entire library. Quickly, I hit the internet because I had other research to do.

Slightly blocking my view, Natalie took the computer directly opposite of me.

"What's your country, Shane?" Her thick dark glasses made her round face wider.

"Not sure yet." I replied. She was so snoopy and stuck her nose into everyone else's business.

To be safe, I popped up another screen and typed in *World Map*.

"Well, I'm researching Brazil." Her voice was confident. Admittedly, she was rather smart and had the best grades in the class. But she liked to rub it into everyone's face. "My father says it's one of the BRIC countries. Brazil, Russia, India and China are supposed to be the next superpower countries."

"Okay. Good for you." I remarked dryly. Natalie's father was a professor at University of Chicago. I think he taught history or law. I was not sure and did not care.

I opened the other browser and typed in *Fischer* that loaded a million hits. I had to be more precise in my words.

"You never said what your country." She insisted. Leaning forward, she strained to see what I was typing.

Next to her, Linda who was always so cheerful piped into the conversation. She stated, "Well I'm researching Canada because my grandparents are from Quebec."

"We didn't ask you—" Natalie began and gave Linda a sour look as if she interrupted an important conversation.

I was glad, so Natalie didn't have to talk to me. Linda was too nice and her long dark curls fluttered in her face. Ignoring Natalie, Linda tugged at the strings on her Gap pink hoodie.

"Well I just like to tell you." Linda smiled and added, "You don't have to be so serious all the time, Nat."

"I told you not to call me 'Nat.'" Natalie seemed to bark.

Looking at the screen, I realized that I never knew Old Man Fischer's first name. So I typed in his address. Soon the screen popped up and saw his name.

"Hans," I said aloud.

"Hans is not a country, Shane." Natalie interjected. Her eyes squinted and shifted her body, moving up in the chair. She wanted to see what I was working on. "What are you really doing over there?"

"None of your business." I stated. I didn't have time for her.

"Better sit down before Mrs. Harris sees you," Linda warned Natalie in a half whisper.

"What are you working on?" Natalie was craning her head over to my screen as I popped onto the World Map.

"My country," I stammered. I could smell her cherry shampoo as her stringy brown long hair fell over the screen. I backed away in disgust.

"Natalie, Mrs. Harris." Linda whispered loudly.

"Shush up," Natalie only said, almost seeing what I was working on.

"What are you doing, Ms. Stills?" Mrs. Harris, who was the librarian, usually addressed us by our last name. How the woman could remember over six hundred some names baffled me. Turning my head to the right, a large robust woman in a thick mauve colored sweater and long brown skirt came headed toward us. Her thin face meant business as her eyes glared over at Natalie who still did not turn away.

"Nothing." Reluctantly, Natalie sat back down and appeared scorned. She was busted!

A smile crept on my face.

"Well to me, looks like you are bothering Mr. O'Conner there." The older woman stood straight and eyed me up.

I tapped my fingers on the keyboard and brought up a picture of Ireland. "No, no, Mrs. Harris. Natalie was helping me brainstorm my topic on Ireland."

Raising her left thick eyebrow, Natalie added sarcastically, "Yes, Shane sometimes does need assistance on big assignments."

Clearing her guttural throat loudly as if she was about to say something, she saw over towards the fiction area where some noise occurred. Doug, Greg and Brian were goofing around, laughing and giggling.

"Fine then," she said as her expression turned sourer. "Ms. Stills, you need to remain planted in your seat for the rest of your time here."

"Yes, ma'am." Natalie replied with a syrupy smile.

Soon, she walked away and headed towards the boys in the far end of the library.

Surprised, Linda remarked in a half-whisper, "You almost got caught."

"Just work on your stuff." Natalie snapped at her and then to me. "Ireland?"

"Hello? O'Conner?" I answered and shrugged my shoulders.

From that point on, Natalie said nothing more and remained quiet. On the occasion, Linda wanted to talk about to Natalie. Natalie rudely shut her down.

Keeping an eye Mrs. Harris, I noticed Mrs. Dolan entered the library. Casually, Mrs. Dolan glanced around the library and headed to the kids in the reference section. As far as I was concern, she could remain there for the whole time.

I needed to find out more information on Old Man Fischer. There had to be some information on him. Before we saw him tonight.

Near me, Sam, who was not at all interested in the assignment, curled his long thin body down into his chair. He then pulled out his iPhone and played a game.

On the screen, I clicked on the first most recent article on Fischer:

"Northwestern University received a substantial donation from Dr. Hans Fischer, an emeritus professor of the science college. His renowned research in ecology, concentrating on deforestation and human damage in rainforests, shaped many current studies on the environmental studies today. Dr. Fischer's kind donation will continue to support..."

I realized he was a doctor. Maybe a medical doctor.

I googled *Dr. Hans Fischer.* A huge list of information generated before me. Thousands and thousands of scholarly articles appeared about or referenced from his work by other scientists. It overwhelmed me. Skimming the bold highlights, his studies in Central America in the late sixties and seventies took were the main source of the information. Never knew Old Man Fischer travelled. *Did Mom know?* As I scrolled through quickly, Fischer was part many other studies throughout the world. Most of the articles centered around his studies on biology and the environment. So many articles! I didn't have time for that. Finally, Fischer wrote five books that were reference guides on tropical insects. Looking at one cover, I knew the library had one of his books. I wonder why the school never offered Fischer to come and talk about it to the classes.

Just as the many articles about his work, the positive reviews about his work were as equal. From the google captions, Fischer's studies were "groundbreaking", "unprecedented", "revolutionized ecological studies" and even "brilliant". Over and over, the science world revered Fischer as a brilliant scientist. Dr. Fischer's last written article was in the early nineties. He was an intelligent, *rather too* intelligent man.

But why did he stop? I only wondered.

Near me, Sam stirred his chair and caused it to squeak slightly. The library was too still, except for the clicks on the keyboards, soft whispers and soft shuffling of footsteps. I stayed focused on the screen, knowing my time so limited. I just played with key words around Fischer and science and life.

About ten or so minutes later, I noticed an unusual article from *International Science Today* from 1991. The title was called, *The Man Whose Voice Brought the Unseen World to Light: An Examination into Dr. Hans Fischer's Revolutionary Discoveries and Evolutionary Trajectories of the Central American Insecta Familia.* Honestly, couldn't they have shortened it? What grabbed my interest was a small black and white picture of Fischer, which revealed a slightly younger, thicker hair man with the same thin face. Still, his face remained the same: icy, somber and murky. In the picture, he seemed rather upset as if he was offended about taking a picture.

"Hey, Shane," Natalie whispered, "Mrs. Dolan is coming over. Better exit out of whatever you are really doing."

Instantly, my eyes searched for our teacher.

I did like Mrs. Dolan because she actually cared for the students. Her smile was sincere and her motherly guidance reflected in her lessons. Now, she was near Linda who began to babble about

Quebec. Maybe Linda was helping me cover up too.

"Thanks," I whispered to Natalie.

She only nodded with a small grin. Did I owe her something now? I hoped not.

Instantly, I minimized the article and opened the world map. I quickly googled Ireland History and popped several articles. I clicked on several of them, Feverishly, I wrote some notes on my pad. I don't think she saw me because Linda distracted her long enough.

"Sam, this is your time of research, not playing," Mrs. Dolan firmly stated as she left Linda.

Banking around the corner, Mrs. Dolan told Sam briefly that he needed to do research on his assignment. "Otherwise, I'll take your phone again," she threatened politely.

Near me, I saw her glance at my screen and smiled. Her face was bright and sincere against the drab grey institutionalized walls.

"What country are you exploring, Shane?" she said to me softly.

Stammering, I responded, "Well, uh, I was thinking about—"

"Yes, Shane, what were you researching?" Natalie spoke up. A devilish speck filled her dark eyes behind her thick lenses.

Keeping her eyes on me, Mrs. Dolan replied, "Natalie, I was not speaking with you. It'll be your turn shortly."

Natalie's mouth pinched a gloating grin and she purposely hid behind her screen. Oh, she was such an instigator! No wonder why she didn't have many friends.

"I was working on Ireland, Mrs. Dolan." My voice cracked slightly.

"That's good," my teacher seemed pleased. "I was hoping so. Ireland is rich in history."

Taking her lead, I remarked, "Yes. And that's why I'm sorta stuck. There's so much. See?"

On the screen I popped open several reference pages that were obnoxiously long. I hoped that she couldn't see the small sweat running down the side of my face.

Leaning over, a subtle whiff of flowers could be detected as Mrs. Dolan skimmed the words. Turning her head slightly, smiling, and she said, "Ireland does have a lengthy history. Do you know where your family is from?"

"Well, my grandmother said that we came from Belfast, Northern Ireland."

"Okay, then." She stood straight back up. "Narrow your search to that area. You'll find Ireland to be fascinating, Shane. How the IRA divided Belfast and the country. Of course, the legendary Michael Collins who spearheaded the labor unions. The great potato famine. The British Monarchy had along hold on the Irish government. Then you go back farther, you will discover the Celtic People."

"Sounds interesting." I only said. Now I felt I had a lot of work ahead of me. No problem though.

"Good. Remember you don't have only today to do research." Mrs. Dolan said softly. "I just wanted all of you to have the opportunity to discover your country and what interests you about it. Good work."

I only nodded.

Moments later, she already went to Natalie. I even think Mrs. Dolan did not tolerate Natalie's know-it-all attitude as Natalie described how she already found topographical, economic and population counts on Brazil. While Natalie spoke, Mrs. Dolan just nodded. Before the teacher left, she asked Natalie, "That's fine information, but what makes you want to research Brazil? Is it the culture? The history? Rio de Jinero? Think about it."

Soon the same boys were goofing again near the copier in the far corner and Mrs. Dolan excused herself.

Next to me, Sam took out his phone and continued to play his game again. Linda was softly talking to Natalie trying to get her for some help. Condescendingly, Natalie spoke to Linda as if she was in second grade and typed in some words to help her search. Now, I would have stood up for Linda, but already time was slipping by.

I needed more information.

I pulled up the article once again.

The length of the article was about fifty pages long. Trying to read quickly, which was impossible, the reporter was evidently a science researcher himself and the content was rather longwinded. Attempting to read the article made me groggy. Even more, the writer kept asking about the discoveries on ants, butterflies, and other things in the rainforests and the 'methodology the cataloguing of the species'. If this was how scientists spoke to each other, I was not going into that career. I just wished that I could print off the article.

About two thirds away through, the writer began to discuss

Fischer's history:

"The enigmatic Dr. Fischer rarely speaks about his personal life and his background. After several accolades about his recent contributions to the scientific community, Dr. Fischer then alluded to his childhood in the Eastern German Block near the Polish border which up until recently was under Soviet control. With a distraught guise, he indicated that his father was a political prisoner and added mournfully, 'He was sent off when I was very young. It was really only my mother and myself.' This reporter researched his father's history, but could not find any shred of evidence or proof of his existence. Perhaps when the Iron Curtain finally falls one day, new information will arise.

Still, I inquired about how he began his relentless fascination with s mall creatures. Fischer responded simply with a rare smile, 'Unknowing, mesmerizing and magnificent.' He further indicated that 'the tiny world allowed me to escape my dismal childhood.'

When this reporter questioned him about his move to United States, Fischer became solemn and refused to discuss any detail. He only discussed briefly that he travelled to Toronto Canada for a new opportunity to earn his first doctorate degree. About six years later, he was offered a research position in Northwestern University where he met his wife..."

"Alright everyone!" Mrs. Dolan called out. "Wrap up your materials. We have to move back to the classroom."

Almost startled, I looked past the screen and saw the others in the class grow restless. Some of the kids closed books on tables, some of the kids stood in line to check out materials, and other kids began to line up. Already noises of chairs and chatter filled up the space.

Next to me, Sam shrugged his shoulders as he stood up, yawning and pocketing his phone. He said to me, "Great research day. Just battled a new realm."

I smiled at him.

While I stood up, stretching me legs, I closed out my articles and logged off. *Why was Old Man Fischer so secretive? Was he really married? Why didn't Mom ever tell me?*

When we went back to class, I could only think about Dr. Hans Fischer.

FIVE

Standing at the top of the stairs, I looked down, straining to see into the living room. I called out again, "Mom? Dad? Maggie? Where are you?"

My pajamas were wet from sweat, but I didn't want to take them off yet. I just felt really groggy, as if my head was in a tunnel or something. I knew I didn't want to go down the stairs, but I didn't see anybody up here. I didn't hear anybody, especially Maggie. She was usually screaming to get me up in the morning, or she was just running around and being her generally noisy self. It sort of felt like a weekend day.

I began to step down, bending over as far as I could to see into the living room. There was nothing.

"Mom? Dad? Maggie? Where are you guys?" I said aloud, but even my own voice was shaky and didn't seem to carry.

As I reached the bottom step I felt the cool breeze from outside when I heard a small meow come from the kitchen.

"Billy Bob, come here," I called out.

On the dining table, I saw the beginning of breakfast, a Sunday breakfast. There was a large stack of steaming chocolate chip pancakes; a plate of hash browns, crispy , salty perfection; a platter of bacon and of course a pecan coffee cake, which was Dad's favorite treat. There were four place settings on the table, and everything was untouched.

But it wasn't Sunday already, I was becoming confused.

I looked into the living room, unlike the usual Maggie craziness of toys, dolls and blankets, it was perfectly straighten up as if Mom was expecting guests. Why would she have company so early in the morning? It was not like her, or any of us, to invite anyone over for breakfast.

I walked toward the kitchen, draft of air got colder and colder as I got closer. I heard Billy Bob's cry again in the distance. I thought it sounded as if he had escaped from the house. He would never leave; he hated being outside and wanted back in any time he found himself outside for even a minute. There was nothing on the fridge, like Dad or Mom had thrown out all of our crayon drawings. The sink and the stove were perfectly cleaned, not a dish or pot to be scrubbed.

I turned slowly to see the door cracked open. Mom and Dad wouldn't leave the house without me.

Slowly, I pushed the door open, calling a little louder, trying to shake off my nervousness, "Mom, Dad, Maggie, where are you?"

Nothing.

I opened the door wider, to see that it was now winter outside and freshly fallen snow covered the ground. The trees were covered in a thick blanket of snow, their branches extending like long claws, reaching to the ground. A slight wind blew over my face, and icy chill washed over me. I didn't turn to get my coat. I needed to find my family. Slowly, I stepped out onto the snow-covered ground, my foot disappearing into the whiteness.

A couple of feet from the house, I saw a large orange bump lump in the street. It had to be Billy Bob. I felt my heart race, and I knew I had to get him inside.

I started to chase him. He saw me and looked frightened and bolted in the opposite direction. I ran down the street in the snow, not caring if my feet were getting wet, not caring if I was shivering from the cold, not caring about leaving the house open. I had to get him and he was so far ahead of me.

"Billy Bob!" I yelled.

The wind picked up the snow, blowing it in my face, making it harder and harder for me to see. I wanted Mom or Dad to come out and help me. Where could they be? I was honestly beginning to worry. What if they disappeared? What would I do? I didn't know the answers. My heart was thumping hard in my chest, and I was beginning to sweat, but my sweat was freezing against me and my hands were becoming numb to the cold.

I seemed to get farther and farther away from the warmth of my house. Farther and farther Billy Bob led me down the street. It was as if he was being drawn to something, though he'd never stepped outside. I knew that we'd adopted him, that he had been out on the street when he was kitten. But he enjoyed being an inside cat now, getting all his treats, being pampered by me, and being brushed. He loved sleeping on my bed with me. What could possibly get him going like this?

I ran further down the street turning the corner. It felt familiar in a way. I knew this path. It was the way to school.

I looked to the right, to count the houses, knowing whose would be next. Even in these houses there seemed to be no one inside. There was no light, no smoke coming out of the smoke stacks. Nothing. The sidewalks were not shoveled. The driveways were not shoveled either. Snow swirled around these houses, piling more to the corners, in the valleys of the roofs, against the chimneys, to the edges of the yards.

It was like an eerie frozen ghost town.

I knew by now that most of the block should be out trying to clear away the snow. A snowplow should be coming by to clear the snow off the street, even putting down a layer of salt to melt the ice.

But there was no one. Anywhere. No movement at all.

I was sliding now, with my cold wet feet unable to get traction to get the momentum I needed to go further. The cold air was filling in my lungs, making breathing harder. I saw my breath as I choked it out, like Dad's old lawnmower sputtering smoke out the side.

I ran faster now to catch my cat.

"Mom! Dad! Maggie! Anybody!" I yelled out, but even the snow swallowed up my voice. I was beginning to freeze now, and my body was shaking harder. My teeth chattered in the bitterly cold air, making an odd rattling sound that sounded like bones shaking together in an empty box.

Then I saw it: Old Man Fischer's house. It was tall and dark, stark against the crisp whiteness of the snow. I could see plumes of dark smoke floating into the sky above it. There were no lights in the house that I could see from the windows. Instead, they seemed to stare back at me with an evil sneer. Is it possible that the house was staring back at me, beckoning me forth with its promise of warmth? The path was shoveled clear, revealing a frozen gravel walkway; the snow along the path had streaks of black dust, edging the path with what looked like a mouthful of jagged black teeth.

And at that very gate, as it blew back and forth in the wind, Billy Bob sat, waiting for me. He patiently licked his front paw, removing the snow from his fur as if he were killing time until our appointment time was called.

I caught up to him, and stood at the entrance of Old Man Fischer's house. I scooped him into my arms where he instantly began to purr, and nestled his chilly head into my sweatshirt.

"What made you run so far, Billy Bob?" I muttered as I worked to catch my breath.

The cat only nestled further into my chest and I truly started to feel the burning numbness in my feet. We had to get back home to look for Mom, Dad and Maggie.

Just as I was about to turn, the front door opened slightly with a creak. I thought I was in one of those trances as I watched the door open. An reddish-orange glow came from inside the house, with such a strong heat that the snow outside the door started to steam and recede. In between the flickers of light, a shape began to take form, a human shape.

Old Man Fischer himself slowly came to edge of the door.

My heart was pounding. I was more from the sight of Old Man Fischer than from the frigid temperatures. I was rooted to the spot, the icy air creating a tight blanket around me.

At that moment, Old Man Fischer said in low voice, "Come to me."

Billy Bob jumped out of my hands onto the gravel path.

"No!" I screeched as I tried to reach for my cat, but my legs were frozen to the spot. I could not break the loose. I was stuck there as I watched my cat slowly pad up the path to the hunched-over old man. His smile grew wider and wider, exposing his wolf like fangs.

The cat made his way to the man and jumped into his arms.

"Mom! Dad! Help!" I screamed.

I kept trying to pull at my legs, but I could not free them.

Snow began to fall harder, larger flakes filling the air and, settling on me. I could not feel my feet anymore. I looked at my hands to see them turn to deep purplish-blue color, squeezing them closed and opened again and again, unable to get any feeling from them. I could barely breathe in the painfully cold air. Without realizing it, I had started to cry, the tears were freezing on my face.

"MOM! DAD! HELP!"

Old Man Fischer looked up at me, grinning wider, the grimace taking up most of his face. He opened his arms letting Billy Bob go. The cat jumped down, sauntered around his decrepit legs and walked into the house, into the intense glow of flames inside the house.

I twisted harder, frantic to stop the scene that was unfolding. "NO! LET MY CAT GO!" I yelled at him.

"Mr. O'Conner, it's time for you," the man growled to me, opening his arms wide.

"NO! NO!"

The cold had becoming so bitter, so bitingly unbearably cold.

"Mr. O'Conner, it's time for you," he repeated without moving.

"NO! NO! MOM! DAD!"

Old Man Fischer seemed to be moving toward me, growing larger, thinner. His sharp smile was tightening on his face, his lips unmoving as he spoke.

"Mr. O'Conner, it's time for you," he repeated.

The cold was making me tremble violently.

"Mr. O'Conner, it's time for you."

"NO! NOOOOOO! MOMMM!"

"Mr. O'Conner, it's time..." He was looming so close now.

I had to leave. I had to run! The snow was too much----

******

"Shane! It's time."

It was Mrs. A.'s voice invading my consciousness. I opened my eyes to find myself in Room B105. She was giving me a concerned look as I tried to get my bearings. I was struggling to erase the images of Old Man Fisher and the snow out of my head.

"Are you okay, Shane?"

I didn't say anything at first, just kept trying to bring myself together the fact that I was at school again. I must have dozed off.

"You were having a bad dream, weren't you?" She leaned closer to me. I could smell the coffee on her breath.

I sat straighter in the hard chair, and felt a cramp in the back of my neck. I must have really been out. There were no other kids in the room, and half of the lights were out. Outside the clouds made the day look dim and gloomy, a typical fall day.

"Yeah, guess so," I said, feeling reality slipping in and out as it battled for space with the images from my nightmare inside my head. I heard the other kids playing on the playground, and when I looked up at the clock it read three fifty-five, only about a half an hour or so until Dad would be here to pick me up.

"Shane, you know that I don't allow naps in the afternoon, but this time you were just too tired," Mrs. A. said as she got up and walked toward the counter. "What were you dreaming about, dear?"

"My cat," I said. I just did not know whether to tell her more. "He was running away from me."

Her body was hunched over the sink as she strained to look outside, at the playground. "This time of year you don't let your pets wander off to far."

I looked at her, willing my heartrate to calm in my chest, feeling like he was still after me.

"I've lived in this town for a long time, thirty-some years, and for a long time before I retired as a teacher from this school," Mrs. A. said. Her voice was distant, as if she was talking out loud to me, or to no one in particular. "But I do know that about this time of year, once the animals begin to disappear, I lock my doors and shut my windows. Ever since Lloyd died, I just don't trust anything."

She was wiping a pan slowly with a yellow towel. "This isn't the first time this has happened. It happens every so often and when it does, a lot of animals disappear. This time, around October. Never before, never after. This month only. I read the reports of the missing dogs and cats in the press. It's so sad for these creatures."

"Why?" I asked, in barely a whisper.

Pausing, her blue-grey eyes cast faint shadows on her long wrinkled face in the fading light. Looking out the window, straightening her back slightly, she continued, "About thirty or so years ago, I was walking through the Forest Reserve just across from Odgen. As a teacher then, I would have to get my walks in early, before school; it was a nice clear fall day, perfect for an early morning walk. That's when I discovered that... that *massacre*," she whispered.

Barely able to mutter a response, I asked, "What massacre?"

Mrs. A. turned to me. From this distance, with the grayness of the sky and the shadows in that corner of the room as the backdrop, I thought for a moment that she seemed transparent. I could see through her then I blinked and she was whole again. My eyes were playing tricks on me.

"There were no leaves on the trees, and the branches were long arms swaying in the brisk wind that day, . I could see for yards all around me. Usually, Joanne Cummings, who lived in the house behind me, would go walking with me, before she went off to her secretarial job in the city. I suppose I was foolish to walk alone, making that choice, thinking that I would be okay, but I liked to get in a brisk walk before I came to teach the kids back then. It woke me up. Really I really didn't notice it; well you wouldn't have noticed it in a blink. There was no one else on the trail, and I slowed down, looking at these mounds of leaves, like they were purposely piled, but their color was peculiar though, for fall colors, too dark. So I got up the courage and went off the path to walk closer to a pile, it wasn't more than fifteen or twenty feet away. I walked slowly, too slowly. I realized later that there were no birds chirping, no other animal noises, just the sound of the branches moving above me.

"As I got closer, I couldn't believe my eyes. There was so much carnage, so much blood and gore!" Pausing, she clutched the small gold crucifix around her neck, and stood straighter. Outside, the kids were running around on the playground, playing tag, basketball, whatever. I sat still, absorbed by her story. "I could not hold down my breakfast, and vomited, and then I screamed. Luckily a man on bicycle was coming toward me, and I flagged him down. I never went back in the Preserve after that day." Mrs. A. was nodding shaking her head 'no' to herself. Not for me. "I won't."

I straightened in my chair. I had to ask, "What was it?"

She set down the dish, and leaned against the counter. Her head turned toward the grey skyline, and said, "Deer. A dozen deer." She paused. "The press never said what got to them, but I know it had to be a large animal, something big enough to bring down those animals. There had to be five animals. What was even more tragic, two of the animals were still barely alive."

I heard a door open and some footsteps running into the classroom.

"The funny thing is that the animals were covered on purpose,"

57

she said, more confidence in her voice. "On purpose."

The footsteps were coming closer. "Mrs. A, do you think that Old Man Fischer has something to do with this?"

"Shane! Come outside!" Jack yelled at me from the doorway. He was breathing hard.

I looked at him. He wore an excited expression, and his cheeks were apple red. Then I looked back at Mrs. A who was tiding up quickly now, and said to me in a hushed voice, "You are not the only one to think that." She looked at Jack, and smiled, "Go on, have some fun before your fathers comes to pick you guys up."

"Come on," Jack urged.

I needed to get in some fresh air, to shake off my foggy-headedness.

"I've got to show you something, !" Jack exclaimed as soon as I reached him. "Something cool that Darryl and I found at the edge of the playground," Jack continued rapidly. "I didn't believe it until I found it. I wish we had found this before, at recess or something. Do you know how cool that would have been?"

His voice was ringing in my ears as I followed him up the stairs, then out into the brisk air. We had past the other two teachers watching the kids on the playground. The one thing that I liked about after school, with such a small number of kids, I felt like I owned the playground and I had space to go anywhere. The other, smaller kids stayed with each and near the teachers, and mostly just played with each other. Jack and I always hung together after school.

I was still feeling groggy.

"You okay Shane?" Jack asked.

"Yeah," I lied.

"You never take naps. I've never seen you take a nap. I know I took a nap once in the second grade and the teacher just about had a fit." Then he looked ahead at a kid with red hair sitting at the edge of the playground. "Hey Darryl!"

"I know," I said. "I just didn't sleep well last night."

"How come?" Jack asked.

I felt winded from running to get to the corner of the playground, opposite of the gym which was on the far side, where it was fenced-off, with the street and the sidewalk just on the other side. Before I could tell Jack about my sleep problems last night, we reached Darryl, who had been waiting for us and hadn't moved from his spot. He was smiling as we approached, and kept looking down.

I stopped running when we got a couple of feet away. There were no other kids around us and the school looked like a huge red-bricked monument behind us.

Without any preamble, Jack pointed and said, "There, down here."

I followed his extended finger to where he and Darryl were both staring into a storm drain that was half-exposed, passing under the fence and sidewalk, which sunk slightly lower than the rest of the playground. I knew Mike and his guys would skip school by crawling under this part of the fence.

I looked down into the darkness and noticed things floating in it, leaves and branches.

"Isn't that cool?" Jack asked. He just stared down there like it was the gates to the promised land or something.

"It's a pipe," I said. The images Mrs. A of her walk through the forest preserve came to my mind then.

"You're sure in a bad mood."

"No, just tired." I leaned against the fence.

"Look at this," Darryl said as he dropped a rock down the drain.

Jack was watching in fascination, excited even just to hear the splash of a rock. "That is so awesome. I bet that went at least ten miles an hour, causing a ripple effect in the tide. I wonder if the leaves sunk down to the bottom. I wonder how far down the bottom is."

Darryl said his mom's car pulled up and ran across the playground, telling Jack that he'd see him tomorrow.

"I am going to Old Man Fischer's house tonight," I said once Darryl was far enough away.

Jack stood up and blinked at me. His face was no longer excited but afraid.

Before I let him talk, I told Mom's story, shortening it a bit, ending with her calling the old man. I didn't say anything about what Mrs. A had just told me. I was still taking that one in.

"Is your mom nuts?" Jack asked.

"No."

"Why did she call him?"

"You know my mom," I said, looking past Jack onto the playground. "They are friends. She wanted to visit with him."

"I don't believe that," Jack said. He the fence with his fingers, and looked away from me into the street. Nearby, Darryl was dropping more rocks into the drain.

"We're going over there after she gets home."

"What are you going to ask him?" Jack was pulling his bodyweight back and forth to the fence. "Do you have something to ask him?"

"I can't think of anything."

"I always ask a lot of questions, Shane. My dad told me to write down all my questions, and I keep them in a notebook. He said if you can't find an answer right away, then I'll find one later. It never hurts to ask questions. My dad's a smart man."

Just then a cold breeze blew through me and I shook uncontrollably for a moment. In the distance, I saw Jack's dad enter the playground and walk over to Mrs. W. Within a couple of seconds, Mrs. W. was calling for Jack.

Jack turned to Mrs. W, and saw his dad, who waved at him that it was time for him to leave.

"Well, I have to go," he said. He looked worried for me. "Be careful tonight, okay?"

"I will."

As he started to run toward the building, he turned back and yelled to me, "You have to ask him something. Write it down. That's what I do." Before I knew it, Jack was sprinting across the playground to his dad. I just sat there and watched them leave.

I started to wander back toward the school, thinking about all the stories I'd heard in the past couple of days and the articles on the old man. I'd gotten a lot more information than I expected, and I just kept thinking that these occurrences might be related to each other somehow. I still didn't have much to go on, but I felt like I held a few pieces of the puzzle at least.

Screams snatched me from my private reflections. Other kids were running around, playing and laughing, I was lost in my own should have slept better last night, but all I could do was to stare at my ceiling, thinking about dark shadows and mysterious, reclusive old men.

In a couple of hours I would meet Old Man Fischer. We would be invited into his creepy old house and forced to make polite conversation and eat pie while Mom made small talk. How weird would that be? Would he notice that I was on to him?

And those were the things I just couldn't seem to get out of my head. The deer massacre, the missing pets, Mike's brother's missing dog from years ago, and the weird black shape my mom swore she spotted creeping through the neighbor's shrubs were just nagging at me. I couldn't shake the feeling that, somehow, someway, this all had something to do with that old man.

"What are you hiding Old Man Fischer?" I whispered.

"Huh?" asked a first-grade girl who was passing by me.

I looked at her in confusion for a second, then realized I must have really asked that question out loud. "Sorry, not talking to you," I answered and walked on.

What was Old Man Fischer hiding in that huge dark house?

You are not the only one to think that.

"Shane!" Mrs. W. called out. "Your Dad is here."

I looked up. and spotted Maggie already running toward me, giggling happily with her arms stretched open.

I shouldn't be nervous. Mom would be with me. So I just tried to keep that in mind and accept that this was really going to happen.

Russell

SIX

Dad was in odd mood today. Well, not odd so much as that he was actually in a good mood for once. I heard him humming a song--something from some band from the eighties, probably a metal band--in the kitchen as he made dinner. He had a full smile on his face; I hadn't seen Dad smile so freely in a while. I sat at the kitchen table trying to do my homework, waiting for Mom to get home.

"Hey buddy," Dad said, his back to me.

"Yeah?" I replied.

"Ready to take a break and have some dinner?" He turned then with two plates of steaming food in hand. He made my favorite, Chicago dogs and his homemade French fries. The fries were all dripping with ketchup.

Maggie kept saying, "Yummy," over and over again from her chair next to me, then she started clapping her hands fast.

Dad sat down opposite of me, and slid a plate in front of me. I was suddenly starving and the smell was making my mouth water. Before I could get a bite in, Dad looked at me and asked,, "Are you sure you want to go there tonight?"

I stopped and looked up at him.

He wore a thin smile that was partially concealed by his recent growth of harsh stubble. When Dad skipped shaving, I didn't like brushing up to his face for a hug, much less receiving a kiss from him. It made him look older as the patches of gray that were threaded along the cheekbones grew thicker and blended into the greying hair at his temples.

I didn't reply, and just started shoving some fries into my mouth.

"I can talk to Mom and call the whole thing off," he added.

While he waited for a response from me, he cut some of his food and handed it to a hungry Maggie who was pulling at his shirt sleeve trying to reach for pieces of food.

"Naw," I said with a mouth full of food.

He looked at me, but I was saved once his phone started ringing in his pocket. The muffled notes of a blaring guitar ringtone was by his favorite all-time favorite band in the world, The Scorpions. It grew louder as he pulled it from his pocket, but his smile turned serious when he looked at the display screen. "You know, I'm not going to answer it," he declared, as he set the small phone on the table. "I just want to have dinner with you guys tonight."

His phone continued its melody for a few seconds longer, the notes playing over and over, until he turned it off. That music really got on my nerves sometimes.

Perhaps this was a nice distraction for me. I did not think about the visit soon, time was flying by. All seemed okay to me. We ate quietly while Maggie belted out some smacking of her lips. I went back to my homework, spelling this time, which kept me busy, but wasn't as painful as math had been last night. I just tried to focus on that one task. Despite the odd dream I had earlier, my little nap seemed to refresh me and made me feel more awake and alert now.

I finished my meal, then Dad said, "Maybe you should go change your shirt. Looks like you got some hot dog business on it. And, brush your teeth, man, you gots some serious nasty French Fry-ness going on in that mouth of yours."

Coyly, dad gave me a wink and then hummed his song as he picked up the dishes.

"Alright," I said, closing my book. I got up and slid my things back into my blue book bag. I took the stairs two at a time. I could hear Maggie being unleashed from her high chair and the sound of her little steps as she started running all over the place. I threw my bag inside the door of my room and walked into our small bathroom. I looked for my tooth brush, feeling like I was going somewhere big tonight. One night I remembered one night when Mom and Dad took me to the Shedd downtown. We had all dressed nice for it. It happened to be on school night, too, so that made it extra exciting. Like now, tonight had the same sense of newness, of unfamiliar ground. I liked it.

But after that greasy dinner, I had a queasy feeling in my

stomach. A surge of nervousness flooded over me as I changed my t-shirt to a long-sleeved shirt. I wanted to dress a little warmer in case Old Man Fischer kept his house freezing. I looked in my side table where I kept a mini flashlight and small notepad. Should I take these along? No, better not. Mom would really have some worries about me then.

Downstairs, I heard Maggie scream and run to the door. Mom must be home. I looked at my clock which read six o'clock. She was right on time tonight.

I left my room and started heading down the stairs, when I saw that Mom coming up.

"Hey, how was school?" she said, smiling.

"Good," I stopped where I was.

"Let me change real quick, okay? Mom does not want to wear a business suit to visit an old friend," she explained, her voice soft. "Go watch a little TV and we'll go shortly."

Maggie was already climbing up the stairs and chasing after Mom.

As I hit the bottom stair to find Dad on his phone, talking to someone at the bakery again. He had a strained look on his face, barking out more instructions to the person on the other end. He was pacing back and forth near the dining table. When he saw me he gave me thumbs up on my clothes. I went to the couch and changed the channel to one of my shows.

In a couple of minutes, he hung up and said out loud, probably not wanting to air out his thoughts, "Why do I hire such stupid people? When I think in the interview that they wonderful, they turn out to be complete morons. Or are they just attracted to me?" Then he looked at me, and said, "Last chance, are sure you want to go?"

"I think so," I said, not looking at him.

"That didn't sound so agreeable."

"Do you know Old Man Fischer?"

"Your Mom knows him better. I used to see him in my shop when I first opened then he stopped coming. Then we just gave the friendly wave, that 'suburban wave'", he gestured with a casual long distance wave, "whenever I see him outside." Then he paused. "Now I don't really see him out that much."

Mom came down the stairs then, with Maggie in-tow. Mom had changed into a black sweater and some dark jeans, and even fixed her

65

makeup a little. She wore big dangling gold hoop earrings on her ears, and pinned back as her long hair.

"Where's the pie?" she asked Dad.

"Fridge." Then his voice was slightly quieter, but I could hear him say, "Are you sure you want to go?"

"Yes, I am just visiting an old friend. Besides, it doesn't hurt for Shane to meet him." She opened the fridge. This time the refrigerator door was normal, not like my dream, full of art work, and pictures of all of us.

"You're being nosy," he accused quietly.

"Me? Nosy? Never," she said as she put a hand dramatically to her chest. She was smiling when she turned to me and asked, "Ready, partner?"

I looked over at Mom then as she started to put on her black coat, covering up her thin frame. I jumped up, pulled my tan coat off the back of the chair and slipping it over me. Still inside the house, I immediately felt warm inside the coat, . I was suddenly ready to be outside, sure that cool night air would counter the sweat that was beginning to form on my forehead. Whether it was really that warm inside or if nervous energy was heating things up I wasn't sure, but I was suddenly itching to get going. And apparently I wasn't the only one.

"Me come, me come," Maggie smiled, jumping up and down at the door.

Dad walked up behind Maggie and lifted her up onto his shoulders. She looked so tiny sitting on his broad shoulders. Her shirt was stained with dinner and chocolate, probably a donut or some other sweet treat from the bakery. "No, Mags. We stay here and play."

Mom kissed Maggie on her cheek, and then gave her a tight squeeze, and said, "See you real quick." Her little body snuggled tighter around Dad's head, peeking around with a small red eye, looking sad, because she really missed Mom or Dad when they left the house, especially when I got to go with them.

Mom kissed Dad quickly on cheek and stated, "See you in an hour or so."

As I walked past Dad he ruffled my hair. "Play nice guys," he said to us.

"What do you mean by that?" I asked.

Mom smirked and said, "He talks about nothing, Shane. Can you get the pie?"

"It's Mr. Fisher's favorite flavor," Dad said following behind me.

Obediently, I took the pie from the counter near the door.

I followed Mom out the door into the cold night air as Dad closed the door behind us, and I heard Maggie begin to wail, and Dad tried calm her down with one of her favorite distractions.

I hadn't realized that darkness had come on so quickly, but it suddenly felt like it was much later at night. I twitched slightly at the chillness of the air as it moved through my body; . Luckily, Mom had just gotten home so her car was still warmer than the outside temp. Mom got in quickly and locked the doors. As we backed out of our driveway onto the street, the heat from the vents was already fighting off the chill from outside.

Mom usually hummed or turned the radio with me in the car. But there was no radio tonight, and she didn't speak at all during our short drive. I looked over at the concerned look on her face glowing in the dim red of the dash board light. Past her the last glimmer of sun peeked over the houses burnishing them in an dark orange and red glow, like large sharp claws had gouged the dark blue sky. On my side, I looked out to see the evening sky clear of any low-hanging clouds. Some stars were still visible in the darkening canopy, which seemed strange, as our usual nighttime view was usually washed out since we lived so close to Chicago. My grandma lived in the middle of nowhere Wisconsin, and whenever we went to visit her, I loved to look out at the huge dark sky there because I could see the zillions of white dots floating in the sky.

Now we were taking the same route that we took during the day to go to school but we seemed to be moving slower. And because it was night, I could see all the things that I usually saw along the way. We both stayed silent in the dark car as we passed shadows on streets, and I noticed that there were hardly any people outside, which made it feel like we were the only ones around. Soon, Mom was turning the car onto Ashland Road.

"Your dad always accuses me of snooping on the neighbors," Mom said quietly as if she did not realize she was speaking aloud. "Like the time I thought the Christens' had a loss in their family couple years back. I swore I saw the Christmas tree up for the longest time, and I hadn't seen Mrs. Christen for a while. I knew she had had some medical problems."

Her sudden story shattered the silence between us. It was nice to listen to her as I counted the houses down as we got closer to the Fischer house. I could see the steep dark roof of his old house. It looked even more menacing as we approached, its blackness giving the illusion of a void in the darkness of the night sky..

"About three months later, I could still see their Christmas tree up. Mrs. Christen had been a sick woman for as long as we had lived here, always in and out of the hospital, usually wearing surgical masks outside between her car and the house. It was already end of March. So I knocked on the door with a sympathy card in hand," she continued. I knew Mom was getting nervous because she began to talk a lot. "Mrs. Christen answered the door, smiling, and pale white. I was so surprised but relieved at the same time to see her. I quickly hid the card in my pocket and handed her the petit fours that your father had made, a told her it was a spring gift. Since then Mrs. Christen and I have been good friends. No matter what, to this day, I still look into their front window to see how long it takes for them to take down their Christmas decorations. They usually leave them up until February. I think now that they are just too damn lazy. Needless to say, Dad thought I was completely bonkers to assume she was dead."

The car came to a stop, and Mom popped the car into park and turned off the engine.

She leaned over the steering wheel to look out at the house, without saying a word. Between the sweetness of the pie and her faint perfume, I felt some comfort in those familiar things before we went got out and start to walk toward the house. She sighed heavily.

"Ready?"

I said nothing. I too was looking out at the house. There were no lights on to greet us. There were no lights anywhere except a sliver of yellow in the room to the left of the front door. There was no sign of welcome from the house, no sign of movement from inside.

Mom opened her door, letting in a gust of chilled night air that filled the car quickly. I glanced past her to the front of the van and open my side. I slide out carefully balancing the weight of Dad's creation in my arms, but my eyes never left the sight of the old house.

"Got the pie?" she asked with a smile.

"Uh, huh."

Behind me she slammed the door shut and locked it. I stood in front of the gate that swung freely in the gusty wind, its rusty hinges unleashing a heavy sounding screech as though each movement was painful.. The black wrought iron fence seemed longer and taller in the night. A nearby streetlight did little to dispose of the long shadows on the lawn.

I scanned the street, noticing how out of place things seemed here. The nearby houses, were brick and one-story, similar in style and design. All around, each seemed to teem with life: they were dimly lit inside, and I could see some signs of movement and flickers of televisions behind the curtains. All seemed well inside these houses, even in such close proximity to this one.

Together, Mom and I walked along the misshapen path of stones. I had to step over the overgrown weeds that were encroaching the borders of the path. I felt the density of the plants under my tennis shoes much like stepping into thick mud after a major downpour. I looked straight ahead as more of the house was exposed in the dim light. I took in the sights of the dark broken siding, the old peeling paint, the broken pieces of the sagging porch seemed to frown at us, with the bottom slats like jagged fangs that might bite our legs when we took the steps to the front door. To the right, a small bird bath, gray and cracked, was filled with leaves and branches, was severely sloping as it was falling into the ground. To the left there was a large tree with weeping branches covered most of the lawn in a carpet of dead leaves stood motionless. All around the yard were brown dark bushes dead and formed in a crazy pattern around small overgrown hedges, as if it had a planned design, at one point.

Mom was quiet, and held onto the back of my arm. From the corner of my eye, I could see that she too was looking at everything. I could hear her soft breath beside me.

My foot landed on the first step, and I heard a loud creak underneath, groaning under my weight. Then Mom stepped up as well, creating a slight shake in the porch. Everywhere I looked things were broken or dead; all of which were in desperate need of repair. She squeezed my arm harder as we approached the door.

The lone porch light gave us a vague idea of where or what we were stepping on. I could see Mom leaning over slightly to peer in the window, but it was well-covered with a thick curtain.

"Here goes nothing," she said and then pressed the doorbell.

A small chime rang behind the door, almost too quietly for such a large house? Surely it would be lost in the emptiness. After that, I heard footsteps slowly coming toward the door. Leaves blew around us and a deep nippy gust of air accosted me, causing strands of my brown hair blow into my face.

The door opened, and a small gush of heat escape from the house as we were bathed in muted yellow light. There stood Old Man Fischer, leaning on his cane.

"Where are my manners?" he said with something resembling a smile, and then he turned to step beside the door. I heard the clicks of switches being flipped and then there was light.

We were nearly blinded by an intrusively bright light that flickered somewhere overhead. I blinked in the spotlight, straining to see past him into the house, but was greeted only by more darkness.

"Good evening, Mr. Fischer," Mom said pleasantly.

"Come in, it is dreadfully cold tonight," he stated simply, almost forcing his words out of his mouth.

"Winter will be here before we know it," Mom chimed in, smiling at him.

I followed her through the entrance, moving past him silently and he didn't immediately look at me. At the far end of the small foyer I could see a large staircase of dark wood rising to the completely darkened second floor. The small light came from a sconce loosely covered in spider webs that lent to the yellowish cast to the light that barely did its job to light the small entrance. To our right, I could see what seemed to be a sitting room with a large couch and two chairs. It was dark, filled with shadows, and looked like it had not been disturbed; it seemed as if it was closed off, purposely not used for some time.

"Yes, isn't that so true?" he said. He had a European accent, much like that of Mrs. Engel, a third-grade teacher. She had come from Poland. His accent was a little different, crisper, because his *s* and *th* blend sounded more like z than anything. How come no other kids talked about that? Then that article about his past could be very true.

I watched him, holding the pie tightly in my arms. Its sweet fragrance was almost overpowering in the musty, thick air.

"We have your favorite, lemon meringue pie," Mom announced., as she patted the large box in my hands.

"That is great, yes," he replied. He looks at me, smiling. His teeth a dark yellow against his snow-white beard which was carefully trimmed on his face highlighting the sunken cheeks and long wrinkles along the sides of his face.. "You must be Shane."

I said nothing. What could I say?

Mom wrapped an arm around me. "You probably don't remember the last time you saw him." She squeezed my shoulders. "Say hello to Mr. Fischer."

"Hello, Mr. Fischer." My voice was small, barely a whisper.

He laughed quickly. "What a fine boy. I only remember you being this small.," he said as he gestured with his hand to his knee at about three feet tall.

My mom smiled. "Yes, he was that young, wasn't he?"

"He was."

An uncomfortable silence fell for a quick moment, and I only look around further into the darkness above, trying to adjust my eyesight, trying to see something.

"It has been that long since we've talked, Mr. Fischer."

He held up his long hand, his thin skeletal fingers had an unusual paleness. "Allison, you know how long we have known each other. Please. Hans. Call me Hans." He grinned, leaning further on his cane.

"Hans," Mom's voice sounded strange speaking his name, "we haven't seen you for so long. I do apologize about that."

"Please, I understand," he said, gesturing his hand up slightly as if to cut off her speech. His voice was low and somehow seemed stronger than I would have expected his long frail body to produce. "Now we must have some of this wonderful creation. And, I must know what has happened recently in your life because it has been far too long. In fact, I brewed fresh coffee for our gathering," then to me, another yellow-toothed grin, "Would you like a glass of milk, for you, young Shane?"

I only nodded my head, unzipping the front of my coat, overwhelmed by the heat in the house. It was so hot. I felt sweat forming on my lower back. I looked away from them and looked into the lit room filled with books.

"Are you sure? Do you need any of my help?" Mom asked.

Old Man Fischer slid the pie gently from my grasp with his free hand. "No, thank you, my dear friend. I have lived alone for so long that I can handle to serve you. I find pleasure to have guests," he grinned.

"Okay then," Mom said.

"Please wait for me in my study," he turned to lift his cane and point at the room of books.

"We will make ourselves comfortable," Mom replied.

As we entered the room, I looked back to see him walk slowly down the dark, almost too dark hallway. He rounded his back over the cane slightly, and his feet shuffled down the hallway, dragging his shoes a little bit. He breathed heavily, wheezing slightly. His shape faded into the darkness, only then when as he turned could I see that he pushed open a pivoting door into a dimly lit room, probably the kitchen. He didn't turn to look back at us and just went on about his business.

I followed Mom into a large room.

"Have you been inside his house before?" I asked in a loud whisper to Mom, who had the same surprised expression as I had on my face.

Along the wall opposite of the window were floor-to-the-ten-foot-ceilings built-in book shelves, filled with thousands of books, bounded in different colors and sizes. There was no obvious way to how the books had been organized, but it was not like a library where every book had its place. Some books were neatly put in their place then were many shelves where books laid on their sides, stacked one on top of the other,   shelves with only two or three books, and then there were shelves with no books at all. Near the windows there was a large fireplace with a large mantle with dozens and dozens of books stacked on top of it.   On the binders, small pictures of insects indicated them to be reference books; all of which had Fischer's name as the author. covering pictures of insects of sorts. And there weren't just books, stacks and stacks of dozens, maybe more, of magazines lay on the floor, creating an almost maze-like path for us to walk through.

"No, never," Mom whispered back, as we both looked back over our shoulders.. I scanned over the spectacle of book shelves, noticing in closer detail that some were filled with books, and others contained metal boxes, that were opened and appeared to contain paper files. In the corners, I could see cobwebs settled into the dark recesses and dust had collected on much of the surfaces. Everywhere there were books, they were covered in a thick layer of dust. Then the most amazing part of Old Man Fischer's study, on the free space of the walls hung different kinds of charts, like a biology lab, of insects of all kinds. There were illustrations of grasshoppers, butterflies, worms, centipedes, spiders, moths, more than I could have ever named.

In the center of the front wall were the windows that overlooked the front yard. They were covered with dark gray curtains that had probably once been white. A large, dark wood table, was parked against it, and was covered with stacks and stacks of books. In the center of the room was a long red and dark wood couch and a matching chair arranged for conversational seating. On either side of the dark red couch two tall, precariously stacked towers of magazines and science journals. In front of the fireplace , which seemed not in use with all the cobwebs, there was a large wooden desk covered in more paperwork, textbooks and hundreds of loose pictures that were shoved in tattered envelopes. I walked slowly around skimming the titles: *Field Guidebook of the Amazon River; Natural Minerals of the Mojave Desert; Plant Species of South America; Small Species of Natural Caves*; and on and on.

On the corner of the desk, between the mess, I had noticed a clear glass globe about the size of large grapefruit and covered in a fine layer of dust. Peering closer, I could see inside that there was a blue butterfly neatly fanned out on a velvet pedestal. It looked like it came from a science lab. I remember seeing this stuff at the science museum, how some animals and insects were preserved and displayed like this. I bent closer to see the details of the beautiful perfectly displayed wings, and noticed its legs straight out and the antennas stretched to their full length.

"Hon, not too close. Don't break anything," Mom cautioned behind me.

"I won't," I said continuing my study of the butterfly. Out of the corner of my eye, I thought I saw something move, and it startled me causing me to jump back, knocking over a couple of books.

"Shane!" Mom hissed at me loudly.

"It is okay, Allison," Old Man Fischer said at the entrance.

"These are only books. They cannot be harmed."

He held a silver tray with two cups of coffee, sugar and cream, a glass of milk and three slices of pie. Immediately, I began to pick up the books off the floor and restack them on the table where they had been, their outline in the dust a clear indication of where they had been on the table. It was obvious that his books had not moved for a while, as if he didn't spend too much time here.

Getting up, Mom was no longer concerned with me, and went to help him. She took the tray carefully from him and allowed the man to lean on her as they walked over to the couch. Thinking I may have smelt a slight ting of body odor coming from him, but I made myself think that maybe it was just the dust in the air. Carefully, he put an arm on my mom's elbow to steady himself and they walked a slow pace into the room. I could not help but to keep looking at all the books and charts on the walls.

"This is like a classroom," I said.

Mom helped him into a chair near the fireplace which had stacks of books in it.

"You are very observant young man," he said. He sat in the chair, while Mom put the tray on the table. She patted the couch next to her, telling me discretely to sit down next to her.

"Thank you, Allison," his sighed heavily.

I sat next to her, still looking around curiously at the books, charts and that butterfly.

"Do you like the *morpho merelaus*?" he asked when he noticed me studying the globe from my seat.

I only stared back at him with a blank look.

"The Blue Morpho Butterfly," he said. "These creatures are found all over Central American jungles. They are beautiful in flight and to observe in the wild."

"I did not realize you knew so much about insects," Mom said as she reached for a coffee cup. "I thought by your beautiful gardens over the years that your passion was in plants. Your exquisite flowers always bloomed all season long."

He smiled. "You are, were always so kind about my gardens. I admit that my passion was not of botany. I had hired gardeners for that, for many years."

"I thought you did that all yourself."

"Please do not misunderstand, I had for some time. It was nice to be outside. Then I had an accident, several years back, going down the back stairs, on some ice," he stated. He rubbed his left leg and then said, "My true obsession was to do with the tiny world, the world hardly seen, but we are in theirs all the time."

Mom only gave a look at him. I turned my head to look at the charts.

"Insects?" I said out loud.

"Shane, you are a great student," Old Man Fischer announced. "Yes, I have my doctorate in both microbiology and entomology."

Mom handed me a slice of Dad's pie, which I set on my lap.

"I never knew," Mom said. "I should call you Dr. Fischer."

"No, Allison. It's just paper degrees, nothing serious." He shook his head slowly. "I would like to be addressed as Mr. Fischer, or by my friends, as Hans. People who address themselves as 'doctor' are pretentious. They only understand themselves and their micro-world of knowledge, claiming to be such a grand professional. Over the many years, I cannot be one of those people."

Soon, he leaned over again with Mom's help, he took the cup of coffee and a piece of pie she offered him. He took a small bite and smiled at Mom.

It felt oddly too quiet in the house. I looked at Old Man Fischer, noticing that his gray jacket was too tight for his body. He was slumped further into his chair, almost allowing his body just to become part of chair. The cane was nestled between his injured leg and the seat cushion.

Again, I looked over all the books on his desk. There just seemed too much stuff on the desk, almost as if there was no point to the amount of papers there. Was he just setting paper and books on top of each other? Was he doing this on purpose? I could see the pictures of people in older color photographs.

I got up from my spot, not knowing if he was watching me.

"So how have you been, Hans?" Mom asked. Her voice was loud, maybe she didn't notice it herself.

One photograph stood out the most: a man and a woman dressed in tan clothes, like they were on a safari, stood in front of a large waterfall. There was so much greenery around them they seemed to be framed by in the scene. The man stood very straight, without a smile, while she was more relaxed, smiling, holding onto to his shoulder. When I looked closer, I noticed how pretty she was, how light her skin was, how dark and curly her hair was. The waterfall behind them was just as beautiful and I could imagine hearing the rush of the water behind them. Still, the man had no interest in the scenery, as though he was trying to not be part of scene. He looked somewhat angry while she was in middle of a laugh.

I picked up the picture, feeling the heaviness of the frame, studying the picture a bit longer.

"Who is this?" I asked, without looking up.

"That is my wife, Jillian. We posed in front of the La Paz waterfall in Costa Rica," Old Man Fischer answered. "That was taken a long time ago, before you were born, even longer still."

Mom looked at me and I handed her the frame.

"She is lovely," Mom stated. "I never knew you were married."

"No, I confess." He replied quickly.

Mom handed me the frame back and appeared to be somewhat befuddled.

"Yes, I had been," he continued before Mom could speak. He looked at Mom with a slight sadness. "She was my only love."

I set the picture back in the same spot.

"How come you never mentioned her to me?" Mom shifted her seat, and set down her cup.

"She never came up in our conversations, Allison. We talked about gardening. I created the gardens for her; I bought this house for her." His voice was deep and hallow. He looked away from us, into the darken hallway. "Speaking about her upsets me."

"Where did you meet her?" Mom asked quickly.

"In college. Long ago, I was an associate professor and she was a graduate student." His voice was deep.

"What happened to her?" I asked aloud, surprising myself with the quickness.

"Shane, Hans may not want to tell us," Mom said to me.

That was Mom's hint to allow a person to tell a story. Mom always loved to hear what happened to someone like at the family reunion couple years back on Dad's side. She was the one getting all the information, asking Dad's cousins, aunts and uncles about any about the family gossip and hidden secrets. Even the stories from Ireland, where I knew we still had long distance relatives. She did her job well, finding out some wild things about Dad's great-grandfather, who had owned a castle.

Here in the low light of this murky den, I looked at Old Man Fischer hoping that he would get this hint.

That's when I heard it again: a sound, a strange sound. I thought that maybe Mom heard it as well, but it was so faint. It was a constant sound though, like humming, a soft humming. I'd swear I'd heard that sound before somewhere. That sound must have always been in the room, but my ears were only now picking it up. It seemed to be so close, but it was so faint.

Was that sound coming from inside my head?

Then Fisher's darkened eyes turned toward us. They had that same dark look that I had seen yesterday morning. It was a cold look, a look that had no feeling in it, and yet there was a sense of hidden obscurity behind it. This time I was not frightened of this look, I was drawn to it. In the meager lighting he suddenly began to look older, as though he was aging before us. He nestled himself deeper into the chair, with its worn armrests and head rest.

Then he cleared his throat before he spoke again, "Would you like to hear a story from an old man?".

My mom shifted in her seat and replied, "If you would be so gracious, we would love to listen."

Outside the wind was beating against the thin windows, causing the sound of tapping. Nearby branches were scratching at the house as if they too wanted to come in and hear his story. The hum sound slowly harmonized with the symphony of other subtle sounds in the house, and I lost my focus on it. I was curious to hear from him.

Please, tell us your story, I urged him silently as a small smile crept over my lips. *Yes, what are you really hiding, Old Man Fischer?*

I sat on the dusty couch, and tried to get comfortable on the hard lumpiness of the red cushion. Next to me, Mom also leaned back but seemed not to mind my fidgeting and only continued to eyeball our host.

"How should I embark on my story? Ah, but to commence," he began, "with how I met Jillian and what fate had in store for both of us…"

Part 2

The Project

"I wish that I'd sail the darkened seas
On a great big clipper ship
Going from this land here to that
In a sailor's suit and cap
Away from the big city
Where a man can not be free
Of all of the evils of this town
And of himself..."

--The Velvet Underground

Russell

SEVEN

Yet, please indulge an elderly man, for I must explain my childhood. My sweet mother who scrupulously cared for me as a young boy as I grew up in the Eastern Republic of Germany, then controlled by the Socialist Parties, which had been brought under the Soviet Union.

I had grown up in a world with fear and dread, and my mother's brown eyes reflected the pain and anguish. Hardly, I had a chance to see her during the long week, leaving before I woke and coming home after I had gone to bed. My mother labored many hours in a factory in Ludendorff, about ten kilometers or so away from our small village. She left early in the morning in order   proper transportation   to catch the only bus that left and returned from factory.

We lived with my uncle and his family in a small apartment on the west side of the town, in a broken area, heavily destroyed during the War years and had not yet recovered. The government had no urgency for reconstruction in the war-torn areas.

My mother was a great woman, resilient in an every sense of the word. We did not have much, no belongings. I went to school with my cousins where we tried to be children state of our community. As years went by, I saw the suffering and sacrifice my mother had to make in order for me to live: her lack of nutrition, her sleep deprivation, and her endless sobs. She dressed me in clothes handed downs from my cousins and my toys were broken left overs. Our only life, the only life I knew, consisted of an eleven by eleven room with a bed and dresser.

My aunt was a decent a woman who took care of me when my mother was not around. She fed me traditional cabbage and potato soups. Getting meat was a luxury in those times. My uncle could not afford enough meat for all of us, so my uncle, aunt and cousins would feast on the meat, while I had received the pitiful ends of the food. My mother worked throughout the years, letting me grow up more or less as one of my aunt and uncle's children. I was never the one to get the first plate at meal times, nor the first new clothes, nor the presents, nor the toys. But they took care of me much like one of their own. My aunt would often tell me stories of my father, her brother, when he was a boy of my age. She never talked about him in the present tense, because he was never to see me or my mother again. My mother had told me that he was taken as a political prisoner and sent to the Soviet Union for life imprisonment. But my aunt had a black and white picture of him. He was tall and round with a full beard. He had such a rounder face than mine, and had great smiling eyes. My aunt had said often that my eyes were his eyes.

When my mother worked, my cousins and I would play around our crumbling apartment building. I often have fond memories of playing in a field, or I should say the city block, of broken crumbling buildings. There were other children who played in this area. I remember the military police always roaming in and out of this area, sometimes there was gunfire, not very often though. Bear in mind, I learned to accept these noises. Much graffiti and crime was a frequent occurrence in the neighborhood. My cousins and I stayed close together and protected each other.

It was around your age, Shane, that my interest in the tiny wonders of the world, the insects, arose. I neither loathed nor feared these little creatures as they came out in the midst of the summer heat, the rainfalls of the season, and then watched as they eventually succumbed to the savage winters. I remember just observing the *tertamonium caepitrum*, or the black ant, create its hills, assemble and gather its food, and attack equally savage predators. Or in a broken window of a fallen building, I had observed intensely the *pholcus phalagiodius*, or the commonly-known daddy long leg spider, as it sat on its fragile web and patiently waited for a *musca domestica,* or common receptacle fly, to get stuck then attacking its prey, devouring its juices. I could watch all these creatures, like the different species of the *lepidotera,* the moth, that fluttered in the twilight sky, in our apartment building around the lights. Or the tiny red *coccineta novemnotata*, the ladybug, that flew in the spring skies. I observed rapturously as these creatures lived their tiny lives and meant no harm to anyone, but were easily destroyed by man's hand or by pesticides. I felt they would come to mean more to my life than I could ever have imagined.

My family found my fascination to be abnormal. They insisted that my interest would not lead me to a useful skill or career and encouraged me to be a factory worker, or a tailor. My uncle would say at the dining table when my mother was not present, "You need a job, to make you strong, and not so weak, to build your arms, and back, and thick through the legs. You are so skinny and pathetic, no wonder why the other kids want to beat on you." In those years, your vocation had been given to you from your social circumstances not your intellect or interest or talent.

Certainly, I did not want this. My cousins would torment me as I studied this fragile kingdom by stomping on the creatures or mashing the mucus out of them. Sometimes they would take large specimens and torture them in front of me, pulling off appendages and antennae malevolently. My mother would not know about my cousins misbehaving, but she realized my passion. In her little free time with me, in my teen years, we would try to escape to the country side, and stand in fields of flowers or the woods, or rarely the river, where I would found more species. It had been at that point when I was cataloging the creatures in a notebook, I had discovered my true passion. My mother had inspired me over these years, allowing me to study the creatures, to understand their place in the world and sketch them in great detail. During this time, I only grew to love my mother more with each moment we had with each other.

And yet, she would change my life in even more significant ways. The day had been dark and snowy, and our ruined city was blanketed in white. Our small room in the apartment was colder as my uncle allowed the coal stove to heat the great room, not our space. It had been my eighteenth birthday. Late that night, as the others slept, my mother came to me, quietly and handed me an envelope full of money.

"Momma, what is this?" I had asked her.

She looked up at me, with great happiness and bittersweet sorrow, and replied, "This is what I worked for, my son. Your freedom to learn is in this gift to you." Her eyes filled with tears.

"You are coming with me, Momma," I said. Naively, I had been so elated.

"No, this is not possible," she explained. "Many people watch me because of your father's actions long ago. I will never be free like you. We had nothing because I saved this for you. Your uncle and your aunt do not know of this."

"Momma", I pleaded. My breath was knocked out of me.

"No. You are a man now. I see your dreams. I make this come true for you." She gave me a tight hug. "Inside, I have a name of someone in East Berlin, your father's friend, who will see you get to the free world. He knows you are coming."

"I don't want to leave you," I whispered. I heard footsteps coming to the door.

Backing away from me, her face was on the closed door, her eyes were full of tears. "Please, you must leave now. He expects you by the morning. Only take yourself and this envelope," she then placed it into my inner pocket.

"I will come back for you, Momma."

She only smiled with red teary eyes. "Yes, you may one day. But until then you are in my prayers."

How long I had held her I could not say. I did not wanted to leave my mother, my only little world. I kept a picture of her, which you see in that small frame on my desk. There, yes. She is, was, a beautiful woman. That had been taken the summer before, at a nearby river beach. We had a great time that summer.

My uncle and aunt had no idea that I was leaving for good. In those days, political asylum was impossible, defecting was rarely talked about, rarely understood. Even at this point, the United Nations was only a thought, not a real power as it is today. When a person left from the Iron Curtain, it was to leave everything behind, all your belongings, taking only your fragile memories as your souvenirs. I had left my mother in that dilapidated room, in that condition, crying, trying not to cry myself. This was where I became strong, where I had held off my emotions, where I learned to truly cherish what I loved.

My journey to America had been an arduous dangerous road for me, unable to trust anyone, but having to count on the help of strangers. Coming from a life where there was no trust to be had to a world where the kindness of strangers was commonplace was a shock to my soul. It took weeks for me to get here, through countless rides in the back of cars, and trains, and boats. I could not take planes due to the risk of discovery; I had no one to rely on until I met my contact person at my destination. I will not give you my real name, because I still fear what could happen to me. I arrived in in Toronto, Canada where I became Hans Fischer, and a citizen of Canada. There, I went into Undergraduate work, and finished with my degree in three years. Then I entered the graduate school and received my first doctoral degree in less than five years. Soon, I was courted by many prestigious American colleges. I accepted one university, who not only made me a staff member but also paid for my next doctorate program. With my new connections, I became a citizen of the United States.

I came to the Midwest because I knew my identity would blend better into the population and large schools. I could become part of the walls, become part of the scholastic endeavors of the library. Yes, I had much difficulty getting into the university; but with the political connections and underground rebellions of those whom I do not disclose, the created my new identification. I did not lie about my knowledge, and no one can ever falsify that. In those days, I had been an over-achiever in my classes, to my professors, so I had not been noticed by the free government.

After many years of studying I left behind any thought of ramifications for my departure from East Germany. During my senior year as an undergraduate I decided to try to find out more information about my mother. It turned out about a week after I had left from the apartment, my uncle turned my mother in to the authorities. My mother became a political prisoner and was sent to the Soviet Siberian prison. I did not know if she had survived her ordeal, nor did I know how long she had been a prisoner there, but the news placed me in a state of despair. But her loss renewed my strength to achieve my goals.

I had many achievements in my academics, many certificates that awarded to me for my outstanding successes, many articles written about my studies and their impacts on the world many awards now put away in boxes somewhere in this house. I remained aloof, if you will, always to myself. I kept to my lab work, not participating in group activities, trying to remain to myself and my thoughts. Was this the life I always dreamed? Not exactly, yet my credentials were accumulating and my work ethic was commended. In my second appointed doctoral years, my focus was on my specific interests in entomology, micro entomology and socio entomology, which were fields that were unheard of at that time, and were something I had created, to some extent.

I guess you could say that I purposely submerged myself in my studies, in teaching in formal classes at the college to the undergraduates, to keep myself preoccupied by my professors' projects. As a young graduate student, you are a slave to the emeritus, tenured professors, and I had to execute a lot of their tasks on a weekly basis, finishing their work such as calculating formulas, cleaning up their experiments, gathering data sets, updating their grading books and other miscellaneous items. Really those years washed over me, and I had no time to myself, or rather I made the choice not to have time for others. I knew people for a time, the people I worked with, but that was as far as I let it go.

However, one day in April as I recall now changed my life for the better. It had been a typical day where the professor who I had been assigned to for the semester called off and I had to teach his introductory science lecture. Interestingly, that day I had been on my way out of the hall, heading for the labs, my usual route against the current of students, when she ran into me.

I had been more than clumsy and just watch her books fall to the ground, as other students step around us, absorbed in their own conversation and, walking to their classes. I really never could understand undergrads.

"Excuse me," I said to her as I bent to scoop up her books before they were trampled on.

She quickly bent over as well. I didn't see her face, but I caught the scent of her sweet perfume, a simple light floral scent that was heavenly.

"No, I am to apologize," she replied. Her voice was sweet and subtle like her scent.

"Here you go," I handed her a book then looked up, into her face. For the first time in my life, I found that I could not speak. She was completely lovely. Her smile gave me true meaning to something genuine I had in long time.

"I was in a rush to my next class over at Stanley Hall." She was beginning to stand up.

I knew that was about a fifteen minute walk from our point, I did not know how she would make it there in time. "That's the graduate hall, correct?"

"Are you implying that I look too young?"

I stumbled for my words.

Her smile widened, "That's a great compliment."

The sounds of other students surrounded us, but I could not force myself to look away from her. I glanced down to one of her books, noticing one was a recently published botany book. "Are you biology major?" I asked.

"Yes, botany to be exact," she said, with a glorious smile. The sunlight glinted off her long dark hair that gently swept her shoulders. "And you?"

"I teach here," I said, not thinking about it.

Her expression changed to a more serious look. "I am sorry, Professor."

"No, I didn't mean to imply that," I interrupted. "I am a researcher for Dr. Kempler's group, and I happen to oversee some of his classes."

Then her face lit up. "The same Dr. Kempler who is creating a bio-diversity group for the natural habitats?"

"Yes, the very one."

"I have been trying for the past year or so to get into that group." Her voice was sincere and kind.

"What specifications of botany are you studying?" I asked, folding my arms over my chest, I could feel my heart swell slightly in my chest. I just wanted to keep talking to her.

"Exotic and tropical sub-plant species in various ranges and elevations of the world." Her statement was true and simple. Then she looked at her thin gold watch, and said, "Shoot, I am already late for class. I must go." She went past me and down the stairs.

"Excuse me, what's your name?" I called after her, watching as she gracefully descended the stairs.

She turned with a smile, and said, "Jillian. Jillian Riviere."

I replied, "Well, Jillian Riviere, would you like to discuss this further?" Never had I been so bold to ask a woman out. Never in my life. But I simply could not let her walk out of my life.

She stopped, and said, "Yes. I would like that very much."

Before I realized it, we made arrangements to meet each other at a small café near the university that night. My nervousness about meeting this beautiful young lady, this Jillian Riviere, was genuine and had me looking at the clock all day long, I watched and waited anxiously as the time slowly slipped by, wishing the minutes to go by quicker rather than focusing on teaching a class. I had to search for a decent, clean pressed shirt. I guess being a single man for so long that I had left the notion of decency out of my priorities. But I managed to make myself presentable and I went to the café as we had arranged.

I waited. You must understand these are times without mobile phones, not being able to text to each other, without beeping each other . We the simple reliance on each other's promise that we show up as agreed, such a novel idea in today's day and age.

The diner filled and emptied as I looked out the window at the night sky as I sipped my coffee.

Jillian came. I only could see her in the light and see her graceful look. She had spotted me, and walked to me. What did I deserve to be appreciated by this beautiful creature?

"I so do apologize," she began, "I got lost in my paper, I looked up and saw the time."

"Please sit," I said. I could only stare at her, looking at her dark hair perfectly pinned up behind her head, her pressed powder blue skirt and crisp white blouse, her black patent leather shoes. And me, the schlump, in a bad shirt and one of my only two pairs of pants, with coffee stains and tattered cuffs. I was not fit to be seen with this exquisite creature.

"I just get so involved in my work, that sometimes I just get so lost," she confessed humbly.

"I can admire that, as I do become lost in my work too," I replied.

The waitress came to offer some coffee, pouring it from a stained carafe, neither offering much by way of conversation, nor specials. Jillian was polite as I ordered food for us, which were two of the specials, two coffees and two slices of pie for dessert.

It turned out that we did not eat, we picked at our plates when the food finally arrived. We talked and talked and listened to each other's opinions about the scientific world, hypothesizing on the theories against our studies. This woman, who was as gorgeous as Jacqueline Kennedy in our time discussed the same theories that I too had argued in my papers. I heard from her gracious pink lips what the philosophies of our scientific world, the very ones that I too criticized and loved. Hearing the same thought patterns come from her was a refreshing connection I hadn't realized that I craved. Not only did I look at this beautiful woman as I possible future mate, but I saw this incredibly intelligent woman as a fellow scientist who challenged me on many levels. How long did we talk and listened and shared our thoughts, I was not exactly sure, but it did occur to me that the people around us could see our commitment to the science world. I had wondered if they could truly see what was beginning to happen in these first hours we spent together.

When we parted ways that night, I thought I would count this as a once in a lifetime experience.

"Oh my gosh, it is already two-thirty!" Jillian announced as she looked down at her watch. "I still have to finish my paper."

I slowly got up from the table, feeling the numbness in my legs. "We should do this again," I suggested, not realizing I was speaking my thoughts out loud.

She smiled and agreed, "Yes, let's do this again."

There was an unusual awkwardness between us, as I was unsure what the next move should have been. But, I leaned over and she gave me a quick hug. The same scent she had worn earlier that day slowly wrapped around me. I came to realize that I very much wanted to see her again.

Over the next day, I found myself hoping that I would see her. I longed for us to bump into each other again. I hoped that she'd had the same emotions that I was beginning to feel for her. Perhaps, it was my many years of self-isolation that developed my dispassionate, coldness towards others. Perhaps, it was my self-induced-seclusion from the world, I then found myself caught in a cocoon, much like the insects I studied. I was not the dominant male to conquer my female mate in order to continue life, to take only one moment from the female. Little had I known that fate had made a decision for a humble man such as myself.

Jillian did call me back, later in the day, to say that she had had lovely time with me and wanted to meet me again. Her voice was as soft, sweet and demure on the phone as I had remembered in the cafe. I could tell by her quickness that she was excited to see me and asked me to meet her at another place, near her apartment. Of course I obliged.

Not too long after these initial meetings, we began to spend more time together, expecting each other's phone calls, planning our next date night where we would talk for hours. Weeks of talking and laughing and seeing each other turned into months of courtship, and I found myself falling in love with her and her feeling the same.

Young man, when you find your true love hold on to her, listen to her, and just love her. You are too young to understand this now, and girls may be far from your list of concerns, but there will be a day when they will pique your interest. Then I hope you will remember what I have said and come to understand what I mean.

But back to my story. As time went on and our conversations were centered on our shared passions, the scientific developments in both botany and entomology, where we could both succeed the most. I found that I wanted to spend more and more time with Jillian. But I was finding that my research was claiming a great deal of my time and I struggled to find a way to make more time in my schedule. I came to the one conclusion that would ultimately change things for both of us, and that was to include her in Kempler's Bio-Diversity project. Professor Kempler had trusted me with great responsibility and it demanded much of my free time, my time with Jillian. One day as he came around to check on the researchers, I pulled him aside and recommended Jillian for the program. I focused on her strengths, naturally discussing her intelligence, and knowledge of exotic plants, indicating that her input would be vastly useful to our group's work. Could he see my feverish attempt to secure a place on the team because I had feelings for this brilliant young woman? No, not exactly, because Kempler was all about Dr. Kempler.

But here I go get ahead of myself.

After some persuasion, and some extra work details thrown on me, Jillian was accepted into the program. However, Dr. Kempler had his own concerns, which he voiced to me privately, "Her youth and limited educational resources are concerns for me. Therefore, her success with me will depend greatly upon your supervision of her work and research. This program will not fail due to anyone's lack of experience."

I never spoke of this to her.

Jillian, of course, was astounded with the news, and wanted to celebrate that night at a local Italian restaurant. In the muted lighting, and a nicely-aged Chianti, she was lovelier than ever. She had giggled at the thought of being involved in the project, explaining how much her input could be an asset to the work. I could not be happier, I was even more thrilled than she was, because it meant that I could have her within easy distance of me during our long research hours.

Now as an old man, I look back affectionately at that following summer and spring, remembering watching her as she gazed into the microscope, watching the curious expression of cross her face, and feeling the exhilaration as she discovered new matter, teaching her what her function would be to the project, working late and being close to her. Recently, I find myself daydreaming of those times, and I cherish that we had. We were becoming closer, and understood ourselves both professionally and personally. It was known among the research team that we were dating, but we respected our team and our work, and kept our distance in the lab. Only outside the lab we would fall into each other's arms.

In December, on a wintry cold night, I asked Jillian for her hand in marriage. She had been completely surprised. I was not a rich man, and the university had not paid well at the time, only enough to pay for my keep and tuition. I purchased a simple gold ring a few blocks from the campus. With a lovely pink, tear-streaked face, she accepted and I fell hopelessly in love. She told me, as I placed the ring on her finger, "Hans, I am the luckiest woman. I have a man that I can share my heart and my love of science with. I will give you as much love as you have always given me in respect. I will always love you."

We married soon after, in late January, just as a severe blizzard moved into the city. We went to the courthouse with her mother who had come from Minnesota. She was a lovely woman with the kindest of eyes and a smile to love as well. I could see in her mother how beautiful Jillian would become in her later life. That is, if she had she lived this long. The ceremony was simple, just us, her mother and Jillian's friend from the school. Jillian was not concerned that I did not have family, only divulging to her that they all had perished. She never knew of my early life, or of my real name. Still it was a great day for us, a beginning a new life for me.

Over that spring time, we adjusted our lives from being fellow students, fellow workers, and fellow lovers to be a married couple, which only enhanced our love greatly. I enjoyed being around her more and more, to listen to her talk, to listen to her sleep, to hear call my name, to look at her from a distance and knew she was my wife. I suppose this was the best time in my life: It was simple and contained much like my specimens that I studied. Had I known now what would eventually happen, I suppose we should have remained in our university based world. No, that would be too simple and opportunity had come to us.

Little did I realize that Dr. Kempler was making his own plans, which were both, unexpected and actually damning.

In hindsight, my fate was already casted.

EIGHT

My doctorial proceedings were only a month away, and then I would stand up and defend my work and cite the data from thousands of man-hours of research. It had been unusually busy March day. At that time, I had completed ninety percent of my work, and I had to meet with my advisor to discuss the status of my project. His critiques and relentless insights would be invaluable and could likely cause us to restructure, perhaps add another section to our research at this late stage. And I still had some minor research to complete and document. To say that I had reached the most pivotal moment of my career was putting it mildly. The last moments before doctoral defense are crucial to success in academia.

Dr. Kempler agreed to meet with me. He called me into his office that overlooked the north part of the campus. It was five minutes or so from the science lab. I had droplets of sweat on my brow from my brisk walk across campus on this unusually warm of day in early spring.

"Come in, Hans," he gestured to me with his hand as he continued talking on his phone. I sat quietly in the chair opposite of the large desk. I overheard his conversation, "I will have my people move as needed. What? I'm sorry, you're breaking up. Better. Yes. Yes. Well, we will talk within the next week. I will phone at that time, once we get the proper approval. Good day."

Past him, I could see dark skies approaching the city, chasing away the warm sun. Many of the students below were walking briskly as to avoid the coming rain.

He hung the phone back on its rest, then leaned back into his chair. He shuffled some paperwork, and a smile caressed his lips. "Hans Fischer. I do not make much time for situations like this one, nor do I spend too much time to ponder any action," he said. "You are one of my prized researchers in the lab division. I found your work to be thorough and complete; better yet I find more definitive evidence in your work than most of the others."

"Thank you—," I began.

"And you are a fine example of what my program on bio-diversity project has to offer. I believe that you exemplify the very essence of the goals ahead." Dr. Kempler liked to talk to any one completely and without hearing much of other's' opinions. I believed he enjoyed his own baritone voice that resounded off the windows of his office. "Our program will be shifting to a new phase of development."

"As you know, most of our research has been provided by the nearby Botanical Society, Zoological Societies and other such facilities in the nearby five-state radius. We have great examples and specimens to gather evidence from, to retain their facts and to obtain the meaning of diversity. Coming from the Galapagos Islands in the eighteen hundreds, the historical research was plain and simple because the evidence was in front of them, and there new ground breaking each and every inch of the way. Today the continued research is of the upmost importance for generational change, emphasizing the effects of pollution and humanity activity. In the early nineteenth century, the researchers benefited from true contact of the developing species and saw how they segmented themselves to become a new, stronger species. This is obvious.

"Much like the leading edge research of that day, I am taking my project, the Bio-Diversity Project, to the next level. How, you may ask. I have acquired enough funding for the university to create a specialized team to go to a special environment and gather actual evidence and document first-hand the interactions between species of insects, plants and animals in their native habitat. What do you think of this?"

I was absorbing his conversation. I listened carefully as he broached the idea, waiting to see where exactly he was going with this new development. Before I could open my mouth, he said, leaning on to his desk.

"Hans, I would like you be part of this team. I am seeking

individuals who will take the risk of dropping their lives here and transplant them in another world. From watching all of your hard work and dedication to the program thus far, I know your passion and dedication to the research, and I truly want you to be on my team."

"I... I don't know what to say," I stuttered. My ambition was grabbing hold of my insides, squeezing the air from my lungs and pulsing endorphins through my body because even before I could speak I realized this was a once-in-a-life time opportunity.

"Before you answer," Dr. Kempler said then, leaning towards me. The stench of his stale coffee-and-cigarette breath wafted toward me from across his desk as he continued pitching the benefits of his long distance field research opportunity. "I am looking for a person who will take charge of the camp site when I'm not there because my duties to the university and the government will call me away at times. I will be in transit a great deal of the time in order to keep things going at both ends. Also, this person must have great leadership skills in order to keep the project running and get things accomplished. I believe I have found this person in you."

I said nothing.

"Please let me know your thoughts," he said as he leaned back in his chair.

My enthusiasm was easily read upon my face, as much as I tried to contain it. I was thinking of everything in my life, of my Jillian. I could not uproot now, nor could she.

"I have one request," I said slowly. "I would like to have one extra researcher come with us."

"Okay, whom?"

"Jillian Riviere."

He just looked at me, his smile began to fade. "I am not sure, Hans."

"Listen, Dr. Kempler. I have been working closely with her. Her brilliant analytical work on the various tropical plants over the recent month have shown incredible breakthroughs, creating new resources for us to gather evidence in this new project of yours. I also believe that—"

"Enough, Hans," he said, sighing heavily. "I have read the work, and yes, these are interesting details. But I have Sloane Connors already selected for the botanist slot in this project. Also, a woman in the field would just *distract* the other male researchers in the camp. Our budget has only enough funds for the allotted researchers, no more. I'm sorry."

"But Dr. Kempler," I said, now shifting in my chair, feeling a slight surge of panic and anger flare in my cheeks. "Connors has horrible skills at drafting evidence, cataloguing species and poor communication skills. I have recommended several times for Jillian to take over his spot for the past several weeks."

"I know. But I like Sloane's take-charge attitude. That is the approach I need for this project."

"Jillian has more analytical detail and forth rightness than most anyone else in the department."

"Without any of your unsolicited guidance, correct?" his voice was deep. "I told you last year to take her under your wing, which you have done. Her reports look oddly like yours. Is the mentor guiding the student's writing, or is the teacher injecting his own input into the pupil's work?"

"No, it's not like that at all," I insisted. I had never mixed our professional and personal lives together.

"That Jillian is also your spouse?" he flatly commented. "It's a small department, Hans. People talk. I need to know that your research is unbiased and undistracted and not swayed by the influence of your *wife's* results."

He stared at me, almost pleased with this statement, as if he knew this had been what he was looking for. I read his look of contentment and silently kicked myself for saying anything. I thought I'd just watched my opportunity disappear in front of me. A disturbing silence fell between us as I watched him, his large face, full of wrinkles, as he puffed on a new cigarette, letting billows of smoke flutter and rise above his head.

"Hans, your work is superior to any other scientist on campus, with unscrupulous detail and continuous emphasis on quality of specimens. I truly cannot go forward on this project without your assistance." He paused taking a strong pull from his cigarette and then exhaled a powerful cloud of white smoke, filling the room with a haze "I do not make exceptions, and take this as your one and only favor from me. I will allow Jillian to come—"

"Thank you, thank you," I said, smiling.

He held up his hand, then said, "I am not finished. Your wife will be able to come along on this adventure, but her pay will be cut in half to the other researchers. I also expect her work to be equal to your quality of work, which I expect you to oversee, personally. If her work fails, in my eyes, so do you. I will not have *my project* jeopardized for the sake of your goddamn personal sacrifices. Got me, Fischer?"

I listened. I was happy then, to agree to whatever stipulations he insisted upon, because I was getting everything that I wanted. "Yes sir."

"Good," he settled back into his chair. "Over the next several weeks I will be calling you into some extra meetings and planning on top of the already rigorous schedule. I'm aware that you have your doctorial defense next month. That being said, I will not make any exceptions on your research for a degree. So I expect you to handle the given workload for the project."

I couldn't say anything. My mind was reeling, planning.

"One more thing, then you may go," he said. "We leave in six weeks. I believe this will be enough time for you to get your situations in order, correct? Which if I looked at my calendar correctly, leaves you four weeks to complete your doctorial phase, tie up your personal affairs and execute my project accordingly." He dragged on the thin cigarette heavily and exhaled a large plume of white mist through his nostrils. "Now, be gone."

I left his office exhilarated. Walking down the steps, I let the intense summer rain soak me, feeling cleansed of this place. I felt like I was starting a new life, as I had once before, a long time ago. This time I made the choice to change my life, and not only my life, but my wife's life as well.

That night we celebrated. Jillian's excitement was equal to mine, if not more so even than my own. Her eyes were wide and bright, and even made a quick trip to the bookstore to find a book on Central America. We talked that night of this new direction, of our lives, and of our futures. In hindsight, I thought this had been a great beginning for us. I thought this would be an incredible point which we would be able to tell our grandchildren, our great grandchildren. Never did I mention what Dr. Kempler had said to me about Jillian. That was never brought up in any conversation. I would realize later that Dr. Kempler had his own personal motivation for Slone Connors' presence in our camp, but what was behind closed doors remained unseen. I had not pursued the truth of the rumors, nor did I want to really understand the truth.

Jillian and I wrapped up our lives at the university. She would have compromise on finishing the doctoral degree she too longed for, even though through her work she would receive several honorary degrees from prestigious universities throughout the world. These I have in box as well in my many cluttered rooms upstairs.

I suppose these last weeks in the States were chaotic, figuring out storage for our small amount of furniture from our apartment, obtaining passports in record time, not realizing how easy it was to receive one then. Dr. Kempler had a connection in the government who helped to expedite our documents quickly. My focus was coming more and more focused on the project as I finished my doctorial defense and received my degree. I had to find my replacement; a great new graduate student by the name of Matthew Borough, whose similar ambitions was able to take in our coming evidence while continuing the project at the university.

Then it hit me during the last week, the third week in May, when our apartment was in boxes, our clothes in suitcases and trunks. Our lives were packaged and ready to go on adventure. Jillian was having coffee at the small white table, devoid of anything we owned, reading a recent book on the political conditions of Honduras, Panama, Costa Rica and Mexico. It was late morning and sun was streaming through the window, casting her face with a golden angelic glow.

I stood next to her, placing my hand on her elbow pulled her up into my arms and presented her with a small narrow box.

She smiled, wrapping her slender arms around my shoulders, emphasizing her small frame in comparison to mine. "What is this for?"

"To commemorate the start of a new life."

She opened the box. Inside was a thin gold chain with a pearl locket. She looked back at me. "This is so beautiful." She hugged me tighter. "Why are you giving this to me?"

"Why?" I asked. "Because you are my world. You are the only woman in the world that could fit so perfectly with me and agree to take on this adventure thousands of miles away from everything you know, start a new future with me. I'm a very lucky man."

"Our future," she said. Her voice was soft and sweet. "I will go anywhere with you, Hans. My life is your life."

Such a wonderful time, those last few days we shared in our little apartment close to the campus and everything we had built for ourselves. I found myself feeling apprehensive, having second thoughts about taking Jillian so far away and embarking on this project in this unfamiliar place. I suddenly wanted to change my mind. I kept hoping that maybe, just maybe, this relocation would be cancelled. Maybe Dr. Kempler would rethink his opinions about me, or about Jillian's participation, or anything that might stop what was to come.

As the plane lifted off the ground, I could feel something in the pit of my stomach, an irreverent sense of change as I held Jillian's hand and felt her squeeze mine back in response.

That day, I saw both equal amounts exhilaration and trepidation in her face as she looked out the window in anticipation of the plane's takeoff. Even the enthusiasm on her expression as the plane began to ascend thousands of kilometers in the air. All the while, her damp hand gripped mine and I kissed it in reassurance, hoping that all this would be great for both us.

I could not have predicted the course of our lives, or that this would be the only the first and only flight that Jillian would ever take while conscious.

Russell

NINE

As the plane descended into the valley leading to San Jose, I was astonished by the topographical features of the area with the steep sloops, rock formations and already dense rainforests below me. I took the window seat, because Jillian had been uneasy by the height after takeoff and had become airsick during the flight. The plane swooped over the landscape and urban metropolis below. As we landed in San José, I was utterly taken aback by its splendid beauty, where the canopy of trees and vegetation anchored solid island in midst of the densely populated urban life. The city was situated in a river valley enveloped by coffee fields, foothills leading into the mountains and dense jungle terrain of Costa Rica's Central Highlands.

We landed in the rainy season. I had enjoyed the changes of summer to fall, and then winter to spring. Here, life revolved around two: dry season and wet season. The latter climate would take a toll on each of us.

Jillian and I stepped out of the airport, and found ourselves intrigued by both the people and the economic conditions of the city. We watched the poorer class of citizens meander about their lives, oblivious to us, the new arrivals. We saw remnants of the regions historical ancestors, signs of the Incan civilizations: darker tan pigmented faces with deep lines and large brown eyes, shorter, more squat statures. I must have seemed a giant amongst them. As we settled into our life there we discovered that I easily incorporated the Spanish language into my own linguistic repertoire, but the others struggled greatly. Americans of that time could not easily adapt to foreign lands.

In those first few hours after we arrived in Central America, our group was transported from the airplane by chartered vans. As we made our way through the bustling metropolis we all silent, tired from the long plane ride. Jillian and I sat together, holding hands. She was excited to be in this new land, and spent most of the trip squeezing my hand to get my attention and pointing out many of the sites and I would casually follow along where she pointed, enjoying being with her as much as I was the scenery. We were both falling in love with the magic of this third-world country, craning our heads in every direction, taking in the passing people and sites. My mind was on the map that I had studied for hours on the plane. It was now tucked away safely in my backpack in the storage area under the bus, but on the plane, I had memorized the place where Jillian and I and the rest of Dr. Kempler's team would call home.

As we headed out of the city into the countryside, passed the last fragments of civilization, dense thick cumulous clouds above turned a familiar deep charcoal grey, the color of which we would all become so well-acquainted with during our time here. Rain swept down from the heavens in gusting waves we would soon come to realize were indicative of life in the equatorial region. The thin roof of the small bus dinged loudly above, as if commanding ordering the bus to slow down. The bus driver, a thin man, who would later be one of our regular drivers, Rafael, a man with seven children to support, maneuvered the bus up the small roads that had he originally been oxen trails a century ago, and has seen little by way of improvement since. Looking along the edge of the narrow roads, the steep sides of the foothills of the volcanic region and the deep crevices of the valley revealed coffee plantations, the sugar cane farms, and the floral nurseries that spread amongst the lines of jungle. Sites that we would become our daily scenery as we drove through the region.

The local people seemed accustomed to the rain. I observed them under the rusty steel awnings that were common on buildings there, as they continued going about their business despite the sheeting rain that fell around them. As we charged up the steep slope toward our remote campsite, I was encouraged to see road signs pointing toward Poas Volcano National Park. Jillian watched in awe at the small town conditions, the running children in the mud filled streets, the casual pace of cars that seemed to drift atop a stream of water where the road had been. For me, this was all a bit reminiscent of a life lived long ago in a provisional towns near Poland, the distant images of my childhood. How very little things differ within a depressed economic conditions.

But, as fascinating as the civilization here was, our mission was not to familiarize ourselves with the people and attempt to theorize any anthropological or sociological studies on their cultures. Nor, we were much less qualified to acknowledge the hierarchy of power within the local and national government, considering the proximity of dictator lead countries just north of here.

Our bus slowly dragged us toward our destiny of setting up a camp which was located near a town called Varablanca. I would like to first point out that Dr. Kempler arranged neither provisions, nor housing for the group. In a way, it was impossible for us to reach back to the town, an easy twenty kilometer journey on foot, and in this rain, none of us were equipped for this rainy season. Most of the other researchers had never been beyond their own neighborhoods, much less beyond the environs of the Midwest. Jillian had been slightly more prepared with my help, but I too felt we were ill-prepared for this part of the journey. We reached our destined location, a literal spot in the woods that the bus could not traverse. With virtually no other option, we all mainly stayed on the bus as the rain poured steadily around us.

I was not nervous about anyone stepping out into the forest to see the wildlife, but I feared the soft earth and the flooding roads. The others in the group would not acclimate to the climate for some weeks. I am afraid to say, Allison, that our grooming during this time was not the best. Over the next week or two I assembled the crates, inventoried supplies and helped with the construction of tents.

These weeks were absolutely miserable for all of us. Most of the researchers did not want to take orders from me, and they would only report to Dr. Kempler. Matt Hughes, Ken Fuerst and Sloane Connors were with us, barely pitching in, directing us laymen, as it were, in the construction. But using my intellect and ease of the native tongue, I was smarter than they realized where I made quick friends with the bus driver. For most of the physical work, the local people who were desperate for money were hired out to create our site. It was unusually hard work during those days. The humid conditions and the unpredictable rainfall set back our work by a month.

About three weeks in, one researcher, Ken Richards, who I questioned Dr. Kempler's decision when he chose him, came to me confessing that he wanted to quit the project. I could see in his eyes that he was not meant for this type of work. His soft porcelain hands were a clear sign that he was not bred for manual labor, nor to do physical research in a large environment, collecting samples, being prepared to live in sufferable circumstances and maintain a work ethic. He was a well enough fellow, to be sure, but the work that was set out for this research was hard.

This presented some challenges for Dr. Richards. According to the research contract, which was a formidable and dubiously long form that each of us had to fill out, included a disclaimer that research findings would be prized to the university accreditation and other legal matters, including researcher accountability for terminating. In any matters, even then, bureaucratic powers held research projects accountable for its results. So if a researcher, like Richards, had a desire to quit his position with the project, he had to fund his own way back to the United States. He would also be required to separate his own future disciplinary studies from the project and forfeit any monetary funds from the project. Dr. Kempler's aim was clearly on the proclaimed glory that would stem from the project. But I digress. And knowing this, Jillian still came to me later asking why I hadn't convinced him to stay. My response had been simple, "He chose to come here and knew the hard tasks that were ahead of us. I believe he did not bring his spirit to the project."

And despite this, Jillian and I became closer, which was more helpful to our work. She was still quite the extrovert, quick to make acquaintances with the fellow researchers while I went about the business of the camp.

In a way, this would help later, but I'll get to that.

We shared a tent for a few days until a group of us decided to rent several rooms in the nearby town. At last we would have our first hot showers after a period of cold dips in the river. I had felt so much like an early colonist, exploring a land that was undiscovered and within the depths of dangerous, hauntingly beautiful terrain, but at the same still a stranger in this foreign land, living primitively, away from the modern comforts of home. In the short of it, we established a working camp within the following month.

That's when our work truly began. Obviously, I had been more distracted with my work and other's guidance to be involved in the key parts of the camp. I was readying us for Dr. Kempler, who had decidedly, at the last minute before our departure to take an extra-long vacation with his family. Honestly, I thought that he had known how hard this part would be, so he conveniently made himself unavailable to avoid both the labor and stress of acquiring equipment and supplies, and the backlash of a band of disgruntled researchers. It was okay, but the sides of the camp truly existed as he would come soon.

Through Jillian's eyes, I began to appreciate the wonders of the rainforest as she explored the lush canopies around the site with guides. I would not let her out of my sight for my fear of losing her. As my Spanish improved, most in our group, I paid extra money to the guides, communicating my concern for Jillian's safety, making sure they had enough food, and enough ammo for their rifles. The samples she was collecting, were startling and amazing in and of themselves., Seeing the beautiful petals, the large leaves of the hidden plants alone hinting at the astounding size of the plants. She had called this forest a "monumental modern discovery" of plant species, feeling totally overwhelmed by the volume of species that had to be catalogued. Here and there she became easily acquainted with the variety of species, and would soon catalogue these botany samples in her research tent. In a nearly fourteen day period, she had easily collected the most species. On our light days, or heavy rainfall days, she would be found in the main tent with the others, settled near my work area, staring scrutinizing the samples, marveling at their beautiful intricacies, and journaling her observations of their minute features.

Dr. Kempler's group hardly performed their tasks. This was to be expected though, because I really had no control over them, and it was quite obvious that there were other researchers who were ready to work. They also knew I did not have the power to rid dismiss these people from our camp site or the project. Impossible circumstances in an impossible, unforgiving environment made me quiet down even more, focusing on the task at hand, trying to guide those motivated by the research to make progress.

Then our camp life worsened when the imperial Dr. Kempler

graced us with a visit to the campsite. I had not been nervous about his arrival because I knew he's appearance was inevitable, much like a dark plague. Dr. Kempler stepped foot onto the camp site, smelling of a fresh shower, bad Central American cigarettes, and a hint of alcohol, and promptly took to barking orders at the workers around us. These native people were used to my stern and direct procedures, respectfully communicated to them in their native language, whereas he just demanded the result in English, getting only more agitated when action wasn't immediate. Such a typical American attitude, I remembered balking at the unwelcome spectacle. His large body was coated in sweat from the humidity of the rainforest, which made his pressed-linen shirts cling to his body. Also, his loyal contingent of lackeys did nothing to help Jillian's or my situations. They encourage the criticisms, usually initiated with a clearly intentional digging or jabbing comment: "Well, I told Hans at the beginning that this would be like this."; "Hans told the locals to do it this way. Honestly, I don't understand their methods."; and my personal favorite, "Hans just doesn't listen to us." I only remained as calm as I could. I had learned then to have a thick skin, allowing comments to fall off me. But even my thick skin was to prickle at their poorly concealed insults.

After a few days, Jillian was becoming upset by their comments and insults about me. She told me that I needed to stand up for myself, not to act like the martyr and take all in and lock it all inside. Smiling, I replied to her, touching her cheek, "I do not care for people with small minds. They serve no purpose to me. This project," and I looked into the jungle, "this project is what we were destined to do." With that, it kept her at bay while I discreetly became more valuable than Dr. Kempler.

With Jillian beside me, she talked to the other researchers and helped to get them to talk to me about concerns with their research. The other guys did not want to talk, let alone approach Dr. Kempler who all within a week's time all but took over the research tent, including taking over my work area. I had let them, but I knew they did not know what they were doing, so it wouldn't have mattered where they perched. In the short time that Dr. Kempler had been onsite the camp's momentum had begun heading in a different direction altogether.

Oddly, I found this brief period to be a relaxation session. I did not decide too much on the others projects although they came to me continuously. Of course, I took Jillian's work over everyone else's. I was indiscreet aiding her supplies, research and other required necessities. Her specimens, perfect in detail and organization, clearly marked her station so she her space and work would not be invaded or interrupted by Kempler's rudeness or his minions meddling. Also, I was responsible for my own research, in addition to running the camp, the workers and supervising the researchers, but, I could not enjoy it. There were things at play that were spiraling out of control.

Dr. Kempler had been in his own world, believing that he was solely in charge of the camp. First, he had decided our camp site was not producing enough key specimens for the project., despite the fact that the valley that we were in was quite untouched landscape, so we had having the nectars of land to ourselves. He had felt that we needed to setup several small camps through the region in order to collect as much evidence to go further. Regrettably, I somewhat agreed with his philosophy, yet I manipulated his idea through his three young researchers. I had explained to him that they should go into the forest and retrieve this information for us, sending them with our best guides, which caused them to made them, leave camp for days on end. With some of the troublemakers out of the camp, the others relaxed some and even thanked me. I did not get the easy end of the stick: , I had to prepare them for their journeys, but I felt the relief once they were actually gone.

Two, he successfully created a great rift among our workers, our local people. His demands and orders in English, caused them great confusion. On purpose, the handful of translators had changed their translations to make him appear a fool. There came a great degree of mistrust between our camp and the local people. In a way, as I watched our contingent of local labor and guides turn over in the next several weeks, I felt embarrassed for us, as though we looked like arrogant Americans taking over the land, as the pretentious Europeans had taken over North America. Even my bus driver had finally had enough of Kempler's endless tirades. He left, saying to me in Spanish, *"Estes le hefe. No esto gringo largo."* Loosely translated, he was telling me, "You are the boss, not that fat American."

Finally, Dr. Kempler's consistent tardiness, and in truth, his idiot minions' tardiness as well, created a major rift in the camp. There were days where I had to wait for him to come before I could go into the field, because he insisted on checking my work and that I didn't forget to cross a T or dot an I. I was tired of waiting for him, especially when his demand was for a flawless camp and research. Typically, Dr. Kempler would come, tired, yawning, around noon at the height of the rain, where I had to be close-quartered with him in a tent. Only these things I mention can I discuss with you, Allison. The good doctor was a vile and filthy man, with eccentric morals and tastes. His vulgar mouth had to be the loudest and foulest that I had heard since I had been in Berlin.

The elements were with me, along with Jillian and our fellow researchers. The rain had been his greatest foe in the forest. We just plainly accepted this as natural course of action, after speaking to the guides, hearing them say that the rainy season lasted for months, and we adjusted our practices accordingly. Dr, Kempler, on the other hand, cursed for hours as the rain fell, as though that would somehow stop the rain from falling out of pity or remorse for inconveniencing him. He also seemed to miss the fact that he had some shelter and somehow felt that he was getting wetter despite the shelter of the tent. He would often say, "Will the goddamn heavens stop pissing on us?!"

Then there were the creatures. As a scientist, I had appreciated the life of the rain forest. I appreciated each element of the forest, the sole reason of my being. I could not count the times he would step on some harmless *arachnids*, *celopetras*, or even swatted at some *leopedratas*. It agitated me to no end. But Dr. Kempler was unnerved constantly, whimpering or grumbling like a child when a small creature crawled its way near him, on his desk, or a page. Many natives snickered behind his back as they purposely caught them and let them go near him.

Still, despite my best efforts to ignore his abrasive character, my tolerance for him was diminishing more and more each week, as I fought to repress my frustrations. He continually piled the work on me, including the administration between shipments of specimens, financials, and other university-related tasks. My hours were getting longer, my research production less and my patience was thinning. Poor Jillian had sensed this, so in return, she would stay out in the field more. During this period, I was the only one who dealt with Dr. Kempler and his erratic behaviors. I was becoming isolated in my own thoughts. I thought it would never end. This is how my research would be, I was convinced of this. The ideals of gathering and producing information that I once had were being stripped away from me, leaving me feeling unfulfilled and raw. I was becoming Dr. Kempler's personal assistant. Again, like before, Jillian and I somewhat distanced ourselves from the others, but now we were separated from each other for extended periods of time as well. Where she had been talking to the others, having her own life, a life without me, I had become increasingly more introverted and withdrawn, isolated from the rest of the team.

Little had I known at the time, but my dear Jillian was discreetly rallying the other men for my side, speaking of my confidence and who I had been, what I had been doing for the camp. In the end, her efforts worked. But while we were in the midst of this tumultuous situation, my mounting jealously was overwhelming my consciousness; I had begun snapping orders at her, I spoke shorter, clipped words with her, at times I was less than kind to her, and Dr. Kempler saw this. Was he admiring the fact that I had been demeaning to my wife? Was he getting a thrill from it? I had never known his real intentions, barely uttering words of instructions to me. These days were challenging me to no end, but soon one would come.

It had been sometime in August, the heat was bearing down on camp, the humidity intensifying, making the forest air even more stifling. That day the work was hard, and everybody was becoming exhausted by the rigorous schedule that Dr. Kempler had imposed. There had been heated discussions to the work detail: . It had been obvious that his minions were taking the least workload, while Jillian and the other men and myself took on more. I had been unusually distant, indifferent that day. Not only was the doctor not on-site, it was about to hit noontime, I had also learned that several more hired staff had not shown up for work. Plus, my desk was lost in a sea of bookkeeping that my wonderful boss had unloaded entirely on me, with notes that all the books had to balance.

The humid air were oppressive, and I could smell my own body odor in the enclosed tent. I'd heard Jillian come into the tent, and ask, "Honey, have you seen the samples I had yesterday?"

I looked at her, completely on edge, and what came next was irreversible. "Am I your personal keeper? Do I have to do everything for you as well?"

She stopped and looked at me. Her beautiful face was serious now. "Listen, Hans," she began to say, "I am working just as hard as everyone in camp—"

"You should know where your items are placed," I interrupted her, tossing my pencil down on my paper. A slight anger fell in me. I could see one of the workers nearby see us in the tent. My tone was harsh and direct, not needed.

"I know you've been working too much yourself." She said, taking one step back. "Seriously, you have to stand up to that man. He is just walking all over you."

As soon as she said that, I saw his car come into the camp. I looked past her, and she turned to see. Then her face turned sour, and she spoke to me: , "You better do it soon, because I am sick of your irritable mood."

I watch her walk out and my heart sank in my chest. She had been right, I was not myself the last few days. I had been an oaf. As Dr. Kempler approached the camp, there was an odd look on his face. He seemed to be stumbling towards the tent. Instantly, Sloane came around the corner and began to help him. It seemed that he reluctant for any help, but he was not steady on his feet.

"Fischer!" he bellowed. I could see in the darken tents that the other men were already looking at me.

The sun already disappeared under the familiar sight of developing billows of dark cumulus clouds rapidly appearing in the sky . Within moments, he was in my tent, and snapped at Sloane, "Leave us."

"But I can help you," Sloane replied.

"You arrogant son of a bitch! Leave us alone. You've helped enough," Dr. Kempler was direct.

Sloane ducked his head, as mist seemed to form in his eyes, then he shot me a stark, hostile look and left the tent.

Dr. Kempler's round face appeared paler even against the growth of dark whiskers on his face, as the beads of sweat ran down his smooth forehead. He produced an already saturated handkerchief from the inner pocket of his tight white sports coat and used it to dab at his neck.

"I must sit," he said, panting for a breath.

I moved to allow him to sit in my chair. Although he was about a meter away from me, the smell of bile and some type of strong medicine syrup wafted from his body. In the confines of the seemingly airless tent, the stench made me slightly nauseous and I held onto the table to steady myself.

"I told you Fischer, no domestic disturbances on the site," he spat out.

"We were just having a discussion," I said simply.

"It seemed pretty intense to me," his breath sounded gargled and low. "But that is not why I am here to talk to you."

I looked briefly around, and I could see Kempler's minions were close to the tent, with Sloane heading the pack. They were all behind the good doctor, so they looked as if they were not eavesdropping.

"Listen to me, Hans," he said. I knew this was going to be one of his lectures. At that very point, when he was done talking about whatever he would tell me, I would tell him I was done with the project. I would quit, and take my beautiful Jillian back to the States. Instead, I only stared back at him, noticing the glassy look in his eyes. Without a peep from me, he continued, "I need to be assured that this project operates smoothly and on a daily basis. In fact, the most important function of this project are the specimens and samples being shipped back to the States, to the University, in a timely fashion. There is so much importance in the scientific data to be encoded here. The future of environmentalism is at stake where our and future generations will look upon the research as pioneering work for future books, lecture tours and National Geographic Specials. This is one the largest goddamn projects in the field. We, you and I, are paving a new foundation of theories that echo much of Darwinism and the like. Bloody hell, the project will give new insight into the very ecosystem that we humans continually destroy. Hans, how can I stress this enough? Yet, it is vital that all materials are absolutely double-checked, final assessments are performed and the shipping process has a final check list intact." He shifted his weight in the chair. "What I am saying is that I am ensuring that you will be doing this all the time."

I was becoming angered. "Dr. Kempler, from the very beginning I have looked after the best interests of this camp and our research goals, the samples, and the specimens. I have been doing key assignments for you and not only that—"

He put his hand up halt my rebuttal, giving me a hint of a smile, but I am not sure that it was just part his alignment. "Hans, I am saying you will be in charge of the research camp."

I said nothing. I heard the rustling of birds in a nearby bush, and the murmurs of conversations in nearby tents. Then my thoughts of quitting evaporated and were replaced by the utmost happiness, a sense of relief oozed from my every pore as he spoke.

"I need to get back to the US as soon as possible." He began to stand, but wobbled slightly. I went to help him, and then I could smell the sweat coming off his body. "I am not so well. I need the States' professional care, not these asshole bush minded doctors down here."

"Can I get a worker to assist you somehow?" I was jumping for joy inside.

"No, I have Sloane to do that for me," he said as we headed out of the tent. "Sloane!"

Instantly, the thin man with a devilish grin beneath his well-groomed mustache, said, "Yes, Frank."

"I am leaving."

"Already?" He was surprised.

"We're going back to the hotel. I need to leave the country," he said simply and loudly. At that point the murmurs stopped in the tents. I saw the workers pause slightly, and then the other men were poking their heads out of their tents. I saw Jillian then, coming toward me. Her face held the same sour expression from earlier.

Sloane took his right arm, almost affectionately, as his other two minions were coming to his side. "Everybody, " Dr. Kempler announced. "Everybody, Can you all come here for one second!"

I felt the wind kick up slightly. Above us the gray skies loomed, ever so heavy and foreboding.

Soon, the camp had formed a semi-circle around Dr. Kempler. I stood opposite of him, wanting to steal Jillian just for a moment.

"I would like to announce some news," he declared. His wheezing breath could be heard over the cicadas' song in the back ground. "As the organizer of this project, I had picked each of you for your distinct capabilities. I regret to inform you that I must leave for the United States immediately. From now on, Hans Fischer, who really has been the backbone of the project here, will be in charge. All decisions and inquires on research or otherwise will be his concern. Should you need any assistance from me, you may mail me your request so that I can make it happen for you."

He stopped and there was such a silence in the group.

"No. I am not staying with him in charge," Sloane said immediately. "I am going back with you."

"God damn it, shut the hell up Sloane! We will discuss that later," Kempler said to him in such a chastising tone that it made several of us bite back our smiles. Then to the group, he said, "Any questions or responses to this?"

Everybody just looked at me with amazement, and possibly relief. I felt Jillian's hand fall into mine, giving it hard squeeze. I looked down at her, even as large droplets of rain fell on her face, she mouthed silently, "I love you."

Without any further pomp or delay, he turned and made to get out of the afternoon deluge , and he cursed something at his three minions who all seemed quite displeased. They each took turns shooting me sour expressions, before following dutifully behind him. Once they their jeep began its ascent toward the ridge, the whole camp erupted in whoops and cheers, accolades were shouted in my direction, and even the local hired laborers joined in the collective cheers. In the rain, they danced and laughed, and soon a bottle of rum was broken out. A radio crackled of a local Spanish station, and the music could be heard over the steady din of the rain. Soon, the everyone was gathered in the largest tent.

Jillian pulled me aside to give me a wonderful kiss as refreshing rain fell over us. We stared at each other for a quick moment. The water dripped around her face, and caused strands of her curly auburn hair to cling to her face and fall into her eyes. I held onto her for so long, believing this would be a fresh start for us.

Behind us, I felt a slight nudge and one of the locals, Luis, was urging us to get inside the tent. Jillian smiled coyly and pulled me towards the crowded tent.

"I cannot believe this!" Don said out loud. He was a great researcher with a specialty in marine biology. He was here in order to find new aquatic species in the nearby rivers and streams of the rainforest, the small crevasses of the land, even in large plant life. Brilliantly, he had been discovering several species of *pimephales promelas*, small minnows, living in nearby pools, replenished only by the constant rain. He was a thin man whose clothes clung to his frame much like a corpse: His skeletal face was eerily covered in a thick beard, and his sunken eyes enhanced his Cro-Magnon appearance.

"I don't even know what to say," Reginald's deep baritone voice came from behind me. He specialized in herpetology. Reginald was a large man, with a solid in his frame, and was slightly taller than me. His skin was a dark, rich color, and his eyes were a glowing hazel.

Some of the workers began talking rapidly amongst each other, so fast for my mind to translate. Luis held up clear bottles of rum and tequila in his hands and gestured for me to sample with him. Of course, I could not refuse and disrupt the cultural balance as their services even more in the coming weeks and months. The liquor burnt my throat and I winced, which made them laugh heartedly at my expense.

The rain was absolutely refreshing, and the warm liquid soaked through my shirt to my skin. This time I welcomed the rain, as if it was washing away the last few months of Dr. Kempler presence here. I really did not know what to say, because I looked at them, all chatting happily amongst themselves. Just minutes earlier I had been resigned to the idea of giving this up, leaving this all behind.

"Darling," Jillian cooed, "you must say something."

Clearing my throat, Reginald hushed the gathered group, and I spoke, without hearing the usual lack of confidence in my throat, "Fellow scientists and fellow workers,, this is a new time. Our goals are the same. We must preserve the university's policies and procedures in conducting research as we continue our work. We each owe our fine disciplines the worth of our work to be set for colleagues and future academia. But our research will be different, I promise you this. We all need to work together in order to get bring this project to paramount success. Honestly, I too was readying myself to quit. Today, we have hope to do we groomed ourselves to do. Tomorrow the work will be there." I paused, seeing the rain dripping off their invigorated faces, then I turned to Jillian, drenched and smiling, , and I continued, "But today, we celebrate!"

Then there was a roar of cheers followed hugs and handshakes for me. I had changed the mood in the camp, a change that was greatly needed. We all celebrated that night. Jillian and I were happy again, content. She forgave me for my earlier rudeness, forgave me for my unintentional dismissal of her affections the last few weeks, and forgave me for being just me. I had loved her more then, loved her more than I could possibly realize.

The next couple of days I had several different meetings which we all took responsibility over the camp. First, I began training a native assistant, who turned out to be one my great friends, Jose Santamos. He was an able man with great English and a willingness to learn. He helped to categorize the samples and create proper storage for them. Paying him double his wage, he went even further to oversee the activities of the other local workers, supervising their abilities and performance around the camp, helping to find new reliable persons as the months passed.

Second, Don helped with packaging and shipping of samples to the university, arranging proper transportation for us and mapping out new study sites as we progressed in our project. Then, Reginald worked on the camp itself, with the help of labor workers to help make it more secure and safe for all of us. Between the two of them, they lifted a great amount of work off of me. I pitched in and helped them as much as I could, but they insisted that I had done enough and that I need to focus on efforts to keep Dr. Kempler as far away from us as possible. They became the very backbone of the project, even cataloguing and discovering species at a staggering rate.

Finally, Jillian took over most of the paperwork and accounting for me, which would lead to her discovering her salary, how low it had been set. She was insulted at first, then through creative accounting I modified her position and then the university recognized her performance. Within a month, the university gave her three times her original rate, and Dr. Kempler could not change it or dispute it. Moreover, Jillian, with her brilliant research and reasoning mind had put that ability to work around the accounting for the camp operation costs too. In fact, she discovered that we had more money allotted to the project than Dr. Kempler had indicated to us. I had always questioned our meager funding from our prestigious institution. This issue, even today, sometimes crosses my mind and I still wonder if he was keeping this portion from ? Was he pocketing this amount for his own selfish reasoning? I could never prove that but I've always remained pensive about that detail.

For the first time, since we all had arrived at the field site, the project was moving forward. We worked in unison, as the *solenopsis invicta,* in which the whole work together to get the food, protect its mound, keep the enemies away and become a solid force. I was no longer burdened by menial, burdensome camp oversight; this was no longer a bad experience. I had been the one in charge, now, I was free to conduct my research, to lead our team and set precedence.

It was about three or so weeks later that I would receive a letter from Dr. Kempler. He was greatly apologetic for his quick departure from the campsite that day, but it had turned out that he had "a serious case of malaria." He had spent an entire week in the hospital in the States, rushing from the plane to the university to get medical care, claiming that he would have perished if he hadn't sought medical attention immediately. Not believing him, I had Jillian call the hospital to check records of his hospitalization. Not that I am immersed in paranoia, but my trust in him was at a minimum. Even in his writing, Dr. Kempler was still condescending and conveyed little personal interest in the need of others. Toward the end, he wrote:

We will discuss business matters within the first of the following month. I will send you a location where we can talk live to discuss the matters at hand.
I do hope you take care, Hans. Should you need any support from me, I will send you help immediately. Until then, please note that
I will be in constant contact.
Sincerely, Dr. F. Kempler.

I showed this to Jillian who laughed out loud. I knew she never took anything he said seriously.

As the months passed, the communication between us and Dr. Kempler came more sporadic. I spoke more to the university administration staff than to the good doctor; in a way, I became extremely independent from the university and Dr. Kempler's needs.

I had been freed of his torment.

TEN

Our biodiversity project was unique in and of itself. We were one of the first research teams to look at the various parts of a habitat, the central highland rainforest, and study all aspects of life there: the animals, the plant life, the climate, the geology, as a whole. Never before had a real team like ours been in practical use to gather this type of information, seeing countries like Costa Rica already creating large nature reserves in order to preserve their native environments. As far as Dr. Kempler's objectives were concerned, I took liberty to magnify his scope to include the continuing devastation that humans reigned upon , and how we had been cataloguing species that eventually became extinct throughout the following years from future researchers.

The deforestation of the land heavily influenced much of our work. Even at the time of study—now, the concept was normalized but back then a radical approach--we connected ourselves with the local government to share critical data and appeal to them to take protective measures to protect those resources. With the books you see around the room, I had been one of the pioneers of ecological preservation, although it might not have felt like it at the time. I would be able to witness how my research been used so much in future evidence. In that time, the land was much more lush and teeming with life as we continued our scientific endeavors.

The area that we were studying is still somewhat isolated wilderness, unaffected by civilization, ensuring that the university's samples were pure and that we had unfettered clearance from the government to survey the territory. At the very least, the following months would enlighten us all to the inner-workings of the sub ecosystems the rainforest canopy.

Moreover, we were heading into a very exciting time in the field of science, the time of a new global consciousness that transcended the old neoclassical mindset that human beings were the superior species, able to dominant the planet and that it was somehow our right to do so. Today the school of ecological minds view the efficient use of resources as paramount to protecting the environment. We're learning to recognize our impact on the ecosystems, and how we as humans, the species with the largest footprint on the planet, can protect and rejuvenate the environment, and go further to explore the farthest, untapped parts of our world. Our group, my group, had been on the frontier of this burgeoning new ideology. I was truly proud of my hard-working team.

That said, I must tell you of these months in order for you to truly comprehend the fate of my dear Jillian. For as the dreary rainy season that we had become so acclimated to, the wonderful dry season was finally upon us. The wonderful sun poured down upon us as if it was a signal for us to renew our research efforts.

As the first couple of months rolled on I had created team meetings at which we would have long discussions about our projects, taking notes from each other, understanding our direction. This truly created a more harmonious laboratory. Each member: Jillian, Don, Reginald and I would each have a chance to speak about their ideals. Jillian naturally assumed the positon of note taker during these sessions. If I felt the research from a member was going off-track, which was typically Reginald, I would have the final say. Consequently, and at first not welcomed by the other researchers, I included some of the native workers, especially Jose, in these meetings because I wanted them to feel connected to the project.

It was an important aspect to the research site, you see. As we identified new species: new animals, new plants, we furthered our knowledge of the area and the habitat. During these meetings, I encouraged the team's needs on improvement, how we could truly benefit the project and the university expectations. Don had come up with a new concept, which I went through the university, not Dr. Kempler, in order to get approval. About three months into the dry season, we would start making our camp smaller and more transportable. Reginald was in-charge of set-up and clean-up. Jillian and I were in-charge of staff, research needs and basic funding. Don with a paid guide scout terrain and would find a new region periodically. In a way, for all us, this constant movement was always a refreshing time as it allowed us to keep a steady pace of collection and cataloguing, a sense of urgency upon us to get as much accomplished before we were uprooted again. And it allowed us to see more of the country. We began from the north, near the Nicaragua border moving down toward the Panama border, creating a tight trajectory towards the Gulf of Mexico for the next year or so.

In order for this to happen, I had suggested purchasing a local house in the San Jose area that we could make a home base, with enough rooms for all of us to reside in at any given time. I was surprised by the team's enthusiastic approval of this idea, they were even more keen to it than I had been initially myself, making a home in this country, this beautiful country in Central America. In fact, it seemed that Jillian loved the idea the most. She said she felt that she established a home for us, creating a private room for us, away from other people's conversations.

For me, I knew this was a great location to store equipment, and have a central location to regroup. And perhaps most important to me at the time, this was a location with a phone. Today the mobile phone is an item a person seems to absolutely need. Back then, our phone number was a particular hotel in a local town, sometimes in Varablanca. With the frequent relocation of our research camp, , our phone usage moved from town to town at times making it difficult for family and associates back home to reach us.

Still, Jillian for a week or so, set up our house with the help of several workers, purchasing furniture and basic necessities of life. Yes, there was at least a woman's touch in that house, having a maid and a housekeeper in there once a week while we traveled was a great help to maintaining some sense of order there. Jillian had essentially taken on the role of house manager there. She said once to me on our way to Puerto Jimenez, "You know, I have to take care of all my men. Don and Reginald are like brothers to me, ones I never had. And you, my darling, who else would take care of you? You can barely get out of the tent looking proper."

After that, the next few months flew by for Jillian and me. We were seemed to be a typical American couple, I was more strict on things and she was carefree. It was her love of the culture that truly inspired her work. One of her favorite things had been exploring new towns, and the local stores and eateries. There she would be able to point out the species of plants that were edible in the local rainforests. There she would have long broken conversations with local people. She had a way of making friends wherever she stepped her foot; the people who looked our house always missed her when we were gone. They would bring local flowers and filling our room with exotic blooms every time we returned.

Jillian really held our group together, giving that extra *je ne c'est quoi*, as the French say, that I could never. I was the leader and made that way, where she helped soften our group of men, allowing us to be more placid and understand the *pura vida* of which the local people were so accustomed. In addition, Jillian had become great friends with both Don and Reginald, often spending more time with them out in the field while I stayed back at the campsite managing other aspects of our operations. I was from a jealous type in any sense of the word. Because these men cared for Jillian as a sister, I saw how they protected her, also made sure she had good guides and assisted with her own research. Perhaps, Reginald and Don could see Jillian's naïve and impractical research approaches as did Dr. Kempler. They never brought it up though. Instead they encouraged to explore the region and gather specimens. And still, at night after a long day, in the house she would crawl into our bed with me, or on our cot in virtually the middle of nowhere, and she would always whisper in my ear how much she loved me.

Little did I realize how much more Jillian was to our team. In hindsight, many years later, I had not known how lucky I really was.

Even as we encountered the next rainy season for which we were all mentally prepared, Jillian and I shared these moments and times so caringly and affectionately. I still maintained the professional end of the relationship, trying not to slip too much in front of the camp, in front of Don or Reginald while we worked, but after site, or around a fire, then I showed my affections. I had enjoyed the minutes with her. What really baffles still me to this day is her book, I have it on the third shelf on the case directly behind me. It is her book, *The Study of Central American Plants: A Discussion on Tropical Beauty, Local Fruits and Edible Legumes of the Local Market*. Inside she had dedicated the book to me with a simple notation: *To Hans, I love you.* Where on earth did she have time to write this? I had thought. Amazingly, with the amount of work that Jillian had performed, she had the leisure time to create such a fine piece of work. Later, in a pile of papers, I found her letter from the publishing house that was most interested in her research .Just recently I received a letter that they would soon be releasing its ninth edition.

We were a scientific group of ecological warriors, as it were, and alone in this pursuit, or at least that is how I had felt. Rarely would we talk about the current world happenings, receiving very little current news at time. Except for me, the group still struggled to read Spanish. The natives would talk about politics with me, about the nearby countries, and in the United States but truly, my concern no longer was with things at home. It was perhaps rude on my part for not wanting that to be part of my life. Yes, the United States was entering the Vietnam War, the Civil Rights movement was underway working to reshape and make new laws and a new subculture was forming, calling themselves Hippies and protesting the War. We were far removed from all of that. It was not a part of my history. Aside from our research all I knew was my homeland, which was still under socialistic power, and I was far removed from any situation, politically and more or less socially as well.

I enjoyed these times in this group. Not once did Dr. Kempler question our samples or specimens. The university hadn't requested any log books, nor questioned our purchases around the countryside. Oddly, my scientific group was an utopia to me. My love of this work that I loved at my fingertips, my dear wife at my side each and every day, my fellow colleagues within my conversational reach, and my life in this foreign land where I was slowly steadily settling into its society.

Yet, all good things do come to an end. And it began with the Reginald's rather abrupt departure.

We had just come back from another successful trek into the area near the Limon region, where I was able to study the rituals of various praying mantis, local big blue butterflies and some other slithering creatures. I actually had discovered several new arthropods while I was there. Jillian herself was in awe of the area, seeing the new plant species thriving outrageously in this Caribbean-like environment. Don and Reginald too had equal triumphs in their pursuit of scientific achievement. We were all tired, and were returning to San Jose late that evening.

I had noticed a particular letter, well more of a note. It had been a telegram from the States, addressed to Reginald. He had just come in from unloading the last of the materials when I handed it to him.

"What's this man?" he asked, letting out a deep sigh.

I only shrugged my shoulders, and sat at the desk to look at some papers from the university. I wasn't really paying attention to him, and Jillian in the other room, so I had noticed that Reginald slumped in the chair.

"No, man, no," he began, and then he was crying.

I got up and called after Jillian. As Jillian came over to console him, "I'm so sorry, Reginald," she said, collapsing with him, silently crying for him. I read the note, which was simple and straight to the point:

Reggie, Joe Jr. died in 'Nam. Come back for funeral. Father.

I could see the pain of this loss of life in his eyes. How long he cried for I can't remember anymore, but Jillian was there holding him.

Then he said, "He was my little brother, the baby of family, at eighteen when he got himself drafted."

Jillian soothed, "There, there."

Between his sobs, he looked at me, "I told Joe that he could have gone to Canada, to Mexico, anywhere. I'd help him." He choked back a sob. "But uh-uh, Dad had to make him go. Dad said, 'We got to make sure us Blacks are represented.' When we moved to Chicago, after JFK was killed, my father was part of the Northern Civil Rights groups so his children could be free. I was just happy being in Memphis."

Don made arrangements for Reginald to leave immediately, which was an unusual request in those days. "Here you go, Reg," he said, handing the needed documents to him.

Reginald just blankly looked at him and said, "I promised him when I saw him off at his plane, before he had to go to boot camp, about two and half years ago, that I would see him again. And when I finally saw him, it was a few months later that we left to come down here, and somehow I knew that when he left to fight I would not see him again."

"You can come back when you are ready," was all I could think to say. I wished I had understood his loss, but I had been an only child. I had felt something for him, a missing cog in our system. I knew without him, that fragile camp I had set-up was leading us down a darker path than I could ever have realized.

I had not arranged to go with him the early morning, although I had given him my support, or at least proclaimed it. Jillian, my sweet Jillian, and Don had decided to go with him. Even our driver was saddened by his obvious grief.

Upon their return, an emptiness descended on our little group that I had not felt in a while, not justifiable, not cohesive to our unit. We did busy ourselves in order to make the time pass, in order for the minutes to click by. Without Reginald, it was extra work for me once again. In fact, learning from my lesson from last time, I allowed Jose to help by hiring two natives temporarily and training them to do Reginald's work. Of course, I notified the university, covering my administration end, not wanting to upset the apple cart.

Some days had passed, when I received a letter par *avion rapide* from Dr. Kempler. He wrote:

> *Hans,*
> *I am briefly jotting this down for you. First, in the wake of Reginald's loss, on behalf our group and the university, I have sent flower arrangements for the funeral. Of course, there is no cost for this to the group; we are doing what is right. Two, if you are overwhelmed with your work load, do not hesitate, I stress, do not hesitate to issue another man for down there.*
> *Our work is much too valuable for any opportunities to be missed or specimens to be overlooked out of carelessness or poor management. Keep the research going, strong and steady.*
> *As always,*
> *Dr. F. Kempler.*

I stared at his letter but didn't share it with anyone else wanting to avoid spreading his toxic influence any further than my own desk. It was unnecessary for him to reach out to us. He hadn't stepped foot in Costa Rica since his departure. In a way, I felt that all my progress over the last few months seemed trivial in his eyes.

Without Jillian's eyes on me, I had filed this letter into my research, letting it sit there amongst my paperwork. Why I didn't tear it up, I can't say.

Still the worst was yet to come.

It had been an unusually gorgeous day. Jillian and I were in a small village in the valley outside San Jose, just getting some supplies for our next research trip. At first, I had felt nothing, but the animals all began to squawk and chatter, and strangely the birds all around us seemed to have been disturbed by something at once. I looked up to see the bright sky filled with different colored feathers. Jillian had not paid attention, and just continued examining the fruits on a nearby stand.

I had never felt an earthquake, nor experienced one before. When you first experience one it is much like floating in still water just on top of the surface when a travelling boat comes near you. You feel that wave wrap around you, you feel the ripple of wake caress you. Yet you anticipate it because you are on a body of water, and your body is finely tuned to this predictable outcome. But that day in late July, I had felt a quick subtle ripple of earth under me. Jillian felt it too. The locals around us went on about their business, their traditional ways, accustomed to the feeling, maybe even ignoring it as a common occurrence here.

"What was that?" Jillian came to me, looking slightly panicked.

"Let me ask this merchant," I said.

Before I opened my lips, the scratching on the radio screamed, "*El Monte Arenal ha estallado! El Monte Arenal ha estalldo!*"

"What does it say?" Jillian asked me, grabbing my arm at the alarmed tone of the voice on the radio.

Around us, there was already silence in the air, as the message repeated over and over.

Before I could open my mouth, a young teenager translated loosely, "Monte Arenal iz boom."

There I realized the beauty around me, in this market, in this small town, the wonderful colors of the buildings, in the alarmed faces around me, watching as many people began to cry. Above all of this, just beyond the town laid the Cloud Forest, pristine and endless. All around us, the forest was still eerily quiet.

Only the voice of the radio announcer was trying to give news of the now erupting Arenal Volcano, describing the path of destruction, the clouds of ash and the imminent death. Jillian gripped my arm and

the news unraveling as her eyes began to tear up.
Such a tragic day in the lives of these native people.

Russell

ELEVEN

The news about Mount Arenal's eruption, a once silent, and believed extinct volcano, a once pristine rainforest on the mountain, came as fast as news could in those days. Unlike today's modern technologies, news came as slow and lethargic as the country itself. I, like rest of this country, waited for information as it crept in at a snail's pace.

Regrettably, the destruction was a great shock to the country and indeed, the death toll was great.. Sometime later, as scientists would discover in the following months, there were some signs the day before: seismic activity that had not been felt but was measured some distance away on seismographs in Cuba. Earthquake prevention and detection equipment was on the cusp of discovery, but it wasn't there yet. The native *ticos* were used to their earthquakes. Unfortunately, in the villages of Pueblo Nuevo and Tabacon, people took these threats with a lack of cautionary plans nor did warnings to prevent loss as they had uniformly contrived that the mountain was just the Arenal Peak, and absolutely harmless.

Costa Rica and much of Central America is situated in a precarious place, a the belt of volcanoes both, active and dormant, that ring the Pacific Ocean. As the science of volcanology came to be, the effectiveness of predicting and understanding the scales of volcanoes had been a mystery. For hundreds of years, Arenal Peak, as it was called by the locals, seemed to be a docile mountain, full of life in the forests that have sprouted from the volcanic soil. Perchance the ancient Mayans recognized its threats and its history, though since the conquering Spaniards of the mid sixteenth century, there had been neither records nor signs of any activity in the Arenal region. Naturally, the locals had grown complacent in the shadow of the seemingly safe peak.

When the quiet mountain began to rumble, much like that of a large plane's engines at takeoff, as the survivors had described it, people knew there was something wrong. As the pressure of magna just meters below the surface pressed toward to the surface, people were still unaware of the magnitude of the devastation to come. There was little visual evidence to the layperson, but the destruction was quite clear. Half the mountain exploded and created three craters, destroying kilometers of wildlife and land. It had sent a large cloud of ashes that would circle the Caribbean and Atlantic Ocean for weeks, blacking out the sky for some days over the area. Nature's brutality continued as winds steadily blew ash over the Gulf of Mexico, the relentless rains continued to pour down the mountain in streams making recovery impossible. In this time, as I had believed that humans had come so far, there were still such limitations in this country.

There had been some American assistance and humanity relief that also arrived to help in the process, but it was honestly pathetic and underwhelming. In the wake of the eruption, seventy-nine people from two towns, Tabacon and Pueblo Nuevo, perished. It was a heavy burden for the people of the land. The country mourned for weeks, as news continued to come in of failed efforts at search and rescue for survivors. Everyone around us felt the pain of this hardship, crying for the loss of people, crying for the victims who witnessed the destruction, crying for the country in its weakest time.

Within a week, much relief had come in and the city of San Jose was alive with military vehicles being sent out toward the active volcano, more military people being escorted around to nearby bases, and new surge of scientists the world came to see the aftermath firsthand and study the newly awakened giant. I had seen it in the papers, read the reports, looked at the flashes of pictures on distorted television sets where the volcano laid in the background. It was a disturbing time for all of us, for our group.

About two days after the destruction, Jose, my great companion, announced that he had to leave to help his family out in Arenal. There were several other men who were also related to victims and had to go as well, to help go through the rubble. They had hope that they would find their family members. Even though survivors encouraged others to stay home; they had witnessed the destruction first hand, witnessing their loved ones perish. There was little that could dissuade Jose and the other men in our camp who left early that morning. Our prayers accompanied the men on their journey; Jillian especially, had cried for their safety and that of their families, as they left us.

By end of the week, the few workers that remained with us were helpful but not as skilled or experienced as the rest. Since Reginald had just left us and now most of crew gone, the camp was slim and piling up with work. I truly felt abandoned in an odd way; though I knew that there were so many elements out of my grasp. It was been a Friday morning when I received the telegram from Dr. Kempler.

The entire day felt off, odd in some way I couldn't put my finger on at the time. That morning, just as the midday rains seemed to have come early, Don discovered that a corner of the lab at the house had a leak inside, probably damaging much of our work. A new worker with little English skills had been helping him, while the house keeper had helped clean-up the area. Jillian had been focusing hard on her work, had stayed up late the night before, so I had let her sleep in, to let her have some rest after a string of stressful days. At least one of us needed that. I had already been up since four that morning, trying to figure out our next plans, how we should adjust our pace. Actually, I was trying to convince myself to hold the project together for at least several weeks more, at least until Jose and the workers or Reginald came back. I had been composing a letter to the university, justifying our slow production during this time, indicating that there were "acts of nature impeding our productivity at the research site." Never before had I caved into any problem, but there had always been ample number of bodies to help achieve our goals.

A growing amount of paperwork was piling up at the corner if my desk, which I desperately needed to attend to. There were daunting specification logs from the university that I had to check, to log costs and verify our monies. I had trusted Jillian implicitly with the accounting tasks, however, I had never trusted the school with equal certainty. There were too many miles and volumes of carbon-copied papers that had to be rectified. In today's world that gross amount of paperwork is now conducted through a labyrinth of computer programs and files are sent electronically through cyberspace. Human error was all but too common in those days, with too many hands and too many stamps of approval before one could see a check, or better yet, the statement from our bank. Jillian always thought I had been too attentive to this detail. I never had money as a child so when I grew I was quite frugal with it, secure in the reality of it only when every penny was accounted for. When it came to the university's money at that time in Costa Rica, I had all but treated it as my own investment. I had lost sleep over this, been a loyal fool at the time, blind to what the reality of the agenda really had been.

So that morning, about nine A.M., I could hear Don and one of the workers banging on the wall with some plumbing work, attempting to fix our central house. There was a knock at the front door and the house keeper answered it. She accepted the delivered telegram, tipped a few coins, and brought the telegram to me in my office. I was already frustrated with the mountain paperwork that had been sent back to me, as it was not balancing against our records. Later, sometime later, a colleague told me that Dr. Kempler had been toying with the numbers back in the university. Where the missing money eventually found itself, what account, what untraceable location, I honestly would never know. Yet during that time, I had been angry at myself, feeling that the unbalanced reports would be my undoing.

I took the orange slip of paper, realizing as soon as I read the sender's address that Dr. Kempler had some message for us. It was simple and straight to the point, as was his particular fashion:

Hans,
I must speak with you about urgent matter. A change in the program. I made arrangement for us to speak at 10 a.m. Saturday, August 7th. I will expect your complete cooperation.
Dr. J. Kempler.

I only stared at the paper for some time, rereading this as an insult from him. How could this man think that he could interfere with my affairs down here? I stood up, trying to clear my head swimming with so many thoughts. I knew then that a shift in power was imminent. I thought I had all the cards in my hands, . Then, seeing this note, only in spite angered me. I flung a stack of papers across the room.

"Didn't know that you would be upset about some leak in the house?" Jillian commented from behind me.

I turned to see her, in khaki pants and a loose white button down shirt. Her hair loose, flowing down over her shoulders, waiting to pin back into its usual style, . There was just a hint of blush on her cheeks and deep burgundy lipstick on her lips. I melted at the sight of her.

"I do apologize," was all I said, slumping into my chair.

She came to me, placing a hand on the back of my head. "You always feel the need to apologize for your emotions, when I do get to see them. What's wrong, Hans?"

I handed her the note.

When she was finished, she said softly but with such force, "What right does he have to say 'Your complete cooperation'? The nerve of that man! He thinks that he can just control us like puppets, even from this a far distance."

"He expects so much from us already," I said. I looked at her. Her face was scrunched in anger.

"Yes he does," she slammed her hand on the desk. "Are we just his minions, disposable bodies at his will?" She put her hands on her hips, and took a deep breath in. "I need coffee."

Jillian left the room, and I could hear the splash of raindrops outside the window, the mounting sounds of traffic splashing through puddles forming on the road, the splashes of some children giggling, talking as they ran by the house.

I could only sit and continue to look at his insulting message, thinking about what he could have to talk to me about: the growing stacks of unbalanced sheets, the specimen samples sent to the States, about any item that he chose to ask.

Shortly, Jillian came in with Don who was soaked and equally upset.

"What's this about, Hans?"

"I thought you were fixing a hole in the ceiling," I said.

"Until Jillian told me what happened. Well, why don't you call him now and ask. Get it over with." Don's voice was quick, sharp, and he breathed heavily.

I shrugged my shoulders, replying, "I just can't pick up the phone. I won't waste time looking for the man."

"I know that it's about me." Don was nodding his head. "He probably thinks that my contribution to the project is insufficient."

"No, Don, it isn't," Jillian piped in.

"Don, I really don't know what Kempler wants this time."

"Well, he never liked my work. Maybe he's calling with news that he's had to make cuts up in the States and I was one of them."

"Relax, Don. You're jumping to conclusions. Knowing Kempler, he probably just wants us to start alphabetizing the specimens as we research according to each region," Jillian added, putting a reassuring hand on his shoulder and took a sip of coffee.

"All I know is that there's no way we can do all this work without the man power," Don stated, speaking exactly what I was thinking. Sometimes, Don frightened me by how often his thought patterns seemed to match mine. Much like soil that contained several kinds of new nutrients to help nurture the layers of the creatures below the leaf line, Don's equal rationale allowed my decisions to be more cohesive.

"Hans, I have a great idea." Jillian was smiling, almost too wide. "Why don't we take a break?"

"Exactly," I replied to Don's comment. "Wait, what do you mean? Break?" I voice sounded odd, hollow. My mind was on the amount of work that I still needed to .

"That is a perfect idea, Jillian. Where should we go?" Don said, his spirits already lifting.

My feelings were more dubious. I had never been one to take breaks; work had been my source of entertainment, I enjoyed being in the lab. That had been my source of calm.

"Who will do the work?" was my only argument.

"Really, Hans? We all have been working especially hard," she began and looked at me. I melted into her beautiful eyes, knowing that it was needed, this break. With that, I agreed and she became instantly animated, and Don had already turned to start to make the plans. In a matter of couple of hours, Jillian had us packed, Don arranged for our travel and accommodations to at our destination. In my disgust toward Dr. Kempler, I had put our retreat on the university's tab, with simple justification in this excursion as a scouting expedition, but truthfully it had been only to get back at him his rudeness and offensive behavior. I loaded the suitcases into the car, then our driver slowly pulled away from the house, away from

San Jose; I did not immediately ask Don where we were headed stowing away my intrepid feelings and following along for a while. I left behind my hard feelings against the university as we passed through the third-world city's limits and relaxed into the serenity of my beloved's hold on my arm and the feel of her next to me.

Jillian was more beautiful than I could ever remember. She wore only simple lipstick, but she radiated a confidence from within and the sheer beauty of her features glowed tan, enhanced by months in the outdoors. Her eyes were trained on the scenery around us, and it had not escaped my notice, but captivated by her, studying her features, her slender face and willowy grace of her arms as they nestled against mine in stark contrast to my thick arms, amply-covered in dark hair. I had long wondered what she had found attractive in me. No other woman would really have found me attractive in my awkward years, and now my age has made me more appealing on the eyes. I was not the friendliest looking person at simple glance, nor did I have much to offer in the way of pleasant company. Despite Don sitting directly in front of us, I swept my arm around her, holding her much like the male blue *morphas* whose mating grasp on his lover is tight and inescapable.

I held her long and tight to me everywhere her body fell against mine. I believe she had fallen asleep at one point during the ride, while I remained alert, surveying the landscape as we passed through into parts of the country we had yet to explore. As the bus sluggishly moved towards the Pacific coastline of the country, Jillian, Don and I did not talk much, only the crackling sounds of the local station penetrated the air in the van, playing hypnotic rhythms of Hispanic melodies and rhythms. It was a drearily wonderful feeling, to be on the bus, away from the responsibility that usually consumed my every waking moment, and much of my dreams as well. I had been with my wife, my Jillian during these last few months but not spending any real quality of time with her. And Don, a new friend whom I hardly knew beyond some forced conversations and hearing his dissertations on his subject species. The scent of the ocean air filled my lungs, reminding me of my first encounter with the ocean on the shores of Great Britain. It had been so cold then, and the air was filled with the rich dampness of sea mist and fish. Here I smelt the ocean as distinctly as I did Jillian at my side, a soft fragrant sweetness that was undeniably fluid and utterly captivating.

By early evening we crawled into the Jaco Beach area, postcard-perfect and busy with the activities of a popular tropical vacation spot. Don had made arrangements for us at a local hotel, which he said he requested as a nice surprise for us. Jillian's curiosity was piqued as she leaned forward to look out the window, while I just wanted to rest. Some desperately needed R&R was an idea that I into.

Stepping off the bus, I immediately felt the gracious hospitality of the locals. The townspeople and tourists alike ambled along in pursuit of Friday night entertainment and the beginning of their weekend. We noticed some American college students with large back packs convening at a youth hostel. The town's main street consisted of several drinking establishments, a couple of restaurants, and several small hotels. And on the other side of the street, as we faced west, between the buildings, was the endless ocean. The glow of the sun shone brilliantly off the curling waves.

Jillian pulled me immediately toward our room, which to our delight and surprise, as Don had promised, opened to beach view. We had a veranda one floor up from beach level, with two ratty blue chairs for sitting. The room itself was typical of the region: small, in need of painting, with a seemingly clean bed, and a small black and white television. During that era there was no expectation of accommodations. We had been lucky to have our own shower, although I had to sacrifice a large arachnoid species in the process.

Having endured these conditions for such a long time, Jillian looked past mistakes and went to stand on the porch. I stood next to her, taking in the sights of Jaco Beach, with its large stony beach stretching for about two kilometers against the Pacific Ocean, and most of the town nestled along the beach and coastline. There was a port about a mile south of the beach, but it did not interfere with the pristine view of the vast ocean. The whole town was settled in lowland between two large ancient volcanic lava flows that flanked either side of the valley that was now covered in boundless tropical beauty. It was quite a large area of flatness between these crevasses of forests. Above us, turbulent skies of intermittent clouds and darkening blue crept out over us from the inland toward the far-off horizon. I felt the warmth of the sun on my skin, combined with the sea breeze, it created the pleasant heat on my skin.

The ocean ahead of us held a beauty all its own. The endless blue of the water, contrasted with the crisp greenish-teal as it faded to a deep, almost magenta hue as it reflected the last of the evening sunset back to us. Ripples of waves, probably a couple of meters tall crashed against the beach, their power wrenching screams and joyful yips from the swimmers. Down the north side of the beach, I watched some surfers, obviously Americans, maybe from California, negotiate their longboards over the rolling curls of water. Surfing was just being discovered and gaining popularity; it was primitive as a sport and looked down upon as a hippie movement. Never would I attempt it, even though Jillian, who stood next to me already promised that she would try it the next day if the ocean was even slightly still.

From below, were heard Don call up to us, already with a drink in his hand, waving us toward a place he found for us to eat. A few minutes and casual stroll later, we happened on upon a local eatery with friendly people that was set directly on the beach. How long we sat I could not tell you, but the sun had long since fallen into the horizon, and the night stars blinked above us. We sat until the first of the beach bonfires were lit and people gathered around them. We really talked very little, talked of nothing really; we talked of American conditions we had no control over, and we barely spoke of science. Jillian and I held hands on the table, really the first time ever I had been this affectionate in public with her.

Eventually Don left us to pursue more interesting nightlife in another cantina down the beach. The rest of the night, we would not see Don, nor for the rest of days either, aside from the morning once or twice during our stay on the coast. Later, it would come out that he had met a local lady friend who hung on his thick arm and laughed at his dry humor.

We left for our room, where we held each other on the squeaky chairs on the veranda and listened to the waves. Even as the noise of the town slowly died down, the soothing sound of the ocean lulled us into a peaceful night of rest.

Over the next couple of days, Jillian and I were one with the beach and the local eateries, the stores, the people. She met a nice older couple, Juanita and Carlos, that ran a local supermarket. They were wonderful with her, and Jillian the same with them. Jillian had watched them interact with their five children and each other as they ran the store, stocking shelves, attending to customers, chatting with the regulars and friends that stopped in. I suppose it should not have been a surprise when, as we sat down for dinner on our last night on the beach, she asked me, "Hans, would you ever like to extend the family?"

I looked at her, seeing the glow of the sunset on her face. "I am willing to bring your mother down here, if you would like."

She laughed, then said, "No, not that. I mean, should we consider extending our family?"

I barely got my fork of food into my mouth. Never had I pondered children, to extend my life, to be a father. I suppose all men have these questions when the opportunity comes. Some men are ready and willing to accept the responsibility, and then there are men who deny their destiny until it was too late. I had not wanted that happen to me, so considering children was quite a brilliant idea to me.

I took her hand, and said, "When you are ready, I will be ready."

A small, wonderful smile caressed her lips. She squeezed my leg under the table. She looked out at the ocean and replied, "Soon, I will be."

Most of that night, we talked of hypothetical situations: . Where we would live, where were the best schools, where we would like to raise our children, what to name them, what we really wanted out of life. Actually Jillian spoke most, I listened diligently, paying attention to each detail, and nodding carefully to her statements and her views. As we talked about the future, I savored the last remnants of sunset that night, as the orange hues bounced off the breaking waves, and couples walked along the beach in the cresting waves and small children skipped through the water. I took a deep breath of salt air into my lungs, listening to the rhythm of waves smashing against the rocky shore. I imagined bringing my, our, children back to this beach, to see the beauty of the sand, to teach them to swim here, have them taste the salty sea water, and to watch them grow. I imagined my life with Jillian as she spoke of aging with her, having our grown kids celebrate our anniversaries, celebrate their birthdays, walk my future daughter, Sonja, down the aisle, watch my son, Gerald, graduate from school as a lawyer. So many dreams to shape that night, so many wishes for the future. I only remember the velvety red sun sink into the ocean, at the edge of the world, and not the silly dreams of a young man.

We walked hand and hand back to our inadequate room

accommodations. She opened the windows letting moonlight fall on her face, then she turned to me. She unbuttoned her blouse revealing her beautiful cleavage. I went to her, placing my rough chapped lips on her silky thin ones. Closing my eyes and hearing the sounds of the Pacific Ocean crash on the shore, I felt her hand slide into my shirt, caressing my flesh. There, in the openness of the night air, we made love on the hard wood floors.

There she would fall asleep next me, and I would stare up into the dark sky, believing our life had changed for the better.

The next day, the driver came for us. I allowed Don to stay longer, for which he so thanked me kindly. It would turn out years later that Don's *mamasita* of that week became his wife, and they had six beautiful children. Jillian and I packed up slowly and left early Saturday morning. I looked at my watch, noting that it was about five hours until the phone call with Kempler. I was not nervous about it anymore. My mind was no longer focused solely on my responsibilities to the university and this project, but on the unknown future that we talked about these past few nights. As the van slowly crept away from the little coastal town, Jillian curled into my lap, to sleep some more. I remained awake, thinking.

I appreciated the surroundings. For the first and only time, I had really acknowledged the beautiful colors of the rainforest, breathed in the humidity, and felt the weight of the air on my skin. I truly felt a part of this land, not a conqueror like early visitors once had been. I was one with nature, if she was willing to take me, to understand me. Would this be a slight signal for me to acknowledge my own existence in my life? Was this to a foreshadowing of my fate? Unknown, you see, I could not foresee the future.

As the bus rolled through the crowded streets, filled will diesel exhaust, then into the urban areas where living conditions were becoming overcrowded, passed the dismal parts of the city, I could only see the sheer beauty of the landscape of the rolling hills, and palm trees, and the subtle chatter of birds in the distant rainforest canopy. I had finally fallen in love with my surroundings which had been the only requisite that I could possibly earn.

Next to me, my wife slowly woke up, knowing the work yet to come. I looked at my watch, about an hour before the call, and we were still a significant distance from the house.

She cuddled next to me kindly and sweetly as if she was reluctant to wake from a deep slumber, and held onto me for protection. I held her tight.

Even as we entered the house, seeing the piles of messages from the housekeeper, I was oblivious to the business at hand. My mind was on my foolish dreams and new love affair with our surroundings. Here, I must point out is the only time in my life I had not been prepared.

At ten o'clock sharp, the phone rang.

"Hello, Hans, this is Dr. Kempler." His voice was hallow, almost like he was calling down a distant tunnel. I realized that he was on speakerphone.

I saw Jillian sit nearby on the couch in the office, barely a couple of meters away from me. She had a notebook of her work that she staring at, but I could tell she was there to listen. I could not have blamed her, either, out of curiosity or apprehension, she had a vested interest in the course of this conversation.

"How are you Dr. Kempler?" I asked. I already had some paper in front of me.

"Spectacular, Hans." His voice echoed slightly. "Your research is quite the catch up here. We are adding several new staff members in order to go through the specimens. . I have certainly enjoyed the preservations you have made to the samples; they are quite the accurate. They are all beautiful to behold."

I made a mental note to myself to thank Jose when he returned. "Well, we do our best down here with the resources that we have."

"Yes, yes. Now, Hans, is there anyone around you?"

I looked at Jillian who was chewing on her pencil. I said, "No, I'm alone."

Jillian looked up, placed her work aside and was now acutely curious.

"Great. Now I can speak openly." And who else was on the other end of this phone line?

There was a long pause as I heard the shuffling of paper.

"Recently, your team has had some setbacks as I gather from your logs sent to the university. One with Reginald leaving for the States. I have not yet found a replacement for his position—"

I interrupted, feeling my cheeks flush. "We do not need a temporary replacement. He said that he would return. Also, we all are taking on the extra burden of his research. Most effectively."

"I am sure of this Hans. You run a tight ship down there, and everyone pitches in to do the work. If this was an ordinary expedition, like the one in the Arctic taking place right now, there would be triple the amount of people you currently have. My hat's off to you. But moving back to your situation, with the rain showers, you have had some damage to your complex."

Jillian came closer to me. "Yes, there has been structural damage to the location, but I have Don repairing the area as we speak. The recent purchases we reported were necessary for this repair." I looked up at her, and took off my glasses, feeling the sweat bead on my forehead.

"Hans, I am not worried about your purchases. I would do the same in a similar situation. You made the right call and took the necessary actions. Seriously, we have enough funding for ten camps for you." He laughed quickly. "This is not what I want to discuss. I would like to share an opportunity for you."

"Opportunity?" I asked. Jillian folded her arms, a discerning look crossed her face.

"Do you remember Dr. Lawrence MacLede, head of the Geology department here on campus?"

"Not especially."

Again he gave an unnecessary chuckle. "That's what I like about you Hans. You are direct. Anyway, Dr. MacLede has been having conversations with a certain geologist in Costa Rica recently, a Dr. Phillippe Ruiz. He is a volcanologist specializing in the turbulent conditions of the Costa Rican area. I will let Dr. MacLede explain."

I heard a shuffle in the background, and a clearing of a throat. "Dr. Fischer?" His voice was monotone, seemingly disinterested in our conversation. I looked at Jillian and wrote down the geologist's name. She only shook her head, and mouthed that she didn't know him. "Dr. Fischer?"

"Yes, I am here." I could sense the growing frustration in my voice, trying not to let it go.

"Good. As you are quite aware from your stand point, Central America is, in geological terms, a relatively a new piece of land. "Over the last several hundreds of thousands of years, as the tectonic plates shift and land masses change and increase in weight from volcanic eruptions and atmospheric effects on the surface, more plate shifting occurs causing the plates to press down into the magma belt creating further change on the surface in the form of earthquakes and volcanic activity, eventually resulting in the land you see today. It's the entire reason Frank put together this research expedition and sent you there to collect samples. Costa Rica in particular is one of the most active areas on the Ring of Fire. As you are probably aware, there are many dormant volcanoes in the area.

The man's contemptuous rattling on about the region annoyed me. But I had nothing to say at this point, and I just sat there listening to him lecture me as though I were a freshman and chewed the inside of my cheek in silent irritation. Jillian looked at me, but I gave no indication of my reaction to the conversation."

"The recent activity and devastation of land from the Arenal Volcano has brought us much interest."

"We are biologists, Dr. MacLede. What does this have to do with us?" I said finally.

"Hans, let the doctor talk," Dr. Kempler spoke loud in the background.

"My good friend, Dr. Ruiz, has discovered something very important. A hidden crevasse of life."

I said nothing. Their agenda was starting to come into focus. They wanted us to go, to explore it. In a way, instantly, my anger subsided and my ambitious interest piqued, but more on the later. There was a long pause on the phone and I could hear some low speaking in the background. How many others were in the room at the other end of the line I could not say.

Jillian put an arm on my shoulder. I shifted my gaze towards her, but I said nothing, my mind honed in on what was going on at the other end of the phone line.

"Dr. Ruiz has not explored this, cave, if you will. Dr. Ruiz's only concern had been the possibility of closure. It isn't a matter of if cave will close, but rather of when the cave will close. In our conferences, Ruiz expressed concern that the time window is relatively short due to the pressure of building magma and rock beneath. I do believe your cooperation in this immediate discovery could be a proven benefit for a great scientific discovery."

"Thank you, Dr. MacLede." Dr. Kempler had shifted closer to the phone. There was a slight shuffle on the phone, some more faint murmurs and finally a door closed. "I have made arrangements for you and the team there to meet with this Dr. Ruiz—"

Before I let him finish, I said, "We are biologists, not explorers. We are here for the mission of this project."

"You will put the current situation on hold." His statement was simple and his voice was stern. "I am not asking you for your opinion on this Hans. I am telling you what the team's next decision will be. With the joint government relationship between Costa Rica and America, and the Biodiversity Program in already in place, my team will be the first Americans to explore the undiscovered cavern." He paused. Even the confidence of his tone uneased my stomach. "The arrangements have been made already. You are to meet Dr. Ruiz."

I leaned back in the chair to look outside. The rain had started to overflow the gutters, pouring in an almost curtain-like fashion that blurred our view of the beautiful clouded hilltops. The nature around us just seemed so distorted now. Anger was rising in me, and I slowly let out a breath.

Dr. Kempler added, lowering his voice a little, "If this claim of new discovery is so true, Hans, you will be rewarded beyond expectation with scientific prizes, monetary purses and circuit lectures. You will have your name in scientific journals for many years to come. So, I expect you will want to cooperate and follow through on this." He stopped, then finally said, "One of Ruiz's people will be contacting you by end of today to make arrangements for you to leave. I suggest that you get there as soon as possible, within the next few days. Lastly, I want to be updated on this and I want a complete report of your findings by end of the month."

I said nothing, thinking of what Dr. Kempler said. The rewards would be beyond belief, the recognition alone would be beyond my expectations, and life would be better. He had played to my ambition, knowing I would give in to it and do this, go to this place.

"Good bye, Hans. Good Luck." The phone went dead.

I stared at the phone in disbelief.

"Well, what did he want? Does he want to cut the funding? Something about the samples?" Jillian began her inquisition. Her voice seemed frantic.

"He wants us to take a side trip to Arenal Volcano.," I said, thinking about the potential for scientific discoveries. I was already becoming more and more consumed by this new prospect as each minute went by.

"I don't understand," Jillian said as she plopped back onto the couch.

I relayed the gist of the conversation, emphasizing the potential discoveries. I could hear it in my voice, I was becoming excited, a new place that hadn't been tapped by mankind. I finally asked her, "Well, what do you think?"

Pulling her hair back into a tight bun, her face was calm and severe, her displeasure was quite evident in her expression. "I don't know Hans," she said. "You've been so bitter at Dr. Kempler since he left, and now he picks up and demands we go to this place, and you're ready to pack up and run out the door? With the assistance of another university, another professional whom we really don't know. I don't know, something doesn't feel right. I just don't like it."

"All we are doing is conducting proper research in an unknown, untouched piece of land." Truthfully, I was only thinking of rewards.

"It just doesn't sound right." She shook her head.

I went to her, and placed my hands into hers. "You want us to start a new life. I think, with this discovery, it will make our future so much better. This is something I have been waiting for."

She said nothing, just turned her eyes away from me. "We have always done things for you, Hans. I have been doing things for you for as long as I have known you." She let out a small sigh. "I just don't know. I have to think about it."

Jillian got up from the couch, and walked out of the room, taking one of our suitcases and headed toward the bedroom.

The desire to see this cave consumed me, much like I was as a child watching the arachnoids spinning silky webs, watching the ants build hills. This was to change us. Jillian's reservations had not deterred my private obsessions, in fact they only worked to inflate them more. I stayed in the office to gather items to together and make some arrangements. She didn't come back into my office or speak to me for the rest of the day.

In retrospect, I should have listened to her. I should have listened to my own gut. Only a fool, hungry for unattainable knowledge, would ignore logic and reason and allow himself to become blinded by glory and fame, and the allure of making such a prestigious discovery.

Such is the fool you see before you today.

TWELVE

Over the next couple of days there was much silence in the house as we prepared for our trip to the Arenal region. I was mostly preoccupied with packing the right equipment and necessary tools in order to make the research quick and efficient. In my head, I was only thinking of the gains that would come from this adventure, this new exploration. No one else was as excited as I had been.

When I'd spoke to Don about our new adventure upon his return from the beach, his reaction was much the same as Jillian's had been, though her attitude toward me had been colder and indirect. He had simply stated, "I trust your judgment on this. However, I just want to point out my hesitation about going because first: it is solely the university's agenda, and second: Dr. Kempler commanded us to go. I hope what we find is worth the trip, but I do not like the scenario."

Of course, he helped to make arrangements for our safe travel. Don also aided me in packing the proper equipment for our expedition. Jillian's displeasure about the new assignment had been noticeable her actions. She was limiting her conversation to facts, there was lots of awkward silence during our down times together and she had a continuously dour look on her face. Did I purposely disregard the interrupted conversation that she had with Don? Did I not want to listen to her as she spoke to the local people about our trip? Did I not notice the locals behaving slightly different with me? I was not concerned; I was falling into my own little world as I always had. I distanced myself from much of the contempt.

On Monday, my rescue had come when Jose and a couple of our regular workers returned. Jose wanted to help us now. In fact, he said that since he had been there he could help us to get there safely.

During all of this, I had made contact with Dr. Ruiz; or rather, I admit, I made contact with one of his researchers who gave me rather cryptic directions to the site, approximately near the volcano. My only reassurance was that he assured me that it was safe. My gut did not feel the same. As the chartered bus arrived at the house, I received another call from the assistant who also added a couple of other minor directions, which Jose took down.

Jillian didn't sit next to me on the ride there; instead she took the seat ahead, and busied herself with reading some her field notes. She did not look out the window much, and her conversations with me were short and monosyllabic. I guess I never realized how much of fool I had been not see her discontent. Next to me Don sat and we spoke of the prior before Reginald left. comparing data, exchanging and reading each other's notes and discussing the findings.

The trip was long and rough, but our intensive conversation seemed to make it easier to withstand. As we entered the Arenal region, navigating up and down the winding curves and steep hills, encountering endless dense rainforest, I found the amount of traffic increasing making the narrow two-lane roads more dangerous to traverse. Jose explained that the normal route to Arenal was never really busy, since it was really the only one to get there. I gave in to the continuous bouncing and jerking of the van on the dirt roads. Jillian's window was open, giving us free access to the heavy miasma of diesel, burning oil and exhaust . It was a nauseating mix, to be sure; still, I was feeling more anxious as we drew closer to our destination. As expected, the local officials had closed most of the back roads due to the potential dangers of rock and mud slides and damaged roads, which had drawn much interest from curious folks from all over the outlying region.

Randomly, it seemed at first, there had been pockets of ruined earth, sunken cracks on the sides of the hills. In one area, near a local market and a fuel station, there were down electric poles, which were bent on their sides like toothpicks. Like Don, who began to point out such sights as we passed. Pulling out her camera from the side bag near her, Jillian began to take photos, without saying much. A series of clicks quietly rattled off. She lowered her camera, craning her head down to look over the increasing devastation.

When the van reached a certain point, we could see Arenal's peak for the first time.

"Jesus," Don whispered.

At his exclamation, I looked up in the direction of his gaze just as Jillian did the same. In the seats beside her, Jose and the other two workers seemed to have fallen asleep because they did not respond to Don's arresting tone.

The van rolled steadily on until we approached a plateau near the newly awakened volcano. I could observe the summit's glowing ruby color. Now, if you were to visit this volcano, you would still see the fierce glowing redness of the molten lava flows against the darkness of the night. Back then, to see the bright scarlet in the daylight alone was a truly remarkable display. Never in my life had I witnessed such an intense crimson, enhanced by the plume of endless murky grey smoke that bellowed out of the crater. Against the normally cloudy skyline of the region's tropical climate, the volcano's unrelenting cloud of black cinder and ash was quite distinctive in contrast, then it slowly blended to grey as it was carried away in the winds of the upper atmosphere.

The van crept ahead, swerving around sinkholes and vents. I could see that a large portion of earth had shifted, exposing differences in the soil itself as it jutted a good foot above the adjacent ground. Not only was this evident, but there a measurable gap had formed, perhaps a meter or so between the two pieces. I wanted the van to stop so I could look, but this crevasse as it were ran several kilometers.

Jillian noticed it too, pointing out, "See the dark mineral earth below? The volcanic layers of the area must have formed from flows many millennia ago to create such rich soil. This may be the inherit explanation of the vast species of botanical life supported in these forests." The expression on her face was both of awe and shock as we passed additional, equally-sized crevasses.

The closer and closer we got to the meeting point, the more my stomach twisted as nerves and raw emotions exceeded my normal levels. I had a sudden uneasy feeling, a sense of foreboding. I thought that I had made the right decision in coming here, yet somehow I knew this was not like that choice. A deep inner voice was silently hoping that the van would get stuck in the road. Or that a sudden mudslide would cross our path and block the way. None of this occurred, of course, only the slowness of frequent stopping for other traffic. Relief vans and military jeeps had exited the opposite side of us, and then soon we came to barricaded roads. Beyond the rows of cars and trucks, beyond the developing crowds of people, beyond the formal tree line, the devastation of the area could be clearly seen. It was a black rocky point, and steam rose slowly off the hot rocks. Huge paths were being created as government rescue crews wore protective gear while the helpers, who were really local villagers, wore their regular button down clothes and jeans. It was a sight of prolific destruction; it took all of us by surprise.

So slowly the van crept past the scene as each of us strained to see what we could of the ruins. "Me, Jorge and Castos been in that last week, Hans. So many people, so little ta do. Hard, man." Jose just shook his head.

Passed the long stretch of road overlooking the remnants of the village, we zig-zagged through the lagging traffic and moved along the main road, which seemed untouched by the volcano. The land beyond the road was unscathed by the volcano's destructive emissions. Before long we were at a dirt path large enough for a farm vehicle to go down. I believe that this had been someone's farm, seeing flatten fields readied for seed to our right, rainforest flanked us on the left. The van jerked frequently here and there where rains had eroded away dirt leaving the jungle version of potholes everywhere making our in the van nearly impossible. I felt my head snap against the ceiling, and saw Don's expression of nausea as he clung to the side window taking in gulps of warm air. Jillian turned to me at one point, and gave me her hand. The rigid road was against our group that day.

After several kilometers on that hellish path we reached the very end and found a small green shack. Pulling closer to the ramshackle house, it felt odd to see it there, as though it's presence there was almost too convenient in its location.

"That is Dr. Ruiz meeting place," I said out loud.

"Sure looks spacious and inviting from here," Don replied sarcastically.

"Don, how scientific you are," Jillian goaded, with a small smile upon her lips, though I could detect a slight nervousness in her voice.

Creeping closer to this shed, a man in his mid-thirties or so, and smoking a cigarette, came out of the shed. He looked to our van then he turned his gaze away, toward the distance forest. There was a shift of motion in the car as we gathered our belongings.

The man opened our side door which Jose leapt from first, speaking immediately in Spanish, discussing the ride up here with the man.

"Dr. Ruiz?" I interrupted the two men.

"No, this is the guide," Jose said. "He doesn't speak good English."

"It's nice that we met this man in middle of nowhere," Don said as he exited the van.

I saw Jillian gathering her journal and small books, placing them into her backpack. I stepped outside, and into the exceptionally warm humid air as it seemed I could squeeze water from mid-air. By the indication of the presence of swarms of small flying gnats, a storm was about be unleashed from the dark clouds overhead. I looked over into the forest, which was fiercely dark and covered in thick brush, a stark contrast the flat dirt field directly behind us, not yet cultivated for the coming growing season.

The shed door swung open with a loud squeak as wind whipped the old rusty screen door open, slamming it against the wall. I turned to look at the tall thin man in dark khaki pants and shirt. His face was long and his beard was grown thick. His eyes were grayish and rimmed with sleepless red lines; his lips were horribly chapped, almost bleeding. It looked as if he had not been among civilization for quite some time.

"Dr. Hans Fischer?" the man inquired, and I recognized the slight English inflection in his words.

"Are you Dr. Ruiz?" I asked, just as Jillian was climbing out of the van, and looking around much the same as I had.

"Good to meet you in person," the man's voice seemed heavy on his Spanish accent, almost purposely. Even from this close distance, a scent of body odor wafted into my nose.

"Yes." At that point, I introduced each of the team, to which he gave a complimentary greeting to each.

Jillian stood next to me, and for the first time in days she touched my hand.

Dr. Ruiz looked at her and smiled, "I am glad to make your acquaintance."

"And you as well," Jillian's voice was pleasant, despite her resentment at the team being sent on this expedition.

"But please forgive me for being rather hasty, but we must continue our journey," he announced. "This location is the easiest access road since the eruption of the volcano. The farmer here has graciously granted us passage through his private land for our access. From here, we must trek through the rainforest for another several kilometers to the site on foot, I'm afraid. It is a not an established path, so please be careful as we go along. I will lead and my partner," he gestured toward the other man who now held a shotgun, "will remain in the back."

"Good. I thought we would be wandering by ourselves," Don said under his breath.

"We have packed up our equipment in various bags for transport, Dr. Ruiz," I said, nodding to Jose, ignoring Don's comment.

"You may not need this," Dr. Ruiz said. "Your Dr. Kempler had already shipped some items for you. I have had them brought to the site and created an area for you and your group to begin immediate research." His attention went back to Jillian.

She squeezed my hand. "How nice that Dr. Kempler was so thoughtful," she said, and then looked at me.

"Yeah, he is such a pleasing man," Don remarked behind her.

"Well, I guess," I looked at my group and Jillian, "Let's begin the final leg of our journey, shall we?"

Just then, Ruiz's man pointed down the road to a car coming toward us, and said something to Dr. Ruiz that I could not make out. Ruiz turned and said to me, "Dr. Fischer, was there something else for us to know about?"

I turned to watch the small *tico* car steadily moving up the road, steering around the holes more easily than our van driver had. As it approached, I noticed that there were two people in the car.

"Oh my god, it's Reggie!" Jillian yelled out. She ran to the car, and Don followed, forcing the car to stop several meters away from us. Reggie was barely out of the car before Jillian was hugging him.

"Is he part of your group?" Dr. Ruiz asked.

"Yes, a vital one."

Reginald got out of his car with his backpack, and made his way to me and I shook his hand. "I got to the house in San Jose probably an hour or so after you left. I saw the note and followed as quickly as I could."

"Good to have you back, Reginald," I said. Turning to Dr. Ruiz, I

148

said, "We are ready now."

With that, we followed Dr. Ruiz down a slender path into a gulley that lead into the forest, where immediately we were entombed in a shadowy darkness. It was unlike the forests we entered throughout the country, where natural light filtered down through the canopy to the forest floor. As we continued forward, in an atoned silence, we heard only the crunch of leaves. The inky shadows made the smallest of sounds seem more threatening than any forest sounds had in the past, because we couldn't clearly see what was making the noise or where it was coming from. And from the very beginning there was something during this introduction into this part of the deep forest that had us all on high alert. Jillian was the first to point out, well whisper to me, "Do you hear that?"

I strained to detect an unusual noise. I craned my neck in every direction as we walked, trying to hear it was she heard. But all I heard was the light tapping of heavy rain on the leaves of the trees hundreds of meters above us.

"There is nothing," Reginald replied with a huff.

"Exactly," Jillian said. "There is none of the usual noise of forest creatures."

Perhaps then I should have been the leader and turned us around, but my team wanted to forge on, to see what await.

There was not much conversation as we climbed up a steep basin. I was in the midst of trying to hear any noise, as I tended to be the skeptical one.

Within the very fiber of my being, I believed that we were on an journey to uncharted discoveries only we were privy to. Or rather, Dr. Kempler's words were still skewing my thoughts during that one moment in time.

Russell

THIRTEEN

The silence in the forest repeated within our group as I noticed the others, including Jillian, scanning the parameter. Creeping darkness loomed across the path and time seemed to crawl slowly as we hiked. Perhaps about a half an hour in, Jillian inquired, "Dr. Ruiz, how far is the new crevasse from the volcano?"

"Ah, Mrs. Fischer, this is why you are a biologist, and I am a geologist." He breathed heavily as the ascent of the climb grew steadily. "I do not mean this as insult, but as fact. We are walking the edges of the volcano as we speak, probably about five to six hundred meters before rock mass. As the dormant Arenal slept for centuries, the rainforest naturally covered its natural crater line and made the image of the mountain rather beautiful to behold. Much like an eel under a crevice of rock on the floor of the ocean, waiting patiently to zap its prey with a death volt; the volcano too lay in wait until the sufficient pressure accumulated to a produce the destructive release we have recently witnessed."

"Then," I chimed in, "how far are we going to reach the site?"

"Less than an hour or so," he surmised, glancing at me out of the corner of his eye, then quickly looking back at my wife.

I heard a grunt from Don, he probably had not counted on this degree of hike.

We continued deeper into the rainforest, the path growing more slippery from the rain runoff following the slope and commands of gravity. In the deep silence, I began to hear a humming sound, a faint thrumming of wings, like that of a rapidly flying insect. It was not near us, but the noise was distinctive, but it would likely take a large swarm of these creatures to reach such a decibel. Ambling along and conquering the path, I suppose I had not really considered pondering the landscape itself. It just seemed as if we stepped into thicker and denser foliage even though the path was clearly defined it was getting narrower along certain passages. Ruiz's man at the end clicked his rifle, preparing it. This man sensed a potential danger.

Behind me, Jillian matched my stride, and she was sweating but not breathing heavily. She looked to the side, and said, "Look Hans."

I stopped with her.

Pointing at a large banana leaf, she said quietly, "Doesn't it look unusually larger than a normal specimen? It looks as if grew exponentially large. In the wild, much like on the coastal areas, mature banana leaves are perhaps four to five feet in diameter, but this..." she said and took a step off the path. She walked towards it without fear.

"Mrs. Fischer, please stay on the path," Dr. Ruiz warned as I saw the guide behind cock his rifle.

"Look at this." She was in awe. I too was gawking in surprise at the grandness of the species. It was unusually immense.

"Amazing," Don said near me as he lit a cigarette.

"Come back slowly, Dr. Fischer," Dr. Ruiz's voice grew louder. I heard then the buzzing sound grow louder as if it was coming closer to us.

Jillian's fingertips touched the leaf, slowly caressing it when a strange movement came from the other side. She brought her hand back quickly and I tried to help her walk back with our eyes still locked firmly on that leaf. Another shifting on the leaf and then large antennae poked out from beneath.

"It's a *solenopisis invicta*," I said calmly.

"What?" Reginald asked as he slid his way between the creature and Jillian. There was fear in his voice.

"A red fire ant," I said. "They are typically perhaps no more than two to three centimeters long. Harmless. But this..."

Then the leaf turned and there it was, a larger than life species in front of us. Jillian let out a scream, and Don grunted in something that sounded like a mix of shock and disgust.

"Please stay on the path everyone," Dr. Ruiz ordered louder this time. "Now!"

Reggie nudged Jillian away from the fascinating spectacle and we all stepped back onto the path.

My eyes were fixed on that magnificent creature, its legs moving in unison carrying on the *mesosoma*, perfectly balanced to support and carry its three body segments; its mandibles opening and closing with such precision as they took hold of the leaf from the underside, with its long legs gripping the stem large glassy black eyes starred back at us, unblinking, eerily, as though assessing our purpose in the forest. It paused for a second, allowing its meter-long dangling antennas, scan the atmosphere, tasting the air for our presence, probably memorizing our scent. I signaled for everyone to stop moving.

Jillian's eyes bulged and she put her hands to her mouth to hold in her impulse to scream, and she seemed to be hiding her face either from the creature looking at her or from her looking at it. Don and Reginald stopped in their steps, frozen completely. Jose and our two workers began mumbling in Spanish, something that sounded much like a prayer.

Above me, the humming of beating wings made me look to the tree canopy where I could see several *vespula vulgari*, or a species of wasps, about two meters long, fly passed us, turning toward the canopy above. Suddenly, a *lepidoptera* of unknown familia classification with wingspan of about a meter and a half fluttered from a nearby tree as its long thick tongue flickered in-and-out, then it was hovering only a few meters above us. Out of the corner of my eye, Jose backed away further down the path and crossing his chest quickly then kissing a small silver cross hanging from his neck.

"Jesus," Reginald whispered, as his eyes grew wide behind me.

Turning my head in the same line direction of his gaze above us into a large tree. A large *chilopoda,* similar to a species I had catalogued, only this one about six-meters long, clung to the bark of the tree trunk above us, using its many legs in synchronize movements it crawled upward towards the sky. The snapping and crackling of the leaves and branches as it passed could be heard seemed to drown out the vibration of wings still hovering above me.

"These creatures will not harm us," Dr. Ruiz announced softly. His eyes darted around him.

"I think your man with the gun believes otherwise," Don said, as he also panned back and forth between the otherworldly beasts moving freely through the air, in the trees and nearby on the ground.

"A precautionary step only," the doctor replied. "We must

continue, quickly, please."

"About how far?" Jillian asked with a slight panic in her voice.

"See the ridge over there?" Dr. Ruiz pointed out as several large insects crept and crawled about the distance between us and our proposed destination about a hundred meters away, over a small valley which now I dared not to cross, nor want to endanger my group. I could see a red glow pour over the shadowed area.

"We are going to *La Boca de la Diabla*," Dr. Ruiz said, his eyes were now darting all over, seeming equally cautious, or perhaps apprehensive. "The Devil's Mouth."

My group, my hired staff and my Jillian, looked at me, both fear and trepidation about the path ahead of us were clear on their faces. I began to walk with Dr. Ruiz, as they followed silently, watching out for anything and seeing everything. It was such a wonderful and splendid sight to behold as we walked, to witness the various forms of life moving around us. Near our path, a large web about ten meters in diameter hung between two trees, carefully spun into the bark. But I could not see the arachnid creature responsible for such a magnificent creation. There had been no evidence of any disturbance to the web, which meant it must have been created just recently. Near me, there was a subtle swarm of flying insects, probably of the *musca* family, or rather a small gnat variation. They were the size of baseballs, with a six-centimeter wing span, probably about a hundred times larger than its cousin seen here in the U.S. The noise from these creatures seemed more amplified in the movement of the forest, even blanketing out the dripping rain from the above.

Everything about the forest itself was larger than was typical for this region, seeing the enormous beautiful flowers on the hibiscus plant, the tailored-look of the palm leaves and the quite spacious spread of the palm tree canopied above us seemed surreal. I felt a tap from Jillian who with amazement pointed at a large species of fern as tall as a two-story house. Its leaves draped over the forest floor probably seven-to-eight-meters in length. At the top, a large mutated *anisoptera* flittered its spectacular translucent blue and green wings.

While the rest were timid and had fearful of what we saw that day, somehow everything that lead up to that moment had brought me to that place, I was meant to be there, to witness these fantastic gorgeous creatures. While before I had had to strain to examine the bodies, I could now see with great detail the exaggerated proportions and markings and colorings of their surfaces. So beautiful, these creatures instinctively executed their tasks at their own carefree pace. I could see their cavities fill with air and watch them exhale. As we approached the site of the red light lava flow it lit the area more and I could observe some of the creatures digest their food through their transparent endoskeletons. Had we then the technology of today, we could have documented so much in that section of forest. Yet that was not our purpose for being there.

Above the growing buzzing of some flying beings that I could not recognize as they moved swiftly, barely a meter above us, oblivious to our presence, Dr. Ruiz finally explained, "When my crew and I came to this location, we first discovered this. I had known then that we were getting to some sort of rich mineral deposit area as it were. Alas, we would soon discover this area surrounding the cavern." He stopped as we allowed a large form similar to a *euborellia annuplies* to crawl slowly across the path, it was way too large to step over. "I believe whatever is happening in that cave has had some effects on the land surrounding it."

"Have you and your men been in the cave?" I asked, looking down towards the native workers huddling near each other, their eyes large and panicked.

Dr. Ruiz hesitated in his response, and then replied, "No, not that much. Our concern is only with rock, and geological implications."

"What implications would that be?" Jillian asked.

I looked ahead to the red glow large and brighter, as if the sky had opened and blood was running down from the endless grey skies.

"Our objective," he said cautiously, "is to monitor the earthquake activity and volcanic eruption from the safe end of the Arenal region. That had been our intentions from the beginning."

"Were you here after the eruption?" I asked, my breathing getting heavy and labored, in the thinner air of the higher elevation.

"No," he said. "We were here about two weeks before the eruption because there had been slight tremors indicating some sort of activity. Back in the local school in San Jose, we the sensors showed significant jumps on the Richter scale of two to three-point-five. Nothing you can image to be defined as major vibrations or that a human could sense, but enough for us to take a serious study in.

"There had been an increase of hot springs and mantel plate

activity in the area over the last several decades from our initial studies, which made us assume that we needed to investigate further. Thus, we came to this location on tips from local villagers who have now lost their homes and lands. In a way, we were trying to predict the inevitable."

"I presume your studies were too late," Reginald remarked as he looked overhead to see a swarm of flying creatures rapidly skimming the tree tops.

"No, our mission had changed a week earlier as our focus was shifted to the crevasse." Dr. Ruiz stopped, pulled a cigarette from his vest and lit it. The amber glow in the misty atmosphere seemed to hover magically. "A local villager who had been one of the victims of the volcano showed us this spot. During our initial hike in, like the one you are on now, I too was in shock, but it was not yet this full. When I saw the insects like you see around us now, I was at first paralyzed in fear. Then my panic dissipated and my fascination took over. The villager and his eldest son had discovered the location while they were hunting some wild boar. They had spotted the luminous red glow, much as you see it now, incandescent in the sky against the lush green of the forest. They were in need of food, and continued to follow the boar they were tracking until they reached the crevasse. As they looked at it, they witnessed these mutated creatures crawling out. They named it la Boca de Diablo. He came back only once with us to show us the path and vowed never to return."

"The locals are always so superstitious," Don commented, wiping sweat off his forehead.

"Only superstitious because they do not understand the unknown," Jillian rebutted.

We walked further along for several moments as the forest began to thin out slightly, which allowed the red iridescent glow to brighten the area, and cast an eerie glow over my skin, and I looked at Jillian whose face seemed transfixed in the glow. The flow turned to black rock, slippery from the recent rain, but slowly became cooler and firmer with each step.

As we emerged from the forest on a minor incline, the skies above us opened up to reveal a silk grayness. I could see the turbulent winds in the upper atmosphere pushing the clouds quickly across the horizon. Then, we turned to our right to find a steep rocky formation and the new Arenal volcano crater. Its top was rigid and formed into a sizeable cone as the lava created a luminous red ring above us. A bellow of white smoke ushered out from the volcano in torrents.

"How safe is my team from the volcano?" I asked, feeling the stares of my colleagues on my back.

"Safe as you want to be," Dr. Ruiz replied. A slithery smile caressed the man's lips which I did not like, but, as we approached a plateau of heated rock, I recognized that we had no choice but to trust him.

Jillian scooped my hand into hers in a reassuring gesture that we needed to press on. Her countenance was that of the confidence and fortitude that I had always loved and admired in her. Feeling the warmth under my feet, I saw ahead of us the Devil's Mouth, a glowing horizontal slit with it's very corners peaked in red light. From this, a vast opening occurred, dark rock emerged from the edges, lava rock, yet it looked much like a mouth frowning. Jagged rocks hung in the back, almost dangerously poised above, and seemed to be too close to the rim. I looked ahead, seeing to the right a tent with some crates set up, and then to the left there was Ruiz's team of three who moved about their business and had no thought in acknowledging our presence.

"What the hell," Reginald had said behind me.

I looked behind us to see the large anthropoid creatures actually at the edge of the rock plateau, gathering and huddling over themselves as if they had no place to go.

"We do not understand why they stop at the edge of the rock and do not come toward us. We feel that we are protected here," Dr. Ruiz said.

Jillian placed her hand on the rock as I did, turning my attention to the crevasse ahead of me. The intense heat was soothing to feel, but to the anthropoid creature it would be devastating. "The mutated insects feel the intensity of the heat, and their instinct is not to stay away, but they could be on the verge of an adaption to this change to their environment, if need be," I hypothesized aloud.

"Yes, that may be the case, Dr. Fischer," Dr. Ruiz replied. "Let me show you where you are set up. Your tent is on this side. I am also giving you my field guide here," he gestured to a man who was large and tall, "as an extra assistant."

"Are you sure you can spare a person?" asked Jillian. She stood up to look at the assistant in the tent.

"Mrs. Fischer, I have a strong group and he is only but a --what you Americans say-- a fifth wheel in my project," he assured us.

"Well, then I'm going to start unpacking, Hans," Don said behind me.

I nodded which he and Jose went over to our designated camp. I shifted in my position slightly from one foot to the other to let them cool.

"Dr. Fischer," Ruiz said to me as he walked towards his tent area. "You may find this rock difficult at first to stand on, but soon your feet will enjoy the therapeutic heat."

"I am not worried about that," I replied. I was growing tired of Dr. Ruiz's haughty rudeness. "May we go into the cave?"

Then Dr. Ruiz stopped and looked to Jillian then me, smiling without much substance. I had at this point followed him across the plateau to his tent with Jillian a few steps behind me. We were in full observation of the very belly of the cavern, the radiant red light covering half our bodies. Above us, I watched the bellowing smoke and plumes of lava ooze out in small rivers. Against the backdrop of the volcano, Dr. Ruiz's profile was painfully thin and his beard seemed too thick for his gaunt face. Behind him, his two other assistants continued their tasks looking at some machines and measuring the spikes on the paper. The generator sound was faint compared to the sounds of the wind and the volcano itself.

I looked over towards the entry where there was a simple rope bridge over a small ravine. "I thought you said that you had not gone into the cave. Why do you have that?" I asked. My blunt words had no effect on Ruiz.

"Dr. Fischer, how else are you and your team going to proceed with your investigations? As I have explained, I am not interested in this aspect of the conditions to be studied here. You and I know the amount of evidence will certainly be enough for esteemed awards in the very near future. You have your science experiments, and I mine," he stated. Looking to the large man he had assigned to us, Ruiz said something quickly in Spanish, and the man gathered up some rope from a nearby table and ambled towards the bridge. "He will take you in. I am to warn you that the carbon dioxide levels are extremely high in there, two days ago, one of my team members reported toxic levels. I have no oxygen tanks here, so I may suggest no more than an hour at the maximum."

"What then?" Jillian asked.

"Then I am not coming to get you," Dr. Ruiz replied. He lit another cigarette.

"He's all charm," Don mumbled behind me.

"Don, would you please start setting up our tent and see what the good doctor from the States has kindly sent us?" I spoke rapidly.

My excitement was filling my chest. I wanted to get inside that place, to get a chance to explore an unfamiliar landscape. Although the night was settling in around us, the amber glow created more shadows and tricked my eyes. Perhaps with little natural light I hoped to enter the cave. At least that was my seemingly young logic at the time. Truthfully, the glow piqued my interest and how this light effected so many species.

I turned my attention to where Reginald, Jose and the other two native workers had begun assisting with unpacking our gear. The other larger man was shuffling his way over to them. When he saw me, Reginald instructed Jose to continue set up of the tent and came toward me.

"Reginald, we are going in, you, Jillian and I," I stated simply.

"That quick?" he responded nervously, his eyes scanned the perimeter of the area.

Jillian looked surprised and began her protest, "Hans, we need to take some measurements of air quality to see if there is—"

I cut Jillian off. "We did come here to look at the cave, did we not?"

A sudden, hurt-filled look of understanding crossed her face. I hated to be so direct, but my decisions needed to be quick and assertive, unlike my methodological stance in the camp.

Reginald grabbed our hiking bags with our pulley systems, and met us at the bridge. We stood there, looking at the red and feeling the radiant heat pulsing from inside. It was not what I was expecting, nor did it appear to be what Jillian, and perhaps Reginald, too, had expected. I looked more closely at the bridge, and couldn't escape the feeling that I did not want to cross over it even though it was a mere five or six meters long. But the ravine below was deep and narrow and dark, and gave off a hideous yellow glow.

"I don't like this, Hans," Jillian said from behind me, with trepidation in her voice.

"Jillian, you have always trusted me before?"

"Yes, of course." Her face glistened in this the red cast, appearing almost translucent in nature.

I placed a hand on her slender shoulder and said, "I won't let anything happen to you."

Reginald came nearer to us and stated, "The ravine looks deep. Let's just be a bit more cautious."

Our new guide went first on the ropes, I listened to them strain under his weight as his movement caused the bridge to sway. As quickly as he had stepped onto the bridge, he stepped off. It was that short and quick, but still seemed perilous. Reginald volunteered to go across first he slowly stepped onto the narrow planks, the taunt, crisp ropes squeaked out a rubbing sound where they were twined together. I let Jillian go next and I held her hand for as long as she would allow me to, then she reached forward to grasped Reginald's long outstretched arm. I zipped along the bridge, my anxiety shut out by the exhilaration of the moment, of the adventure.

Ironically, stepping onto the other side from the plateau, I saw the expanse of the long plateau and the dense rainforest directly behind, stirring with creatures that now looked smaller. Were they looking back at us as well? Why did they not roam beyond the borders of this forest? These questions spun in my mind only until Jillian grasped my hand, then my thoughts returned to the present. I put Jillian between Reginald and myself to allow the guide to walk ahead, letting the gust of wind tug at our clothes. I looked above seeing the grey sky churning with increasing vigor, allowing the first rays of sunlight to penetrate the clouds. The storm clouds seemed to have passed.

We crawled along the side of the cave entrance for a couple of meters, before it was tall enough for us to enter. Even at this point, the heat was penetrating our clothes, feeling the perspiration drip down my face, down my very back. It was hotter than the rainforest in dry season. I looked back to see Jillian crawling along squinting her eyes, only looking above us. This wasn't the first time I had realized her aerophobia; I held her tight for a comforting reassurance before. Could she relax on her own now in these conditions? I highly doubted it. Then the sulfuric smell filled my nostrils, which must have been a combination of rotting plants, the richness of the soil and the stinging fragrance of exotic flowers lingering over the pungent smoke.

I turned slowly to look inside the cave and ambled quietly behind Jillian whose eyes were wide with amazement. What I saw was, well, was something that I would never forget, even in my darkest of dreams. place that was both mesmerizing and stunningly otherworldly. My quivering legs carried me forward despite my dear wife pulling against me with a tensely clutched hand.

Russell

FOURTEEN

I stepped forward on the sloping ledge following the guide carefully, checking my footing against the sandy surface. Carefully ambling into the opening of the cave, I could see only the tops of large palms and bamboo-like trees, indigenous plants of the region such as the *higueron* tree, *mimosa pudica* and *colmillo*. In this atmosphere, the mutated size was unbelievably massive; the veins of the leaves were visible to the naked eye, without the aid of a microscope. I was astounded by the sight of the very trees. Yet as I reached the edge, my eyes could were happily intoxicated from the view. For what seemed for kilometers, the subterranean forest's olive green leaves seemed to blanket the vastness of the space. As I looked above the cave's rock ceiling and walls glistened and magically sparkled. Across to what I assumed to be the end of the cave, the dazzlingly amber glow brightly lit up the cave: Most likely it was the magma of the volcano. Edging toward Ruiz's man, the intense heat of the volcano's magma enveloped me and a sheen coat of perspiration formed on my brow. And I breathed in the lush smell of forest, somewhat sour from decay, pungent new blossoming flowers and a hint of sweet jasmine. .Jagged stalagmites loomed like fangs of a hungry beast poised to chew us up once we ventured further into the cave. Just like in the children's tale, Jack and the Beanstalk, I had the sense that I had been transformed into young Jack, and entered a life above the treetops, in the dense mist of the upper cavern, as I descended, my body was indeed dwarfed by the life thriving all around me.

My eyes never left the trees and plants in front of us, nor the astounding variety and abundance of these specimens covered the landscape. The very space inside the cavern was immense; the valley was deep and long, falling back perhaps two kilometers in some deep shadows. Who know what might lay beyond. We would not discover how vast this valley had been, because as we descended we were overwhelmed by the very Paleogene forest was overwhelming our existence. Quietly, even dare I say breathlessly, we stayed on the path for several meters. The mutated tropical plants swayed as though there was a natural gust of wind. Where or what the source was, I could not say. Imagine of a glass terrarium, a clear vase filled with small plants, sealed from the outside. Yet there is some air that penetrates it, and placing it in front of a large window, the heat of the sunlight causes this biological reaction, trapping the moisture and mist forms. At times the mist hugs the soil near the plants. Just the same in the cave, much of this section of earth had been closed-off bioregion, its own terrarium, of sorts.

There were no words uttered from anyone's lips. Jillian gasped and pointed towards a mammoth specimen of foliage that jutted up and out above the rest of species as its long narrow leaves almost touched the rim of the path. At the same moment, Reginald who was at the edge of the path pointed down. Peering over the edge, we found that the bottom was also dense with plant life, layers and layers of leaves descending to the infinite bottom. How deep was the cavern? Unknown, I would say. The guide's walking cane touched my arm as he gestured with his head for us to step back.

We stopped about midway, when I could feel a slight burn in my lungs. Jillian handed me her canteen, which I drank from. While it was lukewarm and not truly quenching, I felt a slight relief at the back of my throat. I offered it back to Jillian, who refused it. Still there a slight sense of hypertension in my chest, feeling my heart race and a tightening under my dampened shirt.

The ledge, about one meter in width, fell over the edge down into more of the green abyss. I leaned over, straining to see the dark floor below. Just as in an any forest floor, it was embedded with the debris of fallen leaves and plants, carpeted with rotting mulch. When I studied it closer was when I noticed the movement. Concentrating on one spot, I could see various species of *campotomos*, *lumbricus terrestris* and *coleopetra* crawling along the bottom, hugging the bottom, greedily returning the decaying forest floor back to earth. Their antennae flickered about without much notice of our presence. Their long bodies slithered in and out of the rotting leaves, and their claws snipped and snapped at the wood. As I stared closer, I was surprised to realize that there was no other movement on the forest floor, no signs of other natural creatures that would normally be found on the surface. I began to squat down and strained for a clearer view.

"Senior, no move," the guide whispered behind me. I looked at him, then followed his stare past the ledge.

"Hans," Jillian said cautiously. Her hand went to my shoulder, slowly pulling me back.

Ahead of me, perhaps a couple of meters, perched on a strong limb, was a mutated arachnoid species, probably similar to a wolf spider. It had been perched on a web nest, sitting patiently in a silky bed. In great detail I could see the very hairs on the back of its large sack, the spiny tips of its legs, the dark eyes arranged like a frown on the face. It waited in total stillness, not disturbing the air or mist around it, becoming part of the atmosphere. Above us, I noticed for the first time since we began our descent on the narrow path, was the enormous web itself, was spun in an elaborate construction as I had not seen before. The detail as the threads intertwined over the bark and the leaves, the collection of dew forming on the tips was amazing. The danger was quite evident; feeling that my fingertips had touched the web, I was sealed to the hanging sculpture.

"I cannot move," I said simply. "If I move, it will instantly attack us because my vibrations will direct it to us."

"Hans," Reginald said calmly, "there is enough space that it could overcompensate its approach, and hit the rock dead on. From my angle, the right speed would do this."

"I will not move." I did not want any harm to come to Jillian.

"Listen to Reggie," Jillian spoke up. Her breath was becoming thicker, raspier.

I looked up at her, and replied, "Maybe, you should go back—"

Just then, the guide said as his eyes looked beyond us, "*No habla.*"

We all looked at him, and then in the direction he was watching. A flying insect, perhaps a relative of the *coccinellidae*, with bright orange colors covered in black spots, flew casually over our area, oblivious to the inconspicuous web. It hit the web with such force that some dew from a nearby leaves above sprinkled down on us like a brief rain shower. In that instant, the spider jumped from its web-encased perch and shot up towards the creature. I took a knife from my belt and slit the web away. I could hear the fangs dig into the entrapped insect, heard the crunch of shell as the other legs instantly spun it around in midair. There was a quick waft of heat from the activity flowing past us.

I stepped back against the wall, grasping Jillian as she put her arms around me. She whispered softly, "I won't let anything happen to you, either," and she gave me a soft peck on my cheek.

At this point, should I give you the names of the species, it would take a long time for me to discuss proper families and groups, but allow me to paint you a picture, if you will, with some hindsight, what has been the most spectacular sight of my career, of my lifelong passion. Because it was then that the subterranean forest came alive with activity; other mutated species crawled, dug or flew around every curve. There were species of dragonflies with wing spans of at least three meters or more, their beautiful colors glistened against the blackness of the walls, , swooping down and around the plants, landing on them just as you would see in most any landscape, but on such an impressively grand scale. There were species of *morphias*, butterflies, fluttering around collecting the nectars of flowers. They stabbed their long tongues into the pits of the flowers, creating downdrafts of air that would have only been felt on a minute scale among ordinary circumstances. A clash of centipedes occurred over a fallen branch bridge that dangled over the floor of the cave. Each of them were not giving in to each other's strength as they pushed their bodies up, standing about the same size as Reginald as they tussled. Armies of species of fire ants made numerous with their strong pinchers and claws walked up the stalks of plants and trunks of trees, forming infinite lines at nearly every turn, but moving about peacefully undisturbed by the other species. There were groups of orange colored lady bug-like creatures, hovering around a garden of beautiful *corteza amarilla*, much like large yellow daisies. The mutated walking sticks were at an incredible close distance for us to observe from our overlook several meters away. their elongated upper torsos could clearly be seen taking in air, they were breathing. Understanding the fact that these creatures were breathing in this very air that I too breathed was mind-boggling. Such small creatures in our world, I was watching mutated creatures inhale and exhale oxygen without much effort. I could see, in great detail, the wings like stained glass windows of a church, in perfect symmetric detail, what usually looked fragile and delicate now seemed durable and powerful. The very hairs on my neck stood on end as a troop of small flying beetles buzzed past us in a dizzying speed, and in close detail we could see the underbelly of their shells, feel the power of air come off their wings. The life of this small biodiverse world was its own extraordinary gift to the world, much like that of forgotten or undiscovered sea caves under the vastness of the ocean.

We ambled slowly down for not much farther when I notice a marker had been created. Dr. Ruiz had been down here more than once, that I now certain of, but how could I blame him for not wanting to take a glimpse at this untouched Jurassic scenery before us.

There was no discussion between us; our silence was our amazement at the world we had walked into. Yes, I pointed at some creatures, some of the wonders that surrounded us. Jillian scrutinized several species of plants that she recognized instantly, identifying their probable familia class.. But the astounded look on her face had said more than enough, and was probably much like the look on my own face. I would not have wanted to share this amazing scientific discovery with anyone without my beautiful wife next to me. Her hand slipped into mine, and I clung to it graciously.

Behind us, Reginald's nervous breathing was growing harsher and harsher under the stifling conditions in the cave. He spoke little, only a few words here and there to point out his trained observations of the rock formations, stalactites as they dripped into the canopy of the forest below. He also remarked, "Do you notice that there are no mammals or amphibians to be seen or heard, no avian species or marine life either?"

It was true; there was only this anthropoid world, separated, or cut off, from the rest of the natural world.

Upon our first entering this isolated world, I felt the burn of the carbon dioxide in my lungs slowly increase and my eyes stung from the radiated heat. These levels had to be contributors to the development of this world in order for this diversity to exist and sustain itself.

"We leave," the guide said, looking down at his large gold watch. "Been here too long."

"This is just beautiful in an awe-inspiring and dangerous way," Jillian simply stated. Her eyes glistened in the glow of lava, but they were soft and gracious, in stark contrast to the harsh darkness of the rock walls behind her.

"You are right 'bout that, Jill," Reginald agreed.

As I followed the guide back up the same ledge we had just traveled down, all I could do was think of how I would begin my international speeches, how I would graciously accept the Noble Prize for this discovery, and how I and the team would appear in various talk shows and periodicals for months and years to come. I said little as I continued my quiet contemplation of the web and the now large bulb in the very center of the web, where that large spider huddled over it, sucking the fluids from it. Over the buzzing of flying insects I could have sworn I heard the creature extrapolate the essence of its kill. What an odd sound, slow rhythmic, and primal.

Naturally, the extent of this visit was wearing on us; I could hear my own labored breathing over the hums and stirrings of the creatures forest. Reaching the top, my body was drenched with sweat, and my head was feeling light. Jillian who was only steps behind me, constantly looking everywhere at the scenery but said little as she tried to take in as much as she could, I knew there would have been little means for me to stop her from coming back in here.

"The descent is not as steep as the ascent," I rasped. I clung to the outer wall, feeling the fresh air on my hand. I could see the camp from across the way.

"Hans, you're just out of shape," Jillian said as she passed me.

Reginald laughed, with beads of sweat on his forehead.

The cool fresh outside air caressed my face, sending chills through me after being engulfed in the hot steamy conditions of the cave. This time I followed Jillian and Reginald off the side, no longer fearful of this short path, the rocky ledge over a pool of darkness. I looked back, taking a glimpse at the tops of the botanical life, not seeing any insect movement. How I have wished that technology then would have been as it is today, so that we could have captured images digitally and send it to anyone anywhere in an instant. No, it had been our word, now my word, against the billions other souls in the world. The importance of evidence then had been the key to proof of this discovery. Even then, I would have acknowledged the fact of Dr. Kempler's less involvement, distancing him already from this opportunity. This new world was the key to many new hopes and hidden treasure around the globe. Who knew what lie beneath the cap of Arctic ice? Would people reconsider what they thought they understood of our world? For my naïve nature, the discovery of this contained arena of groundbreaking biodiversity would lend itself to arguments for taking greater measures to protect our natural resources all over the world.

"What is your opinion, Dr. Fischer?" Ruiz greeted me at the bridge.

I had not looked at him, instead I only looked up at the very volcano that helped create this world, and simply replied, "We are yet to determine the enormity of this realization."

I would become lost in my own theories as we got back to camp, while Jillian and Reginald shared retellings of our experiences with Don and Jose, who seemed interested. Their combined enthusiasm only led to long conversations that continued long after the sun set behind the ridge of new volcano that night. I eventually joined in the conversations that night, hypothesizing the existence of the creatures we observed, wondering about the natural wonders of the world, reconsidering humankind's insignificant role in the world. We talked and theorized even as a strange auburn glow settled all over us. Ironically, we did not need fire nor light for that night.

Sometime later, Dr. Ruiz and his small group of two would join us, bringing some locally brewed beverages, warm but still refreshing. The warm black stone beneath us and the never-ending billows of clouds above continued as we settled in for the evening. For the first time, as I lay there next to Jillian on our sleeping bags, looking up into the night seeing glimmers of movements of the rainforest creatures rise and fall in the trees, I truly felt amazed and scared at the same time. Most of that night, I could hardly sleep nor could Jillian, our excitement unabated, knowing we were on the threshold of new knowledge. I tossed and turned for most of the night, finding myself watching the glow that emerged from the depths of the planet. I overheard the others occasionally, expecting that they would be restless from the excitement of this new discovery too. But what I had mistaken for their own restless stirrings was little more than their snores caused by the evening of overindulgence.

Eventually, I did drift off to a restless slumber.

Russell

FIFTEEN

It was an unusual sound that woke me. A combination of flutters and clicks. Later, about fifteen years later, I had the opportunity to be witness to a swarm of *robinia visconia*, the ravenous black locust, movement across the northern African deserts. By that point in my career, I had come to be known as a specialist, but only as a consultant to research projects. One morning in my tent, I had heard that sound with such clarity that it would haunt me, sound echoing on the plateau. The absence of wind and eerie stillness of the trees seemed to amplify the very clicks and flutters of the locusts exponentially a hypnotic interminable sound. This unusual sound in our morning camp woke me from my deep sleep.

I turned to see Jillian, Reginald, Don, Jose and our hired men at the entrance of the bridge. As I watched them, taking in the scene, I could see the view at which they were marveling. As though being casted out of la Boca de Diablo, these creatures spewed forth from the cavern. The various species of ants, beetles, spiders and centipede were crawling from the mouth of the cave, slipping into the darkness of the canyon, as many made anthropoid bridges that other species used to make passage. They ran all around us, from the plateau on which we stood, on every side of us only a few meters from us. The winged creatures flew high above us, and gave no indication of being near touching us as they blocked out the sky above. I found myself again reveling in the finite details of their wings, witnessing the transparency of the veins within their membranes, the vividly deep shades of purples and blues and greens. They too had mission to fly into the forest, and disappear from sight, as if the rainforest was devouring them in one immense swallow. I stared at the spectacle for some time, realizing that there was neither incentive nor inclination for these creatures to remain on the rock plateau. I could feel the remnants of sleep dissipate leaving me in this surreal display, grounded only by the feel of Jillian's hand holding mine.

No one spoke, not even a gasp of awe or surprise could be heard from our small audience. I suppose we were all completely and utterly impressed with this scene, realizing we would capture evidence of their existence at some future point, and we would establish new groundbreaking techniques in order for us to do so. I inched my way towards the narrow deep slit in the rock to witness the creatures falling into the murky shadows.

Leaning closer to the edge as I dared, my footing pushed gravel forward into the deep slit in the earth that seemed to have recently cracked open. While some creatures intermediately hung onto various rocks, their own weight alone made them slip into the eternal darkness. Behind me, I felt Jillian place a hand on my back and she too looked into the inky blackness below. As creatures fell, the cracking of their bodies and small thumps of their bodies against the rocks echoed and seemed to fade into the abyss. What lay at the bottom? Did any of the creatures even survive? Logically it would be impossible. Yet seeing these creatures, I believed anything was possible now. .

"They do this every morning at this time, but no other," Dr. Ruiz said behind me.

"From this angle of the mountain," Don said quietly, almost too quietly, "the sunlight enters the mouth of the cave."

"Run into the light, my children," Reginald said.

"Why do they not go onto the rock plateau?" I asked, straining to look deep into the darkness, and then I turned to see several ants attempting to latch onto rock near me, then flinch and fall into the shadows.

"There is a large magma lake about three-to-four hundred meters below the plateau. You can see the faint glow of the lake, and I believe that the glow from cave is created by the same reservoir. One of my men has a probable measure of the cave which concludes that about less than a kilometer down, the lake appears." Dr. Ruiz casually lit a cigarette, and the smoke filled my nostrils. "We are on a rock not meant to sustain life."

"These mutated insects have instinctive senses and know this conclusion already, Dr. Ruiz," I replied. "As for this morning mass exodus, Don, you could be right. But it doesn't give much reason, correct?"

Jillian cleared her throat softly, and spoke, "It appears as if they were fleeing from the cave."

"Look at this," Reginald said, walking over to a beetle specimen we had seen the day before. It had landed on its back, clawing at the sky, similar to the way its modern cousins do when they land in such a precarious position. Because once in this position, it would die. Yet there was another problem here.

Jillian and I walked over to him. Following Reginald's finger, he pointed out the rib cage, watching as it inhaled and exhaled air with great effort.

"It's suffocating," I observed. "Perhaps we should capture one creature and dissect for further analysis." Being the leader of the team, I did not want to jump any conclusions until we had some proof why these creatures reacted violently to life beyond the cave.

"Odd, but relative to amount of carbon dioxide in the cave..." Jillian further added.

Then the noise stopped. We all stopped talking and observed how serene the forest noises faded as the creatures escaped into the trees around us.

I could then hear the rumbles of the volcano above us, a shift in the trees around us and a rush of around us, smelling of smoke and rain. The cave no longer spewed out its contents. A few stragglers remained, but much like the dying beetle near us, these too fell to a quick death, some falling into the ravine below.

"Absolutely incredible," Don said.

Something in the air spurred me into action and I started to organize us quickly. I turned to the tent space that Ruiz had set aside for us to see what we had to work with. During our time in the cave, Don had done some station set-up for us to begin some research immediately, we would need every minute to accomplish what we needed to do.

"Dr. Fischer," Dr. Ruiz said to me.

I didn't look up and began jotting notes down. "Thank you for the allotted space and the extra man, but we can take it from here Doctor."

"One last item," he said, as Jillian and the others came our area of the camp, talking amongst themselves. "We have been noticing incredible spikes in the seismic energy in this location. The force of the magma chamber below us and the released pressure from the volcano.. Both our teams' work here is imperative, but your team's whereabouts must be accounted for at all times. We're likely sitting on a powder train here Doctor. Time is of the essence."

"I will take that under advisement," I replied.

Dr. Ruiz left towards his tent, mumbling something in Spanish, of which I could not quite catch the full meaning.

"What was that all about?" Jillian asked, coming behind me and putting a hand on my back.

"Okay," I stood fully, almost shaking her hand off my back, turning to address the group. "We have a large task at hand, with some danger involved, as was pointed out by Dr. Ruiz's over-concern. First, Reginald and Jose will head back to the car with our equipment. The large part is how we can maneuver our samples through that forest without damaging them getting them down and out of there. You're on that detail, Reginald."

Confidently and saying nothing, Reginald nodded to Jose, who only appeared nervous.

"Second, we need a better system here, and coordination, or at least a temporary area for storage and cataloging. As long as we get it, label it and store it, I think we can study it further back in San Jose. Don, can you make this happen?"

Don nodded of course.

I shifted my gaze past Don and kept an eye on the dying beetle like creature. "I believe you may have a sample right before us. Use our extra man on this." I even saw Don turn his head towards the beast with some fascination. "Let's see what makes these mutated specimens sustain life."

"Got it." Don was already eager to move.

I turned to Jillian. "You and I are going to get the samples."

There were some rumbles of conversation amongst us as everyone set to their tasks, an excitement in the air like before a collective focused purpose: gathering the materials, finding the evidence, studying the collected data. Now the evidence was important to my own well-being, to Jillian's and my future, to my reputation.

Within minutes or so Reginald, the new guide and Jose were

already back for our equipment. In a show of great concession, Ruiz loaned us yet another man to help with some boxes, stating that he could manage his work for a while by himself, even though I could plainly see his last man sitting in a chair watching a meter and reading a recently-translated American novel. My attention turned to Don, who, with some translations had gotten his helper already opening some boxes and setting equipment. He already had his game plan in motion, which was always the case with him.

Next, for our part, Jillian already had her backpack and mine ready. Her journal book was set alongside her pack, sampling tools poking from the edges for ease of access. I barely looked through mine; my only need was already bundled and waiting on top: a length of strong climbing rope to help us descend beyond the designated area, which Ruiz seemed to have blocked off and had stopped us at during our first trek inside.

"Remember we have an hour in there," I said, adjusting my case without looking at her.

"Yes, Dr. Fischer," she replied as she pulled her hair into a bun. She was so well adapted to this fieldwork, perfectly at ease with the direct and to-the-point nature of men from her years of work in science.

"Also, it took about ten minutes to get to that marked-off point on the ledge." I hooked the rope over my torso. "So that subtracts at least twenty minutes of valuable time for collection."

"Yes, Dr. Fischer."

"And one more thing."

She stopped and looked at me.

I leaned into her ear, and whispered, "I love you."

She put an arm around me, firmly and gently. "I love you as well, my husband."

"Dr. Fischer, Ma'am," I replied with a wink.

She pushed me back, smiling. "Then that's employee provocation."

"Site me."

"I will fill out the paperwork when we get back, and have you sign them." She rolled her eyes at me with a smirk. "Let's go exploring," she said as she hoisted her bag onto her back.

We made our way toward the cave.

A growing anxiety began to grow inside me that overtook me, in a way. I felt much like a child again, back in my home village, waiting to be let out of my uncle's house to go searching for my little friends in the field. My heartbeat felt like it skipped in my chest occasionally as we stepped onto the bridge, realizing how close I would be to them. I made my way across the bridge first, then Jillian followed as soon as I hopped to the other side, unsure whether or not that bridge would take our combined weight The smell of the fresh plants mixed with the scent of new smell of fresh elemental rock drifted into my nose. It's a wonderful fragrance, a blend of clean earth and smoke. I will never forget that moment because I turned to look back at the camp then, and at Jillian who clung to the side of the volcano..

I could only wonder at that moment what she could possibly be thinking. Her excitement was plain to see, refusing to let her aerophobia deter her from our goal. She looked at me with angelic eyes, and mesmerized by the scenery as we entered the cave. Our first glances of the area were more logical and methodical than they had been during our initial visit, and I could see the scientific side of her, much like our times in the lab, honed in on her subjects, her mental wheels turning. She was a tactical, hands-on scientist and the plants had been out of reach. Even I could not grasp them. How frustrating this must have been for her. But her eyes were doing the work of all her senses then.

At one point, I allowed her to slip passed me and take the lead down the ledge so that I could see her and keep her steady. While I slipped out my notebook to take my initial notes, she'd already begun rough sketching certain leaves.

As we passed the point where the colossal web had been, we now found that it had been completely destroyed and the arachnoid creature was nowhere to be seen. It may have been waiting again in its layer directly above us. Looking over, the tight ball of web which held the mutated flying species, was half its size. Most of the juices were already sucked out. Even Jillian stopped to look, in equal parts awe and disgust.

Behind us, I heard a crackling of rocks. I turned to look toward the entrance of the cave where one of Ruiz's men was standing; he was waving at us.

"Doctor Fischer, come quick!" he yelled to us.

Her look of joy instantly turned to fear or worry. My concern was now of worry. I allowed Jillian to go first then I followed, breathing heavily, my lungs working harder under the burden of high carbon dioxide levels.

Once, we got to the man, I noticed the anxious look on his face. "Doctor Fischer, one of your men is down."

"What?" Jillian muttered then looked in the direction of the camp site, seeing Reginald's back and Don flagging us.

"This doesn't look good," I said, moving past Jillian.

"Go on ahead," she said.

As quick as my long legs could take me, I went over the bridge, paying no attention to my own safety.

Around the entrance of the plateau, Reginald was on his knees over Jose, telling him to get better. Dr. Ruiz was leaving the area to go to his tent, shaking his head. Don was wrapping Jose in a sleeping blanket already. As I approached them, Jose's friend was near him, the one who has come with us, was tearing up already, muttering prayers to the Holy Father in Spanish under his breath.

In moments, I went to Jose who was lying on his back, shaking, unconscious, having cold sweats.

"What happened, Reginald?" I touched the native man's face and it was on fire.

"I was. Son of a bitch! He was ahead of us." Reginald was shaken, as if he saw something he should not have seen. His eyes were watering with tears.

"Okay, slow down, Reggie. Calm down." It was Jillian who then went passed me, to our colleague and friend, to comfort him as he knelt next to Jose.

"We need to get him to the hospital," Don stated, as he finished wrapping him. "He is going into shock."

"Then a big, um bee, wasp, dunno, came out of nowhere and Goddamnit it," Reginald's voice was shaky and uncertain. He looked at me, drizzles of cold sweat tricking down his face and neck.

"I already radioed ahead to the hospital in the nearby military camp. We will bring him there first." Dr. Ruiz said behind me.

"Thank you," I said to him. Then to Don, I asked, "How long do we have?"

"I cannot really say," he said, pouring water over Jose's forehead. "It depends on the size of the animal, after seeing the sizes of the animals this morning I can only assume that it had great amount of venom—"

"That piece of shit wasp was huge!" Reginald yelled, and then looked into the rainforest, as his eyes darted around wildly, craning his head in every direction. Jillian put a hand on his shoulder to comfort, but he only twitched.

Jose's twitching increased, and his tan complexion was becoming greener and paler. There was not much time. Ruiz and one of his men placed him on a portable cot.

"I will go with Jose to the hospital," I stated, looking at Jillian. She only nodded. "Don, you and Reginald—"

"No damn it! I'm coming with," Reginald said, standing up. "I was with him and saw it. I want to make sure he's okay." He grabbed one end of the cot and Jose's friend took the other.

Jillian just backed off, and with a simple gesture made it clear that this was Reginald's wish.

"Fine," I said, nodding to Don. "You and Jillian stay and figure something out. Maybe organize your thoughts."

I looked down at Jose whose condition seemed to deteriorate by the minute, and there was no time to decide the details. Jillian gave me water, and said, "Be back soon." She lightly kissed my cheek.

"Don, I will radio back to you on Jose's condition and an estimated return," I said. Walking with Jose, moving toward the dense rainforest, seeing the continuous movement ahead of me, my trepidation grew.

As Jillian stopped walking with us, I looked back to see Don standing next to her and her face was red with despair. Already Dr. Ruiz was heading back to his tent with his assistant. "Don'll take care of you," I said.

"Just be careful," Jillian said to me with a concerned look.

I wish that I said one more thing, an important thing that all happy couples say to each other. Instead, I looked away and was focused on Jose, not saying anything to her.

At that moment, I suppose I had done what any great manager would have done, be the support for the injured worker in their time of need, making sure he received the proper care needed, documenting in thought then reiterating on paper. I had only thought of the team, not myself, and not as husband leaving his wife behind. But I had; I left my Jillian behind, waiting for me. In retrospect, the best decision would have been to send Don with Jose and Reginald, and I remain at camp with Jillian and Dr. Ruiz and await word from the hospital.

But one cannot change the past, nor predict our doomed fate.

So, as walked into the forest, we were looking all around, noticing the increase in movements. The mutated creatures seemed even more alert of our presence. Perhaps they sensed our heat or our scents because it felt at times as if they were lingering around us. Reginald himself was shaky, twitching at any movement. Jose's friend, with beads of sweat as he held the cot, was continuing in his recital of prayers. The guide ahead of us was moving rather fast down the trail, which did not feel as long as it had yesterday.

I remained calm, holding up the rear, trying to switch off my scientist mode. There were scores of creatures alive, spinning webs, making nests, digging into the earth; the habitation was too much to take in, and then a gasp from Jose brought me back to our reality. His breathing was becoming looser and fainter. The toxins from the bite had moved through his body quickly, shutting it down. From my distance, I could still see that the blanket around his leg was soaked in blood, dripping to the forest floor. I prayed no creature would find this scent. The expression on Jose's face was discontent and beginning to bloat. Much like the prey of the wasp or bee, or whatever it was, the size of the mutated creature exponentially increased its toxicity.

Onward we moved in the antagonistic darkness of the rainforest. Reginald did not say a word, only kept up his looking around at a paranoid pace. Had I said anything, it would have been irrelevant to him. I remained calm, walking as quickly as I could while watching the path ahead of us and then behind. I tried not to theorize why the species were still maintaining existence outside of the compound of the cave, nor did I allow myself to ponder why the creatures were easily mutating the very creatures around them. However, I had noticed more mammals today, and more birds. There were howler monkeys and pigs scooting here and there, feasting on the oversized creatures. This was to be the end for them; perhaps this had been why they remained in the cave so long. I was not exactly sure, but I tried not to ponder. As I think back, I realize that I wasted much of existence pondering things that could not be controlled, at least, not controlled by me.

This dying man in front of me as we ended our brisk and silent journey was my focus, out of guilt. Yet we all knew the risk involved in this particular journey. It was no less than any other journeys we had taken. This I had rationalized in the jungle, down the descent of the muddy trail. Then there was the silence of the forest that overwhelmed us again, even Reginald and Jose's friend stopped to look around. It was as if there was an invisible boundary for the Devil's Creatures. About twenty years, after Don had published a series of award-winning books, he would write an autobiography called, *Devil's Creatures*, his supposed personal view of this experience. He'd sent me a personal copy, with a personal inscription. To this day I have yet to crack it open.

Ironically, at that moment, as I stood for a brief second with the men, hearing only Jose's lingering wheezing, I actual felt safe again.

Before long, the skies opened up and rain fell steadily maneuvered Jose more carefully and diligently down the trail. Then I saw the field, the farmland and there was no sight of the volcano behind us. The rain itself was refreshing and cleansing to me, but it was cruel to Jose. It seemed to pummel him, disregarding his fragile mortality. It washed over him, making his skin glow a milky-white paleness over the naturally deep tan pigmentation of his skin.

We ran to the jeeps, against the rain and the pits in the trail and the tall grass. I tried to get ahead so I could help load Jose in the back of one. Instantly, I hopped into one while Ruiz's man took the wheel. Reginald and Jose's friend went in the other. The rain had no mercy now, diminishing visibility to almost nothing with buckets of rain. The very sound of the raindrops beat an eerie rhythm in the car. I looked back at Jose, whose mouth was gurgling bubbles from the raindrops that soaked his face. Then over the beating droplets, as the Jeep jerked into gear, Jose began to slightly twitch again, less violently, but more succumbing to the pain. I could not keep my eyes off of him, yet I barely saw the headlights of the second Jeep behind us.

The Jeep dipped into one of the countless potholes, which thrusted my body forward. I looked at Ruiz's man who said, "*Lo siento, Doctor.*" I turned back to watch Jose. His bloody wrapping opened somewhat and then I saw a glimpse of the grapefruit sized puncture wound in his leg. It was already black, oozing out white fluid mixed with his blood. His leg was bloated to twice the size of his other, but the throbbing from the injury seemed to be slowing. I looked at Jose's face and found that his eyes were open, filled with whiteness and blood-tinged.

Jose was gone.

I held back my emotions. I told the driver to stop, and I hopped out of the truck, instantly drenched in the rain. I ran back to Reginald, to tell him the news. He did not take it well. I gave him a few moments , I sent him and Jose's friend on to the hospital to wrap-up any paperwork. Jose's friend would tell the family. Something in my gut told me I had to get back to camp. I needed to figure out what exactly happened.

So, Ruiz's man and I headed back through the rain-soaked, muddy trail. My head was dazed, still full of thought. What I was thinking about at that time, I'm still not sure. Already half the day was gone, and I was exhausted. The rain seemed to be letting up, but I found comfort in it. The walk back through the forest was difficult with the extremely humid conditions. I should have been acclimated to it, but alas I continued to struggle at this altitude. As I ambled closer to the red glow, I watched a large butterfly, mutated into its enormous beautiful form, gently land on a nearby branch, patiently slipping out its tongue to taste the raindrops.. The black markings on its six-meter wingspan were incredibly detailed in a green-aqua metallic color. The round compound eyes saw everything chaotically circled around as the six legs remained still, fine hairs blowing in the nominal wind under the canopy. It seemed almost majestic as perched overhead, indifferent to our presence, seeming entranced by the new world that surrounded it, the openness and freedom it seemed to offer. From this proximity, I could see the abdomen working, exchanging large quantities of air, perhaps gagging on the pure oxygen after spending most of its day inside the oxygen-deprived atmosphere of the Devil's cave. A crackle of branches spooked the creature and it fluttered above me, aerating the stagnant humidity with its graceful wings and I could feel the light, refreshing breeze fall down over my face and shoulders.

At that moment, I saw Dr. Ruiz coming rapidly towards me, probably about twenty meters from the plateau. I knew instantly that something was wrong.

"Dr. Ruiz, Jose is—"

"An accident," he said catching his breath. He looked at me squarely, "Your, wife, . Jillian."

I pushed him aside and ran up the side of the hill onto the plateau.

I called for Jillian where I passed another of Ruiz's men who was pointing at the cave. Then I saw Don. He was carrying my wife's limp form away from the entrance of the cave, scooting against the rock wall. Quickly I ran to them, meeting them at the foot of the bridge.

"Hans, I'm sorry, I'm so sorry," Don kept saying. His face was red with a mix of panic and exertion. He shook his head.

I pulled Jillian into my arms. I put my hand on her face and said, "Honey, come on. Wake up, Jillian." Tears were flowing freely down my face but I didn't pay attention to them.

Dr. Ruiz helped me lie her down on boards covered in a sleeping bag. I could only look at her, telling her to wake up. Behind me I heard Don say, "She just wanted to surprise you, Hans, and get a sample for you. Then there were some loose rocks. She fell and I did my best to follow her with our rigging, and when I got her, I found her on the cave floor, unresponsive."

I could no longer listen to him. What happened next I still cannot remember in too much detail, but we left the camp that day. I got my Jillian down the side of the mountain, into the spare Jeep.

Later that night, she went to the San Jose hospital. It seemed she had been in a coma with a blunt trauma to the head. I requested a private room and I did not leave her side. Don and Reginald came to visit, but soon I would reject their help. By the end of the week, we were boarding a plane to the United States, back to the same University that sent us on that cursed expedition, to their hospital. After a couple weeks of tests, it turned out that her coma was due to some sort of unknown disease. There was no test that could determine the cause or prescribe a cure, which lead to much frustration.

After several months, Jillian's doctors were kind of enough to release her. In that time, I had purchased this house, decorated it and created the garden that you once saw, Allison. I had her hospital equipment transferred here, to a room above us. In her room, I recreated the gardens, much like the ones in Central America, with some Midwest influence. I hired a wonderful full-time nurse, Eleanor Wagner, to take care of her. Although there was not much to attend to in her forever catatonic sleep, she dressed and bathed her in hopes that she would wake up. Had she ever opened her eyes, she would have seen the beautiful gardens outside and known she was home.

Eventually her condition worsened. Jillian passed away quickly in the comfort of our home, a home she would never know or enjoy. I would never hear her speak again, nor receive her tender embrace. Her funeral was small, filled with her favorite orchid species, *chorisia speciosa*, *combretum* and others, lining the desolate hall. I and only a couple of others were in attendance.

Whatever happened in the cave that day had been buried with her. Never once had I thought about leaving her side during that time, during her illness, even as I knew I was watching her slowly dissolve in front of me. So many tears I had shed on her bed, and I still miss her.

When I returned from the second trip after her death, I realized this home was where I needed to be. This home had been where Jillian had laid in a dreamless-state until her body could fight no more. This was our house, what should have held our dreams and our future together.

My sweet Jillian would have wanted it that way.

*****

Mom's phone rang loud.

It made me jump, and I think my mom did too. I looked over at Old Man Fischer. The dim glow of the light made his face look more sunken, which made it more disturbing. He had been in his own thoughts, whether he had been with his wife or not, I honestly could not tell. His expression was solid and straight, almost emotionless, not even paying attention to my mom who fumbled for the phone.

It rang another time and she clicked the button, and said softly, "Yes, we're coming home. Time just got away from us." She glanced at me. "Be home soon."

She placed the phone back into her purse.

The darkness of the house seemed more inviting now. I was no longer afraid of the shadows. How long had we been sitting here listening to this old man's chilling tale? I looked up at the tall ceiling and tried to imagine Jillian lying motionless in the room above me.

"I do apologize for that, M -- Hans," she still could not really say his name, and almost had to force it out. She glanced at her watch. "Didn't realize it was so late already. School night."

183

With that, she placed a hand on the back of my head, and I turned my attention back to Mr. Fischer.

"I understand. Family commitments," he said quietly, barely squeaking out his reassurance with an almost undetectable smirk.

Mom began to stand, and then I followed. Old Man Fischer leaned on his cane, and slowly raised himself from his chair. Mom and I slowly walked toward the foyer. I heard the click of his cane on the floorboards, and the labor of his rasping breaths. Somehow, in my gut, and I could not explain what made me think so, I was sure that he was trying too hard to be that slow. Maybe I was over-thinking.

In the stillness of the house, and as I briefly glimpsed back down the hallway toward the kitchen, I swear I could see an amber light coming from under the door. It was so faint but in this darkness I could see it clearly. Was it a night light in the corner? Or was it something else?

"I am so glad we had a chance to meet again, Hans," Mom said, turning to him. Her hand was on the doorknob.

"The pleasure was all mine, Allison. I hope you don't take too much consideration to the ramblings of an old man," he replied with a smile.

"Well, Thank You for having us and sharing your story this evening. I hope we can do this again."

"Let's not let too much time pass," he looked down at me, "otherwise he will have graduated from high school before I have a chance to tell you anymore of it."

Mom forced a brief laugh. "No, Hans. No, it won't come to that."

That mysterious hum I heard before was suddenly in my ears again, almost as if it surrounded me. I could not tell where it was coming from. Suddenly, a yawn came to my lips which I could not help to hide.

"Yeah, we better go," Mom said.

"Thank you for the delicious pie. Please thank Donald for me," he said dryly.

Mom opened the door and the cool air overwhelmed us. I shivered instantly.

"Have a good evening," Old Man Fischer said.

"Good night," Mom said, putting her arm around me, and we stepped into the night air. The same squeaks in the stairs happened as we went down the porch steps. Then, as my foot hit the cement walkway, the porch light went completely out.

We rushed to the car. The harsh wind blew against me, and a flurry of dead leaves danced around my feet. I had to step on several of the dancers, crushing them into bits as the wind carried them away. The streetlight seemed dimmer and the shadows deeper now.

Once we were inside the car Mom said nothing and quickly started the car. I looked back at the house, images of his story fading and flowing in my mind. There was so much to take in, to absorb, so much to let sink in. There was no movement from the dimly lit room where we had sat, no human shadow going back or forth. Where could Old Man Fischer possibly be in that large house, in all those dark rooms, was beyond me.

"As I returned from the second trip after her death." Dr. Fischer had said. *Why did he go back? Why would Old Man Fischer go back to the place that had ruined his life? Why would he want to?* His story was not finished was something missing. I wanted to know more. And that hum. I knew it came down that same question, and I heard it echoing over and over in my head: *What are you hiding Old Man Fischer?*

Just as quickly as we had jumped in the car, we were home. I was tired, needed sleep.

Believe it or not, I never slept so well as I did that night.

Russell

Part 3

Dr. Fischer's House

"Soon after dark Emily cries...
Gazing through trees in sorrow
Hardly a sound till tomorrow
There is no other day
Let's try it another way
You'll lose your mind and play..."

--Pink Floyd

Russell

SIXTEEN

(Shane)

Friday Nights were always on movie nights at our house. It was a tradition that my dad and I created couple of years ago. These nights, Mom typically worked late at her "events" as she would call them, so Dad and I were left on our own. By end of the week, Dad was usually tired and Saturdays were a fairly slow day at the bakery, and he didn't have to go in until later in the morning. Dad would pop in a DVD and make some extra buttery popcorn. When Maggie entered the picture, we still continued. She liked to play with her toys in front of the television and gnaw on some treats as well.

This particular Friday I was ready for the festivities. I sat on the couch with my big bowl of popcorn and waited for Dad. The bakery had some problems this week, and it showed on his tired face as he attempted to be in a good mood. He liked Movie Night because he could take a nap during half of the movie. Dad had just got into his chair with a large glass of what he called "malted love", when his phone rang.

Whether he wanted to or not, he had to take the call. "Keep watching, okay," he said to me, then ruffled Maggie's hair who paid no attention as she watched the opening scene of the underwater cartoon fish and sea mammal characters singing and dancing. Perhaps I had seen this movie a dozen times, but Maggie hadn't before, so she was not talking. So far at least.

Over in the kitchen, I heard Dad yell into his phone: "What! Did you put it out? Shit, shit, shit! The fire department is on their way? I will be there as soon as possible."

Dad clicked off his phone. He ran his thick fingers through his hair, and his cheeks were becoming a deep shade of crimson. Then I saw him grab his coat.

"Kids, something happened at work. You have to go over to Yvonne's tonight," Dad said loudly. His face was becoming a distressed shade of purplish-red and a more worried look fell over him, a side of him I had not seen for a while.

It was then Maggie perked up with an equal sour look. I really thought Maggie and Dad were more alike than they realized. "No Von. No night." Her eyes were turning red with the threat of a tantrum.

Like me, she truly did not want to leave the house tonight, not now. We just were getting comfortable. I watched Dad run upstairs with Maggie screaming in his arms, to put her in warmer clothes. I turned off the movie, knowing it would have to wait for another Friday night. I was picked up the popcorn bowls and put them in the kitchen, feeling a sense of loss at the disruption. Outside I saw the darkness just beginning to invade the entire neighborhood, the streetlights still too dim to push the looming shadows away.

Selfishly, I really wanted the solitude of Movie Night in order to get the thoughts of Old Man Fischer's story out of my head. For the past couple of nights, my dreams were full of large bugs crawling all over my room as I was running away from the eerie red light in my closet.

Dad was already on the phone when he came back downstairs with Maggie running after him, not so much upset about going to Yvonne's house, more or less upset that Dad had to leave us. He had already changed out of his bakery clothes and was in sweatpants and a concert shirt.

"Thank you, Yvonne. We will be there in less than five. I am calling Allison now." He clicked on his small phone. "This is a bad one, Shane," He looked at Maggie who was now smiling through her tear-filled eyes. "Sorry honey. Dad will make this up to you." Then to me, "Can you help me get her ready and get your coat?"

He walked away in a huff, heading down to the basement, on the phone waiting for Mom to answer.

I pulled Maggie's winter jacket off the hook by the door and got her into it and pulled her hat over her head. "Why do we go ta

Vonz?" She sniffled at me.

I shrugged my shoulders, and said, "Dad's work comes first."

Sometimes, I wished Dad had a normal job, working from nine to five each day, no weekends, no nights and definitively no holidays. Like, it'd be nice to even have him on Easter once, instead of him personally running big deliveries to his most important customers. Or even at some family events, he would come later or not all. Or even just on mornings other than just Sundays. Sometimes I wished that Dad could see how much his job ran his life, all of our lives.

I put on my jacket, and grabbed a book. Usually Yvonne did not have much for me to do since her house was set up for smaller kids like my sister.

Soon, Dad reappeared from the basement and his face was red. He was talking to himself. That usually meant he was making lists in his head.

"I only got Mom's voicemail, but she'll call right back." He looked around briefly, and said, "Let's get in the car."

Opening the screen door, the cold smacked me in the face, and I tried to tuck my face into the hood of my jacket. Maggie walked next to me and she held onto her favorite stuffed dinosaur. I barely put on my seatbelt when Dad already had Maggie strapped in, in the driver's seat. His phone rang.

"Hey. Sorry, Ally, for calling you. Yeah. How long? No, I don't know the damage yet. Taking them to Yvonne's now." Dad started the car, and it hummed to a start and turned backwards with one hand on the wheel. He briefly looked at me and gave me a smile. "Yeah. Yeah. Yeah." He said to the phone. The car slid backward away from the house and into the darkness.

Maggie was shifting in her chair, not saying much, just looking out the window. I felt her discontent as we headed towards Yvonne's. At the end of the street, where Mom usually turned to go to school, towards Old Man Fischer's house, Dad drove the car straight into the newer part of our town. We lived in the historic district, where our house was built in 1903. According to Mom, this newer area was built with fifties and sixties-styled homes which were long, ranch-style one-story homes. Even in the dark, I could see way above the houses and passed the smaller trees.

The car rolled on passed the houses. Yvonne did not live that far away from us plus it was easy for Mom to drop Maggie in the mornings since the Interstate to take to downtown was only a mile away. These houses all looked the same to me: small and flat , with reddish brown bricks in the doorways. They had white-trimmed gutters and flat roofs with a chimney on the back of the house. I knew a few friends that lived over here.

Dad got off the phone with Mom, and announced, "We're here."

Maggie knew the house no matter if it was light or dark. She whimpered in her seat, and held onto to the dinosaur animal. Her eyes were filled with tears.

"Now, now," Dad said softly, opening her door. I felt the cold rush of air come in. "Mom will be here real quick."

"How quick?" I unbuckled my belt.

He looked at me, and said, "She said that she would talk to another manager to cover for her, maybe a half an hour, max. Depends on traffic."

Everything always depended on traffic with Mom. I slid out into the air, looking at the brick-lined doorway with the white door. The porch light was on showing the growing pile of leaves in the planters along the front step. I walked on tight cement pathway to the door, hearing Dad take out Maggie and close the door. Before I got to it, the door opened.

There Yvonne stood with a smile to greet us. "Shane, what a nice surprise." She stood a little taller than me, and she was thin. I already smelled some fresh-baked cookies in the oven. In a way, she was so kind-hearted that it was always relaxing here. I said nothing to her, but gave her a brief hug. "Thanks," she replied to me.

I went into the well-lit living room, taking off my jacket and putting it on the orange chair near the entry. Her living room was filled with older furniture and dated knickknacks, but it was set-up for taking care of Maggie and two other children she watched full-time. Maggie was the youngest, being the "last" child Yvonne will ever watch. The room was long and large, and an area in the far corner with a small kids' table, chalkboard and boxes of small toys. On that end of the room near the children's stuff, there was the television, a much older cousin to our flat screen, the kind that sat on the floor in a large wooden cabinet.

Behind me, I heard her say, "Maggie why are you shying away from me."

"Thank you so much, Yvonne," Dad said.

I turned to see Dad standing in the door, cracked open and letting in some leaves.

"Not a problem. I know what it's like to run a business, Don."

"Ally said she—"

Yvonne interrupted, "She already called and said she'd be here soon."

Dad smiled and gave Maggie, who was now perched on Yvonne's shoulder, a kiss. "Be good, sweetie."

"She always is." Yvonne started taking her coat off, without resisting then gave the older woman a smile.

Then Dad looked at me, and said, "I'll make up movie night another night."

I just nodded at him.

Dad disappeared into the night. From his shadow I could tell that his arm was to his ear, already on his phone.

Yvonne fussed with Maggie, then put her down, and Maggie went straight for the toys in the corner. Though her eyes were still filled with tears, my sister seemed happier now as she clanked about, pulling out toys from the lime green wooden box.

"Cookies will be ready in five minutes," Yvonne said, going towards the kitchen.

I looked at the television. The news was on, and there was a story about a string of bank robberies near the downtown area. The reporter, a Spanish man with a clear voice, stated, "Investigators have no leads at this time. But police have reported that a full investigation has been deployed."

Old Man Fischer's story began floating around in my head as I remembered he talked about when he moved into his house. Maybe Yvonne might know something about him.

I walked into the bright white kitchen where I found Yvonne getting two glasses of milk ready and two small plates out. She was humming a slight melody as she went from cabinet to refrigerator.

When she saw me, she smiled. "Shane, I was going to bring this out to you and Mags."

"Well, I just wanted to see if you needed any help."

"You are so sweet, Shane. Very thoughtful." Her voice was slightly raspy but still had a friendly tone. "It's just cookies and milk."

"They smell good." I had to get her on the right conversation, so I asked, "Yvonne, how long have you lived here?"

She stopped and leaned against the sink. I could see she was figuring something in her head. "Well, uh, I don't know, about thirty-five and some odd years. Frank and I bought this house when Samantha and John were young. We had just moved out of the city and found this a proper place to raise a family."

"So you know most of the neighbors around here still?" I asked. I now sat in the yellow vinyl kitchen chair, the air pushing out of the cushion under me.

"No, no. People come and go." She put her hand on her hip. "Why are you asking?"

"Well, I just had this class at school on history," I had to lie quick. "She told me about how people in our town stay here for good."

"True. She's right. But many people do move away." The timer on her stove rang and she turned pull the cookies from the oven. The chocolate scent filled my nose, and I was instantly hungry.

"But do you know people that stayed around here though?"

Yvonne placed the pan on the electric burner next to a yellow tea pot. "Well, next to me are the Jorgensens. The other side is a new couple, the Bensons. Then behind me there is the nice black couple, The Wrights, who have a lovely small family. I like seeing their kids play in the backyard."

So then I asked boldly, "How about Mr. Fischer, on Ashland Street?" I dared not to say doctor in front of his name.

She stopped putting cookies on the small white plate.

Turning, she looked at me, her small face was rimmed with deep age lines and her white curls dusted her eyelashes. Behind her thick brown glasses, her hazel eyes looked passed me toward the living room then back to me. She took small mouse steps to where I sat and placed the plate in front of me.

Yvonne replied, "No, not me, personally. Sure I've seen him about town. I even see him at mass at St. Paul's once in a while. Frank had more to do with him than I ever did." Then to she asked me, "Why do you ask?"

"Just curious." My voice cracked under the weight of my lie.

She cleared her throat and sat opposite of me in a mismatched wooden chair. It squeaked under the weight of her small frame as she continued, "It didn't dawn on me until now, that the first time I had spoken to him was at Frank's funeral seven years ago. He was an odd man, limping on one side. He only said, 'I am truly sorry for loss.

Frank was a blessed man to have you in his life.'" She paused, looking out the dark window. "All I knew was that Frank did an electrical job for Hans when we first moved here. And he paid Frank well for it."

How Yvonne said 'Hans' seemed almost harsh, with a nervous edge. But I pressed, "What do you mean?"

At that point, she looked toward me, but I could tell she wasn't seeing me. Maybe she was thinking about a different time. "If you knew Frank, he had always been a hardworking, dedicated family man and a great husband. There was nothing he wouldn't do. When he, I mean Hans, approached Frank about the electrical job, I knew Frank was unsure about it. I never met him then, only Frank would go to his house. At the time, Frank was the best electrician in the area, working downtown mainly in those government buildings and such. I asked Frank why he didn't want to do it. He just said that it was an odd request."

"What do you mean?"

"He said to me that it was something he 'didn't want to be a part of' and that was it. But then he told me that he was being paid twenty thousand in cash. We were strapped for money at the time. At the time, John, I told you about him, right?"

"Yes, many-a-times," I said. Her son was a big lawyer in Los Angeles and never had time to see her, his own mother. I could see the sadness on her face, I think she missed him.

"When Johnny was real young, he had a heart problem. Doctors then didn't know what Doctors know now. Well, anyway, John's hospital bills were so much at the time and that twenty thousand would make us even. Frank knew it, but he resisted. Like a good wife, I nagged him about it. Eventually, Frank did it and we got the money." Then she looked at me and smiled.

She got up the table to fetch a cup of coffee.

"So, did he help make something for his wife?" I asked.

She looked down at me, and said, "You ask a lot of questions, don't you?"

"I suppose."

The corner of her lips curled slightly. "Aren't you hungry? Have one of my cookies." Then replied, "You have a gift for making people talk. But you're young, you can ask as many questions as you want. When you are old like me, then you are just called a nosy old fart."

I giggled.

Then, Yvonne turned from the stove and said, "You know what, come to think of it, I never knew Hans had been married. There was talk, of course, but that was all. I thought he was just a single, sorta-crazy man."

The sound of small feet came charging from the living room as Maggie came running into the warm kitchen. "Von, cookie! Smell cookie!" She ran past me and went to the older lady, hugging her hips tight.

"You are always a hungry one, aren't you, Mags?" she cooed at my sister. "Here you go," as she put one on a small plastic plate for her, "remember no spills on the rug, please."

From my seat in the kitchen, I watched how Yvonne took good care of my sister, stroking the back of head, looking after her, like this was her own granddaughter. Yvonne didn't have grandchildren, this much Mom had told me. Her daughter died in a car accident some years ago, and well, the lawyer-son was in California. In a way, Yvonne made me a little sad. But I was happy that Maggie was in her life to make her feel good.

I strolled back into the living room, letting the cookies settle in my stomach, and sat in the orange chair and waited for Mom. The same question circled around in my head: *What are you hiding, Old Man Fischer? What would Yvonne's husband be making for him? If not for Jillian, then for what?*

So many thoughts were in my head, and I just wanted to get them out.

About an hour later, Mom arrived at Yvonne's house. I was beginning to drift off to sleep in the large soft orange chair near the kitchen, but my body slowly went into the routine of retrieving my coat. Maggie had been sleeping near Yvonne on the couch. My sister grunted softly as Mom scooped her up into her arms. Quietly, Mom told Yvonne that we were coming back in the morning because she had some work.

Once home, I gave Mom a quick kiss, said good night and fell into my soft bed. I had dreamless sleep.

The next day, Saturday, Maggie and I had to go over to Yvonne's early, where she already had breakfast waiting for us.

Before we left home though, Dad was getting ready to go into work I overheard the conversation between my Dad and Mom early that morning. He said he felt guilty for taking us over to Yvonne's, but he saw no other way. A small fire had broken out in a small part of the kitchen at the bakery. Luckily no one was injured and his employees knew how to handle the crisis. Dad's new supervisor, who was hired to make Dad's life easier, did not react quickly enough to prevent the fire, or at least that's what the other workers told him. As they talked, Mom was getting Maggie and herself ready for her work, nodding here and there. I could see on her face that she was just tired of the bakery too. Dad had to go back this morning to see what damage had been done, handle insurance things and recover any lost food. "That's it, I am getting rid of that lazy guy I just hired," Dad finally said at the end of the conversation. It would not help us because that would mean his work hours would double, and Mom would be dropping and picking Maggie and I up from school for a while. Again.

Honestly, I was happy to be over at Yvonne's house. I just did not want to think about anything, or at least nothing to do with Mr. Fischer. Yvonne surprised us and we went to the zoo, which was only a couple of miles from her house. Though it was a crisp autumn day, I enjoyed going to the zoo, looking at the animals. Plus, Maggie liked the extra attention Yvonne gave her as we went through the exhibits. So our trip allowed the day to end as quickly as it had begun.

Mom, who looked even more tired, did pick us up later that afternoon, explaining to Yvonne that she was letting another person handle her event. Mom worked hard and a least as much as Dad. I could see on her face the stress that was creating, but she tried not to show it. When she opened the door at Yvonne's, Maggie went running to her.

"Thank you so much for all your help, Yvonne," Mom said, handing her an envelope. "I hope this takes care of it."

We didn't see Dad until later that evening. He smelled of smoke, a dirty wet smell that I would not get out of my nose for a while. He seemed to have bathed in it. Mom, of course, had his beverage ready for him, and threw him into the shower. Lazily, he kissed me on the forehead, not saying anything, and gave Maggie a quick hug. It was late for her, and her bedtime was right around the corner.

While I watched TV in the front room, I could hear Mom and Dad talking.

"I have to go back in tomorrow, assess the production for Monday's deliveries," Dad said, then sipped at his brown bottle.

"Insurance is covering the costs on this, right?" Mom replied, wiping down the same counter top for the past few minutes.

"At least ninety percent of it."

"We can't take out another mortgage on your bakery," she was shaking her head, not looking at him. "Not with Maggie's bills."

"Hon, there will be no problems." He sighed heavily.

"Don, your business is our life too. But it's putting us over the edge." She was shaking her head again, not looking at him.

"I will cut the corners I need to so we float a month there." He stepped towards her. Dad looked so much larger than Mom, almost like a large round mushroom set next to a slender asparagus. "I had been socking away emergency money in an account last year for this."

"When were you going to tell me about it?" Mom stopped. Her face was serious.

"For a time like this, or the kids, or even whatever the house problem." He shrugged his shoulders and finished his bottle then threw it into the trash.

"I am not mad, I just want to know these things," Mom said. Her tone was soft. "The kids and I know the bakery is important to you, it is to all of us. We need it to survive."

"It is," Dad sounded drained. "We have the holiday season coming soon."

From my view, nestled on the couch, I watched as Mom nodded and Dad talked about his "promotions and sales" for the bakery despite this set back. According to Dad, even if one of the three ovens were down they could still crank out the necessary production to turn a profit. He may just have to work a little more. Mom's interest faded from her face and turned into blankness. I think she was tired of Dad's work schedule as well.

I never understood why grownups couldn't just say what they want.

After my show was over, I went to bed, too tired to dream about Old Man Fischer or his cavern in Central America, but about nothing. I woke the next day refreshed. I liked it that way.

SEVENTEEN

(SHANE)

When I went down stairs, Dad was already gone.

Mom was reading the Sunday paper at our large dark wood table in the dining room. Next to her, the comics were already taken out for me, set near the pile of coupons that Mom had already cut out. Somehow, in a way, I enjoyed this time, this quiet moment, because it was just her and me. There was no TV sound and the kitchen window was open. Mom liked the fresh air in the morning, which made the kitchen unusually cool.

"Morning Mom," I said, as I hit the bottom stair.

"Hey. Sleep well?" Her eyes didn't leave the article in the paper. Her thin glasses were balanced on the very tip of her nose.

"Yeah." Down beside my leg was Billy Bob, rubbing his body against my leg, a clear sign that he was looking for a treat.

I went into the kitchen, opening the pantry door to retrieve some cat food for him. Just as I opened the tin, Billy Bob was below me, meowing loudly and sniffing the air. He was rubbing so forcefully against my legs that he pushed me back a step. I giggled softly, then put a good heaping spoonful into his small grey bowl and set it on the floor next to the fridge. Immediately, he went to it, hungrily lapping up the gravy and the bits of unknown meat.

"There you go, boy," I whispered and stoked his soft fur as he arched his back. To me, especially early in the morning, the cat food smelled rank.

I got myself a glass of milk, nice and cold. The creamy taste in my mouth was refreshing. I didn't see any of Dad's usual pastries out, or any types of snacks.

I went to the dining room table and sat opposite of Mom.

199

"How hungry are you?"

I had the comics in front of me. I shrugged my shoulders, and said, "Dunno."

"Well, 'dunno' is not an answer," Mom said, putting down the newspaper just an inch or two. It was a wall of print between us. "How hungry are you?"

"Hungry, I guess."

Now she put down her newspaper wall, and gave me a smirk. "Hungry enough for chocolate chip pancakes with extra whipped cream from Mary Ann's?"

I looked at her with excitement. I loved Mary Ann's restaurant. It was a little place on the other side of our small town, and if you go before the church rush you can get a seat quickly. But if you go after church lets out, then you wait an hour for a table. But it was so worth it! My memories of that place are some of the first I can ever remember. The pancakes were the best!

"Yes!" I said out loud.

"Good, we'll just change fast when your sister wakes up," she said to me. She sighed heavily. "I just don't feel like cookin' today."

For a brief moment, we sat in this awkward silence as she fell back into her newspaper and I started to read my comics.

It had been several days since we had been to Old Man Fischer's house, since we'd listened to his story. I overheard Mom talk about some of it to Dad when we got back that night. I had been too tired to really listen in on the conversation, but we had not talked about it. Was she avoiding talking to me about it? It sure had seemed that way. She talked about her job, my school, and the weather to me, and of course, Dad's fire over the last couple of days, but not the other night.

I had to ask. It was gnawing at me.

"Mom," I said in a small voice. I only looked at my comics, not reading them. Mom was hid behind the wall of print which mentioned record lows in the stock market.

"I know that voice, Shane. What do you want?" Her lips were pinched and her eyes narrowed over the black rims of her glasses with a fierce intensity.

Suddenly, we both heard a thud as if something heavy hit the floor. It made the chandelier move; Maggie's room was directly above.

A faint cry followed, sounding more startled than anything, then Maggie begging for "Momma" over and over again.

Instantly, Mom sprang up from her chair and ran upstairs. Then, I heard footsteps go back and forth and some more crying.

"Shane, come up quick!" Mom called down the stairs.

I ran up the stairs and headed towards Maggie's room which was kitty-corner to mine. I saw Maggie whimpering in Mom's arms, blood was coming from her mouth, nose and ears. Mom was holding her tight, trying to calm her down. I could smell the thickness of pee and blood. The bed sheets was stained in dark red and was torn apart and thrown into a bundle in the corner. Mom thought that I couldn't handle Maggie's messes, but I've learned.

"Can you hold her for a few seconds while I call Doctor Kimberly?" Mom didn't look up at me, just kept looking down at Maggie. She was stroking Maggie's pale face with her hand. She was not really replying, barely whimpering. "Your big brother is going to hold you for a second," Mom reassured her.

I went to Maggie, and took her heavy weight in my arms. Her small body was limp and her limbs dangled in my arms as I sat cross-legged on the floor.

My sister had rare blood condition similar to leukemia. Her small long body filled my arms, and I didn't want to let her go. I wish I could help her, to find a cure for her problem, but only regulated drug schedule could help her. Her sweat was beading against her forehead and her body trembled in my arms. I hadn't felt her like this for a while. I was getting scared for her.

Mom came into the room with her phone as she hung up. She'd pinned her long dark hair into a tight bundle and she was already dressed. She wore a look of concern on her face, a worried expression that had become typical for the longest time when Maggie first got sick and they diagnosed her. She grabbed the bed linens in one scoop and left the room. The tears were building in her eyes yet she would not allow them to fall.

"Maggie, it's okay. Dr. Kimberly will be there. He will take care of you," I said.

"I hurt," she replied softly. Her small blue eyes were barely open.

My throat was choking up. There were some water coming to my eyes, but I pushed them back. I didn't want Maggie to see me worried. I grabbed her small bear and put into her hands. "Here's

Blue Bear," I cooed, slowly rocking her back and forth.

Her breathing became raspy.

Mom came back while on the phone to the doctor. "Yeah, the same symptoms like last time," she bent down looking at Maggie, "we'll meet you at the ER. Yes, time to discuss different meds. Yes." She hung up her phone, and to me she said, "I've got her. Go throw on a pair of jeans, get a book, stuff or something to keep busy. You can go like this."

She'd already thrown on her coat. She scooped Maggie in her arms, talking to her softly, soothing her, tell her that the doctor will fix her, things like that.

I left the room, heading down stairs to the play area. I found my stash of hospital stuff: several word puzzles, a book I'd been meaning to read, and a couple of cars. Of course, I grabbed my phone and charger on the night stand. Behind me, I heard Mom with Maggie in her arms come down the stairs. Mom's footsteps were quick and silent, sneaking up behind me. Without saying a word, I got my coat and hat, and slipped into my shoes.

It was funny, well not funny, I suppose, that we'd gotten ourselves together so quickly for the hospital.

When Maggie had been born, there were many problems with her, and Mom had to be hospitalized as well. Before Dr. Kimberly, there were many doctors, who had all been nice to us, apologizing a lot for not finding a diagnosis. For her first two months, Maggie was in NICU, in a small incubator where we couldn't hold her, and we could only touch her with rubber gloves through a hole like a ship portal on the side. There were so many nights that I had stayed in the hospital, then Grandma came to stay with us. That was a nice a treat, because I can remember all the fresh baked cookies and hot soups she made for us while she was here. She took care of me during those months while Mom and Dad shuffled between their jobs, the hospital and home. Maggie did come home finally with a breathing apparatus and a day nurse for the first couple of weeks. It was such a hard time, but I try not to remember the worst of it, and only thinking about after my sister came home, and the small party we had in her room while she slept.

Now, we hopped into Mom's car, to get Maggie through another rough patch. Mom didn't put Maggie in her car seat like usual, and instead laid her in the front seat next to her, , wrapped in her favorite blanket and her favorite animal poking out. Mom had changed her clothes, but I knew that Maggie would be out of them soon. Once we were out of the driveway, Mom flicked on her phone, and a moment later said, "How are you? Yeah. Well, not to add excitement to the weekend, but Maggie's going in. Don't panic, okay, hon. Yes driving now. No, just happened. We'll see Kimberly in an hour. No, take your time. Can't do anything yet. No, lying next to me. No." I saw her look down at Maggie, but I couldn't see what Mom saw. "No. Not moving. Fine. He's fine." She gave me a quick look back in the rearview mirror. "Yeah. See you shortly. Yeah. Love you too."

The car gently stopped at an intersection.

I heard Mom's voice become shaky. "It's okay, Maggie. It's going to be okay." Her hand wiped couple of tears out of her eyes.

Mom was a strong person. She rarely let her emotions get in the way of anything. Sure, when she got mad, everyone knew it, but there was love in her anger. And when she gave you a hug, she smothered you in her affection. And she had a knack for telling you what she really thought without saying much. She was my mom. She was Maggie's mom. She would do anything for either one of us. But right now, I could see how scared she was for the first time in a long time. Maggie has scared her many times, and those are the times I try to forget.

But I still witnessed them.

Outside the bright glare of the sun spilled in on me. It was only a few seconds later that the shadow of the hospital blocked it out. How many times have I been to this place? The answer was too many times to count. Mom pulled into a parking spot nearest to the door. I slung my backpack over my shoulder and hopped out immediately to open the front passenger door. Mom was calm but moved with swift efficiency as she scooped Maggie up and we ran quickly to the ER entrance. Two nurses behind the reception desk recognized us right away and jumped out of their seats.

"Shane, go wait over there until I come and get you," Mom said, pointing to open chairs near the television in the waiting room.

In a matter of moments, the nurses had Maggie on a bed in one of rooms behind the automated double doors. Mom was answering the necessary questions, explaining that Dr. Kimberly was already notified. Maggie was not moving, and it seemed that her breathing was slow. Her Blue Bear was near her, but Maggie was not conscious enough to notice. Through the double doors that remained opened, I could see everyone as they worked, preparing things, then a third nurse came in and started getting an IV ready. Even as the nurses worked on Maggie, Mom held her hand, and was making sure the nurses would not take Blue Bear away.

I sat on the vinyl couch in front of the television set, which had a church program, praising God. There were many people in the church's auditorium-style sanctuary. The crowd of worshippers were swaying back and forth slowly to the tempo of the music and singing along to the same words as the singers on the stage. The reverend was pacing back and forth, talking about his love of God and how he would share it with the congregation. A telephone number popped on the bottom of the screen, encouraging viewers to dial it to donate and help his cause. It's interesting that God now accepts credit cards.

"Shane?"

I turned to look at the voice behind me. A black woman in a crisp nurse's uniform was leaning next to me. She was holding a television remote.

"Renee, good to see you."

She smiled. "Yeah, I thought I wouldn't have to see you so soon."

"I know." Renee was one of the nicer nurses.

"Did you eat this morning?"

I shook my head.

"Well, I have a Coke in the back. Would you like some chips from the vending machine? Is that okay?" She smelled sterile, like the rest of the hospital, but I was pretty used to the smell.

"Thank you," I accepted with a nod.

"Not a problem," she said, standing back up. "Your Dad will be here soon?"

"On his way."

"That man sure works a lot—"

"HEY! NURSE! SHIT! I'm bleedin' heeeere!" A tall man in his fifties walked into the ER entrance. He had a blue towel was wrapped around his arm, soaked in blood. A small mousy older woman was helping to hold up his arm. The man's voice seemed really loud since there was no else in here. "Someone help ME!"

Her eyes rolled back and yelled at him, "Will you quiet it down? And stop your swearing, we got kids in here!" Then to me, she said quietly, "I'll keep this nut job away from you." She winked.

Renee's smile turned serious and her voice was stern. "Let me look at your wound."

Soon, the man went into the back, sobbing, with a male nurse whose name I couldn't remember. Renee came back with my soda and chips a little while later. Renee and I got along well. We didn't talk much but she sort of protected me. She was a good person. In a short time, the waiting room would fill up but she always kept her eye on me, at least until Dad came.

About half an hour later, Dad came and looked frazzled. His eyes were red, which meant that he had been crying. He loved Maggie just as much as the rest of us, but Dad couldn't really hold back his emotions. He saw me, and came up and gave me a big hug.

"You okay?"

"Yeah, Dad."

"Called Aunt Annabelle. She'll be here later."

"Be safe here." He looked around.

"I have Renee," I said. "I can take care of myself."

"I know, buddy." His eyes were red, full of water. He ruffled my hair, and kissed my forehead. Then he disappeared behind the double doors. I tried to keep myself as busy as possible, trying to stay away from anyone that seemed real sick and watched the others that came in to wait.

A little while later I saw Dr. Kimberly walk in through the ER entrance. He was tall and thin, with thick black glasses. He , not caring about who saw him, and yawned as he walked. *Was he disturbed on this fine Sunday morning by a call for one of his sickest patients?* I wondered, then I watched as he too disappeared through the double doors as he checked his watch. I wanted to go back there and be with Mom, Dad and Maggie, but it wasn't fun. There was never anywhere to sit and I just got in the way. And there was no television, or music, we couldn't talk loud, and people were always rushing down the halls. ER was not a fun place to be.

Later that day, Maggie would be admitted and moved to a private room in the pediatrics wing.

After maybe another hour had passed, Mom came out to me. Her eyes were red, much like Dad's had been. I wondered what the news had been from Dr. Kimberly. Maggie had barely been home a year, a year of craziness, when they found Dr. K. He's a specialist in childhood lymphatic disorders, and he claimed to know the problem.

It turned out that he did, and to their surprise, my parents formed this trust in the doctor. Dr. Kimberly had never struck me as a kid-friendly or patient-friendly doctor, even if his degrees on the wall of his large Oak Brook office said he was well-qualified. I thought he treated Maggie like she was his guinea pig for his 'controversial drug trials' and a subject for his articles in medical journals. Today was proof of that; while my sister lay in pain, her doctor casually walks in to see how she's doing, but has no answers.

Still, I stayed in the waiting room like the good brother, and I kept myself busy reading my books, playing some games on my phone, glancing at the same magazines over and over again, watching whatever programs I wanted (no matter who else was sitting there), and even got extra junk snack from the nurses, like Renee, who pitied me. And on and on my morning stretched. In and out, Dad and Mom came to check on me, sitting with me for a while, saying very little about Maggie's status.

After Maggie was settled in her private room, which Dr. Kimberly so humbly arranged, Dad ushered me up three floors to see my sister. I knew Mom wouldn't be able to leave her side.

Then I saw Maggie. Her little body was covered in so many tubes and wires, like an electric squid was hovering over her body. There was a machine to monitor her heart, and one for her breathing, a machine to add liquid to her body, and a machine for this and a machine for that. Under all that I saw my sister, but I did not tear up. I just stood there and silently hoped she would make it, hoped that her little body could fight her sickness and that she would open her eyes soon. Dr. Kimberly that day gave a seemingly sorrowful, "we'll see you tomorrow morning for a progress report," and left through a green door. Mom, Dad and I said little to each other for a while, the machines filling the room with their own melody.

Maggie was a sick little girl, no way around it.

I stood at the end of her bed, looking down at her for a while, studying all the machines, amazed at how everything worked to help a person's body systems. Medicine had fascinated me over the past few years since we've had this experience with Maggie. I don't know how long I stood there, but when I looked up at the clock it was already one o'clock. The nurses' bags of chips and sodas weren't going to hold me over for much longer. Mom came up behind me then, and tugged me on the shoulder of my jacket.

"Grab some lunch?" Her voice was almost normal again.

I shrugged, then nodded. I didn't want to leave, but my stomach growled, and I realized that Mom hadn't eaten anything yet either.

We went to a fast food restaurant, ordered some stupid burgers, which I gobbled down in like two seconds. It was the best burger I'd had in long time.

Mom just pushed her food around. Her eyes were red and watery. She had been quiet, then finally she said, "Maggie is a little more serious this time, Shane. Dr. Kimberly has to do some extra tests in order to make his prognosis concise. She will have to be in for three days tops this time. They are doing some blood work now."

"Are you giving blood again?" I had to ask. Usually, Mom had to go in for a day or so in order to help out Maggie. That took an extra toll on all of us. Her blood type, the birth mother, had the right chromosomes for Dr. Kimberly's treatments.

She smiled thinly. "No, hon, not this time."

I was relieved, chewing on another bite of burger.

"But, you know the drill." Mom took a sip from her diet iced tea. "I, or Dad, will be with you at home. So fear not, young one, you will be getting some rest. We decided to pull you out of school tomorrow—"

"Good," I said, plucking up a fresh French fry.

Mom held out her finger. "Don't get cocky. You need as much rest as we do."

I didn't want to tell her I was having dreams about large insects. I just chewed on.

"I'm sure you're okay with that, right?" She paused. "I love you, Shane." She put a hand on my hand. No one noticed, and I didn't care anyway.

"Love you too," I replied, smiling, feeling the hot sun through the large windows of the place.

We went back to the hospital.

For the rest of day, I didn't think about much, just did my usual thing when I was stuck at the hospital for a long time: I roamed the floors of hospital. Mom and Dad really didn't care where I went, or who I talked to, as long as didn't bother anyone and I checked-in. In a hospital, you can find a clock anywhere, in military time, in fact. So I knew that riding elevators took about two hours, going from floor to floor about one-and-half hours, watching TV for a few hours, and so on. Once in a while, Mom or Dad would roam the halls with me, but it wasn't as much fun because they were slow at it. I would have to go at a snail's pace.

The point I was there for my sister. Yet when I was home snuggling in my bed, I thought of her. Not being at home. The house felt empty.

Maggie did not leave the hospital for several days.

EIGHTEEN

(SHANE)

When I finally went back to school on Tuesday, Maggie was doing a little better. Mrs. Dolan said she was sorry for the situation, but I wasn't exactly sure she was that sincere about it. I grew tired of grown-ups' empty gestures, whereas the kids in my class, my friends, at least wanted to know if I'd eaten the hospital Jell-O, and if I'd thrown up, how many times I ridden the elevator, if I'd seen anything gross, things like that.

The rest of the week had its ups and downs.

I was truly tired of thinking about Maggie, going to school, and thinking about my parents. In these times, I really felt as if I was alone, cast aside by the family, while Mom and Dad tended to Maggie. Don't think I was at all jealous or envious of her condition, but sometimes I just wanted to stand out and be noticed. I thought that I was different, making that clear in my schooling, my attendance (when permitted), my life.

Probably unlike most of the kids in my class, I enjoyed school. Yes, I'd never admit it aloud. It was a good escape. Science was one of my better subjects because I liked how experiments proved outcomes.   History   was   interesting   to   learn   about   ancient civilizations, the rise and fall of empires and World War I and II. Mom's father, who I never knew because he died long before I was born, served in the second war.   In our dining room, we have a mounted German dagger that my grandfather took off a dead soldier. Still, my favorite subject was English because I enjoyed reading different books.   Mrs. Dolan allows me to get more challenging books from the downtown library to read instead of the ones in the school like Hemingway and Steinbeck. Recently, she emailed my parents that I excelled at writing and reading and encouraged them to put me in more advance classes when Middle School starts. Hopefully, they will do that, if not I'll speak up when signing up for classes.

No matter, while I was happy to at school, I would go back home and wondered who would take me to the hospital.

It was probably Wednesday before reality sank in, after catching up on my homework the night before, I realized that Jack hadn't been in school for the past couple of days. I had been eager to retell the story that Old Man Fischer had told Mom and me, while I could still remember as much as possible.

I realized then that Fischer's story lacked something. He had been very detailed at first. But then, as he got closer to the end, especially when he got to the part about Jillian, he seemed to rush through it, like he wanted to finish it that way. He did it on purpose, much like my reading teacher wanting me to read a story. She would talk to us, hyping the book up, getting us excited about it , making us want to read it. Over and over, I tried to think through the details of the story, until I had realized that it had been missing something. Something important. For these couple of days, my thoughts had been preoccupied with my sister, and helping my parents, and all the distractions that come with the abrupt change to our usual daily activities. But now that I was focusing again on his story, trying to remember everything, in order, something was definitely seemed off.

Thursday, Maggie finally came home from the hospital. Yvonne brought over homemade spaghetti so my parents didn't' have to think about cooking. Mom seemed especially emotional about the thoughtful gesture. I was left alone to eat at the table, and my mind returned to Fisher's story, and I wished I could talk to Mom about it, but she'd been too preoccupied all week. I remembered something odd he said at the very end, right before Mom and I left.

"As I returned from the second trip after her death…"

That phrase kept bothering me. I couldn't really focus on anything else. I tried to concentrate on studying for my spelling and math tests on Friday, but it just wasn't happening. I really needed to talk to somebody about it.

Friday came and I was still lost in my thoughts, thinking that why would Fischer go back to same place he vowed not to go back.

As I was getting up to class in the morning from the Before School Program, I thought that I would see Jack there. But his mom dropped him off at school right before the bell rang. So I wanted to catch him before he got into his class. I had been rounding the staircase, going as fast I could, dodging other kids on the way when I smacked into Mike. His groupies were not around, thank goodness for small miracles.

"Hello Shane." He stopped me in middle of the stairs while others went around us. I could smell his stale breath.

"Mike," I replied.

"Have you thought it over?" He stood only an inch taller than me, not much more. The same food stains were in his shirt as last time when he'd cornered Jack and me on the playground. One thing about Mike, he would pick up a conversation with you in the same exact spot where he left it off.

It took me a second to catch up to his meaning, while I looked up to our floor. I thought I saw Jack's back, and I just wanted to go after him.

"Mike, I don't have time for this," I said, inching my way passed him.

He stopped me with a filthy nail-bitten hand. Had he not taken a bath in a while? His hair was greasy against his scalp too. "You'll make time."

I let out a breath. I looked at him and said, "I am not doing this for you, Mike. Let's make that clear. When I find out what's going on, you will know." I saw a girl look at us, noticing my intense face as she passed us. I turned back to Mike. "You will leave Jack and me alone. Right?"

"Big boy calling the shots here," he said, smiling.

I got in his face and replied quietly, "Well, this big boy doesn't have a urine problem like it smells that you do."

I watched his face twist into an angry knot, then there was a group of kids coming up the stairs as the final bell rang to usher us into class.

"You have this weekend, that's it." Then he walked away, saying loudly so the kids who had just passed could hear, "I'll come and get you on Monday. You and your pretty little boyfriend."

I walked up the stairs quickly, feeling my heart race. Upset, I ran into Jack's room to see him getting his stuff together. The teacher wasn't in the room yet.

"Jack," I said fast.

"Oh my God, I wanted to find you!" he said excitedly, but he looked tired.

I interrupted him, "We have to talk. How about recess?"

"Can't. I have a makeup two tests during breaks and lunch, since I was in New York this week. But I can—," he began explaining, a smile coming to his lips.

"No? After school tonight, then," I said. I looked up and saw his teacher the room, noticing me. I smiled at him, then turned quickly back to Jack. "Lots to tell you. See you then."

I rushed off to my class before my teacher shut her door.

Old Man Fischer's story was churning in my head, and my heart was pounding. I also couldn't believe what I said to Mike. That kind of made my heart skip a beat. I had to calm down. For the rest of the day, I felt nervous and antsy, not taking much time on my tests, and I scored poorly on both when I got grades back later.

My mind was completely fixated now on Old Man Fischer. My dreams over the last few nights were flooded of that mysterious cave in middle of the volcano. A magical place filled with enormous crawling insects with large gardens. Was it still there? What I found odd was the way he condensed the part about Jillian's last moments that threw me off. Why would he just breeze over that? It was his wife. Someone even mom knew nothing about. And if Old Man Fischer was so determined not to go back to Central America, why did he go back another time? As I thought, I had information all along from Mrs. A., Yvonne and Momt was Mike that gave me the push though. Touching the bump in pocket, the collar seemed to burn my skin. Knowingly, I had to prove him that something was wrong.

Just the other night, I had heard about more missing dogs were reported near his house. Then I heard the secretary in the office talking about her cat missing since last week. I even saw couple of posters tacked to trees with other animals missing. All of them near Old Man Fischer's.

These stories were was not a coincidence anymore. There was a pattern.

It was around Social Studies as the teacher droned on about the government and laws that it occurred to me -- I had to get in

Fischer's house. What was he hiding in that large house? The evidence I needed was in there. Once I had it, Mike would leave us alone, people would find out about their pets, the missing and mutilated animals that had been found.

Because Jack only couple blocks away from Old Man Fischer's house, he would have to help me. I could get him there. Anxiously I gathered my book bag together and ran downstairs. I had to talk to Jack right away.

Mrs. A. was setting up for the customary Friday movie. It was a movie I know I have seen a thousand times, so I kindly volunteered Jack and I to clean up the toys from the week.

"How sweet of you, Shane. You are such a nice boy." She smiled at us and gave both of us extra snacks.

When Jack finally came down from his last class I explained the arrangement but I couldn't get into why, so at first he was upset that he do some extra work.

I lowered my voice, and said, "Don't you want to hear about Old Man Fischer?"

A few minutes later, we were in the half-lit cafeteria, along the far wall, far from the After School room. The movie began like clockwork and the muffled sounds of it echoed off the dull white walls. Honestly, both Jack and I were pretending to organize books, crayons, games and the other crap that Mrs. A. had lying around. At first, Jack was talking on and on about his trip, how he saw the Statue of Liberty, how he went to a musical, how he went to Central Park, and this and that. I nodded my head here and there, until I heard the cue from Mrs. A nearby who kindly threaten, "Okay guys, and settle down, it's movie time." Once she turned out those lights, the cafeteria room seemed more shadowy than before.

Mrs. A poked her head in to see that we were okay with our project, and I replied for us both that we were fine. I checked the clock, noting that Jack's Dad would be here shortly.

"Okay Jack, here's the deal," I stammered.

He looked at me blankly. Sometimes I wondered what he thought, then I didn't want to go down that road. "What?"

"Invite me over to your house tomorrow," I said.

"Can you come over to my house?" he said.

"No, idiot, tell your Dad that I'm coming over—"

"Great! You have to see my new train set up—"

"No. We're going to the park."

He said nothing. He stopped picking up the toys and looked at me.

"Look Jack, I have to go into Old Man Fischer's house."

Then Jack's eyes got full and large. "No, no way! I am not going into some old crazy guy's house. That's just wrong, we'll get caught, or worse. Uh, uh, not me, not me." He was shaking his head, starting to stand up.

I yanked him down near me. My voice was low. "Hey, the missing animals all over the place now. All disappeared near his house." I leaned closer to him. "I want to know what he's hiding. Something's there. I feel it. I know it's in there." "No, this is going too far." He shook his head.

"Really, Jack. I'll be in and out real quick, honest. You stand outside and be the guard."

"I don't think it's right. And how do you know he won't be there."

"You."

He looked puzzled.

"I remember you saying that you saw Old Man Fischer drive past your house on Saturdays around four o'clock to go to your church."

He looked like he was thinking back. "I did, I guess. But he'll only be gone for a little while. Church is only an hour—"

"Jack, simple in and out." I smiled. "I will get the stuff that we need together tonight. I'll come over about three forty-five, or so, then we'll go the park. But instead of going to the park, we'll hop the fence of the neighbor's yard behind Fischer' house and get in through the back."

Jack shook his head. "No, no. I can't do this. I can't lie to my parents. We'll get caught."

"No we won't. And you're not lying," I reassured him. "You're just not telling the whole truth about where you're actually going."

"No, I can't." He went back to our clean-up duties.

"Jack," I begged.

Jack was upset. Could I tell him then and there about my deal with Mike? That this was for his benefit? I looked at the clock and saw it was almost time for his dad to show up. He kept shaking his head and angrily threw the piles of books together.

a brief moment, I heard only the small hum of the overhead lights echo in my ears. That humming sound was so familiar. Was that like the hum in Old Man Fisher's house? What would he need with large powered lights? Is this what Frank, Yvonne's husband, installed?

I looked at Jack. I needed answers, and I couldn't let go off the certainty that whatever it was had to be in Old Man Fischer's house.

Finally, I said, "Jack. Please?"

He said nothing.

"Fine. I will just have to go by myself," I told him. If I had to, I would go alone.

"Jack, your Dad's here!" Mrs. A. called from the door.

I only looked at Jack.

Jack's father came into the room, wearing holey jeans and a paint-splattered t-shirt covered by a large tan jacket. His father was a large man, built like a pro-wrestler from TV. "Hey J," he said, smiling. "Hey, O'Conner," his baritone voice rattled his greeting to me over the empty cafeteria walls.

I nodded and gave a small wave. I looked back to Jack who was looking at me. I could see he was scared, and didn't want to ask, but that didn't matter. I was already figuring out how to do it myself.

"What's wrong, J?" his dad asked, ruffling his hair.

"Um," Jack said, clearing his throat.

I pretended not to be listening and continued putting away games.

"What's up, buddy?" As his father came closer, I could smell the fresh fall air around him.

"Um, I was wondering if Shane can come over to play," he said.

I looked at him. His father looked at me. "Only if it's okay with your family."

"Mom will be okay with it." I told his father, who smiled to Jack. "It'll be fun."

Jack didn't respond; he just glanced at me and left.

Nervousness overtook my stomach. Was I doing the right thing?

Russell

NINETEEN

(Shane)

Dad's car swung onto Ravine Road, the street just behind Ashland. As the car turned, I saw the top of Old Man Fischer's house.

"I'm glad that you're going to have good time today, especially after this last week," Dad said, lighting up a cigarette and inhaling deeply from the thin white stick. He released a large billow of smoke a moment later. Dad's car was small enough anyway, and the smoke just hovered in the small space. I didn't like it when Dad smoked in the car, it made my then my clothes and skin smell like him.

He always smoked when his stress level was high, and I guess it had been especially high lately. I just didn't like to be near him when he smoked. I think sometimes it seemed like he forgot I was around. He was lost in his own thoughts.

"Yeah," I replied, reluctantly sucking in the smoke.

"What are you guys going to do?" He cranked down the window slightly, letting the cool air into the car.

I dared not say anything about our trip and the contents of the backpack between my legs. "Mr. Richardson has been constructing a large layout for Jack's new HO train set that he just got for his birthday. We're going to run it on the track."

"Sounds like fun," Dad replied. There were dark circles under his eyes like the other times Maggie had been in the hospital. In an instant, his phone rang; He looked down with a frown. "Sorry, Shane."

"No problem." This time I had been happy for a call from his work. Dad was still talking loudly to one of his bakers as our car quickly approached Jack's house. The car hit a bump and my backpack rattled, and I turned to see if Dad had heard. No, he was preoccupied with his conversation of cookies that needed to be fired up for a large group early next week.

Dad ended his call as we pulled up to the curb in front of Jack's house.

We both saw Mr. Richardson and a man talking at the doorway. The man was giving him a flyer, and Jack's father looked down at it.

"That's Bob Voss. He comes every Friday to the bakery and buys five dozen donuts for his team. It is a large load, but he gets it on the train to get downtown. Wonder what's going on?" Dad's voice was low and monotone, then to me he said, "You have fun. Mom will pick you up later. I have to swing by work and check on a couple of things."

"Okay," I said as I flung open the door feeling the cool wind wrap around me. I lugged my heavy backpack over my shoulder.

Dad gave me an odd look. "What the heck is in that?"

I smiled. "You know the basic playing stuff."

"Alright. I love you, Mr. Man." He smiled, and finished his cigarette. He waved at Mr. Richardson through passenger window.

"Love you, too," then I shut the door.

He pulled away from the curb, and Mr. Richardson gave me a nod while he spoke to Mr. Voss.

"Just let me know if you see them," Mr. Voss was looking directly at Jack's father. He seemed quite saddened.

"I'll let you know, if I do, Bob," Mr. Richardson replied.

I had sneaked behind him as he moved slightly to the side to let me by, giving me a smirk.

Behind me, Mr. Voss said, "Barb has been really distressed today, and the police aren't doing much about it. Or any of the other missing animals."

Glancing down at the flyer of two beautiful German Sheppard's, Fifi and Giggles, were standing in a large green yard. The faces were savage with a loving appeal. Then it said that they had been missing since this morning. Mr. Voss was on the ball to get the word out about his dogs. He was just as faithful to them as they had been to him and his wife. Mr. Voss looked at me, his eyes were puffy, blood shot.

"Down in the basement, Shane," Mr. Richardson nodded his head toward the warm house.

I only shook my head.

From behind me, I heard, "Bob, again, sorry about this. I will make sure if I hear anything to call you."

On went Mr. Voss about his dogs. I shrugged off my coat because I was too hot in the house, even though we'd only be here for a few minutes. I shouldered my backpack, feeling the weight press against my back. I passed their living room, the oldness of their house echoed in its building designs, the large baseboards and antique windows stained in different colors. I noticed one section of the wallpaper in the far corner was still partially pulled off revealing older yellow floral wallpaper underneath. There was a sawhorse in the near corner with a power sander covered in dust, undisturbed for some time by the looks of it. Going towards the basement, an open closet filled with hammers, screwdrivers, nails, tape and the typical contents of a large heavy toolbox set in middle of the pile. I hadn't been here about two months, yet everything remained the same. Mr. Richardson was a contractor for a large company, always going around the city at crazy hours of the day, building new homes and offices. Mrs. Richardson was a real estate agent, but since the "economy slowed her down" (as Jack had said recently) she went back to her previous job as an accountant. His parents were always busy, even on the weekends, not spending time on the house, letting items stay where they had been.

Mom called the Richardsons "Do-It-Yourselfers at a snail's pace", and I had to agree with her assessment. The house was cool, big open stairs, wood, but there were so many projects that needed to be completed, it almost needed to be rebuilt completely. They loved to buy these old homes that needed the love and fix them their way. In the process, though, Jack always had rooms that were "in progress", and he just got used to walking around construction sites. It was no wonder why when the school had some city workers fixing the sidewalk last year, that he made no qualms about maneuvering easily around the blocked off path; it was second nature to him.

Near the kitchen, the basement was open completely, since the door still leaned in the corner on the opposite side of the room. I looked down to see the dim light on in the basement, barely illuminating the old dark wooden steps, which gave a low groan as I stepped on each one. When I reached the bottom step, I saw Jack in the far corner, the track board was three or four feet tall and open in the center. Jack standing in the opening in the center of the table just watching the large scaled train zip around the thick tracks.

Jack's basement was old, half the walls had crumbling cement and the other half was still dirt. Mom said that meant that the foundation was likely failing, and wondered if the Richardsons would bother fixing it. Recently, I saw that some thick wood boards were now on the ground and some boxes were set down here. Next to that was Mr. Richardson's work area; covered in more tools, nails, wood pieces, an open dusty red cabinet was open full of screws and nails, all collecting dust. Near the bench on the dirt floor were some large pails of paint, now dirty at the bottom.

When Jack looked up and saw me, a smile lit up his face. "Shane! You have to see this!" he yelled at me over the noise.

I went to him. The set up was simple. The track was anchored on the board, with the power station in the center, a simple O-configuration, and with two houses on the far side then a train station set up on the opposite end. Of course, there was a Y-track with two pieces of track for additional cars that were lined up. The boards hadn't been painted yet, nor had they set-up other figures, cars or animals for the scenery. But the middle of the board was hollowed out so the operator, Jack, could stand in the middle to run the train while it zipped along the tracks.

"Neat," I said. I was beginning to feel nervous. "What did you say to your mom?"

"Look at this red boxcar. It is a replicated version the old Wisconsin Central circa 1939. You can see what the original brakes would have looked like and the custom painting on the sides. I even helped to pick this one out. I love it when it swings around the curves." Jack's face made it apparently that he was completely thrilled with his train set.

"That is nice, Jack. But remember we have to go to the 'park'." I said.

"This train is so cool," he said, then he stopped it, ducked under the boards and looked at me and said, "I thought we were going to Old Man—"

"Shhh," I said, looking up the stairs. "Don't say that. We're going to the park."

Jack's parents allowed him to go to a park near the corner of

Ashland Road, on the corner of Old Man Fischer's block.

"Oh, right. The park." Now his happy smiley face turned sour. "Really, Shane, do you think this is a good idea?"

I bit my top lip. "Jack, you can't back out now."

"I mean, can't we just stay here and play with my cool new train?"

"No," I said, then I smiled, placating him. "I packed some things in this backpack for our adventure."

He smiled at that. "Can I see inside? Please?"

"No, no. Not until we're outside," I replied. Sometimes I had find creative ways to get Jack moving.

"Alright," he groaned.

"Let's get our jackets." I slung the backpack firmly on my back, and followed Jack back up the stairs.

At the top of the stairs, Jack whispered to me, "I'll get my jacket, it's in my room."

"Make it fast."

Jack took the stairs by two, making heavy thudding noises with each hasty stomp then he disappeared. I looked into the living room where Mr. Richardson had returned inside and was watching a football game, drinking a malted beverage, yelling at the screen. His father was as big as one of the players on TV, all the way down to the snug-fitting, long sleeved jersey he wore. Without him noticing me, I grabbed my jacket off the chair.

I quietly made my way into the kitchen where I found Mrs. Richardson, at the counter chopping some vegetables with a sharp knife. Her features were delicate and petite, and the long dark dress she wore tapered at her waist. I could smell her sweet, flowery fragrance even before I entered the kitchen.

I thought somehow I could just watch her chop vegetables all day long. She turned to look at me. She smiled at me. "It's good to see you, Shane." She took a sip from her glass, smiling and then returned to her work. Her face was extraordinary, simple makeup and her long blonde hair was tied back loosely at the nape of her neck. She wore a pair of small square reading glasses that clung onto the tip of her nose, as she lingered over an open cookbook with a glass of red wine. "I'm making a new recipe tonight," she proudly said. "*La bouef au pouivre*: a tasty roast with savory carrots and peppercorn sauce, and rosemary roasted potatoes. Sound delicious?" She looked at me with a small smile as though she was hoping I would approve of her menu choice.

I only nodded, trying uselessly to put on my coat. "Uh huh," was all I could manage in response.

Without turning, she asked, "Are you going to stay for dinner?" Her voice was sweet and elegant.

"Um yes," I croaked. What a time for my voice to crack.

"You are such a good friend to Jack." She took a sip from her glass and smiled at me. "Plus your father has the best brioche this side of the Atlantic."

"I, uh, will," I could only muster. "You see the stuff he, um, brings after done working."

"Can only imagine." Her voice was elegant and soft.

I couldn't seem to pull my eyes away from her, which was not an unpleasant experience, at all. But she was my friend's mother. Still -- her eyes alone --

"Ready," Jack announced behind me.

"Where are you boys going?" Mrs. Richardson said. She continued to chop the vegetables in front of her.

"Mom, I told you earlier, the park," Jack said. He rolled his eyes at me.

Now, I had my coat on and was headed to the back door. I could smell the beef now cooking in the oven, a great aroma of garlic and onion coming from the vent. My mouth began to water and my stomach rumbled. I was suddenly famished.

"Alright then," she said, smiling, then adjusted Jack's zipper on his coat. "Got your phone?"

"Yeah." Jack pulled out a thin black phone from his pocket.

"Good. If you don't come back in an hour I'll be calling you." She smiled. "You don't want me to hunt you boys down."

I smiled sheepishly at her. "No, Mrs. Richardson."

"Good. You boys go have some fun."

At her directive, we were out of the door.

Once outside with the door closed tight behind us, I looked up to the see the billowing dark grey clouds moving fast across the sky, casting a dark, hazy green-grey color to the afternoon light. It seemed that whatever daylight from the sun was being absorbed with a mist. It was far from damp, but it felt like November air when the hints of the first snowflakes came. That day was cold, icy in our neighborhood. The cool air hugged me like an ice blanket, for which

I stopped and put on my gloves and hat from the back pack.   I zipped it up and put it on my back, with a grunt.

I dared not to look back at Jack's house, I kept my eyes turned to the sidewalk, trying to push back my growing nervousness.

I have come this far, time to go all the way.

Russell

TWENTY

(SHANE)

We began our walk in silence. It was fine with me; I didn't want to talk yet. There was no one else on the streets, not even Mr. Voss was handing out flyers any longer. Not even a car passed on the vacant street. Was it the temperature drop had sent everyone inside, or the eerie feeling in the murky, overcast afternoon. It seemed as though Jack and I were the only two people left in the world.

I'd heard of movies like that, ones that my parents wouldn't let me watch: a nuclear blast, taking all people -- adults and kids, all the animals -- everything; or a zombie apocalypse: everyone in hiding and at any moment we might happen upon the mass of vile, mindless, flesh-eating creatures. That thought raised the hairs on the back of my neck and had me quickening my pace. The stillness of the streets of our neighborhood was haunting, the darkness slowly seeping from the shadows around us.

I could hear Jack's uneven breaths. I could tell he was nervous. So was I. I had to stop my legs from trembling.

We crossed the street, walking past the small park on the corner at the end of his street. Jack's head tilted towards it then went straight. The leaves had already blanketed the ground like a sea of brown curls flooding park, slow moving waves on the tiniest of breezes pushing them along.

Ahead of us, a few houses displayed Halloween decorations: playful ghosts with smiling faces, dancing witches, rubber skeletons dangling from a porch cocooned in cobwebs, large skulls and paper lanterns were stuck on the large bay window of the next, nicely carved pumpkins sitting on steps covered in artificial cobwebs at the following house. It was hard to believe Halloween was less than a week away.

Old Man Fischer's rooftop came into view behind those houses. An involuntary shiver overtook my body and I pulled my jacket tighter around me as I looked over to Jack, now keeping pace with me.

"Are you cold?" I asked him. We were about five houses away from our destination. I was trying to distract myself from the invading sense of foreboding as we drew closer to the enigmatic house of the equally enigmatic Doctor Fisher.

He only shook his head in response as his eyes glanced up at the roofline of Fisher's house. "I'm not sure about this Shane."

I stopped and looked at him. "Jack. We have now less than an hour. I'll be in and out in no time." Again, I found myself warring with the decision to tell him about my motivation for going through with this: my deal with Mike to leave Jack alone if I could get to bottom of these mysterious occurrences.

Jack's eyes were a solid black, and glazed from the chill of the air. "In and out," he muttered as he nodded in acquiesce, repressing shiver. I couldn't be sure if it was from the cold or from nerves at what we were about to do.

We started to walk again, our pace changing unconsciously as we got closer. I think we were both trying not to look like we were up to something, trying to keep our countenance nonchalant, just two friends walking through the neighborhood. We could have been on our way anywhere. No reason to draw attention to ourselves. Not that anyone else was out here in this menacing haze.

In the dim light of early evening, Old Man Fischer's house was creepier than it had been in the dark just a few days ago when I'd been here last. From this perspective, it became more obvious that the roof was badly in need of repair, as shingles were falling off and gutters were dangling from the corners, spilling over with dead leaves and other debris. I could see enormous cracks between the bricks of the chimney, white smoke slowly seeping out. Even from our distance a few houses away and dozens of feet below, the slate tiles of the siding were obviously cracked and falling off the back of the house. A section of the back looked as though there was no siding at all, only the dark black of the substructure underneath. Paint from the trim and windows was peeling off in strips like banana peels, hanging and flapping lightly in the wind.

"Jack, here. Let's go this way," I said, looking toward the brick house. The red brick house before us was just behind the Fisher house, and it appeared dark and silent. Beyond the backyard, we could see the very tall, dark grey wood slats of the fence that divided the two yards. Spikes of brown branches and dead leaves poked over the top.

Without a word, he looked around, just as I had then we walked quickly across the yard toward the back yard and nearer to the fence. Jack was only steps behind me, but I could hear him breathe heavily; it was quick and loose, his face betraying his emotions. His eyes were sunken back now and his cheeks were tight, no indication of eagerness or delight in the thrill of our adventure right now. But he had wanted to come with me. Or did he feel the need to come? I couldn't know for sure.

As I crouched against the fence, I was glad I was not alone.

"Why are we not going through the front door?" Jack asked.

"What do you think the neighbors would say if they saw two young boys on the old man's doorstep trying to get in?" I replied, feeling my own jitters sneak up on me.

"Yeah, gotcha." He looked at me with unease.

"We have to get over this somehow." I touched the grey wood, feeling its cold refusal through my gloves. "You go that way, and I'll check this way. There has to be an easy way in."

Probably when Old Man Fischer created the gardens, he made the fencing to protect his landscape. Even the neglect of the front probably was in the back and I didn't know what shrubbery or trees held stead-fast to the rotting fence. Like at my grandmother's house, her bushes grew into the steel fence at the end of her property. God only knows what was behind the grey line.

Jack scooted to the left and I went to the right. I looked all around me, at the neighbor's house, into the dark sky above, then began feeling along the fence. It was sturdy, very strong. Unlike the rooftop, there were signs of some replacement pieces, no holes, no cracks, and no way to get in. It seemed like this the wall between us and his house. Why such a tall fence? Maybe the overgrown was a camouflage for something else. Maybe he just let the backyard just go to concentrate on other things. Obviously if he had enough money to donate to a college, then I was sure that he could easily hire someone to maintain the yard.

227

"Hey, found a way in," Jack said behind me.

I followed him around the corner of the yard, near the tool shed of neighbor's yard and a garage of the next door neighbor. As we entered the narrow space between the garage and fence, I noticed the sides of the tool shed were worn from the middle down, and the adjacent garage paneling was also worn.

"Here," Jack said. A small smile came to his lips as he pushed on a piece of the wooden fence then several slates of the fence moved like a door. It was no more than four feet tall, and one side of the opening looked newer, like it had been replaced more recently.

I squatted down, looking through the opening into secluded yard, which seemed darker somehow. I looked up at Jack. "Great! Let's go." I crept through and turned to hold it open with one arm so Jack could sneak in as well.

We stood, a silence between us, as we both stared up at Fischer's house. It was nestled in a sea of overgrown weeds, plants and trees, except for a narrow, worn path from our hidden entrance leading in the direction of the house. There was no lawn, no sign of mowing; it was wild, absolutely overgrown. We began to move slowly along the path, a mix of crushed, icy mud. It was obvious that despite the deserted appearance of the rest of the yard that this path was well-used. Inside this tall grey fence, it felt as if we'd entered some other world, shielded from the life outside from which no noises entered. It was a short walk passed the dense dead forest of weeds and grasses to the back of the decaying house. Near the mid-point in the yard, we came to a large tree, turning grey and its branches reached toward the heavens as if reaching for a last grasp at survival in its quagmire. Old man Fischer had stopped using his gardeners years ago, leaving the plants to become overtake the space. This forgotten garden merged with the fence ensuring that no one could see over, and I was sure the neighbor's windows couldn't be seen from the house. That meant that the neighbors couldn't see anything of significance on this side of the fence either.

So much trouble must have come from letting the yard go like this. Surely, neighbors must have reported him or something? Or, maybe the neighbors thought he was too feeble to take care of his land anymore and had taken pity on the old man. Maybe sympathy for him had allowed this to go on. The smell of rotting leaves and decayed earth filled the air around us as the wind picked up. The intensity of the stench seemed too great for the size of the space we were in.

I stepped onto the back steps, watching the back door for any signs of life, noting that the house was fairly dark from this view, Jack pointed to something. "Look."

"What do you mean?" Jack was standing on the bottom step. He looked scared.

The path we had followed to the house didn't stop at the steps we were on now. Taking two more steps up the porch, we could see over an overgrown bush, to where the path terminated. There was a black door where the trail stopped. It appeared to be some kind of old cellar door, leading under the house. "There," I declared.

Jack stood next to me, indecisive. "I don't know about this."

I looked blankly at him. I was arrested by the force of my curiosity. *What are you hiding Old Man Fischer?*

At the top step, right at the door, I asked, "What time is it?"

"Uh, four o'clock."

"He's at church, right?"

Jack only nodded.

I stopped at the door, shrugging off my backpack. I opened it to pull out two flashlights, and handed one to Jack. Then I pulled out two hammers, and gave one to Jack. He only looked at them, as I returned the backpack to my shoulders.

"I'll go in real quick." I said overconfidently, masking my nervousness. "You stand here and let me know when he comes."

"Stand here? By the creeping doors? In the dark?" Jack's eyes were wide and glossy as they surveyed the yard. "I'll come with you."

"Alright, this is what we will do," I said, in a low whisper. "When we go in, I will take the top floor and you go through the bottom. Use the flashlight only if you need to. I don't want the neighbors to see us. Now the hammer is for anything else, protection."

Suddenly, the neighbor's garage door opened slowly.

We both jerked to life and crouched near the stairs, breathing heavily as we listened to the car backed out and down their driveway. A porch light turned on, dusting the tops of the weeds with light, as we shrank further into the shadows. I heard a loud a radio, then two people talking over the volume. Then a moment later, the car continued out of the driveway, into the street and then sped away.

Once I no longer heard the car, I continued to explain our game plan to Jack. "Then—"

"I am scared. I can't do it." Jack , looking as scared as I was becoming.

"Don't worry." I had to lie. I needed to get in there. "Jack, in and out."

"How do you know the door isn't locked?"

"He doesn't lock it."

"How do you know?"

I shrugged my shoulders. I glimpsed through the stained window into the darken kitchen and saw very little features of the kitchen.

Now Jack looked at me with large, deer-in-headlight eyes.

"We need to hurry, Jack. This will go twice as fast if you go in with me and go through the first floor while I search upstairs, OK?" I said. I turned and put my hand on the doorknob. "No talking unless we find something."

The door clicked open, and I pushed the door open.

I took my hat and gloves off, unzipping my coat enough to shove them inside. A blast of warm air hit me in the face as I pushed the door open further. It was unusually humid, and hot. The elderly man had an obsession for the heat on a cool day.

Instantly, the floor seemed to move away from us, the tile white floor was showing our shadows. I put my finger to my mouth to 'shush' Jack who was looking at the floor and I heard him gulp.

We stepped fully inside the kitchen, adjusting to the dim light of the day.

Jack stood right next to me, breathing hard.

"There're so many bugs," Jack moaned.

"Shh, yeah. Roaches. Don't step on them, if you can," I instructed. "Keep your voice down."

I could make out the old look of this kitchen with its white yellowish cabinets, an older looking refrigerator and stove. The stove's burners seemed to be moving. I flicked on my flashlight toward an old pot and something went scurrying away from the beam of light.

"Shh, go quietly," I whispered. The counters were lined with dirty dishes and glasses that were caked with green mold and crusty food. A sour smell that I was familiar with from Dad's bakery when one of the baker's hadn't cleaned out a cooler in a timely fashion filled my nose. I tried to not breathe too deeply and took breaths through my mouth, not that it helped much.

A small breakfast table set against one wall was cluttered with stacks of newspapers and magazines laid carelessly over each other. Next to it was what I suspected was the basement door. That's when I noticed that odd humming sound again, as it filled my ears, slightly louder than I'd heard it during my previous visits here. It seemed to come from the basement. I was more than a little curious about that sound, but wanted to check upstairs first. I could only hope we'd have enough time to investigate the basement, too.

I nudged Jack forward, through the kitchen and on into the hallway. He took one quick look back at me and nodded, then I watched him as he resumed his inspection further down the hall.

Now that I was on this end of the kitchen I could get a better look at the basement door. It was partially open, and there was a small light on and a faint, red glow emanated from something down below. I craned my neck to see the old stairs leading down.

I paused where I stood for only a moment. I felt a pull to the odd glow in the basement, but my goal had been to get a look upstairs first, so I needed to stick to the plan.

I found a narrow staircase in the corner leading upstairs that must have been the servant's staircase. My mom had explained to me that the large, old mansion homes in our town, like Old Man Fisher's, had been built by well-to-do families of the day and that they often employed servants. It was customary that they not be seen by guests during their work duties, so separate staircases were built for the workers to move about the large houses.

At the bottom of these secluded, utility stairs, it was dark, but a bluish light shone at the top. The darkness shrouded me as I forced my legs to climb up, on step at a time. Slowly, I turned back to look down at the kitchen in time to see the roaches began to swarm out from their hiding places and race the floor. I certainly had no desire to linger there any longer, so I resumed my ascent. Even in this dim light, I could see the hanging cobwebs from in the corners and the deep cracks in the plaster walls. Heavy dust was in the air, tickling my nose and making me want to sneeze. But I dared not, so I held my breath hoped the urge would pass.

Once at the top, the hallway was dimly lit from the single blue light covered in flowered wallpaper, ripping at certain corners and peeling from the seams. The tall, dark wood baseboards and large wood doors made the shadows seem to leap out at me. Oh, how I wanted to turn on my flashlight. But I remained calm long enough to let my eyes adjust to the low, grey light coming from the small dirt-laden window covered with a curtain of cobwebs. I crept ahead, slowly and carefully. A couple of feet into the hallway, I noticed sconces on the wall were lined in webs, some with cracked glass bulbs jutting jaggedly from the sockets. *Old man Fisher must not come up here, otherwise why would he leave the lights like this?* My stomach was full knots, my legs trembling, as I made my way through the humid second story. Outside, the wind played a soft, dark tune that made my legs tremble.

Maybe, it was the murky atmosphere or my fears playing tricks on me. The long hallway seemed almost endless with closed doors. From the outside, the immensity of the house could not be really seen. Here, I could now understand the size of Fischer's house. Mom told me once that old Victorian houses like these were gigantic spaces: A reason why she didn't care for them because she would have to fill each room with furniture. I wondered what possibly be filled inside these room. I imagined that they were filled with his research and books from yesteryear. Much like the study, I could only bet that his obsession in saving everything filled each of these rooms. My curiosity was at its highest and I so longed to peek inside. Looking above, a small window was right above the doorframe. If I had enough time, I would have figured out a way to get up there and try to look through the glass.

Time was against me.

I ambled forward as I reached the first closed door.

I took a slow, deep breath and turned the jeweled knob. It was locked. There was no time for a thorough search, I had to search to find something, anything. Old Man Fischer had these doors locked for a reason. He would close off his memories only to open when he decided it was the right time. Much like why he told us his story. When I reached the next door, which was locked, the past was tightly locked away behind the thick dark stained doors. Ahead of me, the upstairs seemed to be large than it seemed. Passing already two rooms, there were at least three more on either side.

Turning back, the staircase was so far away. My ears attempted to tune into any slightest noise. As I went forward again, the sweaty palms barely held onto the flashlight. It was unusually warm in the house, like the other night.

Checking the locked doors as I went, Old Man Fischer was leading me to what he wanted to me see. At the end of the hallway, in the darkness, from an open door, there was a dim yellowish light.

As I crept forward in the darkness, daring not to turn on my flashlight, turning to see behind me, shadows seemed to close in around me. Beads of sweat clung to my forehead, my heart racing as I stepped forward softly, surprised to not hear any squeaks in the floorboards. I forced myself to make my breathing slow and steady. I wondered what Jack was doing, if he had even managed to move from his spot in the hallway. Once I reached the central staircase, I hugged the wall and tried to lean over the banister to look down into a dark, empty foyer. A large dusty chandelier with huge crystals covered in webs hung from the ceiling down passed the second floor landing. I listened for any movement from Jack. What was taking him so long?

A small knock could be heard.

I froze in my place, barely breathing. There was no other sound in the house, not even the mysterious hum that had always carried up here. Cautiously I leaned over the banister, looking into the shadowy entrance and seeing the doorway. I waited for a few seconds, making my heart beat slow down. Those seconds dragged out as I strained to hear anything. It wasn't below. It had to come from the open room.

I needed to go in there.

I paused for a moment; it was a moment we did not have.

Slowly I walked into the deserted room. A hospital bed sat empty on the left. Next to it: old medical equipment, an IV stand, a computer monitor. *Just like he had described.* I walked further into the room and noticed a closet, the door partly opened, was full of old women's clothes, now dusty and full of cobwebs. On a dresser was a jewelry box filled with once beautiful necklaces, now dulled with time and dust . Past the IV hookup stand, at the far end of the room, was an entire wall of windows. I crossed the dark and tarnished room to the bank of wavy glass, obscured by yellow curtains. Closer I got to the window; I could see the street below, and the expansive, forgotten garden. Dreary grey clouds were darker in the sky.

This was Jillian's room. *Why did he preserve Jillian's room? Why didn't he throw anything out? It's like a dusty museum.*

I looked down into the gardens below me to the wasted vision

Fisher had created for Jillian: flowers that would have bloomed in the right season, trees perfectly trimmed, and lawn sculpted around the intricate brick borders. Here, I could see what passersby could not spot from their cordoned-off vantage point this was Old Man Fischer's pledge to his wife. She would wake up, out of her coma, to his spectacular tribute to his first love.

A chill went down my spine and I began to shake uncontrollably.

I looked out to the empty street, to see the rooftops of the houses and buildings of our town, and realized that he did truly love her.

I turned from the windows, letting my eyes adjust to the darkness of the abandoned room, and noticed something concealed in shadows on the dresser.

As I moved closer I realized they were jars, filled with yellow liquid and something else inside. About two dozen glass jars contained something black suspended in the liquid. I walked closer, probably too slowly, trying to make sense of what I was seeing. Craning my neck and slightly bending over, I swore that they were black eggs with long spiral strings floating around it. The jars in front looked as if they had been there for a while, with layer of dust settled over the tops, making them look even more murky. Then, on the left side near the window, there seemed to be newer jar. It was a large black thing inside. Despite my sense of dread, my curiosity took over and I had to take a closer look.

Out of the corner of my eye, I saw a glimmer of movement and I turned.

Old Man Fischer hit me in the head with large piece of wood. I fell hard, backward to the floor.

My eyes were swirling in my head, severe pain surged through me. I was really not with it, couldn't quite focus my eyes, but I knew he was still there because I had heard him curse under his breath. I could just make out the shadow of his presence, noticing as I was fighting the ringing in my ears and the violent whirl of pain and dizziness in my head that he stood straight, his back strong, his posture perfect, unlike when we had seen him before.

"What are doing in my house, Young Shane?" he growled, his voice was stronger, deeper than I'd ever heard it.

Old Man Fischer didn't wait for my response, and stooped down and grabbed my ankle and pulled me out of the room by my leg. I looked back up to the jars, the one that had caught my attention before I was nearly knocked out. Did it move in that liquid. whatever was in there? Or was it my imagination and the swirling feeling in my own head? My head was starting to get my thinking back, but there was a sharp pain in the back of my neck. I had tasted some blood in the back of my mouth.

"Why are you snooping in my house?" he demanded.

His strong grip on my ankle and the quickness of his movements as my body slid across the dirty floor. I tried to grab the banister before we went down the stairs, but spinning head made my movements too jerky, delayed, my grip too weak.

"I shouldn't have known better than to talk to you and your dear mother," he said. He took the stairs quickly. The stench of his body odor filled into my nose, making me gag as he began to drag me down. My head back hit the hard steps, banging my head back and forth against the hardwood causing flashes of light in my brain with each painful impact. I began to kick at him, trying to get him to release my ankle and stop our abusive descent when he rapt me hard on my knee with the piece of wood making my leg go instantly numb then he wrapped a very strong arm around both ankles and resumed dragging me down the steps.

"You can't struggle against me," he growled in the dim light. His grip was like a vise around my lower legs.

"You were faking that Old Man thing," I grunted. We reached the bottom of the stairs then and I began to scream, though it came out sounding more like a gargled whimper.

Fischer reached down, grabbed me by the shoulders of my coat and suddenly slung me over his shoulder. My head was hurrying to catch up to the ease with which he lifted me up when he dropped me back to the floor of the foyer like a wrestler on TV. I heard a loud crack sound from my shoulder and instant white-hot pain ripped through me. I couldn't hold back the scream that burst from my mouth.

"You can try to scream," he leaned over me, smiling. His eyes were large, and the web of wrinkles expanding around them tightened as he glared at me. "But it will not help you. The police will know that you came to break into my house to steal all my precious valuables."

"No! Not true," I whispered back, my lungs fighting for air through the sharp pains in my torso.

His voice changed suddenly to that feeble, slow tempo I had come to recognize as Mr. Fisher's voice, "Officer, I believed this young man was an innocent child, wouldn't do any crime. But alas, I found him poking around my house attempting to abscond with my dead wife's jewelry." In the dim light, the darkness of his eyes overtook the white as though they were owl eyes, a predator's eyes, probing and scanning the shadows. Out of his pocket, he pulled out a thick diamond necklace letting it dangle over my face for a moment. Then his accent became strong again, his voice heavy and faraway sounding, and his breath was thick and musty, "Such a boy needs to be taught a lesson."

He stood abruptly and turned, pulling at my legs and dragged me along the floor again. In my peripheral vision, I saw roaches, and other things, bugs maybe, creeping along the baseboards, crawling in and out of the cracks of the plaster, and running in every direction from us into the shadows.

"Where's Jack?" I grunted, staring at the mass of spider webs in the corners of the ceiling.

"Don't worry, he's safe."

Old Man Fischer seemed taller now; his hardened face and wrinkly skin glowed in the dusk of the hallway. He stopped and looked down at me, smiling. He asked lowly, "Why did you come here, Mr. O'Conner? I would think my story had scared you and your mother off."

"I wanted, to uh," catching my breath, gathering my thoughts, grasping for a suitable excuse. "To hear the ending, the *real ending*, of your story," I panted back, struggling subtly to move my feet as he tightened his grip.

He chirped out a quick laugh. "You are a curious young man, aren't you? Why do you say that 'real ending'?"

We had paused in the hallway, near the doorway of into the study, I could see the dusty books, more insects scurrying about the darkened room. I thought back to his story, all my mounting questions, my growing suspicions. I wouldn't get an opportunity to ask many questions of this puzzling old man, so my only reply was in earnest. I looked straight in his haunted, astute gaze, and whispered, "Why did you go back, Dr. Fischer?"

He responded slowly, his voice heavy, a threat in his tone lay just under the surface, "You ask too many questions, Mr. O'Conner. But if you want answers. I'll give them to you." A slow smirk curved across his lips. He stood taller, letting out a deep breath. He yanked me hard, quickly down the hallway into the kitchen that was teeming with roaches that all quickly disappeared into the dark corners.

I suddenly didn't want to know where this was going. I tried to grab onto a nearby chair, but I couldn't reach it in time. My fingertips raking at anything to stop him from dragging me any further, but the ache in my right shoulder had caught fire, and my left arm was not my strongest.

In a quick move, he leaned over and grabbed my arm forceful and pulled me across the floor.

"So many things you do not know, so many things you don't understand yet" he grumbled as we headed toward the basement, now more brightly lit. Where was Jack? Had he been down there the whole time? Old Man Fisher interrupted my thought of our situation. "You have your whole life to be inquisitive, to discover, yet why do insist on understanding me? Like a chimpanzee? Am I one of your species to be studied under your young feeble, adolescent brain? What must I do in order for to support your evidence? While many fools would find it adorable, this juvenile game is rather hilarious and insulting. Thus, I propose to you, Young Shane, if I am your intended subject, then are you willing to be part of the next stage of *my own study*?"

Suddenly, we went down the stairs. My legs thumped crazily against the wooden stairs to make the pain on my right shoulder throb, but I dared not to scream or cry. I try to latch onto to the railing, but I could barely touch it.

At that moment, about half down the stairs, I saw Jack strapped to a chair, an empty one next to him. He face was red, tearing up as he saw me. There were several pieces of duct tape over his mouth. He was sitting on a platform built several inches above the floor. The floor was different here, it seemed to be moving. Fischer was moving so fast though. The temperature was hotter down here, more humid, too, and my clothes were quickly fusing to my body.

Swiftly, Fischer lifted me and placed me on the chair. My head, still spinning from the blows I had taken and my sudden up-righting, before I knew it Fisher had a rope tied around me restraining me tightly to the straight-back chair..

"Ah, that should hold you," he said. A deep breath released from his mouth and a raw raspy smell wash over me. I choked.

On the platform, I was at his shoulder level as he stood straight in front of me.

This was not any ordinary basement. To the left, there was a laboratory set up, with a table just beyond the staircase and some tubes with strange colored water in them, a bright light above, and a computer on the far corner. Behind the table, in the red shadows there were fifteen aquariums, five across and three down, against the dark brick walls, moldy and contained different insects moving about in there, some standing in corners, large legs and webs were only visible in others. Beyond the wall of tanks bathed in red light, I could tell it was another room with more aquariums and I thought I detected small increments of movements from the dark creatures inside.

"Welcome to my lab," he announced proudly, smiling when he noticed where my gaze had fallen. He put his hands behind his back, and looked at us, almost proudly, which made me more nervous. I could not see well behind him, he was standing too close for me to see past him. "You and your friend are the first ever to be privileged to be down here. Isn't it just grand?"

I finally answered, "Is this what you are hiding? This lab for your experiments?"

He guffawed. To the right of us, beyond large white containers labeled "TOXIC", the basement window with a nest of webs showed the dark outside. Was it already that late? . Mrs. Richardson should be calling her son soon. I looked over to Jack next to me, but his eyes were trained on Old Man Fischer.

"No, my young friend, you have it all wrong. My lab is not about experimenting. My life's work is in research, finding the cause to an effect. That has always been my passion." I looked over to Jack. His gaze was fixed on Old Man Fisher's left pant leg. When I turned to see what held his attention I saw the focus of his disgust: a very large, very ugly beetle, crawling up the old man's pant leg. I could see the hook-like feet as they clung to the fabric, moving quickly enough to cause an involuntary shudder to run through me. I glanced back at Jack who seemed to be withdrawing further into his chair as though he was trying to get further away from me. Underneath him was actual dirt, mulch which was alive with a floor of moving insects of all kids, slithering and crawling over each other.

Noticing he'd been robbed of our attention, he scanned the area we had focused on. He bent over to scoop up the vile-looking creature, and stated, "This is the *dynastes titus*, the Hercules's beetle, as it is known in Costa Rica. It is the largest species of beetle known to mankind. It is both frightfully disturbing to look at with its large horn, and deceitfully ominous as it prowls silently up my leg. And yet, to humans, it is utterly harmless and misunderstood. Its habitats are on trees throughout the rainforest, crawling about, finding food, seeking shelter from the rain. Here, he is only part of the eco-system that I've created here, my basement floor. He serves a greater purpose." Gently, he placed the insect onto the ground, and we all watched as it dug into the many churning layers beneath.

Turning from Jack, I asked, "Dr. Fischer, why are you letting me see your laboratory?"

The smirk he wore turned into a proud grin. Slowly, he turned to walk toward the shadows at the back of the lab. There was a wall of red light on one side, and the familiar low-resonance hum emanated from somewhere within. "You are quite observant, Young Shane O'Conner."

Because there was a bright light above us, shining almost directly in our faces, our view of where Old Man Fischer stood was partially obstructed. I couldn't tell exactly what was going on behind him, there was only enough visibility to make out his tall slender shape. I could see the old furnace tucked under the stairs as if it had been purposely moved.

"Why do you have all this?" I asked. My voice was becoming shaky with nervousness. .

Beside me, Jack whimpered softly, water dripping from his chin. *It's okay Jack, we'll get out of this.* I thought.

I hope.

"I did not create this lab to carry on studies of all species," Fischer said lowly, seemingly distracted.

"What was it for then?" I insisted.

"No," he ignored me, "the work that cannot be done here for that purpose. It's a new experiment." He turned towards the glass aquariums near the staircase.

"What is your experiment then?"

Next to me, Jack glared at me with large bulging eyes.

Shaking his head, one step going backward, he rambled, "That has all been covered already. No, I created this for one purpose and one purpose alone." Old Man Fischer said in a low voice. He held up his hand and turned away from us and pointed at the basement stairs. "No gentlemen, this is not university property anymore."

At that point, I was distracted by what was behind Fischer.

In the deep shadows, , I began to recognize the outline of what looked like a large steel cage with thick black bars, like that in a zoo, perhaps for a large animal, not agile enough to fit between the bars, but strong enough to require a steel to hold it. Even from here, I could see Frank's wiring and thick circuits jetting from out of the ground. As Old Man Fischer turned back towards us, I thought I caught the briefest glimpse of something shift inside the cage, something large.

Fisher came near me, and his face was serious. "No, all this is to study Jillian's murderer."

I heard a--

Click! Click! --

sound.

Could this be the same sound that my Mom heard so many years ago? Could this have been the sound that Mike's brother heard coming from the basement? There was more shifting in darkness, as if it dared not to get near the red light.

The air was so thick down here, my chest was on fire. Frantically, I was figuring how we could manage to get out of this situation, out this basement, away from this sneering old man and his cold, penetrating glare.

I watched him, then looked down to the floor. There was something near his foot that caught my eye: a ripped black and white collar on the living carpet under our feet. I squinted at it, trying to get a clearer look at the engraved tag on the front of it: GIGGLES.

He continued to drone on, absorbed in his own story, oblivious to what I had just discovered.

"As Jillian's unconscious body and I reached back to the States," he stated clearly, slowly strolling towards us, much as the same tone of a teacher, the same one he spoke to me and Mom. We were his students, strapped in chairs against our wills to listen, to hear the ending of his true story.

Old Man Fischer began: "I knew life had changed once again..."

And my suspicions had been confirmed: Old Man Fisher most

definitely knew something about Mike's brother's missing dog, and no telling how much more he was hiding. But I was beginning to get an idea.

Russell

TWENTY-ONE

(DR. FISCHER)

My darling Jillian remained in her catatonic state, oblivious to the cramped private room, to the huge equipment keeping her alive, to the constant wave of presumed medical professionals examining her body, and even oblivious to me. The aspirations for our future dwindled as she slipped further into her deeper unconscious state. I resided at the hospital for the first days, and only there, looking at our luggage in the corner. I had no longer any domicile, or home, if you will, we had given that all up. Everything was sold, gone. Anything that I truly treasured were in those battered suitcases.

My life, my Jillian, you see, was my only home.

The disheartened, audacious doctor ran many tests his disposal to bring forth a diagnosis of her unknown paralysis. I had not been easily satisfied, and asked for specialists and neurologists, fields that were, at the time, just entering the gateway of discovery. Unlike now, so much could have been implemented for treatment and an improved prognosis. Needless to say, I had requested different doctors for my wife, and soon realized that their empathetic attempts to discover the true nature of her illness resulted in the same outcome. I had grown impatient, frustrated by their lack of knowledge. Somehow I realized that I had just as much chance of finding the source of her disease, but had it not been for my reluctance to leave her side, which pained me greatly. I watched the nurses tend to her needs as I crawled into my chair. They would not speak to me nor would I engage them in conversation, there was no need for it.

How I fought the nagging urge to contact Don and Reginald during those dark months, but the guilt of leaving her side tore deeply insides. Seeing her undisturbed body, eyes closed, fed through a tube, there was no hope in me; my ambition to continue lie in that bed with her. I lived at the hospital that first month, hardly leaving her room, living out of my suitcase from the trip. I had not bothered with my hygiene or appearance, and it became apparent from the looks of the staff and visitors at the hospital that it had not gone unnoticed. I didn't have the energy to care. My focus was completely absorbed by Jillian.

About three weeks or so after our return, still no visitors came to check on us, even to check on Jillian. For long time, I debated calling her mother, but was too ashamed do so.

On an early Saturday afternoon, a month after our arrival, Dr. Kempler came to pay us a visit. His large body filled the small room to an uncomfortable degree. I was shocked and angry at his gall in showing his face there. Immediately, I stood up ready to eject him from the room through the window.

"How are you holding up, Hans?" He reached out with his large hand for a handshake, but I remained still. "I was going to stop by sooner , but I knew you had," taking a breath, "had issues to contend with."

I said nothing, trying to remain calm. I could feel my anger building from stomach. This was Dr. Kempler's fault, for demanding we go to that damnable place.

Clearing his throat as though sensing my hostility, he took one small step back, eyes on me warily, and he said, "Hans, I do not know where to begin—"

"You forced us to go," I stated, the strain in my voice evident, even as my accent came out more pronounced than it had in years.

"What do you mean, Hans? Can you elaborate?" Dr. Kempler questioned, folding his large arms over his barrel chest.

"You told us that we did not have a choice to go to Mount Arenal." My voice grew louder.

"I did not force anyone to do anything, you made the choice," he replied simply.

"No, you threatened to pull our team out of the original assignment, if we didn't meet your demands."

"You are mistaken, Hans," Dr. Kempler stood straighter and puffed his chest out, attempting to make himself look larger, trying to intimidate me into backing down from my mounting accusations. "I just wanted to protect and enhance the project. I did not know that you agreed to go to Mount Arenal. On my end, I already had another team ready to go."

Anger swept through me instantly. How dare Dr. Kempler attempt to place the blame on me! He was an ignorant bastard!

"What team are you speaking of? Then why didn't you tell me that over the phone?" My heart was racing.

"I didn't want." He gave heavy sigh. "I didn't want to bruise your ego, Hans. While you are a fine researcher, your mood swings can certainly be unpredictable." He made his way to the door. "Listen, I personally spoke with the chancellor of the university about your current situation. The university will take care all of Jillian's hospital stay, and any of her future medical concerns. And it will pay for a hotel or apartment for you, so you can live—"

"If I stay quiet," I said. I looked at Jillian.

Dr. Kempler understood how much it meant for me to bring Jillian on the project. Now, his project was destroyed and his name could be destroyed. Essentially, bureaucratic policies of the school protected him once more. He again was controlling my fate.

"Hans, we only want wants best for your wife." He paused, glancing at her. Then he looked at me. "Hans, you need to get some rest, take a shower, take some time for yourself."

I could only stared down at Jillian, perhaps taking in all that he was saying.

"Is there anything else that I can get for you, anything else the university can do?" His voice was monotone, mechanical. The effect was quite unsympathetic.

"Yes, there is," I said now looking up at him.

"What would it be, Hans? Really, anything you want." Dr. Kempler shifted slightly in his stance. The heavy jowls of his lower face jiggled with the movement.

"Leave us alone," I said forcefully.

"What?" He looked stunned.

"I said, get the hell out of here," I said louder, and took a deliberate step closer to him.

Dr. Kempler took a couple of hasty steps backward, getting to the door, and said, "You will see that I did what was the best. I am truly sorry."

"Get the hell out! Now!" My hands were tight fists at my sides in an attempt to keep my rage from flow up into my hands and giving them a life of their own. They ached for it, wanted it badly. I could feel the adrenaline pulsing through my veins, heating my neck and face as my heart hammered a war beat.

He fumbled for the latch, and left us.

That was the last time I would ever see Dr. Kempler. Jillian would no longer need to be plagued by his presence.

Yet there she laid --on her bed, undisturbed -- without a sound.

By end of the weekend, I had taken the offer of an apartment. It was an efficiency studio near the hospital meant for the medical students, with very meager furnishings, a twin bed, an outdated washroom, and a small kitchenette with a single burner cooktop. It was nothing spectacular, but life was not spectacular at that time, my sole focus was only to be close to the hospital. I rarely ate anything but hospital food, and probably had lost more weight than Jillian. I was suffering her disease through my guilt.

When initially arrived to the hospital, I made several attempts to contact Jillian's mother. An older man typically answered the phone and I left a brief message for her. But she did not respond.

Her mother never liked how I stole her only daughter from her. She did not come to our wedding nor say good bye to Jillian when we left for Central America. From Jillian's brief stories about her childhood, her mother was overly protective of her after her father passed away. Even when Jillian decided to attend school in the Midwest far from the Virginia coast line, her mother thought it was a horrible idea. I hardly spoke much to her mother other than answering the phone and handing it over to Jillian. Our relationship in a word was tumultuous.

When Jillian's mother arrived to hospital unannounced, two or so weeks after Dr. Kempler's visit, she neither acknowledged me or registered my presence in the room. Her small body was rigid, and swathed in a black dress.

Her mother, who was sobbing, pulled up a chair next her daughter and held Jillian's motionless hand. "Hello, Mrs. Riviere," I began. Not once did her mother look at me, nor console nor speak to me. I observed her for a long time, watching her grief swell from her inside, repeating under her breath "My Baby, only baby" and sobbing. I noticed the striking resemblance of Jillian in her mother's face, her incredible features in this stark environment. Her mother's hand clenched her daughter.

A nurse came in, her mother demanded between sobs, "Please, leave us alone. I want to be with my daughter."

"I understand," the nurse responded softly, then to me said, "I'll check on her in about an hour."

Once she left, I leaned on my chair and proceeded to lie to her mother. "Jillian will soon wake up and be healthy, responsive and okay."

Her mother's head whipped in my direction and she glared at me, acknowledging my presence for the first time with such rancor and hostility, and hissed, "Liar! Liar, Hans! You are a horrible liar and husband, just like Jillian's father was. At least he had alcohol to blame. What's your excuse?" Her mother shook her head back and forth as her eyes filled with tears and she fell back into sobbing over her daughter's motionless hand.

After some time she regained some of her composure, and wiped her eyes with a tissue. Without looking at me, still gripping her daughter's hand, she finally uttered, "You think I am so, so stupid. That I'm not a brilliant, educated person like you? I've already talked to her doctor, they've told me that she will never open her eyes again. That they believe she is brain dead. And you think I am such a fool to believe you?"

She paused for a second, letting go of Jillian's hand, her lips for a moment as her eyes bore into me. "You are to blame for this. I hold you responsible for my daughter's illness, her... her... death. And for that, I will never forgive you for it." She inhaled sharply, and said, "I've said my goodbyes to my daughter. When you die, God forgive me for saying this, I hope you die a lonely old man. You deserve that."

I sat straight in my chair, shocked. No words would come to me. I suppose, deep down, I agreed with her mother's harsh words, words I hadn't been able to say out loud, much less to myself. But they were true. I was to blame for this, and I was already suffering the life of loneliness she had just cursed me with.

Her mother looked down, eyes overflowing with renewed tears, "I love you, Jillian. We'll be together again, soon."

She composed herself and slowly stood up, bending to kiss her daughter's forehead then she turned and walked out of the room, quietly sobbing.

I wanted to call after her, beg her not to leave but nothing came to my lips. Her mother had every right to convict me of her daughter's dire circumstances. I sat motionless, listening to the sounds of Jillian's respirator whirring relentlessly as it circulated air through her lungs that would not work on their own. I longed for Jillian to open her eyes, for this all to be a bad dream. I longed to hear her to say my name again, just once more. I stared at the door for a long time until the nurse returned to check on Jillian.

It would turn out that later that same year her mother would perish in a terrible auto accident. A lawyer, who was a cousin of the family, contacted me about her death and her belongings which I had shipped here, to the house. All of it remains in the far bedroom at the top of the servant's staircase, still packed just as it had been when it arrived. I never did go through those boxes, hoping that Jillian would recover and want to go through her mother's belongings. I was still clinging to hope that my Jillian was in there somewhere. I remained even more pigheaded and faithful over the next few weeks and months, letting time pass me by.

My life was in that hospital room, sitting there, holding her hand. I had no other purpose in my life at that point, only Jillian, who remained in her coma, something I could not fix. My time in the apartment was the longest for me, and I came to the hospital everyday beginning early from five and stay until ten or so. I drank horrible coffee, and ate out of vending machines and the cafeteria. There were no phone calls, no visitors, no friends. Much like a specter, I crept along the halls of that hospital, waiting for my wife.

Today, in the modern world, had I been acting this way, a nurse would put me on some medication or force me to talk to a grief counselor. No, I did not need that, didn't want it, didn't deserve it. In hindsight, I suppose I was recharging my energy for what was to come.

I looked at her to appreciate my life with her.

In the endless spiral decent which I launched myself into for weeks, the time passed through me without much cause or hurt to my senses, just blinding numbness, I watched occasionally the news to see the bloodshed in Vietnam, to see many American soldiers dying, to see a country being torn apart. This made no effect on me. I only cared about my Jillian, knowing she slipped away from me more and more.

About three months later, a telegram arrived that would reopen my world once again. A nurse brought it to me lingering for a moment after, casting curious glances at me as she busied herself with checking Jillian for the second time that hour. I remember exactly what it had said. I must have read it at least two dozen times.

Hans,
Please contact me soon. Possible diagnosis to Jillian's illness.
Don

Suddenly, for the first time in that whole dismal period of my life of mine, I had hope in front of me. Don suggested a possibility of a cure for Jillian's condition. I even read the note to her, to which, of course, there was no response, just the hum of the breathing machine. I thought of our talk on that beach that seemed so long ago, about the life, the future we planned to share. And foolishly, I did believe in that because I was absolutely and deeply in love with her. There had to be some possibility of Jillian coming back to me, of hearing her voice again, of seeing her beautiful face smiling at me again. I thought to be true that the seemingly lifeless hand I held now would one day squeeze mine back. At that point, my heart was still firmly in control of my head.

Coincidentally, it was about three days after receiving the telegram that Reginald came to the hospital.

I had just gone down to the cafeteria to grab a snack, the same as I did every night at that time, hoping to avoid crowds and doctors. How I loathed meeting or speaking to anyone in that place. As I opened her room, I found Reginald there at her bedside, holding Jillian's hand. He looked worn, his face was distressed and even disappointed. In retrospect, he and my wife spent a great deal of time together during our time in Costa Rica, talking and sharing stories, of their discoveries, of themselves. I had been busy, preoccupied in my own work to really keep track of them. The look of compassion and heartbreak on his face suggested that maybe Jillian had been more than a friend to Reginald. If there had been a secret liaison between them, I never knew. At the very least, it was evident to me in that moment that Reggie cared for her a great deal.

249

"Reginald," I whispered, my own voice shaky laced with tension at the bittersweet feelings at seeing him there. "How did you find us?"

He didn't speak as I stood near just inside the door, watching him with Jillian. Central America had taken a toll on him. He had lost some weight, his tan leather jacket seemed too large for his now slim frame, his full thick hair made his face seem small. Slowly, he looked up at me, and all I could see was frustration, anger and sadness. His eyes were bright red, full of tears, their tracks shimmered against his dark skin of his cheeks.

"Don't flatter yourself so easily, man. I didn't really come to see you." His voice was steady, barreling at me like a machine gun. His posture was rigid as his bloodshot eyes seemed to stab me. "Why did you take her away from us? You had us to lean on, but you just up and left without so much as a word?"

"I don't understand," I replied then I closed the door behind me. I didn't want anyone who passed by to overhear us.

"Typical Hans," he said bluntly. He looked down upon Jillian with a great careful look.

"Please sit," I suggested, moving towards him.

"No."

After a moment, he said in a low voice, "You know I respected you, Hans. I admired your work and what you did at the university. When I was offered to be on the project, I jumped at the chance to work with you. Unlike Dr. Kempler and others alike, you saw my capabilities and intelligence as researcher. Nothing beyond that. When I meant Jillian, she completed you. She gave life to the team. As we grew in our research, and as individuals. We were so separated from the ugly world here, of any preconceived tension. In Costa Rica, I thought of you and Jillian as friends. Almost a brother and sister. Had so much respect for you, man. Even the way you treated the local people down there, moving us all around, giving me new jobs that were only reserved for other white people. Your talent down in the camp had shined through. And you had Jillian, the one that gave life to our team. I truly felt part of a team." He stopped for a second and squeezed Jillian's hand. "You know, when my brother died from the war in 'Nam, I had lost almost everything and knew I could come back to a family, our family, in Costa Rica."

"Reginald, I never knew you felt that way," I said, taking a seat in the chair near my wife. "No you wouldn't have," Reginald spat back, almost in a lower voice. He threw his hand up in the air. "Just, just be quiet and listen. Damn it, listen to someone else for once. I came to Jillian only when I had problems with you, when you snapped at us for our deadlines, or when you were quiet and you had decisions to make. You were just being Hans   just a pensive dictator   you were just more subtle than Dr. Kempler, in how you always got your way. But Jillian, saw something in you, always had faith in you, rallied for you to the others, behind your back, when everyone else was on the verge of mutiny. She might have been your right hand, but she was the glue that held our team together. But you never seemed to appreciate her enough. She body." He looked down at her with water in his eyes, and then he blinked.

I could only stare back at him, letting him release the rage he'd obviously held in for a long time. Oddly, I was not angry, just numbed, or maybe stunned, by his words. "That day at the volcano, I realized I was wrong. That Kempler hadn't put a gun to your head. No, *your* damned ambition to be the best, Hans, put us there. You made the decision for all us to go, despite the obvious dangers. I thought you were better than that. All you white people are the same. I believed in you, that's why I followed you there. And why we all witnessed what we did. Why Jillian lays here, like this, now."

He paused for a second, stepping away from the bedside, he turned to amble toward the window. With his back to me, I could see his rigid posture tense with his hostility. I was not comfortable in the room, in the heavy silence. The sounds of the machines were the only noise and the ambient noises of the evening hospital just behind the closed door.

"I will never forgive you for Jose's death, not that you would try to understand." His voice was slightly louder, amplified by the window he was facing. What he saw I could not say. The view from the room's vantage point was of the inner quad of the square of hospital buildings and the roofline of the entrance. "I still have the same nightmare almost every night: that enormous wasp-thing swooping down, impaling Jose. I can still hear it, the crush of his body as he was stung, his screams. He was my friend, man. I was only inches away from the man, but I couldn't help him. I was frozen in place, too shocked to move, too afraid I would be next. It coulda been me." He paused for a few moments, as he seemed to try to catch his breath.

"You weren't there. I had to tell his family that week what had happened to him." He inhaled some air briefly as if he needed to control himself.

"You left the camp before I got back, leaving Don there crying like a little baby. Then poof! Gone! Out of the country without a word? Nothing, man!" His voice was booming now. He took a steadying breath, and returned to looking out the window. "You ignored our calls. I won't spare my breath on you anymore. All my respect and dedication for you and your work, it is all gone man, all gone."

"I didn't know how you felt," I managed to say.

In the dim light, I could see a slight smirk on his face in the reflection of the dark glass. "I am doing this only for Jillian, and if she ever wakes up, I hope she will see what you really are. I don't owe you a goddamn thing, Hans. Nothing," He stated bitterly. "I'm sure you received that note from Don, though I don't understand why you didn't bother to respond. I promised Don I would come to find you, but that's all. After this, I am done with all of it."

Reginald took in a deep breath. "If you really love her, if you ever cared about us, Don and me, you would have picked up the phone. You knew where we were, you had the number. And we waited, going through the research, thinking that you would call, give us information, to give any word. Nothing for us to know. We had called the hospital ourselves and found out what Jillian's diagnosis. We tried to reach numerous of times, tried you here without any success. The only response that we received from the nurse had been 'the family is not accepting any phone calls'.

"Being so dedicated to your," he paused for a moment and shook his head. "Don was always in the shadow, a place he should never have been. But Don wanted for us to go back to the volcano, to that opening. He thought he could find answers to Jillian's condition. In a way, I agreed with him, anything to help her. By end of the month, Don had informed Dr. Ruiz that we would be returning to continue our research. When we arrived with barely any supplies, Dr. Ruiz said, 'I had phoned the university to see the legitimacy of your research. It seems that they were puzzled about this recent investigation.'

"'Doctor,' Don said to him. Don could think up of something real quick. 'We are just doing a follow up investigation to the recent happening of the others in our camp. We will not want the university to be directly involved.'"

"Not sure if Dr. Ruiz accepted that, but he still smiled at us, a smile like only a devil would give. Never trusted that man. He told us, 'Well, then, your area is as it was. I do not have any men to spare, since I am down in numbers myself. Also, the seismic activity in the volcano has increased significantly over the last week. Whatever you must do must happen fast.'"

"Don and I had already planned that he would do solo investigations in the cave while I would take the forests. Over the next couple of days, I knew I had to get past my trauma from Jose's death. The forest near the cave was different already. All plants and insects life that we'd encountered during our first expedition was starting to die off. And the smell of decay was horrible. It took me back to my time in Korea in the early fifties, on the frontlines during the war and scouting the small towns for enemy soldiers and smelling the rotting bodies.

"In the forest I walked carefully, stepping only where I needed to. Alone in that stench, I thought a lot, reminding myself this was all for Jillian, to hopefully find a way to save her. The answer could have lie anywhere, so I grabbed samples from everything.

"As we gathered samples to be tested back the Main House, Don already packed containers of potential samples. Though we worked together, we were silent, focused, while Ruiz's team talked and joked, smoking cigars and drinking Imperial from cans. We worked hard in that limited time, with almost no sleep, in the warm humidity of the rainforest. I did anything I could to avoid going into the cave at all. Don went in with a worker, a friend of Jose's.

"Don spoke occasionally here and there, but he was more exhausted then I was, had been working tirelessly. He was fixated on finding something. He would say over and over, 'Beyond my living expectations,' and keep going back into the cave. He would give himself only short breaks, so his work was in nearly constant motion.

"The third morning, I woke feeling sick to my stomach. The wind was hard and the smell of the volcano was overwhelming. I felt that I was moving slower than normal. Don was heading into the cave just as I was sitting up on my cot, rubbing my head from the tremendous headache when I felt the rock under my feet tremble. My cot and the tables were shook. Don came rushing back, and I saw Dr. Ruiz and his men scramble from their tent. It lasted for such a long time, unlike a typical earthquake tremor. Our work sampled were falling off the tables, glass breaking everywhere. Suddenly, a flame shot up out of the ravine, lava bombs rocketing hundreds and thousands of feet into the air, some landing not far from our site. We started to run down the mountain as quickly as we could in the treacherous environment, as more ejecta shot into the air. Dr. Ruiz kept screaming, 'This is it! This is it!' in exultation, a euphoric expression upon his face. As the others fled the site and Don and I stood watching in awe and terror at the seven other men were trying to cover their equipment while a fire began to grow in our tent. All the samples, all the proof was going up in flames. Destroyed. I tried to move as quickly as Don, grabbing our stuff. The crates were breaking open. Flames were everywhere. I told Don we had to go. At the top of the volcano, thick black smoke was billowing thousands of feet up into the sky, blocking out the sunlight. It looked like a wall of smoke was coming towards us.

"In that moment, another strong earthquake jolted us, sections of rock down the sheer cliff faces, eventually closing off the entrance to the cave. Don was in hysterics, and raced back into the tent, yelling, 'The box! I need the box!'

"We ran like hell for cover into the forest. It turned out that the heavy winds that typically flowed through the ravine carried the ash fallout away from us."

Reginald stopped, sighing heavily, his breath fogging the window in front of him. "That was the second time I'd escaped death in that forsaken place. God saved me again. Those demonic creatures were a sign for me, telling me to find salvation. I vowed after that never to talk about what I saw in that Godforsaken rainforest. Nuh-uh, never again, 'cause I know we saw what the devil can do. Every time I speak of it, the devil wins. I quit all this." He turned to me, his hands shaking as he said, "Don asked me to find you. The box he saved from the tent holds the answers to Jillian's illness."

He reached into his front pocket to pull out a small key. His face was solemn and placid, almost as if he was confessing his sin to me. "This is to unlock the box. If it really contains what Don says it does, and you can find it, then you will find the cure she needs."

He placed the key on the table. He gave Jillian a long final look, and began to move toward the door. My heart was pumping fiercely, adrenaline ramping up my heartrate and increasing my breathing to the point I thought I would hyperventilate. I stood up as he reached for the door.

"Listen, Reginald. I deeply apologize for not understanding your position." I could only say.

"Such a Hans response," Reginald responded dryly.

A flush of anger enveloped my cheeks and I then asked, "but how will I find this box?"

He stopped, giving a small smile, and replied, "How would you ship something so important that would go undetected by the university and only for your eyes?"

"What do you mean?" I was anxious. I wanted the cure.

"You're an intelligent man. Figure it out," he mused, then opened the door then he turned slightly to look me directly at me. His dark eyes were full of sublime anger. "And Hans, I'm finished with all of this. I just hope God brings Jillian into His arms when she finally passes."

With his back to me, he said, "And don't ever, ever come looking for me. I will make you regret it. "

Reginald disappeared down the corridor forever.

TWENTY-TWO

(DR. FISCHER)

That night I sat in the chair staring at the key. Don had gone into a burning tent for whatever this protected, to save Jillian. He said the locked box held a possible cure.

I watched her lying there, as the oxygen was forced into her lungs. I couldn't let Reginald's grievances or his opinions of me or my character distract me from the real purpose of his visit. While I look at Jillian in her restful state, new questions arise about their friendship. Throughout those years, they usually conducted sampling within the same areas in the forest, researched in the same manner and complimented each other's work frequently. And there was always that sublime look Jillian gave Reginald, here and there. Was I too naïve about the actual situation? Did I trust Jillian too much? Perhaps these dark inquiries were only fueled by Reginald's spiteful words. It will be always unsettled for I will never have the right answers. And part of me, deep down, did not want to face the truth.

Yet what overlapped my dark thread of thinking was Don because but he brought me something more valuable back: the motivation to move forward again. During the night, as I sat there by Jillian's bedside contemplating what Don had discovered and where I could find this box he'd returned to the States despite the fact that he hadn't physically come back into the country, a new hope blossomed inside me fueling thoughts of the future. The key in my hand was Jillian's possible future, or so I'd hoped. As I sat that night, I realized I needed to get Jillian out of that hospital room, because when she awoke I wanted her to wake up in a beautiful environment.

I envisioned the great gardens that I maintained for many years. Now these gardens are nothing but overgrown mess, a forest of weeds, bushes and tall grasses. This very house that you have intruded upon, snooping through our rooms. This home was for us, for my Jillian to come home to heal. She lived in the very bedroom where I found you, my little deviant friend, with the view of the street, and the forests preserve, some of the downtown, the very view I knew you saw only minutes ago.

In a feverish, ambitious renovation period over several weeks, I hired a designer and a gardener to prepare the house for Jillian. There was much work during this time, and they worked hard, seeming to sympathize with the time-sensitivity of the situation and Jillian's illness. They pushed their crews harder than normal to ensure that the house would be ready. At the time, my old neighbors all questioned who was moving in here when they saw all the work being done to the old place, when the medical equipment was delivered, on the day Jillian arrived home by ambulance. I did not want to answer to those silly nosy housewives, but I could see them peeking out through their curtains on that cold morning when the medical transport brought her home, attached to a breathing apparatus and other monitors. Eventually they all moved away, which pleased me, the fewer around to disturb me the better. Though some still meddle in my business and have tried to threaten me to clean up my house and grounds. Money can make troubles disappear, and covert donations to city hall may have help me stay off the radar. Still, the day she came, I had the house filled with tropical flowers fit to welcome a queen. The fragrances were astounding.

In a manner I'm sure was more intent on protecting themselves than on genuine concern for Jillian's well-being, the University offered provided private nurses and doctor visitations for Jillian. Eleanor Wagner was her best nurse, and someone I came to trust the most for the night-time monitoring. They had someone here at all hours to care for her, to bathe her, check her vitals, and perform necessary tasks to monitor her slowly deteriorating health. I also hired a house manager, June Stewart, for the house and the grounds, though June's most important duty was to make sure that Jillian was dressed and that fresh flowers were placed in her room several times a week. I had such hope that she would wake up in a normal state and I wanted everything to be perfect for her when she did. But June was also my saving grace, as it was really I who needed to be fed and looked after in my state of depression and research-fueled obsession left little room in my awareness for much else.

Over the course of those months, moving Jillian from the confines of the dreary hospital room to our grand home allowed me some sense of normalcy for the first time in my adult life. With Jillian's book already , the purse of her rewards provided us a comfortable life that felt long overdue. I found that I did not wallow during that time, and instead I was able to start looking forward to the shaping of my future goals.

My first order of business was to have my credentials at the University reinstated. Once I was settled in the house and Jillian's care was established, I contacted the chancellor of the University. Initially, my calls were ignored and my appointments were cancelled periodically. I could have given up, gone about pursuing some other aspect of research in my field, but I had too much invested in this project, everything really. I had even sacrificed my wife, our future together. Perhaps it was my protectiveness over my research, my findings that kept me from letting go. But once Jillian and I were comfortable in the house, I drew my full attention toward the school.

I decided to go to the chancellor's office one day when my frustrations and angst had finally reached a crescendo. I walked in, unannounced, to the Chancellor's office, past his squarely-built secretary and opened his door without so much as a knock. He was on the phone and upon my abrupt entry looked up at me in surprise.

"What's this about?" he grumbled at me. He was a thin man in a white shirt, a thick black glasses hugging his nose.

"My name is Hans Fischer. I'm a former researcher in the Biodiversity Project in Central America. I have been trying to—"

"This gentleman," the square woman interrupted from behind me, "was overly rude coming here without an appointment or without even bothering to announce himself to me before interrupting you, sir. Should I call the campus police?"

The chancellor continued to look at me then said into the phone, "I'll call you back." To me, "Mr. Fisher, was it? I was wondering how long it would be until I'd see you here."

"Sir, I'll get the police," the secretary was turning to leave.

"Not necessary, Mrs. Huntington. You may leave us. Please close the door behind you."

I heard her leave, muttering something under her breath. The chancellor sat straighter in high back red leather chair.

"Please, have a seat, Mr. Fisher."

"No, I will stand, Thank you," I said. My voice was deep and shaky in the quietness of the office.

"Very well. State your business."

"I would like to retain my research laboratory to continue the studies on Biodiversity Project."

He cleared his throat. "As you well know, the economy and the War have caused a downturn in applications to the school in the past few years, and will likely continue to do so over the next few years. As of now, we are fully staffed with professors and researchers alike. I would love to have your knowledge and experience here, you've been a great asset to the University and you're ongoing research here would no doubt attract new students. But there are simply no positions of your caliber available at the moment."

His phone rang.

"Excuse me," he said, reaching for his phone.

I clenched my fists, feeling the heat of rage surging within me. I approached his desk in a few quick strides and placed my hand over the receiver button, disconnecting his call.

"Hans, now that is out of line," he began as he looked up at me with the phone to his ear.

"I need your full attention," I replied, my voice low, my eyes burning into his.

Casually, he replaced the phone on the cradle, and I took a step back, my eyes still firmly on his.

"You have it." He folded his arms on the desk.

"You may wish to rethink your response to my request. Surely, you would not want me to go to the Board of Trustees of this fine institution to explain to them how a beautiful young woman was tricked under Dr. Kempler's supervision into entering a dangerous part of the world, and who is right now in a catatonic, state and fighting for her life. And surely, Mr. Chancellor, you would not want me to explain to them about how you personally signed all the medical orders for her treatment at the University hospital, and authorized medical expenses paid by the University for her ongoing care. In total, you have helped sign a nice pension for this young lady whom may or may not be in conscious state ever again." I paused, and then added, "Or I may just go to the Tribune. They like stories like this."

There was an awkward silence. I could see in his grey eyes that thought was occurring, probably carefully planning his words. He took a sip from the glass of water near him.

"You seem to have the upper hand here," he stated. "You put me in a bit of a quandary as to how to satisfy your request. First: Kempler is no longer an employee of this university. Yet I am still dealing with the burden in the wake of his abrupt departure. Second: I will grant you access to a laboratory you seek. It will be set up—"

"I will also need access to all of the materials and samples from the Biodiversity Project." I said. I tried not to show my eagerness to get my hands on the research materials.

"It is all yours. You will have access to the remainder of the projects financial funding, as well. I will make arrangements." He noted something on his steno pad.

"I have one more request," I told him. What you see before you, this lovely laboratory was constructed by the university in the years that followed Jillian's death.

Never had I been one to threaten someone or something, not for my pleasure, but it was a necessity for Jillian's health, and I needed to secure his confidentiality as I worked through the materials. I didn't want any of Kempler's possible minions catching wind of what I was doing and trying to sabotage my work or reporting anything back to him. I couldn't let anything disrupt the work I was finally beginning. Jillian couldn't afford anymore wasted time. So a threat felt warranted in this situation and I took great care in choosing my words. It was two or three days later, when my lab at the campus had been set up, that the Chancellor's secretary called me personally ensure that I had the necessary tools in order to do the proper research. They even made sure that my work there was undisturbed by painting 'AUTHORIZED PERSONNEL ONLY' over the door, and on the mailbox nearby. My name was not mentioned anywhere, masking my presence on the campus, which I was pleased with. I received an envelope with the access keys to the exterior storage unit in the basement that contained the samples and, I hoped, the box with the sample that Don had collected for us.

I didn't waste time with lab set up as I normally would have. Instead I hurried into the depths below into the shadows of the basement, blanketed in long strands of cobwebs, where I eventually found the samples that we had captured and cataloged in Central

America. As I began the arduous process of sifting through the crates of samples I thought back to how I had been so worried back then about the preservation, the packaging and placement of the samples that were going back to the University for further analysis. I recalled how I had trained Jose myself to carefully control the samples for our future studies. The crates were stacked haphazardly in the space and were not arranged for ease of access.. It also appeared that the crates had never been opened. There was no sign of tampering, no sign that anyone had ever opened the crates to check the samples or verify the shipping inventory for accuracy. I couldn't help but note with some misapprehension that no one had bothered to check them after the constant memos and lectures we had received from Dr. Kempler on the proper packing and shipping of the samples. It had been such a bone of contention between us and a great source of tension and anxiety in the early stages of our camp that I thought it might have caused the collapse of the project before it even got underway.

In a way, I felt completely insulted by what I found there in that storage closet. Dr. Kempler had lied about continuing research back at the campus and that they were making great strides with the materials we were collecting. All that painstaking effort, all that time spent combing over every fine detail to make sure the samples arrived safely back at the lab and that the information was thorough for the scientists we believed were hard at work there as an extension of our efforts in the field. The basement of crates lay as evidence of my personal foolishness; proof that our work had been only a ridiculous joke to the rest of the campus and to the greater scientific community, as well. Here, in the damp storage area, I saw the hundreds of crates just parked, untouched, against the wall. And despite all our months of diligent efforts, all the blood, sweat, and tears that our team had poured out uselessly in that rainforest, I was exhilarated the crates were unsullied, that for all Kempler's appalling actions, at least he had not damaged or discarded the samples.

I would know each crate, each container would have borne the fruits of my meticulous labors. But in this mess, the task of sifting through it all had been difficult and time-consuming, and time wasn't something I had in great abundance. I had no help in moving them, and they were heavy and cumbersome. I knew I needed to work smart.

The real question was: *How would ship something so important but it would go undetected by the university, preserving it for my eyes only?*

My astute colleague had some to the conclusion I had been to blind to see at the time: that Kempler had been neglecting the actual research and simply storing the samples away.

The days seemed to pass by slowly, though time was slipping away from Jillian in her fragile condition. My body hurt from moving the crates and coming close to what I thought was my holy grail, but it was not there. Despite my frustration, I was able to make progress with our helped my project, the very one Dr. Kempler left in disarray. In a moment of epiphany I had the idea to start sending some of the crates of samples to the corresponding departments for further study. That's when I was struck with an epiphany. I enlisted the assistance of the lead professor from the necessary departments and sent samples with a simple note that read: *Please classify and identify these samples.*

As you have witnessed from my library, a great many researchers benefited from my project and my work. I received some accolades from it, because even though my presence on campus was not public knowledge at that time, the University's research project was well-known throughout the scientific community and those who knew me knew that I had been the main source of the final phases of the research. They understood the political angle. The broad opinion of Dr. Kempler was that he was not a scientist and had been only an administrative blowhard. Later, because of the doors that my early research provided, I would receive many rewards that were beyond my dreams. Years later, even the University could not deny the scope of our project and dedicated a laboratory wing in Jillian's honor. I would not attend that ceremony because my own project was taking flight.

But that is a story for another time.

With a significant amount of the crates sorted and sent off to other labs within those couple of weeks, I still had not found Don's box. Trepidation was building because Jillian's health was declining. I knew I was losing time with her, but my need to find this box was relentless. Fate, it would seem, had a different course set for me.

One night, I returned later than normal to my lab because I had a long conversation with the doctor about Jillian's condition. With my frantic efforts to discover answers to our questions about what was happening to her that I had not realized how much time had gone by, that Jillian was slipping away. I needed more time: more time to be with her, more time to find a cure and save her. I desperately wanted to hear her say my name once more, to look at me once more, to hold me once more. Oh, the lengths a desperate man will go to for his true love he would defy the natural order of things, work day and night without sleep, forget his own limitations until he's convinced himself that he's invincible. I had thought I was that man, but I had let my own desolation take over; I became obsessed with my research, aiming hopelessly for a box.

When I arrived in my office, I found a simple package had been placed on my chair. The note attached to it said it was from the desk of the chancellor. It simply read: 'This must be yours.' The address was from the San Jose camp and it was addressed to Dr. Kempler. A normal person might have questioned what to do with the package addressed to someone else. I considered those answers briefly: I could send a sample to Dr. Kempler directly, but he would never open it. He would have felt it was beneath him to do actual research work.

After only a moment's hesitation to contemplate my options, I tore open the box, digging through the clumps of straw used for packing material to cushion and stabilize the samples we were shipping home. As I rummaged through my fingers grazed something. It felt like a tin box wrapped in paper. I pulled it from the package, my breath was caught in my throat. On the outside, attached to the paper, was an envelope with my name written on it. A 'Do not open box' message was scrawled on it in . It was Don's awful handwriting. A smile caressed my lips; finally, I had struck gold. The letter inside read:

Hans,
I have an important sample for Jillian's illness. Do not handle this with your hands. Be extremely careful.
The cause is in this box. You must find the effect.
Contact me soon.

Sincerely,
Don

I set the letter aside absentmindedly as I turned my eyes to the box. All my hope lay inside that small tin box. I grabbed the key that I had carried in my pocket every moment of every day since Reginald's visit. I pulled off the paper, and inserted the key.

A perfect fit. I turned the key, and I was sure that the click of the internal mechanism could be heard all over campus. Returning home the next day, I went immediately to Jillian's room. The soft morning light fell over Jillian's face. As I sat down next to her, I studied the details of her face. I knew that finding a solution would take more hours for me, I knew this time with her was important. I whispered in her ear about the box, telling her she will wake up soon. Her still face and the quiet whir of the oxygen machine were subtle reminders of our reality before it was quickly washed away as my daydreams of her precious smile overtook returned. I would see that smile again soon, I was sure.

Finally, I could begin my work. I returned to the campus after a night of insomnia. The enigma of that sample taunted me. Carefully, I opened the box, wearing protective mask and gloves. The inside of the box was lined in plastic and filled with a hunk of compost from the cave floor. Even to the casual observer, one could see the decaying pieces spiny legs and rigid claws, dozens pieces. I sifted through the top layer of the sample to observe some botanical matter a tangle of undergrowth and foliage that continued to decay in this preserved trap.

I weighed the compost which came to about a kilo or so. The texture of it was light and brittle as I carefully pushed small scoops of it aside to see what lie beneath. That's when I smelled that acidic odor of carbon dioxide that had assaulted my nostrils on my first visit to the cave. *Ok, Don, what is so special about this sample?* On the surface I could come up with some potential answers, not the cause. I methodically tested pieces of the compost for any known bacteria or virus, much like the hospital had tried over the last months; I was testing for the direct cause, and finding nothing.

Yes, there were a number of ways that things could have gone badly for Jillian. Further analysis of the samples proved that high levels of carbon dioxide were infused into the creatures that inhabited the cave, as well as the vegetation and even the water droplets contained elevated levels of carbon dioxide gas. Of course, carbon dioxide is a waste product of the human and animal bodies, and so it would be toxic to humans, especially at the levels I discovered in that sample. CO2 gas inhalation can induce irregular breathing and heartrate and eventually render a person unconscious, or a catatonic condition, or death. Even absorption through the skin could cause severe burns.

Elevated levels of primitive viral diseases also appeared on the severed appendages of several of the insect specimens that were included with the sample. Yes this these were a natural state for these creatures and would have been commonplace. And certainly in the case of human patients exposed to these viruses, a healthy person's natural immune system would have produced antibodies that would ward off the infections, especially with the medical support that Jillian had been receiving for weeks by that point. Essentially, Jillian should have awoken after a month or so from either of these conditions, under the worst-case scenario. However, it would seem that her disease was mutated, more sophisticated, in a sense, than the strains I found on the *Insecta* parts.

Eventually, after much testing, I felt my hopes being dashed by the dwindling probability of finding the solution in that compost. Perhaps Don was wrong in his assumptions that this was the held the answers we sought. I was beginning to acknowledge to myself that I had come to a dead end, when I took one last look through the sample crate and inspected the very bottom of the box. There was material still down there. I was sure I had taken a sample of every centimeter of the remaining compost, when I noticed some specks of soil on the base, actual rock. There was no plant nor species matter on it and I wondered to myself how it would have gotten there. I realized it must have come from the cliff face she had fallen from. It still didn't answer how the bits of rock would have ended up in the soil sample, but in desperation and dedication to the scientific process, I ran the same battery of tests on the remaining material in the sample.

No, I was not a disciplined medical doctor; however, my background in microbiology and chemistry gave me the knowledge I needed to seek the culprit organisms at the root of my wife's illness. Thus, knowing that toxin levels were acutely elevated in Jillian's blood, I focused more toward searching for a single cell structure, breaking down the rock sample to its simplicity. Removing the mineral makeup, I was able to finally expose the bacterium involved. My reasoning allowed me to find a possible cause: *Clostridrium Botulinum*. This particular bacterium could be found in much of the earth, surviving in environments with little to no oxygen. In fact, it is commonly referred to botulism, which plays havoc on the restaurants, hotels, and public institutions, causing widespread illness and occasionally deaths. In my day, we were just becoming aware of the impact of the bacterium, how it spread and how to eliminate it, as health departments and centers of disease control were being established throughout the country.

Upon my positive identification, I sat in the chair knowing the correct course of treatment and feeling confident in my conclusion, certain that the doctors would not have checked nor conceived of checking for such a widespread bacteria strain. This was not some exotic, new disease we'd unearthed in the rainforest, as the doctors had implied. In fact, it was something that should not have been beyond their expertise in the least. I wrestled with second guessing myself, that I should have known that I was the best person to take control over her diagnosis and her evaluations so much sooner than I had. But there was no time for me to gloat; I had to make sure I was right about my findings. I tested a sample of her blood that I had taken from her previously. Later, I would produce that report in court when I sued the University and won a handsome settlement for their negligence and malpractice. When results came back with ninety percent accuracy, I was excited. We finally had an answer, and my Jillian was still with me.

As I hurriedly packed my belongings and the results of my testing, I thought back to the cave, recalling the creature's behavior and how they would not go near the base of the cave. It seemed that the mutant anthropoids instinctively avoided moving toward the bottom of the cavern.

In hindsight, I realized that it was likely due to the temperature flux caused by the molten magma hundreds of meters below the surface. I stopped and stared at the dirt, the compost, realizing there was another strong possible reason for their behavior. For every habitat, there is a food chain. Given the enormous proportions size of these insects, there had to be something greater in the midst of that Pleistocene-like ecosystem, which must have formed during the last global warming. Was this what Jillian was trying to uncover during her fateful solo trek into the cave? Had she seen something in there and formed a hypothesis and gone to collect samples before it was wiped out by the volcano?

For the first time in weeks, I left the lab believing in Jillian's recovery.

But, in my self-reclusive phase, as I was attempting to discover the cause of Jillian's coma, I had lost track of Jillian's deterioration. Her body had begun to shutdown, the bacterium infecting vital tissues. Her doctor was honest about her condition, clearly explaining that her metabolism had slowed and her body was no longer accepting nutrition. Her brain activity had been reduced to the point of barely allowing any function for the rest her body. As I sat with her in those final days, I could see the frailness of her body, the pale yellow hue of her skin. I failed in my fight for Jillian. My last hope for her to ever open her eyes so that I might look into them for a moment, had been taken away from me. In the Jillian's remaining days, I stayed by her bedside as she rapidly withered away. She had always been a strong woman, independent in thought and lovely to behold. I looked out over the gardens that she would never see, imagining her standing in them, smelling the bouquet of fragrances. The nurses came around to check on Jillian's state, and tried to comfort me, but I was numb to their kind words of sympathy.

I sat next to Jillian until her death in the third week of July. She went quietly as Eleanor and I looked over her. I had no more tears left to shed, though some tears did come, I later realized, in relief, perhaps for Jillian who no longer suffered, perhaps more for myself.

On the day of her burial, I laid on the couch in the den, having barely slept, drinking whiskey, and feeling so alone in this immense house. It was the first day of August, and a terrible lightning storm was brewing outside on that hot summer day. The night was extra humid and warm. The phone rang through the silent house, which I had planned to ignore. I looked at the clock, it had read ten forty-five. So late for a call. Such an odd time; who would be calling me so late?

I staggered to the phone and picked it up.

"Hans!" A familiar voice shouted at me over static crackling in the receiver.

"Da Don?" I could barely speak.

"It's Don!" He was shouting. There was a lot of noise on his end.

"The box was too late—"

"Can't hear you, Hans!"

"The box was too—"

"I found your killer! Jillian's murderer!"

Then I was alert, the adrenaline pumping in my veins.

"Where are you?"

His line was breaking up. "Central house...I will leave directions. Don't have time Come quickly."

Then the phone went dead.

I looked down at the receiver. Within moments, I was climbing the stairs to pack.

I had vowed I would never return yet there I was on the phone to acquire tickets to go back to Costa Rica.

TWENTY-THREE

(SHANE)

The basement air was thick and hard to breathe, too hot and sticky like a balmy summer night. It seemed that it was full dark outside now; the bright lights glanced off the dusty windows making it harder to see out. The stench of decay from the floor beneath us filled my mouth with each breath, and I choked on the taste of coppery, sulfuric funk.

More beetles had worked their up the side of our platform, probably drawn to the scent of our sweat or blood. Slowly, they crawled towards us, as centipedes ran over them. The edges of the platform were becoming blacker and blacker, as more and more insects approached to inspect us.

Dr. Fischer casually paced back and forth in front of us, rambling incessantly about things I could only half pay attention to. Occasionally, he would drift far enough to the side that I could see catch a glimpse of what was behind him. He was deep in thought, lost in his own world, in the past, his eyes harsh and alert as he recalled his story. Even his thin long arms floated in the air as if he was conducting an orchestra. Pausing for a moment, Fischer's chapped lips still spoke silently, probably to someone else, or something else. And his frame was strong and sturdy as he paced with his clasped hands were in a tight ball behind him. This was a different man than I had met the other night.

I strained to see behind him, trying to make out a shape, or anything, but only getting peeks at shifting shadows.

I returned my attention to Jack, who's wide, black eyes were frantically scanning the platform, flinching as the creatures slowly inched their way along the edge. I watched as beads of sweat dripped down the side of his face.

For a brief second, I saw the light of Jack's phone inside his pocket again. His phone was on. It lit up again. Mrs. Richardson was calling her boy, surely wondering where we were.

I assure you, Mrs. Richardson, Jack is definitely not at the park, I thought.

Slightly shaking his head, Dr. Fischer was gathering his thoughts. Maybe, the truth was coming out of him because he could no longer conceal his mess. "When I arrived in Costa Rica " he continued, his voice somber. " memories of Jillian washed over me. I tried to block them out, focus on deplaning and making my way across the tarmac, on the heat of the country as it enveloped me. It was as if I had never left. From the west, a billowing wall of dark grey clouds loomed with the promise of heavy rains. The smell of sweet, salty ocean mist filled my senses with memories of Jillian, sharing our tent in the rainforest, of the thrill of getting lost in my work with her by my side. At the gate, many of the local people greeted me kindly with nods and smiles, some with fewer teeth than others. They remembered me, and were likely wondering where Jillian was; she had always been the one to take time to getting to know them, no matter the circumstance.

"I moved on through the crowd quickly, not wanting to waste any time. I needed to get to the Central House, collect the directions to Don's location and head out of town as soon as possible. As I went through customs, heading near the baggage claim, I had noticed a series of people with signs waiting for incoming foreigners, diplomats, etc. A young woman held one with my name on it.

"'*Me llamo, Hans Fischer. Que te m'ayuda?*' I asked.

"In perfect English, she replied, 'You do not recognize me, Dr. Fischer?'"

"'I apologize, senorita, but I do not.'

"'I am Jose Santamos' eldest daughter, Maria Caterina. You came to house once. I remember your beautiful wife.' She paused. 'I am truly sorry for your loss.'

"Thank you,' I replied.

"'Are these your bags, Dr. Fischer?' Maria asked matter-of-factly.

"Yes. I am planning to go to—"

"She interrupted, 'Yes, the Central House. Plans have changed. I will be taking to Dr. Marche myself. I will get the driver to get your belongings.'

"Don you work for Don?"

"Suddenly, there was a loud percussive bang in the airport and many people went scrambling. It sounded like gunfire."

"'We must leave,' she said simply. Her face was serious as she looked into the crowd. Her black eyes were much like her father's eyes: fathomless, intelligent, and cunning. Within moments, we were out of the airport with little conversation.

"A tall, overweight man, who I discovered was our driver, took my bags and pack them into a rusty, sky blue Volkswagen bus. Maria took her seat in the front beside the driver, while I positioned myself a row back near an open window. We began our trek through the city just as the storm let loose a deluge as the van sluggishly negotiated the sharp corners and ambling people of the bustling metropolis.

"I was listening to Maria and the driver conversing in Spanish about the weather and then news information that crackled over the music. There were landslides in the direction we were headed, and the driver decided to take us the long way. I sat on the hard seat with my carryon bag between my legs, I pulled out my flask of whiskey and took a sip of the warm liquid. I leaned against the thin walls of the van, felt a splash of rain over my face, and thought about Jillian. Perhaps, Jillian, in a way, was encouraging me to press on. The crumpled picture, the very one you saw in the library, was the one that I carried with me on that trip. I fell into a slumber not wanting to look at the familiar landscapes, although still beautiful, even in the rain, there was nothing for me in that country anymore.

"Some time later, Maria woke me up. 'We'll have some dinner,' she said.

"I was not in the mood for food. Yet, I was able to change into some proper clothes and refresh myself in a poorly sanitized lavatory. I was quickly adapting back to the harsh lifestyle of the area. When I came out, I saw Maria leaving the pay phone to meet the driver at the table. There were three plates of food; I just wanted a refill on my flask.

"'You need to eat, Dr. Fischer,' Maria urged. She drank a cold beer. The driver, who said little, as he consumed the *gallo pinto*.

"'I'm not in the mood for it,' I said. I took a sip of the lager that tasted too weak and rather flat.

"Behind us, inside the cantina, a couple of younger men from the town were shouting at the television. There was a soccer game on.

"I watched Maria for a few moments as she looked out on the dirt road that ran through the sleepy village. 'I am sorry about your father,' I told her.

"Silence was her only response. A few minutes later, after what sounded like the favorite team among the locals had scored a goal, she sighed and turned to me.

"'Doctor, your apologies are too late for me and for my family.' Her voice was thick with resentment. 'I have moved beyond my father's death.'"

"Why are you working for Don?

"Maria took a sip of lager, only staring ahead of her, and avoided my question. 'My father died from unfortunate circumstances. Something he could have avoided if he had not worked for you.'

We said nothing for a while as the rain eventually stopped. She rose then said, 'Really, doctor, you need to eat. It is an insult to the Tico woman in the kitchen who prepared your meal.'

"I shooed the flies away, in earnest, from my dish and ate some pieces of tortilla shell with some shredded pork in it. While the pork melted in my mouth, the taste was delicious, spicy and slightly salty. I just was not hungry, just didn't want any food. Before I knew it, we were stomping in piles of mud and back in the van. Although the driver had parked haphazardly, he easily pulled the van out of a deep mud puddle. The windows became crusted with chunks of mud. In Spanish, Maria told the driver to 'stop playing around and move it'.

"With the heavy rains, the van seemed to move leisurely as we encountered more unpaved, mud slicked roads through towns I had not remembered, driving through smaller areas where only a random house and a cantina stood. I looked to see some children running and chasing each other on the side of the alleyway, barefoot, near a broken down dwelling. They had no care about the possible dangers in the mud, the possible nails or pieces of wood that could go into their feet, nor did the assumed mother on the weathered colorless portico. I had chosen not to look anymore at the villages, seeing the depleting towns, the abandoned homes or farms, the broken fences. Instead, I looked above towards the surrounding cloud forests, trying to catch a glimpse of an animal, seeing if there were birds in the sky, any mammal that would indicate real life in these harsh conditions.

"After some time, several hours if I had to judge without looking at my watch, we reached our destination, the dreaded and magnificent region that I remembered. When we had originally reached the foothills of the Arenal volcano we had approached from the bumpy dirt path that served as our access road to the region around the volcano was bordered by tall sugar cane that had matured to its full height. The plants smacked violently against the sides of the van creating sounds like the whipping of small animals. After several spine-jarring minutes, I could finally see the small dilapidated green shed that marked the trailhead for our footpath into the research site. I noticed a light on the inside when the door opened and a man stepped out looking in the direction of our vehicle. Most likely, he was stationed there to wait for our arrival. I could not be sure.

"'Are you ready for a hike, Dr. Fischer?' Maria asked, a smirk appearing on her face as she climbed out of the van.

"As I'll ever be," I replied as I gathered my backpack. How I dreaded coming back to this place. Sudden images of Maria's father lying in the van filtered into my mind, watching Jose slowly die in front of me. The anguish for losing him that day was right at the front of my mind and I wanted to sob like a small child. Instead, I took another swig of my whiskey to bury those thoughts.

"Quickly the man from the shack began helping to unload the van of our belongings. Stepping out into tall grass, I looked over at the path. I could see a more striking trail than before. Studying in the heavily filtered light of the rainforest canopy had been treacherous because of the additional venomous threats hiding in the depths of the foliage. It was nearly impossible to concentrate on the task at hand while constantly swatting away biting flies and insects and having to watch over our shoulders.

"The driver went into the shack and came back with two shotguns. In that moment, Maria pulled out her pistol from the glove compartment of the van, instructing the two men to lock up. They nodded and went about their duties quickly. The man from the shack already strapped my suitcase onto his back securely.

"'Dr. Donald Marche has a cabin less than two kilometers from here.' Maria said. Her expression was serious as her tone. 'Please stay close to us, Dr. Fischer. These forests are filled with eye lash vipers. Ricardo,' she nodded, indicating the driver, 'had seen some other animals prowling around.'

"With that, we began our journey into the dark forest. Around me, the forest came more alive with its chirps of birds, crackles of chirps, and the last shouts of holler monkeys over the rise and decent of the cicadas' melody. My eyes adjusted well enough for me to see the creatures, the insects to come alive more. The darkness of the forest was creeping around us, which Maria handed me a flashlight. Between the four of us, there was barely enough light to penetrate the thickness of the wooded area. Carefully I stepped over *phoneutria nigriventer*, running over the path, or even some large field pests following them.

"About a half an hour later, I saw a glimmer of a light, in middle of this nowhere. Creeping closer to the house on the steep path, the house looked more like a small shack. The faint redness could be seen on the outside walls, which all the windows glowed with light. I heard a generator kicking over slowly, and the smell of a wood fire enough to get the chill off.

"No more than ten or so meters, the screen door flew open knocking. 'Hans!' Don said loudly, almost joyfully.

"I had never received such a reception because I could see the smile on his face. He came to me much like a long lost brother, wrapping his arms around me. I actually liked it.

"'Don, good to see you again,' I said breathlessly. I forgot about the steep grade of the mountains and the elevation of the place.

"'Maria, please get the man some water', Don said and then took me carefully out of the darkness into the one room place. Having the door closed, I felt slightly protected from the exterior forest; even though I heard the faint sounds of rustling animals.

"'Thank you,' I said to Maria as she handed me a cup of brown tinted liquid while I saw Ricardo drop my belongings by the four cots opposite us, near the wood stove. It was warm in the one room better then cool dampness of the rainforest.

"Maria went about talking lowly to Ricardo and the man from the shack.

"Don's expression changed, and said, 'I wish my box had come to you earlier, maybe Jillian's condition would have changed.'

I said nothing, feeling suddenly drained after our long journey today. Over in the far right corner, near the burner and make shift pantry, a work table had been set up with test tubes and some equipment. On a stool, a man with a long gaunt face and thinning black hair peered into a microscope in the dim light. He hadn't let the arrival of our party interrupt his work with the slides.

"So, Don, please, tell me about your work here. What have you discovered?" I asked him.

"Don's weak smile as he replied betrayed his weariness, , 'Tomorrow you will know everything. Tonight you need to rest, get some sleep.' He went to the shelf above the electric burner, and grabbed a bottle of dark liquid and two cups, generously poured the liquid into both and handed one to me. "Let's just remember good times."

***

Old Man Fischer stopped talking, which roused my attention. Looking down at Jack's pocket, I noticed that his phone was sticking out more. From my angle, the time read quarter to seven. We left Jack's house it was three-thirty or so. God, his parents are going to pissed. Knowing my mother and being the worry wart, she was already in her car riding up and down the blocks.

That's when I heard clicking, coming from behind him and it sent a chill up my spine. I wasn't sure what was causing that sound, but all I could think about was getting free from the rope that held my hands tightly together behind me. I could barely feel my fingertips.

Jack was nearly hyperventilating, and I knew his state of panic was going to lead to his need for his inhaler. It was in his front of his jacket pocket, but we were both bound tightly.

On my leg, I felt a pinch. I looked down to see a beetle was crawling up my leg already. There were two on my shoe. I let out a great breath. I couldn't scream, but my hands were trembling.

Next to me, I saw Jack wobble his legs to get two centipedes off of him; they dropped on a layer of beetles near him.

These bugs were so close to us.

Dr. Fischer's voice was louder over the hum behind him as he stood within the shadows in the far corner and continued: "The next day, Don announced that we were walking to the plateau. It was a shorter distance than the initial walk maybe thirty to forty minutes. We still talked casually about anything and nothing. Maria had slept overnight along with Ricardo, plus the unknown man. I walked into the forest again, looking up seeing some small pockets of blue sky. That was always misleading because the rain clouds were brewing closer.

"As we began our journey, Don began discussing his time since Jillian and I had left. I said very little, just concentrating on the steep climb ahead of me.

"'It took a lot of convincing to get Reginald to get back to that spot. I knew there had to be answer to Jillian's illness. It must lie in the cave, because her toxin levels were usually spiked but she still maintained her body for a long time. Therefore I theorized as we rode back here that some sort of contaminate had to be the source in that cave. Reginald complained the entire time while I quickly ignored him. Honestly, Hans, I have no idea why Jillian liked him so much.

"'Upon our arrival, I was expecting to encounter all that life. Instead, we smelled the stench of carcasses rotting all around us. It made the common life even more active, with regular insects and animals busily devouring the mutated creatures. It was such a sight to behold, but I did not have much of that. Reginald insisted to investigate Jose Santamos' death.'

And that point, I looked up at Maria whose view was strictly on the forest landscape. Her pistol was clutched in her hand.

"But Don kept talking. 'He believed he would find research in the decomposition of the forest floor. While that would have been approach, the cave held the answers, which I adamantly explained to him. No matter, he had no desire to be in the cave. I wanted to go in more than ever.

"'We reached the very plateau meeting Dr. Ruiz whose suspicions were quite evident, but I was sure he did not let the whole Jillian matter get back to his own university. Or at least at that point.

"'Finding our equipment and tent very much undisturbed, I began my work, for Jillian, for you, to continue what we started. I had to work alone without choice or consideration from Ruiz which suited me fine. Once I crossed that bridge and set my eyes on that cave seeing the beauty as I am sure you had, I wanted more. I tried to take samples of species and plants as much as I could hold. I gave myself plenty of time for breaks having short controlled stays.'

"Don had always talked and talked about such fine details that in a way his useless banter about the cave made the walk seem to go faster. Ricardo had been ahead of us carrying the shotgun in both hands, leading us. Behind me, much like a soldier, her eyes were on movements on the trees, the ground and the air.

"'It was my second day at that cave towards the end of the day,' Don continued. I could hear his breathing getting heavy. 'It was then

I had noticed a booklet, a journal, Jillian's journal. I recognized her handwriting. I opened to the last entry which simply read: Creatures afraid of ground? Why? Simple as that.'

"I stopped for a second and thought of her handwriting. Seeing myself in the lab about a month earlier, finding the cause of the dirt. Where I too had the same conclusion of what was the meaning behind the bacterium laced soil.

"Not interrupting because it would take precious air from my lungs, Don continued: 'I then stopped where I had I looked over the side of the ledge, probably as she had. Carefully, I strained to see the bottom, past the plants. I watched as long as I could, then I noticed the movement. My lungs were on fire, but it was this location I noticed the other creatures avoiding the dirt, purposely. I noticed a huge string of fire ants forming a dangerously long living bridge. Foolishly and desperately I ran for a quick breath.

"'When I returned, there were a dozen or so of ants on the ground. It was then I noticed they had the same twitching as Jillian had; it was not the fall because no more than several feet, and compost would be a softer landing if anything. It was the ground itself. Somehow, someway I grabbed the largest bottle to scoop that dirt. I had felt victorious, but it didn't last. When the last burst from Arenal overtook the camp, I wanted to save everything, all the evidence of this great discovery. It all went except for the box of dirt.'

"Then we reached the plateau. Above the sky was filling rapidly with dark rain clouds, gusts of wind was coming around us, hot and humid, I looked to the left causally eyeing the volcano in which the top was concealed with floating grey vapors. I had considered for a moment I could see it gaze back at me, a glowing scarlet eye but only the scorching magma was twisting steadily down the other surface. The plateau felt warmer under my feet. Ruiz's area still remained now weathered and ripped from abandonment and neglect, with the seismic instruments broken on the rock. I could see the scorches of whiteness that had been the cause of the fire. Near where the original bridge a tent with sides stood, fairly small. Don, Maria and Ricardo walked into it, there was some talking. In front of me, large black boulders had covered the entrance, no glimmer of red light, no smell, no arthropods, and no movement. Already a moss was forming over the rocks as if nature itself was sealing it forever again, to be hidden.

"Don came to me. 'Is it not amazing how nature can conceal the most beautiful of wonders?' he asked.

"'Don, when I was testing the soil, to me it did not seem like normal dirt. That high concentration building up for years was not natural.' I said.

"Don smiled. 'Dr. Fischer, Hans, your mind is always thinking several steps ahead. I had learned much from you. Come.' He turned and went into the tent. I joined him. In the small tent, a black iron cage held two multicolored chickens, which were clucking madly, a back pack and another gun, a tranquilizer gun. Maria was testing the rope that Ricardo had put on, tightening and securing the rope. Soon she was putting the rope on herself with Ricardo's guidance.

"'When did you know that the soil was a trap for something bigger?' I asked. My heart began to flutter, the idea of seeing and witnessing such a new creature. My old self was coming back to me, I felt reinvigorated. I was in my element again, reunited with my first passion.

"'Hans this is why I asked you to witness this. The day I reached for the soil, I saw the bushes move, something coming towards me, something coming towards the ants that had fallen. Honestly, I was scared. I wasn't prepared that day, and I thought I had another chance to see it. But no, everything was destroyed. Except this.' He pulled out Jillian's last journal, handing it to me."

"In creeping shadows, Old Man Fischer stepped towards an old work bench, draped in webs, crunching on the anthropoid-laden floor, and reached for an old book, dusty, plain and brown. Tenderly, his thin fingers stoked the hard brown binding..."

***

Out of the corner of my eye, I could see the flashing of Jack's phone in his pocket. There were now seven beetles crawling slowly up my legs as more followed. I looked over at Jack whose eyes were large staring down his shirt at a large beetle climbing up to his chest.

I looked back at Fisher, still staring down at the book when he began to read from it. The book was a small tattered leather book piece as if it been read a million times.

Below him, the living carpet seemed more active as pinchers, legs and bodies crawled around. Bugs slowly crawled up Fischer's legs as well, and some slipped down the top of his tall boots. He seemed so distracted. So lost.

Looking at Jack briefly, he was jerking his body trying to get the bug off.

I only stared at the centipede that slowly crawled onto the platform, making its way to my tennis shoe. I hope it would not crawl up my pants.

Then Fisher continued once again, in the same dark voice...

***

"My Jillian," he said, "had seen what was happening in that short time in the cave. She had observed everything, taking in more details as I could never. When she went alone back into that cave, she probably had noticed the same as Don. She probably leaned too far, she hadn't known. Ultimately, it was her incessant curiosity that lead to her demise, I imagine. Even I listened to Don that day, heeded his warnings. I could imagine my Jillian plummeting to her final moments of consciousness, lying helpless on that cave floor, enduring the slight pinches of the small creatures that had been laced with the contamination, so hazardous to her existence.

"'All I know I thought I saw a shell, a large black shell.' Don had said to me as he was ready for the next climb. I too was suited up in the rope.

"'I don't understand,' I said.

"'Hans, neither did I. I really wrecked myself over Jillian, knowing I had been so close. I mourned her too. Reginald left some months after. He had had enough, and I didn't blame him. Our prestigious University was no longer sending any support. There was nothing in that house for me. We'd heard nothing. Until a couple of months ago Dr. Ruiz sent a telegram   an important one.'

As we exited the tent, I saw Don put the tranquilizer gun into his knapsack. pointed up towards the west side of the mountain, with a steep slope covered mostly in dense rainforest except for a bald spot at the very top. "There," he said. ?Do you see it?"

"Looking to where he pointed, I spotted the thin ring, glowing electric-red in stark contrast against the pale grey sky. 'My God,' I gasped.

"Yes, Hans,' he said. "Ruiz had come here about four months ago to survey the area as post-analytical work, when his team discovered the opening. He didn't investigate any further, for fear, I think, of coming in contact with the same gigantic mutants as before. He eventually reached me and explained everything they have witnessed. I came immediately, with the aid of Maria and her cousin Ricardo. Ricardo's family is native to this area, and they lost a couple of family members to the eruption.'

"We had reached the ravine by then, now filled with rock and debris from the volcano. Ricardo used a sling rope across his body and strapped the crate with the live chickens, now covered in a tarp, to his back as they clucked in protest at being jostled. Ricardo climbed up and over the jagged rocks that had filled the ravine eliminating the need for a footbridge like we'd had before. Carefully, he grasped onto the rocks slowly began to make his way across . 'Follow us carefully, Doctor. It is not a hard climb, but the rocks are loose." Don informed me as he began to get his footing. We had ropes between us, connecting us together in a chain, his rope to Ricardo, and my rope to Maria's. "Follow my exact footsteps.

"Of course, every eco-system has a supreme predator, a species at the top of the food chain to control the havoc, keep everything else in check, if you will," Don said out loud.

I felt the dusty rocks slip under my hand as I pulled my body up as I listened to Don begin to lay out his hypothesis to me.

"He continued from above me, "So, What if, in this case, in this cave, sealed away from the world for centuries, the natural order had to evolve with little-to-no threat? Over time, as you could tell by the obvious mutations of the insects and plant life alone."

"True,' I grunted as I traversed a particularly large grouping of rocks. "Then we must theorize that something larger was controlling the elimination cycle, the hunting cycle if you will. This black shell creature can be matched with several hundred species alone in our existing catalog of known rainforest coleopteran suborders."

"'Or perhaps it was not only a natural scavenger, but an opportunistic predator, itself.' Don was leaning against the rock, looking down at me. "Like a hyena in the Africa wild, pursuing after victims, food, desperate for food.'

Maria joined the conversation then, "Our family came from the ancient Inca Tribe, decedents if you will," her tone somber. I dared not to look at her directly for I was only concentrating ahead on the ledges, keeping one eye to the darkening skies above. "For generations, our family had a celebratory custom once a year around the first day of summer. My grandfather would gather the men and the boys of the village, and they would go into the forest in search of a certain beetle: the king beetle. They would come back with a bucket, overflowing, beetles crawling around trying to escape. The entire family, all the wives, the girls and babies, too, would come outside and surround the men with their fresh catch. Each of us would take one, even myself and the other children, and raise our beetle to the sun. My grandfather would speak, in combination of Spanish and Incan language, 'To you, Inti, we offer the sacrifice of true power for the soil of the land.' Then we would eat the creatures alive, crunching the shells and the squirm of their bodies. When I grew older, a teenager, I asked my grandfather why we did it. He replied, 'Child, we must sacrifice to have plenty. The beetle has the power we need: it eats, it devours the waste, and it makes soil plentiful. We are the entire beetle.'"

I had turned to behind and below me, she was grabbing a piece of ledge only inches from my foot. "'The cave was not meant to be discovered by us. Humans believe they must conquer everything," she said. "'My father's death should have been a warning to you.'"

"Ancient beliefs are not applicable to modern science," I remarked then continued behind Don. In hindsight, perhaps she had been right. Or maybe my age is making me more cognizant of my own ignorance.

"As we climbed, the howling wind was the only sound to break through the tense silence of our climbing party.

"Soon, we had reached the most treacherous part of our climb, up the steep side of the mountain where there were fewer handholds and we were more exposed to the gusting wind as we navigated the narrow ledge. The only consolation at that point was that the cave entrance and the red glow were now visible and only meters away.

The chickens incessant clucking was echoing against the rocks. I looked down over the top of the forest canopy, barely able to make out the beautiful tropical birds flying from tree to tree, the black shadows of howler monkeys as they moved about. Ahead of us, Ricardo had already made it to the entrance. He placed himself in the crook, and then quickly began pulling Don up. In a matter of minutes we were cramped in the small cavity in the rock face. Ricardo's acidic dank breath wafted into my nostrils as I passed him. Then the familiar warmth slowly washed over my body, the humidity of the secret world took over me.

"I will go first down the ledge. Be careful, there's a lot of loose gravel," Don said. The cave entrance was barely two meters high by a width of three meters. The rock walls amplified the chickens' clucking like a megaphone and the effect was deafening.

"Don slid, legs first, down the grade of the cave, and soon we were all doing the same, looking for anything that moved. The glow intensified as we moved deeper into the cavern. A chrysalis of a butterfly species was near the opening which hung from a thick tree limb. It's size was about nine meters in length and four meters in width with a brilliant ivory shell. More spectacular, the thin member of the chrysalis was transparent and I could see the beautiful markings of large butterfly inside.

"Had I realized that I would cross the threshold into this unfathomable Otherworld again, I would have better mentally readied myself. I don't think I had been truly awake on my journey here, not until this moment.

"As I stood there, pondering the punching bag-size chrysalis and blinking away the cobwebs in my brain, I heard the rustle of pebbles behind me. Something was sliding down the path in my direction. I started to move forward, before I looked over my shoulder to see what was coming toward me.

"Maria was only a meter away from me when I reached a narrow passage that opened up to a long ledge, high above the cave floor. Don was crouching near the edge. From this location, we could see the vastness of the cavern. I took in the unnerving, majestic beauty of this hidden world.

"I have only been this way once, to check the safety of the ledge," Don whispered, almost reverentially. "It was not until recently that I had found that shed you met me at last night. The man there is the farmer's son. He offered us the use of their shed in exchange for his access to look at our specimens under the microscope. He is stone deaf."

"Maria reached our spot then and crouched next to me, breathing hard. Her eyes had softened in wonder in the incandescent crimson light. "This is amazing," she said.

"'The cave is also lethal,,' I replied, looking over the forest. I then saw the life appear, under the massive foliage, on peak of the branches. I felt the warmth in my chest.

"She said nothing even as she awed at the forest ahead of her.

"Shortly, I heard the clucking fowl and Ricardo bent over slightly. Next to me, already Don was pulling an arrow gun out, snapping the pieces together. He pulled out a separate hook, handing to me. 'Here Hans, screw tight into the rock right there,' Don said.

"Next to me, Maria had her gun out, eyeing the area around us, guarding us.

With the rope tied securely around my waist, I leaned further over the edge. It took a moment for my eyes to adjust to peering into the inky darkness and I tried to steady my breathing. Luckily, we were so close to the side opening, the cool wind brushed over me. As my eyes started to make out shapes below, I scanned the area. Just when I was beginning to think, "Or course it wouldn't be this easy to find...," I catch a twitch of movement in the periphery. I look straight down along the cliff wall below, and that's when I saw it: an enormous creature of about fifteen meters with elongated antennae clinging silently to the vertical cavern wall, about five meters below us. Gently, trying not to make vibrations, I screwed in the hook."

***

At that moment, Dr. Fischer turned his back to us; his form was straight and rigid much that of a soldier.

He walked towards the back of the basement and further into the shadows of the dark basement. The floor was crawling around him, slithering and striking at his shoes but he didn't seem to pay any mind to any of it.

Jack suddenly began squirming excitedly in his chair drawing my attention to the beetle that was now lay on his chest. He was breathing hard, his eyes were bulging in his head as he gawked in fear and disgust at the thing. Sweat poured down the sides of his face, as his hands were twitching behind him, and I craned my head back to look at his movements.

I glanced between where Dr. Fischer had disappeared and Jack, a longtime Boy Scout, has he was working furiously on the knot that held the rope tight around his wrists.

A smile of relief and excitement overtook my lips.

Until I felt a sharp pinch on my leg. I jumped and immediately shook my leg out at the beetle clinging to my jeans. It was pinching at my skin with its sharp beak-like pinchers. But it wasn't my primary concern at that moment. No, my eyes were now locked on the black scorpion that was creeping over the corner of the platform only a few feet away from me.

***

"With much trepidation," Dr. Fischer began again from somewhere in the dark depths of the basement. "I moved back onto the ledge, as Don was already preparing the tranquilizer gun with enough toxin to put a herd of elephants to sleep. Don poured ether over one of the hens, provoking more spirited though odd sounding clucks from the bird, the echoing sounds seemed alien in the stillness of the cave.

"'*Ta bien, Ricardo,*' Don said, nodding at the man who already had the dart gun ready, a cable attached to the end. Don looked down, not seeing the creature below us from his vantage point. He pointed to a dark spot, and said, '*Estes, Por favor.*'"

"Maria's eyes darted in every direction, her body tense, as she scanned every possible direction in our fantastical surroundings, trying to detect even threats or where they might come from. But I knew; I knew all of it was a threat, even the immense *hetereocera* flapping its delicate brown wings from under a nearby fern leaf. I watched as it changed directions and flew towards the intense red glow of the cave. What else was down there? from the corner of my eye an five meter arachnid creature inching closer to us as its long spiny legs ambled forward It had probably sensed our movements in the vibrations in the air and come in for a closer look. Ricardo looked like he planned to make the creature regret his curiosity.

"'*Va! Va!* Don said to Ricardo."

In an instant a small crack sounded off and the arrow flew into the cave, near the dark spot where the floor was seen. Quickly, Ricardo took the cage latching a hook onto the cable, and then placed the other end onto the nearby hook. Within seconds, the cage was released and I could hear the high pitch squeal of the cage fade into the cave, barely audible over the echoes of other unfamiliar sounds around us. In a snap, the cage stopped just inches above the ground.

"I turned my gaze back to the arachnid. Don was too interested in the chicken to care about my actions, so I took his light from him and scanned up the walls of the cave. For a moment, everything seemed so still, so unnaturally still, as if everything had stopped in unison, on cue. Then, there, on the ceiling above us, the arachnid clung to the rocks a couple of meters over us.

"'Maria! There!' I shouted to her, tugging on her arm. Instantly, in soldier-like precision, her arm shot up in the direction I was looking and fired at the creature. A couple of shots hit the beast then it was falling swiftly toward, then past us, one of its flailing legs slicing open Maria's free arm as it passed. A spray of her arterial blood splashed over my face, blinding me as I tried to grab her arm to keep her from falling with the creature. In the next instant Ricardo was beside her, pulling her back and ripping a section of his shirt to wrap around the wound. I leaned toward them where we were all sitting or kneeling on the rough foundation of gravel and rock.

"Strangely, I saw Ricardo was looking with Don towards the cave, when he muttered, '*Oh dios mio.*'

"As I looked the same way, Don said proudly, 'There she is...'"

Russell

TWENTY-FOUR

(SHANE)

Dr. Fischer stood next to a dark box and flicked a switch. large red light came on Jack's tape-muffled screams were soon followed by my own quick yelp.

Inside the previously dark alcove of the basement was something large. As the red bulb reached full luminescence, banishing the shadows to the far corners of the space behind heavy metal bars we were being watched by a large, black beetle-like creature. It was immense in size: nearly that of a small hybrid car, standing on six spiny legs, its shell black as coal. It stood almost to Dr. Fischer's chest, or even taller, as it squirmed about. In the bright red light, the insect seemed to move more, its large pinchers were zapped as it grazed the electric fence that contained it.

That hum, I now realized, was the electrical fence stopping the hideous creature from escaping. My hands were sweating, and I could feel the moisture soak through my layers of clothes. My heart raced, feeling slightly out of breath, and I thought I knew we couldn't escape.

"Let me introduce you to *Coleoptera Hanium Jillium,* or Hans and Jillian's Beetle. I named her myself," Dr. Fischer announced with pride as if he were introducing his first born. He hadn't bothered to look at us as he spoke but I could hear the sneer on face as he spoke. "This is what emerged from that cave floor. This is what would have devoured my Jillian should she not have been discovered in time, not that her fate hadn't already been sealed. This is what nature did not what humanity to find." He paused, watching the beetle intensely. "Isn't she... isn't she just so beautiful?"

Jack was shifting back and forth in his chair, trying desperately to shake off the beetle that was now nipping at his neck. His movements were shifting the phone closer to the edge of his jacket pocket and I could see the flashing light clearly now.

I was about to find myself in as desperate a situation as Jack, if that black scorpion moved any closer to me. I took advantage of the increased lighting to look around the basement frantically for something, anything that might help us since we could see more.

In my frenzied attempt to lay eyes on something to get us out of whatever this was, I glanced at the window hoping to see someone passing by, a car, anything, so that I could yell for help. I knew I couldn't just scream in panic.

I had to figure a way out.

"I brought her back thirty-five years ago," he said proudly. His was still turned away from us, our movements masked by the crazy thrashing of that strange beast inside its cage banging against the fence showering sparks everywhere.

"Why?" I asked, barely hearing a sound. "Why would you bring that here?"

It was then I realized that Jillian knew of its discovery, and Don knew of it as well. Fischer took this much farther, and captured the creature, the source of the danger.

"I am scientist, and a researcher," he stated matter-of-factly. He paused, seeming to admire his work for another moment. "I needed to know how it survived in that soil when everything else seemed to die in it, how it thrived even, how it differed from the other mutant creatures in that magical cavern. So many questions to be answered! Sure it took a little bit of forged documentation to get the specimen here, but really was well worth it."

If I could keep him talking while I thought of how to escape... I asked a little louder, "Didn't anyone see you bring it in?"

"Of course not, dear boy," Fischer commented disdainfully, "I had been meticulously careful in my planning, bringing her here in middle of the night. I paid handsome salaries to the delivery people for their discretion. In fact, Frank Stanislaw designed her enclosure and its inner workings. I hid the creature in the tool shed from viewing until her place was ready here. Or course, I hadn't planned for every possibility. I thought I had an adequate amount time while he created this beautiful containment unit. About a week after she was delivered here, she escaped the tool shed and disappeared. When I found her a few days later in the Forest Reserve several kilometers from here. She'd slaughtered a herd of deer there and was still lingering amidst the remains of the carcasses. I presumed that it had been her first taste, and that she'd developed a desire for animal blood at that point. I had to tranquilize her and have her transported back to the house."

As though the creature understood that we were talking about her, it went wild, tossing its body back and forth in the enclosed space, clicking its mandibles and its claws clattered on the patch of the cement floor, which had deep roots and scaring from years of abuse from "Cleo". More sparks flew as it rammed the bars with its helmet-like head.

The plastic jars jiggled violently against the wall, the liquid swirling violently inside.

"Now, now, Cleo, just relax. They are guests," he said to the thing like it understood him. He looked only at it like a father over his young toddler, lovingly and madly. "When Frank finished his project, the specimen went dormant."

"How long did that last?" I asked, surprisingly distracted by my curiosity.

Jack was leaning back as far as he could not to let the beetle pinch at his neck. Some nicks had been made as trickles of blood went down into his shirt. But his fists were loosening under his movements. In one final jerk of his body, the beetle flew off of his shirt and disappeared into the crawling floor. I began to sway my body side-to-side in hopes to loosen the bolted chair.

Old Man Fischer remained staring at the insect; I think he was lost in his own world. "Seven years to be exact, and that would be her pattern. During her hibernation, I created this mock-up environment with her cousin familia on the floor, the compost, and the conditions for the bacteria to thrive. I created this habitat with conditions similar to what she would have lived in, even adding the extra humidity with a large commercial humidifier. In the beginning I had tried to establish some ferns, palms, and other plant species, but that was too much immense of a task to maintain.

"The most challenging aspect of her care was her feeding. I tried processed ground meat and poultry for her, but Cleo would have nothing to do with it. So I tried the one thing I knew she would go after, as she had when we first encountered her: live chickens. I set up the platform that you are on now. I turned off the cage and let her out. How strange and unique her eating habits had been in a caged environment, seeing the claws snap the chickens, the tongue come out to drain the liquid, the simplicity of the kill. Amazingly, she devoured the four chickens in less than thirty seconds and wanted more.

"That night she came towards me. Of course I shot a tranquilizer in her, but it bounced off her shell. I ran up the stairs to save myself. I heard a loud crash and she went out the storm cellar, and escaped. I had to go after her, I didn't want anyone to discover this. That time, once I wrangled her down, I just placed the chickens into her cage until she went dormant again."

The giant black insect was now thrashing about, ramming against the cage door. Dr. Fischer never flinched at the shower of sparks, like he was used to this thing acting so crazy, but he had his back to us, so I couldn't tell what expression he wore.

I looked back to Jack, who still struggled with his ropes, but at least the beetle seemed to have stopped attacking the delicate flesh of his neck.

Then things started to happen in quick succession. I heard crashing and the sound of liquid, and turned to see one giant flash from the thrashing animal violently shake the cage wall in its frame, jostling the ten gallon bottles of liquid on the uneven floor. With just a few solid bumps they rocked and tilted, nearly spilling over.

Then I could have sworn I saw headlights flash in the basement window. *Could a car pass by that close to this side of the house?* I was turned around and couldn't seem to orient myself to which side was exposed to the street. *What were those lights? Did I imagine them?* I found myself silently praying someone would hear the crazy commotion inside and come investigate. My stomach was full of knots. How are we going to get out of this? What was the old man planning to do?

"What about the other animals? The neighborhood pets?" I asked. "Someone will discover this."

Then he turned. Jack and I froze.

There was a long, peculiar smile on his face, and in the red light he looked angry and insane. His eyes had a sinister gleam in them and his form tall, imposing. His voice broke slightly as he spoke, slow and menacingly, "Yes, there were a few that have tried, but I shooed them away. It's easy, when I'm the mean old man on the block, no? There was one boy, can't remember his name, but he tried to knock on my door when he found his dog's collar in my yard. I just yelled at him and scared him off. He knew better not to come snooping around here anymore."

He paused, eyeing me then Jack then back to me.

"The animals are a necessary sacrifice to the whole greater cause of science and research," he said so bitter, matter-of-factly. "During her first dormant stage thirty five years ago, here with me, I was able to determine her age to be about one hundred fifty years old. In that way, she is much like that of a giant sea turtle, one the oldest living species on the globe. That intrigued me greatly because nowhere else in the Insecta phylum is any creature known to have a long lifespan. That discovery alone would turn the natural science community on its head. After she awoke from her seven-year sleep, she needed feeding again and became difficult to contain. Unfortunately, by that time Frank, my trusted electrician and handyman on her original enclosure had died and I was forced to do the work myself to fortify her accommodations. Once her hunger was sated, she tried to spawn You probably noticed the eggs that resulted, preserved in the jars in Jillian's room. Unfortunately, I only realized after her second spawning that the eggs' failure to thrive was due to the low level of carbon in my makeshift habitat. there is not enough carbon in the air. By the third spawn attempt, I learned that her eggs would need the carbon in-take to remain consistent for at least a year, but there was little I could do about raising carbon to that level for her to spawn successfully without drawing attention to my little laboratory here, or risk poisoning myself in the process. Cleo's fully developed adult stage allowed her to adapt easily to this higher-oxygenated atmosphere and the reduced carbon concentration.

"But I have rambled far too long. You two young men are to be key players in the next phase of my experiments," he said, smiling as though we should be thrilled with the honor he'd bestowed upon us. He stepped toward us, crushing various beetles, worms, centipedes and spiders that were underfoot, as the living nightmare behind him hit the cage harder showering sparks across the width of the basement, some landing on the platform at our feet.

As if is there was no worry, he was so close to me. His wrinkly thin pale lips grew wide, and I could look deep into his red-veins in his yellowing eyes, see that his sanity was slipping and there was no reasoning with him. Dr. Fischer's mind was set, and then croaked:

"For my next experiment, I plan to introduce Cleo to human species And see how she reacts to direct contact with people. What do you suppose will happens when I open the cage?" he asked me, a devilish grin loomed large on his face.

Then there was a ringing, coming from somewhere far away. At first, I looked to Jack thinking it might be his phone ringing in his pocket and we were just now hearing it for the first time. But when I turned to Jack, he was staring at the stairs and up toward the ceiling. Then I heard it again, and I looked at Dr. Fisher. He'd heard it too. A look of irritation crossed his face, as I heard it ring a again, and we all turned toward the stairs.

It was the ring of the doorbell.

Then there was knocking at the door, then pounding.

Dr. Fischer was frozen to the spot for a moment. Then he reached over with a long finger and put it to my mouth. Mechanically, his head shifted back toward the steps and his face turned sour. He stormed to his workbench, grabbing the duct tape, and said to me, "Now, I don't want anyone to hear you scream. Or I will have to make this much more painful for you both." He looked from me to Jack and back before placing a fresh strip of the heavy grey utility tape over our mouths.

Both Jack and I let out simultaneous groans of panic as Dr. Fisher discovered Jack's loosened ties on his wrists. His response was to look into Jack's alarmed face, and tell him, "I liked you the most because you didn't ask any questions. You listened so quietly."

He tore a long strip of tape and wrapped it forcibly around Jack's wrists, over the loose rope, then leaned in to Jack's ear, and hissed, "I guess you will get to meet Cleo first."

Another bell rang and more knocks came from upstairs, sounding more urgent and demanding, and Fisher growled in irritation as he pushed away from Jack and turned toward the stairs.

He cleared his voice, and in a deep gurgling voice, "Coming!" We watched him as he ambled toward the stairs and began to slump over, with a limp on the right, and grabbed his cane hanging near the bottom step It was rather fascinating to see him morph before our eyes into a weak old man, as we all had known him to be, the other adults seeing him as harmless Old Man Fischer: the fragile and grumpy old man on the corner, failing to see the real secrets he was hiding.

The basement door closed behind him.

Jack looked at me and his muffled cries came from under his tape.

I began to rock my body hard in the chair. I didn't know what I was going to do when I was free, but I would do something I had to, and it had to be now.

A large crash sounded from next to us.

The beast's ramming against the cage had finally dropped the jugs. They toppled over, cracking and spilling onto the ground, soaking the floor. Whatever chemicals where in those containers was killing the floor, all the slithering and motion stopped. Some insects rushed onto the platform to escape the waves of the poisonous sea. The odor was overwhelming, and smelt of gasoline that had sat in our garage for a long time, only this smelled much, much worse.

I tried to shake off more of the insects off the platform into the lake of death below but in same moment, Cleo, the enormous mutant beetle, went insane. It forced itself hard against the cage, repeatedly. I could hear the crackles of electricity singe the shell. Jack was screaming again beside to me.

Above us, I heard shouting and stomping on the floor boards. I looked up at the old rafters and tried to scream.

The beetle was making headway with the bars, and I heard a snap of wood and groan of straining metal. I began to shake my chair harder. Sparks from the cage were becoming brighter in the dim red light. Then I saw the panel of red bulbs fall to the cement, splitting open. Unknown to the beetle as it twirled itself in the small cage, its back legs crushing it until it sparked a fire from the frayed electrical wires.

This was it! We needed to escape, and it had to be now, before the fire or that creature reached us.

The insect squealed suddenly and so loudly that both Jack and I stopped our muffled screaming and stared at it for a moment. The thing was trying to unfold its wings, which were large, probably more than fifteen feet across, instinctively knowing it too needed to escape the fire that was now crawling up the back wall of its enclosure. From where I sat, I knew the cage was too cramped for full extension of her wingspan. Fisher had purposely kept her cage too small. It rammed its body against the bars, breaking the wood that held the metal bars in place. Ah, Dr. Fisher's fatal design flaw. It was amazing that it hadn't broken free of the cage before now. It's power was impressive.

A loud thud came from the floor above us, then I watched as a layer of smoke overtook the floor joists above our heads, and then filled my nose. I was suddenly gasping for air, unable to breath with the tape over my mouth and the smoke stealing my air.

Jack was breathing heavily through his nose. He looked at me with wide, scared eyes.

The caged insect renewed its attempts to escape. That was what it wanted: to be free. Dr. Fischer had caged an animal, a wild thing that wasn't meant to be kept by humans.

The fire was growing larger, and the insect was crouching against the voltage.

The door of the basement flew open with a bang.

Then hurried footsteps as someone was coming down the stairs. In the shower of sparks, I saw my mom fly down the stairs.

"Shane! Jack!" Mom gasped.

Another thud hit the floor, but heavier.

She ran to us and looked over at the cage. She shrieked but her shook off her shock and amazement quickly and she came to us, ripping the tape off my mouth.

"Mom, we have to go!" I yelled as I struggled with my ropes.

"You are okay?" She asked. She looked back over her shoulder, at the giant the bug striking the cage relentlessly, and turned, wide-eyed to Jack and ripped his tape off his face.

"WHAT THE HELL IS THAT?!" My mom yelled and she began to tear frantically at the rope around my legs while she squashed dozens of dead and dying bugs around us. "What the hell did he do to you guys? Are you both okay?"

"Mom, we're fine! That thing is trying to escape! We HAVE to go!"

The beetle's nudging against the fence was making the electric cage surge. The hum turned to hissing, and I could smell the shell burning then.

Jack caught his breath enough to say, "Mrs. O'Conner, there's a knife in my front pocket!"

Mom groped in his jacket pockets and found the knife and in seconds she had freed Jack. "Go! Go! Your Dad's up there!"

Jack leapt off the platform and he didn't look back.

The fire was getting intense now, licking its way across the ceiling coming toward us. As Mom cut my last leg free, the floor ignited in a flash of flame. We both screamed as we grabbed for each other. I spared one last look at the insect trapped in the cage, squealing against the heat and flames. Its legs were squirming and its antennae were curling from the heat.

"COME ON!" Mom yelled pulling at me.

The sudden pain in my shoulder erupted again, but I ran: up the stairs, taking two at a time, with Mom was right behind me as we pushed through the door.

I looked back to the basement stairs and past her, catching a glimpse of the flames as they followed us up the stairs, crawling along the walls as if it were trying to beat us to the top.

I bolted down the hallway, and found Mr. Richardson picking up Dr. Fischer up from the floor and throwing him over his shoulder. He yelled at Jack to get outside, then yelled in general for everyone to get out quickly. There was smoke from the basement now beginning to fill the main floor.

"RUN! RUN!" Mom yelled from behind me.

She didn't need to tell me again: I was running as fast as I could. Behind me, I heard a loud pop then everything went black.

When I could see again there was ringing in my ears. I was still on my feet somehow and I just ran: past the study, over the cracks in the floor where smoke was oozing up and flames were just beginning to creep through.

I reached the door, Mom right behind me then I saw Mr. Richardson putting Dr. Fischer down on the weeds outside in the yard. Already, cars were stopping in front of the house, some of them running over to us. Mr. Richardson went to Jack who was on the ground gasping for air, then looking up at us.

Suddenly, a rush of intense explosion from behind me. The force of the blast carried me off the porch and I was airborne. I landed solidly against the stone sidewalk where the pain of my shoulder exploded inside me, then my head bounce once on the immovable concrete. I wanted to scream at the intensity of the pain, but my breath was stolen from me in that moment and I couldn't make a sound. That seemed to somehow amplify the pain! Around me the world seemed to be flashing and spinning. I blinked several times, trying to see my mom who was now hovering over me.

"Shane!" Her lips moved but there was no sound. Why wasn't she talking louder? She had the same look she got when she was with Maggie during one of her episodes: a look of sadness and concern? Was Maggie sick again? What was wrong now, I wondered? The siren echoing inside my head but suddenly all I could feel was the cool night air, and I suddenly felt very comfortable and sleepy.

I was rolled onto my back and once I was looking up I could see fire eating up Dr. Fischer's house. I looked up toward Jillian's room as yellow-orange flames burst through the windows; there would be no more of Jillian's memories.

The sky seemed to come alive, the cold air mixing with the smoke. Was if it the insects also trying to escape from Dr. Fischer's prison? My confused thoughts were being squeezed in on all sides by darkness. Was the fire dying?

I looked to my mom, as my heavy eyes greeted the darkness.

EPILOGUE

"I am a lineman for the county
and I drive the main road
Searchin' in the sun for another overload
I hear you singin' in the wire, I can hear you through the whine
And the Wichita Lineman is still on the line..."

--Glen Campbell

Halloween finally arrived!

"Mom, are you ready?" I called through the from out on the porch.

Looking down the block, as the sun set, many kids were already on the street, dressed as princesses and goblins, witches, dogs, everything else, too. Porch lights dotted the landscape and kids were marching up and down the sidewalks with their bags and pillow cases for treats.

"I am getting Maggie ready!" she shouted after a second.

The weather was actually warmer now than it had been a few weeks ago. It changed just in time for the holiday, and I was glad because I didn't wear a winter coat over my costume.

At school, we had our annual Halloween parade, which would be my last one: I was dressed as a Mummy because of the cast on my right arm. I had broken it in several places and needed some stitches, too. I spent a couple of days in the hospital. According to the doctor, I really took a hit to my head when the explosion pushed me out of the house. Mom stayed home with me for one day and Dad another once I got home. I really couldn't do much with my extra time at home; the pain medicine really knocked me out. I suppose it wasn't until yesterday that I began to feel like normal.

Mom had suggested the mummy costume in the hospital, and I liked the idea. Dad thought I shouldn't wear something like that. I was not sure yet if Dad was angry with me, or proud of me, after what had happened. We hadn't talked about it yet, and whatever he felt, he had an odd way of showing it.

"Trick or treat!" a voice said behind me.

I turned to see a couple of girls, fourth graders, I think, walking up our sidewalk to the porch.

They all looked surprised to see me sitting there. On the sidewalk near the street, I saw two parents talking and pointing at me.

"Aren't you the one that was held up by Old Man Fischer?" one girl, dressed up as a ballet dancer, asked me.

"Yeah, he is!" the other, in a large doll costume, replied.

"I'm glad you got rid of him," the ballet dancer whispered.

"He creeped us out," the doll followed.

I didn't say anything, just watched them as they took some candy from the bowl. The dancer said, "You're a hero."

They skipped off to their parents.

Dad came out, carrying a pumpkin carved with a fancy witch's face. People on our block were always jealous of his carved pumpkins. "Last one," he huffed and walked past me.

"It looks scary," I said to him.

Turning to me, he smiled, "Not as scary as you."

From behind me I heard some muffled screams on the television, and noticed Dad look up through the window. He didn't really care about the walking part of treat or treating, he liked to stay home to hand out the candy and watch scary movies.

"I heard someone was scary," sang Mom's voice from behind me.

When I turned to look at her, she stood in the doorway, her face painted like a tiger, and she was wearing some black yoga pants and a black shirt. I could see the orange and black striped tail dangle dangling behind her. The paint brought out the scratches on her face. She'd needed some stitches to close some gashes from being thrown by the explosion. She'd landed on a broken tree and a branch impaled her arm and her face was nicked from the thorns. She also had a couple of broken ribs, but from the tight shirt that she wore no one could see the bandages she wore underneath.

"Who was that on the phone?" Dad asked.

"Dr. Kimberly," Mom said, smiling. "Looks like these new meds for Maggie are going to work for a while. The test results came back good."

"So, it's a double celebration today?" Dad said, pulling Mom in closer to him.

"You'd like to think so," Mom said.

"You are such a tiger," Dad said, quickly climbing the last steps to wrap an arm around her.

Mom smiled and kissed him. "You out did yourself on the pumpkins."

"You outdid yourself on this costume," he said to her. Dad kissed her neck.

"Guys!" I said. "Eww!"

"Boooo, booo," a small voice came from the screen door, and out came Maggie the Ghost. Her tiny body was covered in a sheet with two simple eye holes cut out.

"And you look adorable!" Dad crooned as he scooped up Maggie.

"No me scar-ee 'host!" Maggie screamed back.

"Yes, you are a scary ghost," Mom said.

I saw Jack's parents' car pull up to the curb then. Mr. Richardson was in a Hawaiian shirt and long tropical shorts. A large straw hat covered his head and he had white stuff painted on his nose. Mrs. Richardson was dressed as a witch with a large black hat. Jack climbed out of the backseat and was running at me in an train engineer's hat and overalls, but his face was white and there was fake blood all over his neck.

"Shane!" He joined us on the porch. "I only went down the block at our house and look in my bag." He opened his pillow case to show me his take.

"I like the dead train conductor outfit, Jack. Looks even better at night." I said.

"Mr. Richardson," Dad said, shaking Mr. Richardson's hand.

"Where's the costume, Donnie?" Mr. Richardson asked.

"I am an insane baker in plainclothes," Dad replied deadpan.

They laughed.

"So, you stay in and watch slasher movies, too?"

"What you got?" Mr. Richardson put a hand to his square jaw, looking interested.

"Just your normal everyday couple who are stranded in middle of nowhere and a homicidal maniac is hunting them down in the middle of the night."

"Sounds great to me!"

Dad looked serious, and said, "You will be forced to have a malted beverage."

"May I, dearest one?" Mr. Richardson turned to his wife.

"If you must," she replied and kissed him on the cheek.

They went inside the house, and Mom and Mrs. Richardson began talking about Maggie and her costume.

Jack and I were on the steps.

"Did you know our picture was in the paper this week?" he asked me. He was twisting a licorice piece in his mouth.

While I was in the hospital, Jack told everyone at school about what happened to us. He could never keep his mouth shut! Many kids and adults did not believe the story until I confirmed it when I came back. Even some of the people who witnessed the fire claimed to have seen all the bugs dying in the fire. Mom reluctantly spoke to a reporter for a small interview in the local paper. The same article that Jack just mentioned feature our faces and Old Man Fischer's house in ruins.

"Yeah, I did, I guess. I only glanced at it. I really didn't want to read what it said," I lied.

"You know, yesterday, Mike came up to me and apologized for everything he had ever done to me? Can you believe that? In front of a hundred people on the playground. I couldn't believe it," Jack had only told me the story for the tenth time today.

Guess I never will tell him the *real truth*.

"Are we ready?" I asked Mom, interrupting her.

"Well, are you?"

I smiled, "Yeah, it's getting dark."

"Don't you want it to get darker for trick or treat?" Mrs. Richardson asked. Even in her green makeup, her smile still mesmerized me. She reached from under her cape, and pulled out several glow sticks. "Here you guys," and Maggie came to her, "for you, too, sweetie."

"Alright!" Jack screamed, cracking and putting it around his neck.

Mom put one around my neck and one on my cast. "That should do it."

"Allison," Mrs. Richardson said softly, "Are they really putting Hans away in a psychiatric hospital?"

I stepped a couple of feet away, watching Maggie and Jack chase each other, Maggie haunting the dead train conductor. They were laughing and giggling, but I stayed close to the porch to listen to the conversation.

"Yes, you don't have to worry," she paused. "Detective Regis came this morning to explain to us that he went berserk in his cell, started rambling some nonsense about his late wife and large insects, and someone named 'Cleo'. He kept repeating that Cleo was alive, and insisted that he had to look for her."

"Oh my," Mrs. Richardson said.

Just then, I noticed that there were some more kids coming our way.

"He'll be put away forever," Mom said. "I thought I pitied him. I guess you really never know a person, I suppose."

"Yeah."

"Come on, Mom!" Jack whined.

"Hey Shane!" A kid from across the street yelled. "That was sweet what you did! You, too, Jack!"

"Thanks!" Jack yelled back with a huge grin.

"That's the other worry I have," Mom said to Mrs. Richardson.

"What's that?"

"Containing the preteen ego," she said then looked at me.

Mrs. Richardson started laughing, "I guess I will tell the big boys that we are leaving."

"Okay, Mary."

"Can I use your bathroom, Mrs. O'Conner?" Jack asked.

"If you must," Mom replied.

Jack ran up the stairs, catching up to his mother. They went inside the house together where I could hear a burst of laughter from the living room.

Mom looked at me, and whispered, "I'm proud of you."

I looked at her, then asked, "Did Detective Regis say if they found that thing's body?"

"No, Shane. Dr. Fischer had a lot of flammable materials in that basement. Everything was burned to ash." She paused. "You have nothing to worry about, okay?"

"Mom?"

"Yes, Shane." She was adjusting her tiger ears.

"How did you know where to find us?"

She stopped, and looked down at me. "I saw your notes on Mr. Fischer, with your questions about the disappearances."

"You went through my bag?" I whined, rolling my eyes.

"Yes, got a problem with that?"

I had to smile at her expression, then I shook my head, and quietly answered, "No."

Maggie came up to Mom and gave her a hug around her legs. Mom started talking to her.

I watched the people out on the darkening street, heard the giggles of the young kids and screams of the older ones in mock terror. Today had been my first day back to school, and many kids came up to talk to me, wanting to hear the story, but I didn't have much I wanted to tell them. Even Mike told me that I was good with him. Mrs. A. came up to me to thank me for giving her morning walks back to her.

But despite from being told that I have restored a sense of peace and safety in the neighborhood, I couldn't get his story out of my head. I couldn't escape the feeling like I had been with him on his scientific trips. I will never get the image of Cleo out of my head, not for a long while, at least. In the middle of the night for the last couple of days, I would turn on my light and swear that I saw things moving in the dark corners of my room.

Dr. Fischer was no longer hiding in his house. He was being sent away, locked in a mental hospital. Perhaps it would be safer around here now.

As the tale of Old Man Fisher still swirled in my head like haunting whispers, my bravery helped to answer some our town's legends. The experience in his basement made me a stronger kid than I could possibly image. The fact that I witnessed something extraordinary both intrigued and frightened me for years to come. What it proved was that anything was possible.

Next time, I would be prepared for anything…

July 2016

Your Purchase Means a Donation...

A portion of proceeds from my book sales will be donated to the Autism Society.

The Autism Society supports, advocates and networks for Autistic people and their families. Most importantly, the organization is an essential source of information for seeking medical professionals and gathering resources for Autistic people and their family members and direct them to the right local facility.

Autism effects individuals on different levels, categorizing them from high-functioning (those who able to blend into society) to low-functioning (those who are needing constant care and support). Despite the diagnosis, Autistic girls, boys, teenagers and adults need continuous help to adapt to rudimentary daily tasks for the rest of their lives. A family, who has someone with Autism, understands and appreciates these individuals' uniqueness and gifts to share with the world.

I am lucky to be a parent of a gifted and talented Autistic young adult.

Mental illness robs the individual of functioning in life. Please be kind to help those who cannot support themselves on a daily basis.

Russell

A Preview of Russell's

Next Dark Thriller...

Gavin

Coming Soon

(Unedited)

PROLOGUE

He travelled ninety percent of the time for his job, wrangling in new customers from the competition, reaching his bonus marks each period and assessing monthly goals for his team. He loved his job; travel was the perfect excuse. Even more importantly, he could escape his pathetic home life. On his business trips, he could be what he *wished to be*, what he *longed to be*, and become *who he should have been*.

No matter what, the liaisons were *his* personal treats.

Never had his indiscretions interrupted his work schedule. He worked especially hard, meeting with his clients, going to early dinners, creating a tight schedule, so he could have time for his fun. He could be the lover of many men. He did not care about the person's history, their past lovers, their race…he just cared about the pending pleasure.

The bathroom light stretched out over the shadows, and soon the hard sound of water drummed against the granite surfaces. The Latino hummed softly, breaking the tranquility of the atmosphere. It wasn't the first time he had been with this man. Just so coincidental that he got the email from the Latino the other day, how quick the Latin man had responded.

Ubiquitous internet sites allowed him to have discreet interactions. Sometimes he remained anonymous, other times he used aliases, and times, like now, he gave out his true name. In the case of the latter, saying his real name to his partners probably made him the most adventurous and seductive.

Slowly, he swung his legs from underneath the sweaty hotel sheets. He was not a fit man: the surface of his stomach was bloated, his hairline receding, and his body was speckled with salt and pepper hair. He had to catch his breath walking up a single flight of stairs. Lately, he found himself having to buy larger clothes. Yet men still found him attractive, or was it the money he flashed? In the glass picture frame, the faint reflection of his bare torso catching his eye as he was tried to ignore the large mirror on the opposite wall. *"Am I supposed to look like this as I go into my forties?"* he thought. In the darken shadow of his image, he could have sworn he saw his father.

A brief tremble shook his body. So long it had been since he thought about his father. That had been a lifetime ago, another lifetime.

"Asshole," he mumbled under his breath, then he stood up and ambled towards the window.

Carelessly, his hand clutched one of the two white rods of the thick French embroidered curtains and slid it open. The brilliance of the hot afternoon sun filled the room instantly; the Chicago North Shore skyline presented itself. Below, the beach, filled with nearly-naked men and women, sunning themselves, playing in the water and even running along the path. Ahead, tall apartment buildings lined Lincoln Park in a faint blur, as they merged with the northern horizon. The Park was dotted with people setting up picnics and getting ready for some soccer or soft ball game. Between these islands of greenery and sand, Lake Shore Drive was at a crawl; cars sluggishly making their way north or south. While he was twenty stories above, in a well air conditioned room, the people outside were enjoying the oppressive heat of summer.

Chicago, had always made him uneasy. Much of business had been in the area, and he dreaded coming here. For one, it was too close to his own home just across the Wisconsin border in Milwaukee. And, it was a place he longed to forget; a life he had once lived, and a life no longer cared to be part of.

But the city did have its perks; the men there were abundant, lively and exciting.

Behind him, the shower continued to echo off the stone walls. Snippets of this morning, and of last night, drifted through his thoughts, brief flashed of his Latino pleasing him in many different ways. He found himself savoring the memories until he was nearly aroused all over again. This morning, at the Home Office, he anxiously finished up his work and lied about needing to get back home sooner, so that he could get back to the room quickly. He returned only to find his companion was still naked and sleeping on the bed.

He looked at the clock, which read 2:33. He already regretted having to go home; he wanted to stay here for another day and indulge a bit more in the Latino.

He reveled in his state of undress as he moved from the window. His wife never allow him to walk the house stark naked. She could not bear to see him naked, always insisting they be in complete darkness when they--

How long was it since we had sex? A year? Two? he wondered as he scratched his chest hairs. Then he said aloud, "Don't care. I get enough on my own."

When he moved to Milwaukee, he first met his wife at a bar on the East Side, and he had thought she was the one. At the time, he had been desperate for a change, and her family had enough money to allow him to reinvent himself and become someone new. At the beginning of their marriage he had been happy with her—or at least he thought he was happy.He worked for her father's company, but then things changed; life had changed, and not for the better. It had been especially bad after she lost their first child. Then the promotions had leapt at him, but he couldn't go much further in the small family company. So he looked for another job and took a new job when a friend offered him a position. While his wife was not pleased, his new job paid even more money and more bonuses, and that had kept her mouth shut. Of course, it also allowed him the benefit of travelling on a bi-weekly, if not weekly, basis all across the country. When their first child was born, she was completely absorbed in taking care of the baby who needed so much attention, so much hospitalization...and just so much goddamn work for a little thing.

He had no patience.

When he encountered his first lover while on his travels (a subtly and sublimely casual affair that had lasted three full days), it was then that he created a new world for himself. Each time he left, he craved it more.

His two worlds evolved over the last decade. The first world founded on a legal, loveless marriage to an ungrateful, sour women and a retard of a child, which his salary floated and secured. The second world of carnal madness, where his inner desires could flourish. Over the years, the second world of his inner yearning, craving the primal desires gnawed more and more at him each time he returned to the first.

But soon, very soon, he would have his second world all the time. He needed a few more days, a few more trips, then the transactions would clear—a plan that he cultivated for long time—

And at that thought a smile caressed his lips. He turned away from the brilliant sunlit day, he was no longer in his reality.

Casually, he walked towards the coffee table and turned on the television. The dull silence of the room was splintered by the sounds of the newscaster reporting from O'Hare. A large Middle Eastern delegation would be descending upon the city this weekend for a special conference. While the reporter with her crystal green eyes and blonde ponytail pulled back tightly against her scalp alluded to a "benign summit", the camera panned to the rows of protesters that were opposing the visit, flashing their signs of *No Oil for Blood* and *Chicago Doesn't Need Blood Money*. That was another reason why he disliked coming to Chicago, too many useless opinions.

"Stupid, liberal assholes," he whispered, shaking his head in disgust.

There was a brief knock at the door that broke his attention.

"Babe, I told you I didn't have time for any room service," he called out as he walked towards the door. His scratchy voice was barely audible as his mouth was still thick with the taste his lover.

Only the echoes of water answered him.

He opened the door, announcing a bit more loudly, "I think you have the wrong room."

No one was there. He found only an empty hallway decorated in fine touches of gold and burgundy carpets. Peering around the edge of his door, he listened for a moment but no movement could be heard. Shrugging his shoulders, he turned and closed the door.

The view ahead of him, the crescent of Lake Michigan, was a deep aqua color that bordered the Northern Suburbs, looking almost like a surrealistic Dali landscape as the water melted into the tall apartment buildings and the sunlight seeped into the sapphire-colored water.

He took a couple of steps back into the room and craned his head towards the bathroom. Maybe he should invite himself in. His desire began to pique painfully. He noted that he had at least a half an hour before check out, as a sly smile crept over his lips.

There was another brief knock on the door.

Pivoting on his heel, he looked at the door, the smile dropping from his face. That retard child, his child, always knocked on the bathroom door, playing games with him, especially when he was trying to take a shit. She thought it was funny. How it pissed him off.

His patience was at its end. He stood straighter and went to the door. "Listen," he began as he opened the door again, "Who the --," and stopped.

No one.

He could hear the ring of the elevator closing. He stepped into the hallway, not thinking about his crude nakedness, looking both ways, hearing only the hum of electricity that powered the sconces on the wall. He could smell the disinfectant from the freshly clean rooms nearby and the sound of the television coming from his suite.

There was unordinary stillness.

Backing up, he kept his eyes on the hallway and closed the door. Behind him, the water splattered in the bathroom. On the television, a commercial was advertising Blues Fest in Grant Park with innocuous jazz tones softly drifting behind the speaker's soulful words.

As he stepped towards the bathroom, he noticed a red smear on the tiles as water washed over it creating a lighter hue like that of melted cotton candy.

"What the hell? Hey, are you alright in there?" he asked. His voice cracked and seemed loud in the large bathroom.

Behind him, a heavy blow came down on the back of his head, sending his body stumbling forward. He collapsed against the wall in bathroom. Near him, barely a few feet away, the Latino's body was slumped in the corner of stone shower stall. Red liquid poured from the long red smile on his neck. He wanted to say his name but he was dizzy from the blunt force he had received.

Sliding down the wall, a strap went around his neck and a great force pulled him backwards. His body fell backwards onto the floor with a thud and caused him to gasp for what little air that he was allowed. The strap choked him harder as he felt himself being dragged away from the bathroom. He seemed not to be reacting as fast as he felt he should. He pulled at the belt, and he craned his head up to see the outline of another man but the brilliance of the sunlight made it hard to see his face.

The stranger was pulling harder at the belt. He was long and lean, shirtless, and so pale. For a quick moment, the other man's body pressed against his back.

The man was naked as well.

As a surge of adrenaline began to pour into him. He kicked his legs and clawed at the strap, feeling his nails dig into in his own flesh. His reaction was too late; the man was tightening the strap. Only muffled gargles escaped his collapsing throat, choking on his last breaths, choking on the coppery taste of blood as he bit his tongue repeatedly. Seeing the last glimmers of blurry light, he realized that his wife would finally be able to see his other world.

That last thought gave birth to a small grin to cross his lips as he gasped for air.

Darkness soon enveloped him.

One

Metal music of his favorite band, *Slipknot*, pulsated in Gavin's ear buds. The steely rips of the guitar, the raw guttural singing and the rhythmic drum pounding created a resurgence of raw energy that increased the length of his stride and the quickness in his pace. While this particular album was quintessential Paul Gray, the inspirational bass rips were from the second to last recordings with the band before his death. Respecting the posthumous honor, Gavin enjoyed the music more as he ran along Lake Shore drive.

The tingling in his left leg meant that he had been pushing himself harder on this particular run. He could feel himself reaching the twelve mile point. A glistening layer of sweat coated his naked torso and he felt the radiant heat of the bright sun on his skin. Even though the music was deafening, he could still hear his rasping breaths.

Today was the first real day of summer.

He was an avid runner though not as neurotic as some runners. He did not wear the expensive shorts and breathable shirts, or the specialized hats, or any of the distinctive runner's gear. Well, he did cave in to the shoes; that he would spend money on. He also did not wear a timing watch anymore. At first, he did, for in a way, it seemed to help him with his pace. When he had forgotten it for his first half marathon three years ago, he discovered after viewing the results that his pace was actually better when he was less focused on the counting and listened to his body instead.

So now, he just ran.

Gavin liked it simple; his beat up White Sox hat, a cheap MP3 player with his tunes, a thermo water bottle clutched in his hand, good shoes and a pair of shorts. He caught glimpses of women turning their heads as he passed them. Perhaps his half-naked body was what made them take a good second look. As was standard runner etiquette, he received the cursory polite runner's nod from men, probably eyeing him up as well. Honestly, he did not care. Before, he would have felt slightly conscious of their stares, but today, especially today, on this hot summer afternoon, he absorbed their looks, relished them.

His faded, slightly-torn baseball cap was tight on his head. His eyes darted side-to-side, taking in his surroundings. Ahead, the glorious tall buildings of Chicago jutted jaggedly towards the sky like shimmering steel and glass stalagmites, reaching towards the brilliant azure sky above. To the left, he saw the beach filling with people; kids and dogs all playing in the rough, choppy water. Although the heat was intense, and he would have welcomed a quick dip in the cool water, he instead ran towards the pedestrian bridge that crossed over Lake Shore Drive. He was halfway across the overpass, where he looked the steel fence to the Friday afternoon traffic below, already filling all eight lanes. The distant echo of horn blasts could be heard over the music that still filled his ears. No matter, he was heading for his apartment building on Wells, which was less than a mile away.

Running for Gavin helped him to purge his thoughts of the day, to find solutions to problems, and to even work on cases. The more stressed he had been at work, or in life, the longer he would run. The concrete was his therapist.

Last year, around the time he was training for his first marathon, he had been working on a sex trade case that had involved several extremely influential aldermen. The highly-stationed men had covered up their on-the-side escort service of which the women were illegal, underage Eastern European girls. These girls had been promised fame as a model or actress if they left their homes for opportunities in the U.S. But upon arriving in The States, they became victims to the streets, forced into acting only as cheaply-paid prostitutes. More so, some of the girls were given incentive money to become smuggling mules, made to carrying drugs inside their orifices.

Later, as the case developed, Alderman Allen La Baron had been the man to strike a deal with Russian drug czars to bring over highly-potent Ecstasy and heroin. With Gavin's stint in drug enforcement, La Baron had been the key to the case. Following the alderman, monitoring the money trail, and striking deals with the small dealers in exchange for information. It had taken so much time and energy, Gavin worked the case day and night for a better part of three years. But the careful handling of their traffickers funds made it difficult, if not impossible prove which of the politically-influential men were involved in the elaborate operation.

The three aldermen's political connections ensured that they were neat and securely covered by a labyrinth of middlemen: third-party dealers, johns and accountants; it was a sophisticated nightmare, in a nutshell. At the preliminary hearing, just last month, Alderman John Coleman, a small bulbous man in his mid-fifties, plead guilty to all charges. His lawyer read his letter of statement to the public, stating at one point, "I can only apologize to my constituents, who recently re-elected me to my present position, for failing them as an aldermen. The voters trusted me to be a leader of their community and to work for strengthening the bond of communal well-being. In my private actions, I was actually disbanding and disrupting the neighborhood harmony. I can only apologize to the women who were used as prostitutes for our financial gain. They had been promised a better life in America, when in fact, I aided in the destroying their minds, and abusing their bodies, as well. I can only apologize to the many people who bought our narcotics, while I preached a message of No Drugs to our youth. I was the supplier for the whole. And finally, I must apologize to my family, my two daughters and my son, for bringing them such shame. You are always in my heart. To my wife, I hope in the years ahead that she will forgive me and my horrible actions. As I await sentencing, I will repent of my sins." At that point, John lowered his head and sobbed uncontrollably like a spoiled teenager caught with a nickel bag of marijuana. The press had a good time with the event and glorified the destruction of the seedy alderman. Over the course of the following year, many suspects further down the food chain were easily caught and turned state's witness, assisting the investigating officers and precincts in other cases involving drug trafficking and distribution, prostitution rings and counterfeiting.

Alderman Robert Masterson was the ring leader, and now the main target of the investigation. He was a smug man in his early fifties who took great care of himself with weekly skin treatments, massages, and an eccentric aerobic workout routine that made him rail thin. He had been the Alderman in the near North Side for twenty years. On the surface, Masterson was a devout family man, married thirty-some-odd years; father to four children who all went to Northwestern; lived in an audacious home in prestigious Lincoln Park, and was the perfect Catholic, attending mass every Sunday at ten o'clock. He appeared successful, accumulating a vast number of antique cars, good land in key development areas in the suburbs, and took a unique interest in the arts; Robert seemed to be an entrepreneurial emperor, yet his pretentiously deep pockets with highly-esteemed Chicago business executives, state representatives of surrounding districts and a congressman who frequented Robert's lesser-known business ventures, had a distinct taste for Robert's bevvy of women a regular basis.

As the right people turned blind eyes to his activities, he orchestrated a dark operation of human trafficking where young women were mere products for purchase and client use, and where the drugs were marketing tools to draw in fresh clientele, and the purpose of the business was merely to support his outrageously extravagant lifestyle.

Last year in early fall, while training for a full marathon -- when Gavin had been attempting to crack twenty-three miles -- Gavin recalled the details of a recent arrest of a young Yersi Meeranova. While the police officer was booking her for prostitution she claimed to have some important information to offer. In her brief interview, Yersi spoke about a man she referred to as "t'in man," who would take in one special "girl" for the month. Unfortunately, Yersi had been the girl for the past month. According to her, he was a "mean man" and liked to "inspect flock." What's more, "t'in man" always took one for "private in'pection." That night that the cop found her on the street, she explained, "t'in man" had finished with her, had beaten her and dumped her, bleeding and unconscious, where the officer found her. Gavin could tell from her mug shot that her face was black and blue, one eye swollen shut. Where her shoulders were exposed in the photo bruises were evident in the area around her collar bones, and there was a faint impression of a handprint around her neck. The picture could not hide her pain nor her fragile youth.

In his gut, Gavin knew that Robert Materson was "t'in man". Yet when Gavin went looking for Yersi, she had disappeared. Gavin realized that her disappearance was conveniently-timed for Materson, and that drove Gavin to persist in locating her. Several witnesses came forward to place Materson in the location where Yersi had been picked up, but still no tangible evidence connected Materson to the girl. Finally, an anonymous call came in and gave instructions to the whereabouts of the young girl. Her body had been discovered near one Masterson's building developments. Through Gavin's experience, the guilty, especially the extremely idiotic ones, always messed up the simple crimes by touting an inflated-opinion of their own intelligence.

Around last year's holiday season, an avalanche of evidence arose and arrests were made. While the aldermen arrogantly believed that their sanctimonious bubbles would never get punctured, Gavin personally brought in Masterson for Yersi. Waiting patiently outside, Gavin personally arrested the gaunt alderman as soon as the man stepped foot onto the sidewalk outside his church just after Sunday mass.

While his family had been moved to shock and accusations, as Materson was shoved in the unmarked car he muttered softly to Gavin, "You have just ruined your career, officer."

Contrary to the alderman's threats, the case put Gavin on the map in the CPD. In the last months, he passed up interviews from news stations, his face was in the union paper, named as a hero and his precinct threw him a large party. When he began his case, his only concern was for the young women. Once the aldermen were arrested, he helped rescue forty-three illegally-immigrated new recruits who had been housed at a rundown shack of a house on the West Side. Since then, more women had come forward to testify against the men.

That was old news though. That was not why he was running today.

Rounding the corner on Wells, he drank the last swallow of lukewarm water and saw his apartment building within blocks.

Old Town was always busy and congested, but it was one of his favorite neighborhoods, with good restaurants, it was located close to work and the gym. He now had the chance to live here. The sidewalks were already filling with people as he passed by beach chairs, swimsuits, fellow runners all heading towards the lake. On the street, taxis and cars drove past him in each direction. He maneuvered around cars, through the crossways hearing an occasional honk of a horn and garnering a couple of one-finger salutes from drivers as he cut across crawling lanes of traffic, his legs continued to propel him forward at his usual pace.

Today Gavin commenced his new life as a single man, all over again. Hours earlier, he had signed the final documents of his divorce. Gavin could not easily forget Emily. He could not blame her either. The Aldermen case consumed all of his waking hours...then again, he has willingly thrown himself into it. Their marriage had had its problems for a long time. But he didn't want to think about that now, so he quicken his strides and increased his pace in an attempt to forget those years with her. Even during this last year of separation, of selling their home, moving recently into his new apartment, he still could not forget all of it. No matter how hard he tried.

Suddenly, a blast of a car horn made him look to his right at the cab driver who was throwing his hands up and probably cursing him in his Middle Eastern dialect.

He picked up his pace and continued down the street, darting through pedestrians as he went. When he was about a block from him, he saw a familiar face in the crowd. His partner, Derrick, was leaning against an unmarked black police car, he was almost too obvious. His crisp, white shirt was tightly tailored, cinched at the waist and stretched taunt over his arms showing off his thick, bulbous biceps. Yes, his attempt to blend failed just as if it were an attempt by a pro-wrestler to walk incognito amongst the people.

As he got closer to his partner of , Gavin ripped the earpieces from his ears, and the city sounds of traffic, people whistling, dogs barking, screeching brakes, people talking and far distance sirens invaded his senses.

"How can you run when it is this hot?" Derrick asked, wiping his brow with the back of his hand.

"I have," he huffed, "to train." His lungs heaved in his chest, and without the benefit of his movement to create a breeze he was now feeling the heat of the day on his body.

"You're insane," his partner commented drolly, then looked towards some young women in bathing suits as they passed.

Still panting, Gavin bent over and gripped his calves, to feel the stretch in his lower back down through his hamstrings, his sweat dripping onto the pavement. "No, no, problem, Derrick. Why the social call?" He poured the remaining water from his bottle over his head. In his periphery he saw a couple of young women smiling at him, eyeing him up.

"I promised not disturb you today...."

Gavin interrupted, "It's fine, really," releasing another heavy breath. "Nothing planned tonight anyway." Even through his dark sunglasses he felt Derrick's eyes on him, "What's up?"

"Business, business only," he replied, then queried, "How did it go today?" his partner's bass voice resonated in the noisy street, carrying with it his unspoken concern.

I don't want to talk about it, Gavin thought to himself, but instead he remarked cryptically, "I signed. It's done. I'm free."

"Was he there?" Another unwelcome, probing question, followed by another swipe of his forehead. Behind them Derrick's Charger car moaned slightly as the air conditioner re-cycled.

"Yes," Emily's new boyfriend had been there, but sitting in the lobby. He did not escort her to the preceding.

"What does the asshole look like?" Derrick shifted his stance.

He's tall, blond hair, blue-eyed, good-looking, perfect teeth, probably an accountant. "A Ken doll, maybe with all the working parts, and shorter than me," Gavin recalled, stretching more, flaying some sweat towards Derrick.

His partner stepped back to avoid the droplets. "Goddamn it, don't get that on me. You're nasty," he chided. "Go take a shower, quick too. I can smell you from here, even over all the exhaust fumes."

"Why?" he challenged, his lungs still burned and his legs tingled. He was going to pay later for his lengthy run in this heat.

"It happened again."

Gavin stopped his stretching, stood and looked up at Derrick.

"This time, two people. Close to here, at the Drake," his partner explained as he started chewing on a new piece of gum that he fished out of his pocket.

"No one's touched the scene yet?" Gavin's voice was serious. He made it perfectly clear to the department that if it was their scene, no one goes in.

"No. They're waiting on us."

"Fine. I'll be down in ten."

"Ain't going nowhere, G," Derrick was already on the driver's side of the car, opening the door. "Sweet Jesus, it's a nice iceberg in here."

With that, he headed for his apartment building with purpose, deciding to take the stairs because it would be faster. Gavin had to get ready fast. He always had a set of clothes waiting, just in case of emergency. They needed to be on the scene first this time. He took the stairs two at a time. His legs trembled as he huffed each set of stairs, catching whiffs of his own stale body sweat here and there.

Two bodies meant things were getting serious now. *Our guy's upping his spree,* Gavin thought as he realized he was only a floor from his apartment.

Shit.

ABOUT THE AUTHOR

For over twenty years, Russell has been an Executive Chef and Manager in the Restaurant Industry, in which he has created succulent entrees and managed various types of kitchen operations. In the recent years, he began to teach future culinarians achieve their professional goals in hands-on classroom and lecture settings. With his recent graduate work in the field of Sociology, his interests centered on organizational behaviorism, social theory and food insecurity. His current book, *The Tale of Old Man Fischer*, is published and available on Amazon.com. Due out next year, Russell's latest project is a thriller series based in Chicago, Illinois.

Currently, he lives in Up State New York with his wife, two children and several cats.

Please visit him on:

Facebook Page: Russell_The_Author
Twitter: @Russell_Writer
Instagram: or follow him on Twitter. @Russell_Writer

End Notes

A-ZLyrics. 2014. "Wichita Lineman." Glen Campbell.
http://www.azlyrics.com/lyrics/glencampbell/wichitalineman.html

Campbell, Glen. "Wichita Lineman". Glen Campbell. Capitol Recording Studio. 1968.

Lyrics Freak. 2014. "Heroin." The Velvet Underground.
http://www.lyricsfreak.com/v/velvet+underground/heroin_20143880.html

Lyrics Freak. 2014. "I Can't Explain." The Who.
http://www.lyricsfreak.com/w/who/

Lyrics Freak. 2014. "See Emily Play." Pink Floyd.
http://www.lyricsfreak.com/p/pink+floyd/see+emily+play_20108721.html

Melville, Herman. 2001. "The Swamp Angel." Battle Pieces and Aspects of War. Prometheus Books. Pp.365

Pink Floyd. "See Emily Play" Single. Sound Techniques, London. 1967.

The Velvet Underground. "Heroin". The Velvet Underground & Nico.

The Who. "I Can't Explain" Single. Brunswick, Decca 1965.

37129348R00189

Made in the USA
Middletown, DE
20 November 2016